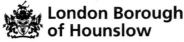
The Sudden Departure
of the Frasers

Louise Candlish studied English at University College London and worked as an editor in art publishing and as a copywriter before writing fiction. Though her stories are about people facing dramatic dilemmas, she tries to live an uncomplicated life in London with her husband and daughter.

The Sudden Departure
of the Frasers

LOUISE CANDLISH

PENGUIN BOOKS

PENGUIN BOOKS

UK | USA | Canada | Ireland | Australia
India | New Zealand | South Africa

Penguin Books is part of the Penguin Random House group of companies
whose addresses can be found at global.penguinrandomhouse.com.

First published 2015
001

Copyright © Louise Candlish, 2015

The moral right of the author has been asserted

Set in 12.5/15.25pt Garamond MT Std
Typeset by Jouve (UK), Milton Keynes
Printed in Great Britain by Clays Ltd, St Ives plc

A CIP catalogue record for this book is available from the British Library

PAPERBACK ISBN: 978–1–405–91984–5
TRADE PAPERBACK ISBN: 978–1–405–91985–2

www.greenpenguin.co.uk

For Sheila Crowley, saviour of this story

'There was no trap involved, no trick: he was a wolf in wolf's clothing. And I went right up to his door and asked him his name.'

Amber Fraser

Prologue

15 January 2013

'I hate you,' I said, trembling.

I love you, a voice replied, but it was not the one I wanted to hear; only my own, inside my head, the words incarcerated there forever.

He said nothing. His mouth made vile movements, a bully's gathering saliva to spit at an object of repugnance, a victim. In his eyes there pooled pure savagery.

And then he sprang.

Chapter 1

Christy, April 2013

Right from the moment she first held the keys in her hand, something felt wrong.

Later, she would regret ignoring that instinct, but at the time she put it down to the simple fact of Joe not being there with her. It couldn't be helped, of course, it was just one of those things – or several of them. A rescheduled client meeting that could under no circumstances be missed; the estate agent's half-day closure for staff training (or, as Joe suspected, plans for a long lunch courtesy of the commission earned on *their* house); her own eagerness to get into the property and start their new life: all conspired to bring her there that morning to pick up the keys alone.

'Well, congratulations, Mrs Davenport,' said the agent, and he placed the keys with a ceremonial flourish on the release document for her to sign. There were two sets, one attached to a costly-looking silver key ring with a pretty dragonfly charm – the previous owners', presumably.

'Thank you.' Hand shaking, Christy scrawled her name before snatching up the keys and defending them in a clenched fist – as if someone might step forward and battle her for them! For these were the keys to a house on

3

Lime Park Road, and never in her wildest dreams had she thought she would come to own a property on that street. Yes, she and Joe had always aimed high, but this, this was rags-to-riches stuff, the fairy-tale ending you wouldn't normally trust.

'I hope you and your husband have many happy years in your new home,' the agent said. He was different from the one who'd handled the sale, younger and less sincere: could that be why the encounter felt, somehow, illicit? He could be a con artist, she and Joe the innocent victims of some elaborate sting. Or maybe it was the previous agent who'd been the fraudster?

Illicit? Con artist? Fraudster? What had got into her? She could tell by the way the man was frowning that her smile looked as problematic as it felt; it was causing disquiet, the way it might if a clown put his face too close. Managing a last choked thank you, she made her exit to the street. It's just nerves, she told herself; or excitement, the pure, debilitating kind that was hard to distinguish from terror.

Either way, she could have walked the route in her sleep, for she knew Lime Park as well as any postman from the countless occasions she and Joe had roamed it together since first viewing the house. She knew the short parade that masqueraded as a high street, with its mix of cafés, boutiques and estate agents, and the florist's on the corner that spilled its colours far across the pavement, as if cans of paint had been flung from the windows above. She knew the famous old art school that had stood empty for years before being redeveloped into the complex of luxury flats it was today. She knew the little park, the main gates of which she passed through now, walking in the shade of the old limes that lent the area its name, catching the scent of cut grass on the breeze. And she knew the web of streets beyond, including the one that curved around the park's southern edge, the one that contained the house to which she held the keys (she was gripping them in her hand still, as if to relax a single finger would be to render the whole business null and void; the fine edge of a dragonfly wing cut painfully into her palm).

And here it was: Lime Park Road, lined as far as the eye could see with cherry trees in full bloom, like giant sticks of candyfloss, casting dancing black patterns on the sun-bleached car lanes. It was a festive sight, could almost be the gateway to a carnival – until you noticed there wasn't a soul to be seen. No one was parking a car or closing a gate; no one was pushing a baby or walking a dog; no one was arriving or departing.

There was only her.

As the road swept eastward, the façade of their new home came into view. The houses on Lime Park Road were brick villas built in pairs in the late nineteenth century, their matching chimney stacks positioned at the outer edges of the roofs like cocked dog ears, and number 40 was the right hand of its twosome. Hers now, hers and Joe's, and yet it was with the furtive air of a trespasser that she pushed open the gate and teetered towards the glossy Oxford-blue door. She lifted the key to the lock, her breath held. How unfamiliar each element of entry was: that brief resistance followed by a sudden sweet give, the weight of good timber against her palm, the cool hardness of tile underfoot, and the smell in the broad hallway of ... not so much temporary disuse as reckless abandonment.

But maybe that was because she knew the previous owners had left in a hurry. Virtually overnight, in fact. Lord Lucan's got nothing on this pair, the agent had joked.

She wished she hadn't remembered that detail, for the sight of the bare hall walls and closed internal doors caused wild thoughts to surface: what might she find behind these doors? Bloodstains on the floor? A decomposing body? Some sort of weapon that linked the murder to Joe and her?

Ashamed, she turned brisk, throwing open the first door she came to, the one to the large square sitting room at the front. Everything was perfectly in order, of course, and quite devoid of signs of crime. There was the grand and glamorous marble fireplace they had so admired; and the pair of thickset ribbed radiators, the type torn from Victorian schoolhouses and reconditioned for the nostalgic wealthy; and the deep bay with its shining triptych of panes. She'd forgotten its original oak seat, newly upholstered in a textured linen print that looked far too expensive to actually sit on.

Christy marched across the room and hurled herself onto it, if only to prove that she was not the kind of person you could intimidate with *fabric*. The view onto the street was glorious, a collage of green leaf and golden brick unfettered by the low-level planting in the front garden; it was like looking through a giant camera lens at a scene lit to perfection by a master cinematographer. This was where she would come to watch the seasons change, she thought, during those many happy years the agent had wished her.

On her feet once more, she moved to the rear of the ground floor, actually gasping at the sight of the vast kitchen, just as she had when she'd first seen it. The fittings were high-end and handmade (the agent had mentioned a designer neither she nor Joe had heard of but whose name, when invoked in earshot of her boss, Laurie, had caused swooning), the cabinet doors made of opaque glass with brass fittings, the worktop a glittering slice of quartz. Family and friends were going to be not so much impressed as astonished, she thought, and to picture them assembled amid the hard, gleaming angles was like imagining villagers circling a spaceship that had just landed in their field, lights flashing in colours never before seen on earth. With the image came a fresh swell of unease, a recognition of its true source. Who are we fooling? she thought: this house is worth far more than we paid for it. There *must* be a catch.

She remembered with perfect clarity the day the agent had rung with news of an unusually well-priced house in Lime Park, a once-in-a-lifetime deal for a buyer who could act fast – so fast that only the chain-free were invited to bid. How she and Joe had patted themselves on the back for having already sold their two-bed in New Cross and rented just before the market had suffered a fortuitous downturn. But even so, this house was beyond 'well-priced', it was a gift, and in the whirlwind of the transaction they had perhaps not been diligent enough in asking the crucial, central question:

Why?

'They're leaving for personal reasons,' was all the agent had been able to tell them of the sellers, which made Joe suspect financial ruin.

'No,' Christy said. 'Why would they sell at such a good price if they need the money? They'd hold out for top whack.'

'Not if they need the cash quickly,' Joe said. 'Maybe a debt's been called in and they have to cut their losses. It must happen all the time in a recession.'

The agent agreed that times were harder in the outer suburbs. It wasn't Chelsea, after all.

But Christy's instinct pulled in a different direction. 'No. This is something emotional. It must be divorce or illness. They need to pay for treatment, perhaps.' Whatever it was it had to be something catastrophic for a couple to give up a home they'd plainly only just finished renovating, for the place was box-fresh throughout; you could smell the newness of it, hear it squeaking. 'Are they leaving London?'

But the agent didn't know, had no forwarding address on file, the sale being conducted by the couple's solicitor. He admitted he'd not met the couple – Jeremy and Amber Fraser, they were called – face to face.

A sharp rap at the front door startled her and, laughing at herself, she opened up to the postman. He had an item

too big to fit through the letter box, an oversized brochure of some sort for Mrs A. Fraser. There was other
post, too, all of it for the outgoing couple.

'Didn't the Frasers redirect their mail?' she asked.

'There's sometimes a bit of an overlap,' the postman
said, 'but it'll kick in in a few days, don't worry.'

'I'll collect it all up and send it on to them in one batch,'
she promised.

Alone again, she inspected the items. Only two were
not junk or publicity mail-outs and both were addressed
to Amber Fraser: one was a postcard with a picture of an
old *Vogue* cover, the model an alluring redhead with a
plum-coloured pout; the other a white envelope with 'Private & Confidential' stamped on it. Christy experienced a
sudden desire to tear the letter open – an extension of
that peculiar sensation of being in the house unlawfully –
but resisted the urge and satisfied herself by reading the
postcard:

Hi Amber,

*How are you? Hope you're still loving your forever home! Have
tried emailing and phoning you, but no luck. Couple of loose ends
to tie up – call me when you have a spare moment?*

Love, Hetty xxx

Below the name a mobile phone number had been
scribbled, 'just in case'.

On cue, Christy's phone began ringing: Joe.

'Your meeting's finished?'

'Just this second. How's the house?'

She was honestly not sure how to answer this. 'It feels a bit strange, like I'm going to be arrested for breaking and entering. Does that sound crazy?'

Joe chuckled. 'That's just Imposter Syndrome. Happens to everyone.'

Well, not *everyone*, she thought, not the entitled Oxbridge types with whom he worked and routinely lost out to in promotions, but she knew what he meant: everyone ordinary, like them.

'But don't worry, the solicitor sent the confirmation email, we've definitely completed, otherwise they wouldn't have released the keys. We're the owners now.'

Christy felt her heart contract, and with its unclenching came the first flood of joy. 'It just seems too good to be true, Joe.'

'I know.' But his tone was unambiguously triumphant because as far as he was concerned all good things came true if you worked hard enough to get them. In the seventeen years that had passed since they'd met at university, he had never stopped remembering that he had something to prove.

'Are you on your way?'

'Leaving right this minute, just setting my stopwatch to time the commute. One minute longer than an hour and we're giving the house back.'

Laughing, Christy hung up and looked once more at the handful of post for the Frasers. Then she slotted the postcard and the 'Private & Confidential' letter between two larger envelopes, out of sight. Joe's right, she thought, you're not an imposter.

You're just lucky.

'And look what else I've got!' Along with a chilled bottle of Veuve Clicquot, a gift from Marcus, the partner at Jermyn Richards who was his boss and long-time mentor, Joe waved a copy of *Metro* under her nose. It was open at an article titled 'Top Ten London Streets for Families':

6. LIME PARK ROAD (NEW ENTRY)

It's a miracle that this Victorian beauty has kept itself below the radar for as long as it has – blame the Lottery-funded revamp of the park last year and the newly opened Canvas restaurant for its breakout moment. This is the most sought-after street in the neighbourhood thanks to its handsome brick villas, once chaotic shares for the students of the Lime Park Art School. While there's still a smattering of the old boho crowd amid the incoming well-heeled families, don't let that deceive you: the days of snapping up a property for the price of a couple of watercolours are long gone.

'Talk about being in the right place at the right time,' Joe crowed. 'We've probably made a ten per cent capital gain on the house since this morning! Shame we've hardly got anything to put in it, mind you.'

'I know. It's a bit embarrassing.' Christy's glance swept the spacious zone between kitchen units and garden doors that had been furnished by the Frasers with such memorable elan. There'd been a vintage dresser stacked with coloured glassware and a leaf-green velvet sofa with wittily mismatched cushions. The dining table and chairs had been of the same bold contemporary style she'd seen through the window of Canvas, all curved lines and vibrant hues.

Wherever they'd gone, the Frasers would not have arrived, as she and Joe had, with nothing but sleeping bags and a change of clothes. The cut-price van-hire company the Davenports were using to transport their possessions from the storage facility did not have the smaller van size available till the next day. Perched now on bar stools to eat the cheese-and-tomato sandwiches Christy had made that morning – it seemed too prosaic a snack for so glossy a setting – they were grateful to their predecessors for having left them and saved them from sitting cross-legged on the floor. (Another reason to discount the theory that the Frasers had fallen on hard times: the stools looked like design classics; you could probably get hundreds of pounds for them on eBay.)

But none of that worried Joe as he poured the champagne into plastic beakers. Smart in his office suit and only a few days into a new haircut, he looked like a man who'd earned his spot on that designer stool; a man entering his prime. His eyes, the colour of cognac and the only exotic touch in a solidly Anglo-Saxon face, glowed warm with glee as he touched his cup to hers and popped the discarded ends of her sandwich into his mouth. 'Here's to a new life of bread crusts and eye-watering debt!'

Christy grimaced. 'Let's not think about debt today. Let's pretend we own the house outright.'

In reality, she would not forget as long as she lived that adrenalin-drenched sprint to pull together the finance for the house, how they'd tossed into the pot the proceeds of their flat, life savings and a loan from Christy's parents (Joe's had nothing to lend; her own, little enough to cause her guilt pangs for having had the nerve to take it), not to mention a mortgage brokered in haste by a friend of a friend and regarded thereafter by the couple as too hor-rifyingly colossal to be real. Even then, they'd fallen short, had had to resort to punishing forgotten credit cards to cover their solicitor's fees.

'Cash-poor' didn't scratch the surface of it.

And then there was the other sacrifice, agreed between the two of them in what already felt to Christy like a deal with the devil: babies. There could be none yet, not until one – or both – of them had been promoted. After all, you could decide to have a family any time, couldn't you, but a house like 40 Lime Park Road was a rare and special thing and they might never have had this chance again.

Yes, they were agreed on it.

The arrival and unloading of their possessions the next day did not attract the curiosity they might have expected on a Saturday morning in suburbia. The street remained as deserted as it had been the day before, the atmosphere reminding Christy of that resettling of energy the morn-ing after a party – a party so eventful that its highlights and lowlights could not yet be told apart.

'Where are all the neighbours?'

'It's the Easter holidays, don't forget,' Joe pointed out.

'They'll all have houses in Cornwall or France or take their kids on amazing safaris.'

'That must be it,' Christy said, marvelling again that they should find themselves joining such an affluent group. Would they fit in? Their backgrounds, their accents, the fact that they even had to ask: would they pass muster in an area like Lime Park?

She hoped so. After all, part of her desire to live here was the idea of an established and sociable community; nothing *too* grand or exclusive, of course, but certainly something more substantial than the anonymous, interchangeable relationships of their previous neighbourhoods. And perhaps the first local convention to be observed was that it was up to newcomers to introduce themselves and not the other way around.

Waiting until a civilized hour the next day, she began with the adjoining house, number 38, which was divided into two flats. She tried the downstairs bell first. After some delay, there were reluctant footsteps within and a heavy-set middle-aged woman appeared at the door, politely putting Christy off before she could even open her mouth: 'Felicity's not here. She's down in Dorset at her daughter's. I'm just checking on the place for her.'

The place in question, glimpsed through the half-opened door, had polished oak floorboards and walls painted a rich Venetian yellow. Christy noticed on the hall table a stack of mail that suggested several weeks' absence, as well as a beautiful hourglass bottle of scent.

'That's a shame,' she said warmly. 'We've just moved in

next door and wanted to say hello. So Felicity is the owner, is she?'

The woman eyed her with circumspection. 'Yes, but not for much longer. She's just agreed a sale.'

'Really? Sounds like everyone's moving out.' But Christy knew it was not uncommon to find two properties side by side on the market at the same time; the appearance of one 'For Sale' sign on a street often encouraged neighbours to have their own houses valued. 'Well, she might decide to stay after that piece in the paper on Friday,' she joked. 'It was quite a write-up.'

The woman did not smile. 'Oh, believe me, no amount of money could keep her here.'

Christy was taken aback. 'Sorry, I –'

'In fact, I doubt you'll see Felicity back here at all before she moves out for good.'

'What do you mean? Why not?'

But the woman already had her hand on the door, ready to close it. 'I'm afraid I have to go, I'm right in the middle of cooking . . .'

The kitchen was partially visible on the far side of the hall, its lights off and worktop cleared; there were no smells of cooking. In any case, hadn't she said she was only here to check on the place?

'Do you know if they're in upstairs?' Christy said, her tone persistently bright, though she addressed only a sliver of the woman as the door advanced towards her. And then it was in her face, clicking shut, causing her to step suddenly back.

Not a very promising start.

She rang the bell for the upper flat, but there was no reply.

In the front garden of number 40, Joe was spraying the Frasers' immaculate topiary with a hose he'd found in their garden shed. 'There was definitely someone in the upstairs flat a minute ago. I saw a dark-haired bloke at the window.'

'Weird that he didn't answer his doorbell.'

'On the phone, maybe. What about the other side?'

But it was obvious there was no one in at number 42; the off-street parking bay had been empty since Friday.

Just then a man walked by their gate, a black Lab at his feet. Both human and canine eyes were cast determinedly to the pavement.

'Hi there,' Christy called brightly. 'We've just moved in!'

The man didn't glance up, the dog only briefly, and the two walked resolutely on.

Joe cracked up. 'You can't just shout out to random passers-by! He probably doesn't even live around here.'

'I saw him coming out of a house further up.'

'Er, he could have just been visiting someone. He's parked down there, see? The Volvo? Just wait till the neighbours come to us,' Joe added, continuing his watering. The hose spat and hissed in his hand like a threatened animal. 'It's not like we've joined a commune, it's just a regular street.'

The two exchanged a grin: it was certainly not regular by *their* standards.

'You're right,' she agreed, 'we've got years to get to know people. I'm just excited to see who else lives here.'

'Well, don't get your hopes up. Just because we live next door doesn't mean we're going to be best buddies … Damn!' As he reached to twist free a dead shoot, the hose slipped and water shot at Christy, soaking her feet.

'Urgh, it's freezing!'

If this were a TV show, the Joe character would have squirted the hose upwards, soaked her to the skin, then she would have seized it and returned the insult, leading to shrieking and kissing and his lifting her over the threshold and chasing her upstairs to conceive their first child. But it was not TV and anyway they had their pact, didn't they?

'Coffee?' she offered.

'You're not going to fire up the space-age monster?'

'I was going to boil the kettle for economy-brand instant, actually.' There was no way they could splurge on the imported capsules needed for the Frasers' fitted appliance, assuming she could figure out how to operate the thing in the first place. 'We might have to steal coffee from work from now on. Milk and loo rolls as well. We'll take it in turns to evade suspicion.'

'It might come to that,' Joe said cheerfully.

Before heading indoors, Christy glanced up again at the neighbour's flat, the overhanging bay visible above the dividing hedge. It was a dim day and there were no lights on, but Joe was right, there *was* someone up there.

She looked again at her wet feet and felt a shiver pass through her.

Chapter 2

My name is Amber Fraser and I suppose you could call this a confession.

Of course, I don't mean in a religious sense, or even a criminal one, but it occurs to me that if I were unlucky enough to be on the plane that crashed, the boat that overturned, the taxi struck by lightning, then there should be a written account of the truth available. God knows, Jeremy couldn't be expected to give it. Sometimes I think he's forgotten what the truth is, so committed is he to believing our lies.

My lies.

The need for deception began almost as soon as we moved into the house on Lime Park Road. It was April 2012. I can't believe it's not quite eighteen months ago, not when my eyes in the mirror suggest a period closer to eighteen years, but I guess it's always difficult to recognize your pre-revolutionary self, isn't it?

We'd been living in an apartment on the river in Battersea and the move to suburbia was both serendipitous and carefully plotted: serendipitous in that Jeremy's childless uncle had died suddenly and left him enough money to fund the purchase and renovation of a new house, and carefully plotted in that we had been in agreement for some time that we would make the move as soon as I was ready to give up work. And now, at thirty-five, I was.

I can picture you wincing as you read this, checking that the date above really is from the twenty-first century: ready to give up work! What kind of a shameful throwback is she? But when your husband is wealthy enough for two and you have been selected in the first place for your youth and good looks, then I guess you are qualified to make staggeringly anachronistic statements like that (if not so easily forgiven). And some of my fantasies *were* very 1950s, I have to confess. I imagined myself soaking up the sun in the garden for hours on end, lying on one of those old art deco steamer chairs, a pile of magazines and a jug of daiquiris by my side — should the weather turn miraculously Wisteria Lane on us, that was. In Lime Park in drizzly south London the equivalent would be to laze in bed and then swim in the pool at the gym, mooch about the little boutiques on the Parade or lunch with fellow wastrels up in town. I know women who have done little else for years and, when challenged, they all say exactly the same: Don't knock it till you've tried it.

But don't worry, I wasn't planning on doing nothing. We hadn't bought a family house without intending to fill it with a family. First, I would oversee the renovations (or oversee the project manager who would oversee the renovations) and then I would have a baby. And even an indulged hedonist like me knew that looking after a baby was the hardest job of all.

By the time we moved in, Jeremy and I had been trying for several months to conceive. It wasn't long enough for us to have investigated fertility treatments, but it was long enough to suspect that something was stuck that might need an expert to loosen it. He had had a girlfriend at university who'd become pregnant and so it stood to reason that the blockage was mine. Our amateur diagnosis was stress, of the work-related variety: somehow my media-buying job managed to be at once over-stimulating and completely stultifying. Without the commute, without the office politics, without the *work*, I could ease my body into a more fecund state; I could relax into the soft green bower of Lime Park and await impregnation.

As I say, the lies began almost as soon as we arrived that rain-splashed weekend in April. Now, when I think about it, it's as if I'd become a different person by the Sunday from the one I'd been on the Friday, but I know that can't be true. This wasn't a case of life-altering epiphanies, it was simply a matter of the old me resurrecting – Amber Speed, party girl, hellraiser, law-breaker. I'd convinced myself she was dead, invoking her now and then with nostalgic regret, but I think I'd known all along she was not dead. She was merely sleeping off a hangover.

So, on the Friday, when I was still his devoted wife and the committed future mother of his children, Jeremy suggested we leave the new house and go for a walk in the park while it was still light. We used our private gate at the end of the garden, which like everything else in the property had not been painted this millennium. I was fond of that little gate. It was like having access to a generously sized communal garden, one reason for the rising prices both of the houses themselves and, as Jeremy pointed out, the insurance premiums they carried.

'I wonder if easy to get *out* also means easy to get *in*,' he said, carefully clicking the latch shut behind us.

'Oh, don't be such a bore,' I said, laughing. 'Anyway, burglars would have to go through a hundred sealed boxes before they found anything worth stealing.' We'd agreed there was no point unpacking ninety per cent of our belongings until the works were complete; within days the whole lot would be buried in dust. 'They'd just give up and leave.'

'Not if they hit the jackpot of your wardrobe,' he said, hooking my hand under his elbow and squeezing the ends of my gloved fingers. 'Then they'd be quids in.'

Quids in: one of the many terms he used that reminded me of the difference in our ages. At fifty-one, he was sixteen years older than me.

'They would.' I pressed myself closer to him as we walked, resting my head on his shoulder and admiring the way my hair tumbled over his waxed jacket, shiny and vivid as spilled blood.

The park was a compact rectangle and a circuit took only ten or fifteen minutes along paths bordered with daffodils. It was one of those days when wet weather seems appealing, even romantic, when the rain is soft and the circumstances hopeful. There was a lovely corner of meadow where the grass had been allowed to grow wild, and I imagined settling there in warmer weather, whiling away whole afternoons with music or a book. Maybe, one day, I'd be taking a toddler there to romp. But that was a long way off. In the meantime, I wondered if I'd be able to persuade more centrally based friends to join me or if they'd baulk at the train journey. Lime Park was not on the Tube and the overland service was chronically over-crowded according to Jeremy, who'd have no choice but to start using it daily from Monday. I'd need to make new friends locally.

'It's nice, this area, isn't it?' he said. 'I've always thought there was something special about it.'

'Yes. It feels so much more relaxed out here. And secret, like we're the only ones who know about it.'

In Battersea Park even in the soggiest weather you were in danger of being dragged underfoot by stampedes of runners, or stalled by the tourists who clogged its paths in that oblivious way of out-of-towners so intent on experi-encing every local detail they forget there are natives with lives to get on with. Lime Park, I was to discover, was deemed too small to run around and too lacking in statu-ary for tourists. In spite of a recent regeneration programme, word had not yet spread and I wonder now if that atmosphere of secrecy, of removal, was a factor in the events that followed.

'I hope there'll be some fun to be had around here,' I added.

'Oh, I'm sure there will,' Jeremy said. 'Aren't the sticks supposed to be more debauched than the centre of town?'

'I think that's only an urban myth. Or a suburban myth.'

'Well, you'll find the party people, darling, wherever they are.'

You see, I hadn't changed *completely* from my earlier

libertine self, I was still known to be fun-loving and flirta-tious. But the crucial thing was I was always faithful. Since Jeremy and I had become involved almost five and a half years ago, I had not for a moment considered encourag-ing another man, not even to remind myself that I could (conceited as it sounds, I *knew* how attractive I was; it was sort of the point of me). In any case, he was not the sus-picious sort. He trusted me.

I trusted myself; it's worth my remembering that.

Returning to the house, we toured the rooms once more and studied the plans of our designer, Hetty, for the kitchen extension and new bathrooms while reassuring each other that if it all became too much we would simply decamp to a short-term rental or hotel. We stayed up late, drinking champagne, before heading to bed in our tem-porary quarters at the top of the house. It was cold that night and a decent heating system had yet to be installed, so we piled on the blankets as if camping out in the open. We fell asleep touching.

I remember all of this because there was no premon-ition, not a whisper of an instinct to warn me that only two days later I would suffer a catastrophic malfunction. *I'd need to make friends locally . . . I hope there'll be some fun*: how portentous the lines sound when I read them back, but I'd meant only that I hoped for amusement, a mild diversion every now and then, the company of someone who knew how to mix a decent cocktail and tell a good story.

But by Sunday I'd met him and at a stroke Lime Park had lost its innocence, those banks of rain-washed daffo-dils emblems of hope only in the most ironic sense. And

I can't even blame him because I actively sought him out. There was no trap involved, no trick: he was a wolf in wolf's clothing.

And I went right up to his door and asked him his name.

'We need to speak to the neighbours before Monday,' Jeremy said on the Saturday evening, our first full day as owners coming to a close. We sat with a takeaway curry at our tulip dining table in the kitchen that would within forty-eight hours become a demolition site. The outdated cabinets and appliances, the chipped floor tiles, even the newly fitted worktop (a token attempt at a pre-sale facelift that wasn't fooling anyone, Hetty said, least of all her): everything would be in a skip the following week and we'd be cooking in a makeshift kitchen on the top floor. In reality, I'd skip lunch and we'd eat out most nights.

'I haven't seen a soul on that side,' I agreed. By contrast, the family at number 42 had introduced themselves within hours of our arrival, at least the wife had, taking the lead in the self-confident, emphatic way you'd expect of residents of a road like this. She'd come to the door with a potted lily and home-made chocolate cake, exclaiming, 'You *must* come for drinks as *soon* as you're settled in! We've all been *dying* to meet you.' She'd been gracious about the building works, too. 'Oh, we expected that. No offence to Rachel and Tom, they were great friends of ours, but that kitchen was on its last legs and they didn't touch the bathrooms the whole ten years they were there. I think they thought with young children anything new would just get trashed . . .' On she gossiped about our predecessors, who had gone off to Beijing in pursuit of the dragon dollar, before concluding, 'Anyway, we're not attached, are we, so the noise won't be too bad for us.'

The ones it *would* be bad for were on our other side, number 38, our Siamese twin (I came in time to think of our master bedroom and its counterpart on the other side of the wall as conjoined hearts). A charm offensive was in order and I'd been keeping half an eye out for comings and goings, an opportunity to introduce myself, but so far no occupants had made themselves known or even been spotted at the window.

'It's flats, not a single residence,' Jeremy said now, with a trace of superiority. 'They probably rent.'

'What, if you rent you can't possibly come out and say hello?' I scoffed. 'You have to own a "single residence" to have any manners? *I* was renting when we met, remember?' Naturally, I didn't add that my last flat had been well known to council environmental officers owing to complaints about parties, and Jeremy conceded the point with a fond little tut. I challenged him increasingly these days, especially when he said anything snobbish or entitled like that last comment. Having married into comfort, I was able now to admit – and occasionally defend – my earlier experiences of the opposite. It was nothing that suggested we were drifting apart, you understand, but more a case that I was growing up and he was giving me the space to do so.

'Anyway, they'll have been out at work all day yesterday,' I said. 'The only reason – what was her name? Caroline

Sellers, that's it – the only reason Caroline Sellers came by on a Friday was because she's a stay-at-home mum.'

'I hate that term,' Jeremy said, wrinkling his nose. 'As if they're under house arrest with electronic tags around their ankles.'

'Maybe that's how it feels?' I hoped there might be a different way of phrasing it by the time I became one – and, perhaps, a different way of *feeling* it. 'Anyway, people will have been doing Saturday stuff today, or nursing a hangover after office drinks. I remember it well.' I smiled, mock nostalgic. 'Friday always was the best day of the week.'

Jeremy ladled another helping of biryani onto his plate; he was lucky with his metabolism and, while not vain, kept himself in the kind of shape you'd expect of a successful man with a younger wife. 'You sound as if you wish you'd been there yourself, darling. You can always go back, you know. I have no wish to enslave you in domesticity.' He looked at me, amused. 'Make you *stay at home*. Or you could change careers? Retrain?'

I dismissed the very idea. Retrain? I'd never been trained in anything in the first place. Since I'd walked away from my job at Christmas I hadn't regretted it for a moment; I wouldn't have gone to Friday night drinks with my old colleagues if they'd been handing out tickets to the moon. 'I'll have masses to do here,' I told him. 'You're right, though, we do need to warn the neighbours about the work starting. There'll be a skip in the drive at eight o'clock on Monday morning.'

'And builders do like to get straight on to smashing everything up,' Jeremy said. 'It's the only part they seem to enjoy. It'll be bedlam by eight-thirty.' He spoke with the relish of someone who knew the upheaval would be brutal but expected to experience it only second hand, passing through in the dark, silent hours to admire progress or admonish the lack of it.

'We'll go around tomorrow morning and take them a bottle of wine as a bribe,' I suggested.

'Shares in a Bordeaux vineyard might be more appropriate. Better you go, babe, since you'll be in the firing line once it starts. And you're so much prettier than I am.'

'I certainly am.'

Thus armed, I headed next door the following morning. Though I used the parallel garden paths, I could easily have shimmied through the hedge between the two front doors, for there was no dividing fence. I considered idly whether we should put one up, the wrought-iron kind that seemed to be the fortification of choice on Lime Park Road, rows of spears painted in Farrow & Ball Off-black. Warrior chic, Hetty would call it.

Number 38 had not been extended into the loft as ours had, or to the rear as ours was about to, and there were just two floors, each containing a good-sized flat of identical footprint. I tried the downstairs flat first. A woman who looked in her seventies came to the door, smiling and expectant. She had an iPad in her hands and in the background country music played.

'I'm Amber Fraser,' I began.

'You've just moved in next door,' she told me before I could tell her. 'Felicity Boyd, pleased to meet you. I saw the vans on Friday. That was quite a convoy you had there.'

'Wasn't it? I'm not sure how we managed to fit so much into our old place. It was a bit of a shock when it came to boxing it all up.' Or watching a team of professionals box it up for me, as had been the case.

'Which is exactly why I would never dream of moving again,' she said cheerfully. 'I'm here for the duration. I couldn't face the packing.'

'Well, why would you need to move? We're already loving it here. The park is beautiful, isn't it?'

'The daffodils!' she agreed. 'And there'll be poppies soon too. They lasted for ages last year.'

'Well, I *love* poppies.'

It was all rather jolly and I felt sorry to have to tell her that her flower-filled idyll was about to be destroyed. But when I began to detail the improvements she only exclaimed with pleasure – 'How exciting for you!' – as thrilled as if it were her own home set to be refurbished.

'So, except for the kitchen extension, it's nothing structural. If you'd like to come over for a coffee one day, I'll show you exactly what we're planning.'

'Lovely.'

'Of course, we'll have a proper house-warming when it's all done – champagne, the works. It will be such a good party you'll all forget the horror that came before.'

She was delighted with the bottle I offered; I would give regular alms, I decided, pleased I had stocked up on hostess gifts on a recent trip to the West End. I got her to repeat her name before I went. I didn't want one of those awkward situations where you call someone the wrong name for years on end or have to avoid using one at all because you're too embarrassed to admit you weren't listening in the first place. (How mindful, how forward-thinking Amber Fraser could be, how dedicated to her new role as suburban homemaker and pillar of the community!)

When I pressed the bell for the upstairs flat there was initially no response and it was only as I was about to give up that there finally come a gruff male 'Yep?'

'Could I come up for a moment? I've just moved in next door and wanted to have a quick word.'

'Huh?'

It was obvious he was irritated by the rude awakening and I smiled to myself, remembering a time when noon on a Sunday had been offensively early to me too.

'Fine, come up,' he added, and I heard him clear the phlegm from his lungs as he resigned himself to the nuisance of my visit.

I still think sometimes about that short walk up the stairs to his flat, one of those moments of sweet, ordinary innocence you don't appreciate until it's gone – like the liberty you take for granted in the minutes before you get in your car and run someone over.

It was as I turned onto the narrow landing that I saw him. He was tall and broad, black-haired, dark-eyed, pale-skinned; he was both young enough and old enough, both too much and not enough: in other words a police photo-fit of what I remembered as my type. He was also dishevelled, hung-over and entirely unrepentant of being in no fit state to greet his caller – in fact, he was still dressing as he stood in his doorway. He had his jeans on and his arms in the sleeves of his shirt – yesterday's shirt,

29

I guessed, plucked from the floor – but he was looking down at the open front as if he couldn't quite remember how buttons worked. He radiated Saturday night debauchery, reeked of it, and the yearning it evoked in me was startling in its violence, just how I imagine a ghost taking bodily possession. By the time I'd thought to stop it, it was too late.

'Hi,' I said.

He raised his gaze to me, doubtless expecting some middle-aged crone, and at once his fingers halted, hovering a while as if he might change his mind and undress again. It goes without saying that I'd made myself presentable before setting out on this errand, my hair soft and loose over pale cashmere shoulders, lashes long, lips baby-pink. I was as demure and clean as he was louche and unwashed, and I could have curled up and purred on the lap of the god of vanity to see his response.

'Hi,' he echoed, and in this single appreciative syllable I was able to detect that casual wickedness I'd found so addictive in the men I'd gone out with before I came to my senses and married Jeremy. He was so like them, in fact, that I almost gasped one of their names aloud in recognition (Pete! Phil! Or, briefly and most dangerously, Matt!). I knew his kind inside out, had no doubt that regardless of his day job (if he had one) he was in his own mind a rock star or a poet or both. What he was doing on a street like Lime Park Road I couldn't begin to imagine, but, then again, since we were on the subject, what was *I* doing? Putting in high-end flooring with the aim of pushing an overpriced baby buggy back and forth across it, picking the neighbours' brains about school applications and piano lessons: was that really what I'd chosen for myself for *the rest of my life*?

I was momentarily speechless, frightened that I should suddenly be having these thoughts when I'd had no such ones for years. *Years*. Since the earliest days of being with Jeremy, I had only congratulated myself on my propitious and mature change of direction; I'd had no cold feet whatsoever, not a hint of a shiver. I'd managed my weakness for dissolute creatures like this one as you'd manage alcohol addiction or self-harming or any other disorder. I'd thought I was its master.

Why, then, was I relapsing now? Who *was* this man?

Clenching my toes inside my boots, I composed myself, heard my voice emerge in a low, cool purr: 'I'm Amber Fraser, your new neighbour. In the Lockes' old house?'

He did not reply, merely abandoned the intricacies of the shirt buttons once and for all to set about memorizing my face. I repaid the compliment, noting the length of his nose, the range of his thin mouth, a dark slash across the stain of an unshaven lower face. His eyes, under dense straight brows, were downturned at the outer corners, lids heavy with insolence.

'Am I allowed to ask *your* name?' I prompted.

'You are,' he mocked, giving it.

I had to ask him to repeat it because I hadn't caught the words, and he cleared his throat to do so. 'Rob Whalen.' He looked up and down the length of me very candidly then, making me grateful, blasphemously grateful, for not yet being pregnant and for not gorging on biryani takeaways or anything else that might jeopardize the narrow waist so vital in making sense of the dimensions above and below it.

I held out the bottle of wine. 'Well, Rob Whalen, I'm sorry to get you out of bed. I just wanted to give you this.'

He took it from me, squinting at the label as if it emitted difficult bright light, before his lips parted, mouth broadening into a smile. 'Looks like a nice one, cheers. But I might wait till later before I crack it open, know what I mean?' He had a faint south London accent, the kind that had probably begun as an affectation and stuck, the tone sleep-roughened and seductive. Belatedly, those under-slept eyes turned suspicious. 'Why are you giving *me* a gift? I don't get it. If you've just moved in, shouldn't I be the one with the offering? I could have brought you, what, a muffin basket? Or is that just in American films?' He chuckled, pleased with himself. 'How long before I've left it too late and you start suspecting me of darker motives?'

I thought then, He's not into music or poetry, but film. That's his passion; he'll be writing a screenplay, dreaming of Academy Awards and a beach house in Malibu.

'You don't need to bring us anything,' I said smoothly. (Actually, maybe I didn't say 'us'; maybe 'us' is a false memory.) 'But I have to admit there *are* dark motives, on my part, anyway. You see, I came to warn you there'll be building work starting first thing tomorrow and it will get a bit noisy. I don't know what time you leave for work, but I want you to know I'll be making sure everyone is careful about sticking to the hours permitted by the council.'

'That won't help me,' Rob Whalen said. 'I work from home.'

'Oh, that's not good.' But already, criminally, I was thinking the opposite: that *was* good. He was at home all day, I was at home all day, we could get together and –

Stop!

'I have a horrible feeling we're going to make your life a misery then,' I said. By then I had definitely introduced the plural; I could hardly conceal for long the fact of my marriage, even if I wanted to. 'It's going to go on for a few months, I'm afraid.'

He shrugged. 'It's no big deal. I usually have head-phones on when I work. Or I take my laptop to the café in the park.'

'What about your . . . ? Or do you live alone?'

When he said yes, he lived alone, I was thrilled. Girl-choosing-a-birthday-balloon-and-being-told-she-can-have-two thrilled. Girl-who-didn't-already-have-a-mate-for-life-and-thought-she-might-just-have-met-him thrilled. (Was that Jeremy I could hear on the other side of the wall? Dragging a box up the stairs to our temporary marital chamber in the eaves?) Oh, how different it would all have been if Rob Whalen had answered instead, 'This isn't my place, I'm just staying with a friend before I leave for a flight this afternoon to start a new life in New Zealand.'

If he had, I'd – we'd – still be living in Lime Park now.

Because it was instant, my attraction to him, incontest-able. And had it been one-way, just my craving him because I was entering a new bored-housewife phase and was open to suggestion, it would have been possible – just – to conquer it. I had my pride; I would not have chased indifferent prey. But it was recognizably mutual, obscenely so. We were edging towards one another, millimetre by millimetre, not speaking, only staring. It was outrageous, indecent *already*.

'Well, goodbye,' I said, feeling myself frown as I turned to leave. I was confused, mildly nauseous. 'Enjoy the wine.'

'I'll let you know,' he drawled.

'If it's any good?'

'No, when the misery starts. I'll let you know and you can decide how you're going to compensate me.'

This was candid even by my standards and I blushed as I went down the stairs. There was not the sound of his door closing, I noticed: he must have stayed in the doorway or come out onto the landing to watch me depart.

Behind Felicity's door her music played.

With some effort, I composed myself as I scurried the few steps home. Jeremy was on the top floor, unpacking clothing and cramming it into a chest of drawers on the landing. The room at the back, our makeshift living room, was a jumble of furniture and boxes and items unpacked and displaced: shoes, underwear, a rogue table-tennis bat I hadn't known we owned.

'Did it go OK? What're they like?'

'Fine. Both really nice.' And when his hands next became free I took one and gripped it in mine – as if that could stop the unstoppable, the brief knitting of fingers!

He paused to smile at me in indulgent surprise. 'And?'

'There's an old woman with an iPad downstairs and a bloke with a hangover upstairs.'

Typically, he ignored the latter to seize on the former. 'When you say old, what do you mean?' As if somehow personally exempt, Jeremy was wryly amused by societal attitudes to ageing; it tickled him when I made blithe remarks about someone being over the hill.

'Oh, seventy or something. Though she's got the iPad, so I guess she must be quite with it.'

'"With it"? You're a bit young for an expression like that.'

'I must have picked it up from you. I'm entering middle age prematurely. Thanks for that.'

'You're very welcome,' Jeremy said.

How old was hard-living, hard-chested Rob Whalen? I wondered. My age, a year or two younger, perhaps. But he might have been ten years older for all it mattered, or twenty, for he was one of those eternal bachelors who were easy to catch and hard to keep, interested only in the pleasures of the present.

I swallowed hard.

Still with his hand in mine, Jeremy looked out of the window. Where the view from our old flat had contained the iconic Thames, here in Lime Park it was of an anonymous wedge of garden, complete with the children's swings left by the Lockes. Trees whose type I could not hope to identify had yet to blossom, not persuaded by the city's first attempts at spring. Next door, in Caroline Sellers' garden, her children sprang about on a damp trampoline, their mouths circular with screams that our sealed windows rendered silent, dreamlike. I pictured them rising to superhuman heights, clearing the wall in a perfect trajectory to land on the grass in the park, brushing themselves off completely unhurt.

'The garden will be great for kids,' Jeremy said, as he had when we viewed the house. 'Looks like they've got three next door. The Lockes had three as well, didn't they? The place is teeming with them. Maybe they put fertility hormones in the water.'

'Urgh, what a horrible idea.'

He grinned as if he'd said something naughty, dirty, but he hadn't and he never would. He couldn't alter the cleanness of him, the neat and predictable well-brought-up wholesomeness of him. He was over fifty but he was boyish, and there were times, like when you'd just been confronted with your preferred type, your archetype, when boyishness was not an aphrodisiac.

No matter: talk of children had led logically to thoughts of creating them, and before I knew it I was being carted into the bedroom for the latest stab at conception. Which was fine, which was what we both wanted, which was the plan. But on this occasion Jeremy halted mid-unbuckling, distracted perhaps by the sight of the myriad repairs and renewals the room needed before it could be considered half-habitable. He didn't say anything, but I guessed his thoughts – We *must* ask Hetty about that ceiling, the plasterboard looks bowed. And does that window need replacing? – before he remembered why he'd brought me in here in the first place.

'Come on, then,' I said from the bed, my tone

encouraging but also leavened with a new emotion, not guilt yet but some furtive precursor of it. I'd never used that tone with him before. To someone listening at the bedroom door, I could have been his mother about to tuck him into bed for a nap, or an escort with a bashful first-timer on her hands.

In order not to think about Rob Whalen, I thought about nothing.

Chapter 3

Christy, April 2013

It would be a source of consolation in time to come that their families visited the new house while fortune still favoured the brave; when she and Joe had the pleasure of presenting their new home as a proud gain rather than a potential loss.

And what a pleasure it was!

Eager as greyhounds, her parents raced to Lime Park on that first Sunday afternoon, tearing through the door with flowers and champagne and a card with no shortage of exclamation marks in the message: *Good luck in your new home, Joe & Christy! Congratulations! You did it!!*

'What is this, ten times bigger than your old place?' her mother said, as the tour ascended to the suite of rooms at the top.

'Maybe not *ten*,' Christy said. 'But I have to admit there was a moment yesterday when I forgot we had this extra floor up here. It was more than my mind could process. How weird is that?'

'Very weird,' her father said drily. 'Some might say immoral when you think there are families in this city living six to a room. Or no room at all, just one of those halfway-house hellholes, waiting for permanent accommodation.'

As a teacher at a Croydon comprehensive with police officers at the gates and social workers on speed dial, he had always been going to draw comparisons, but not at the expense of letting his daughter and son-in-law know how delighted he was by their remarkable leap up the property ladder. It would be like refusing to be thrilled by magic.

'You could always get a lodger up here; you'd hardly notice they were there, would you?' He was thinking, possibly, of the five-figure sum – pretty much all her parents had to spare – he'd lent them in that scramble to amass the funds for completion. 'If you ever fall on hard times,' he added good-humouredly.

'I'll remember that,' Christy said.

Joe's parents were united with hers in their stupefaction. 'You're getting a bit posh for us now,' they told Joe, and Christy saw the flush of pride in their faces.

'Oh, that'll never happen,' he said, grinning. 'Will it, Christy? We'll never crack the enigma of gracious living.'

'Not while we're with each other, anyway,' she said. 'Maybe in our second marriages?' How she loved seeing their families together in the new house. She was already having visions of big noisy Christmases, everyone gathered in the living room like something out of *It's a Wonderful Life* (there was a lot more furniture in these visions; as things stood, most of the family would have to cram together in the window seat).

'What must this other couple have been like?' Joe's mother marvelled on entering one of their three glittering bathrooms, the master en suite ('master en suite': it was like a foreign vocabulary). 'Were they Russian or something?'

Joe chuckled. 'No, but Amber Baby had *very* expensive tastes.'

'Amber Baby?'

'That's what we call her, don't we, Christy?'

'We do.'

Closer inspection of the dragonfly key ring had revealed the inscription '*Amber Baby*' on the insect's belly and had been immediately adopted by the Davenports. Christy, who could not imagine Joe even *saying* 'Christy Baby', much less having it engraved on a charm for her, though she knew exactly the type of woman who inspired the immortalization of intimate nicknames on trinkets she then discarded without a care. A different species altogether from her. 'I'll send the key ring on with the mail,' she had told him, though she already had the faint suspicion that she was going to keep it.

'Expensive tastes? You can say that again,' said Joe's mother. 'I haven't seen *those* taps in B&Q, have you? And what's the bath made of?'

'Copper,' Christy supplied. 'A vintage Mexican tub, the agent said.'

'Who on earth would think to import a bath from *Mexico*?' her mother asked.

'Amber Baby,' Joe and Christy chorused. 'Insane, isn't it?' Christy added.

Even so, the insanity was surprisingly infectious. Standing in front of the mirror an hour earlier, she had found herself scrutinizing her discreetly pencilled eyes ('honest brown' was probably the most generous description of them, though they were not without a sparkle of their

40

own) and sprouting dark roots with a vanity that was both uncharacteristic and – she would be the first to admit it – unwarranted. She'd even stood on tiptoe and straightened her spine; it was as if the Frasers' mirror demanded proper respect of all whose reflections it granted.

'Well, now we know how the other half live, eh,' Joe's father said, a phrase he used more than once that afternoon, exaggerating his accent for effect.

'Yes, and apparently it's without the Internet,' Joe said. 'At least it is for the foreseeable future. We've gone back to the nineties.'

'We're using a different supplier from the Frasers,' Christy explained, thinking, For different read cut-price, 'and I can't get them to come out here for three weeks.' Forty-five minutes she'd been held in the helpline queue the previous Tuesday morning, carefully avoiding Laurie's eye when she patrolled, only to be told that an express service would incur a surcharge. Regular (slow) service was going to have to do. 'Joe goes back to work tomorrow and I'm here on my own for a week,' she added. 'I'm quite looking forward to being cut off from the world.'

The group meandered into the garden. After a dim, overcast morning the sun had found a fault line in the cloud cover, causing them to screw up their eyes and make visors of their hands, cavers emerging from the underworld. Early spring in a well-tended garden, what a picture of new hope it was: the gleaming close-shorn lawn, the clutch of trees (identified by Christy's mother as blackthorns) heavy with blossom, the pale flagstones gilded with sunlight. The four parents strolled the length of the path like visiting dignitaries on a town-twinning scheme, and peeked in turn through the gate into the park, surprising a spaniel sniffing on the other side.

'The people before had young children, did they?' her mother said, motioning to the set of swings.

'I don't think they did,' Christy said. 'At least there were no kids' bedrooms when we looked around. The swings must be from the family before them.'

Her mother nodded, unconvincingly casual. 'I suppose you wouldn't bother tearing out something like that if there's a fair chance you'd be needing it yourself at some point.'

'You have to pour concrete,' Joe's father agreed. 'It's a right palaver.'

Though she chose not to look, Christy had no doubt the elders were exchanging glances, united in their expectations of a grandchild. She knew her own would have decided it was a done deal the moment she and Joe had gone begging for a loan (maybe their generosity had been in good faith: cash for babies!). Certainly the sight now of multiple spare bedrooms, a lawn for kicking a ball about, and those swings, semi-permanent and wholly symbolic, would only have served to strengthen the belief. How she hated to disappoint them all, hoped Joe wouldn't decide to lay bare their postponement plan. Better if he hinted vaguely that they would be trying soon and then, when next quizzed, suggested it was taking a little longer than expected, just one of those things. His casual diminishment of it – even in this imaginary form – brought a lump to her throat.

After the tour they had coffee in the kitchen. Their old pine table looked completely wrong amid the Frasers' state-of-the-art modernity and there was talk of sanding it and smartening it up with a coat of paint.

'What's this?' her mother asked, spotting the hotel brochure that had come in the post for Amber Fraser. Since the acetate was already torn, Christy had thought it harmless to open it and leaf through the photographs. 'Treetop Suites, I've heard about this hotel. It's not far from Granny's place in Sussex. Isn't it extortionately pricey?'

Christy nodded. 'Don't worry, it's not ours.' She didn't mention that she had read the letter that had come with the brochure: *Dear Mrs Fraser, following your recent stay, we are delighted to confirm your automatic membership of the Treetops Club . . .* It had made Christy think of the mile-high club; she imagined the Frasers in their luxury cabin under the canopy, lounging about in silk robes and cashmere slippers, feeding one another woodland-themed canapés before falling onto a bed strewn with apple blossom. *Oh, Amber, baby . . .*

She suppressed a giggle.

'Shouldn't you be forwarding any mail that's not yours?' her father said, ever the upstanding citizen.

'Yes, I'll send it on in the week with the rest.'

'No point keeping it, anyway,' Joe said, tossing the brochure aside with mock regret. 'It'll be a long time before we can even afford a drink at a place like that.' He and Christy beamed at each other: incredible how quickly you could get used to being phenomenally in debt.

At the door, about to leave, her mother delivered her

43

official verdict: 'It's a wonderful house, Christy. I see why you decided to risk everything to get it.'

And Christy accepted her congratulations in the who-dares-wins spirit in which the words were intended. After all, did anyone who dared win actually believe they might lose?

Did anyone who risked everything expect to fail?

Christy had met Joe at Cocktail Night in the union bar during their second year of university (the lowest-ranking of any to grace a Jermyn Richards CV). Delivering her White Russian to their table, he'd remarked on her sweet tooth and when she told him that he'd already discovered the most dangerous thing about her, he'd laughed and said, Good, because he didn't know how to cope with dangerous women. Perhaps that was why their attraction had been less a fireworks display than a quiet mutual ignition; neither having fallen in love before, they were not in a position to tip the other off as to what was happening between them, and only when they'd resurfaced did they understand that they had plunged.

Unlike other couples, they had developed no mythology around their early years together, nor around their respective childhoods. If hers had been unremarkable – the only child of a teacher and an assistant manager at a branch of Boots – then his might be described as a struggle. His father had worked for decades in recovery patrol for the AA, routinely absent on weekend and night shifts, while his mother raised four children and cleaned part-time for a chain of kitchen showrooms. The family

44

home was – still was – a rented terrace on the east London–Essex border.

(Once, at a Jermyn Richards drinks, Christy had heard Marcus and another senior partner discussing Joe in terms such as 'salt of the earth' and a 'genuine Londoner', as if he'd been raised by pearly kings and queens, but she'd noted the affection in their voices.)

Physically, he was not striking, at least at first glance, being short and wiry and possessed of the kind of gentle colouring that would fade prematurely, but Christy knew herself well enough to understand that she did not have the self-confidence to handle a conspicuously attractive man – were she to have caught his eye in the first place, which history suggested she would not. Integrity, kindness, intelligence: those were the attractions that mattered to her, and Joe had them in such quantities that they *glowed*. And while he was not one of those people who had reinvented themselves so convincingly it came as a discombobulating experience to meet their parents, twelve years in a City law firm had nonetheless smoothed the accent somewhat and furnished him with most of the cultural references his colleagues had possessed from childhood. (She'd done her best to keep pace.)

Still, he'd suffered for his lack of an expensive education. Once the euphoria of winning the JR training contract had faded, he'd intuited swiftly that he had not made the cut as a one to watch. That decentness of his was no advantage; he was too useful a wingman in the ever-more dangerous flying environment that was Mergers & Acquisitions to ever be given a crack at lead pilot.

'I'm starting to think I have to work twice as hard as them just to get the same credit,' he said of his socially superior counterparts.

'Now you know how it feels to be a woman,' Christy told him.

It was not until the end of the first week that she had her first encounters with the neighbours – or, in the case of the guy upstairs, 'sighting' was a better definition. He was an unkempt figure, it transpired, and of indeterminate age: either young and out of condition or older and *in* condition, it was hard to tell with someone so bedraggled. His black hair was an overgrown thicket that obscured his eyes, and the rest of his features and neck were buried beneath a pelt of facial hair. Tall, almost towering, and heavy of gait, he was a bear of a man – but not the cuddly, protective kind; more the kind that came down from the mountain to rampage through your bins.

Christy was in the front garden, enjoying the novelty of weeding, when he came out of his house and paused at the gate, fishing in his jacket pocket for something or other, his back to her. He did not respond to her call of hello from barely ten feet away, and when he ignored a second, louder greeting, slipping away without so much as a glance over his shoulder, she seriously wondered if he might be deaf.

But of course he wasn't deaf; he was just rude.

Oh dear. Perhaps it wouldn't have been such a disappointment had not the woman on the other side been so cool with her the next day.

Caroline Sellers introduced herself when she and Christy were leaving their houses at the same time and came face to face on the pavement. Older than Christy by about five years, she gave an immediate impression of bluntness, short not only in stature but also in facial feature, nose a little flat, brow abbreviated, jawbone not quite strong enough. Pony-tailed, heavily mascaraed and dressed in jeans, blazer and high-heeled ankle boots, she had the capable but burdened air of someone in middle management who regularly threatened to walk out of her job but never actually did.

'Sorry I haven't had the chance to say hello before,' she said, and her voice was exactly what Christy had expected of her Lime Park neighbours: fine-grained accent, tone of utter dauntlessness. 'We were away over Easter.'

'Anywhere nice?' Christy asked.

'Just our place on the Ile de Ré. The kids went back to school this week.'

'How old are they?'

'Eleven next week, almost-but-not-quite eight and a half, and just turned four.'

Christy wondered why she didn't just say eleven, eight and four.

'Do you have any?' Caroline asked.

'No, it's just my husband and me.'

This dismayed Caroline; you could see it in the slow slide of her half-smile, a perceptible withdrawal of warmth.

'Would you like to come in for a coffee?' Christy said, forgetting they were both on their way out, her own errand involving a trip to the hardware store on the Parade for light bulbs.

'Thank you,' Caroline said, 'but I need to dash. I'm just picking up my youngest from school. He's in kindergarten and finishes a bit earlier than the other two.'

'Is it a local school they go to?'

'Yes, Lime Park Primary, just behind the Parade.'

'I'm going in that direction, as well. Maybe we could walk together and you can fill me in on the local gossip?'

This Christy said quite playfully and yet the other woman looked startled, almost insulted, by her suggestion. Suddenly she was digging in her bag and extracting a set of car keys; she had been going to walk (and why wouldn't she, the school was ten minutes away?), but now she'd decided to drive.

'You're based at home, are you?' she asked, apparently not entirely incurious.

Christy smiled. 'No, I've just been off work this week to unpack and get the utilities sorted out. I thought I might need to do some decorating but the couple before us left the house in such perfect condition there's nothing for me to do.' When Caroline failed to react, Christy continued to voice her thoughts, forgetting this was not always the most successful basis for conversation: 'We're not online yet, either, and my phone doesn't get a very good signal down here so I feel a bit cut off. I can't wait to get back to work, to be honest. The street feels so dead. There's no way I could do this full time . . .' Too late she heard how the words might have sounded and felt her cheeks flush. 'I didn't mean . . . Well, maybe you don't work and I didn't mean it how it sounded.'

A week out of the office and already she was a gibbering idiot.

'Excuse me, but I certainly *do* work,' Caroline said, frowning rather fiercely. Her voice rang clear and confident in the quiet street, audible surely to anyone with an inch of open window. 'I have three children under eleven and if *that's* not work then I don't know what is.'

'Of course. I only meant —'

'Real work, eh? A contribution to the Exchequer, something in the interests of society and not for my own selfish hormonal ends? Yes, I know what you *only* meant. Well, future taxpayers don't raise themselves, you know.'

'I . . .' Christy's face burned. She was not sure how this could have escalated so rapidly. Was this one of those unfortunate situations when you find yourself bearing the brunt of someone's pre-existing frustrations? Had Caroline been criticized before and not had the opportunity to defend herself? 'I'm sure you're right,' she said apologetically. 'Forget I said anything.'

But Caroline only looked at her with exasperated disbelief, as if she could not credit that *this* was what had emerged from number 40. 'You think very differently from Amber, I see,' she said, as if that settled it.

'Amber?' In her confusion it took Christy a second or two to place the name. 'Oh. I didn't ever meet —' she began, but it was too late, Caroline had turned from her to point her key fob at a nearby Mini, the lights of which began to flash as the locks released. Christy wondered how a family of five could fit into the tiny cabin, but then she remembered the enormous Audi on the drive. She and Joe had never owned a car in their lives, let alone two.

'Bye,' Christy called after her. 'Another time, maybe?' But the question was obliterated by the angry crunch of the car door closing.

Oh dear, she thought. So far she wasn't seeing much evidence of the open-armed community she had so confidently expected of Lime Park Road. But there were plenty more fish in the sea, she told herself, and the law of averages dictated they couldn't *all* have spines as prickly as this one.

Besides, she had dinner at Canvas to look forward to.

Joe had suggested it, Joe had booked it, and presumably Joe was also now going to explain how they would justify paying for it in the light of the crushing budget they'd drawn up together (if it didn't permit good coffee, then it certainly prohibited meals in restaurants like Canvas).

She'd studied the menu on her way back from the hardware store and concluded that it was both intimidatingly fashionable (crab foam and grated bottarga – they'd not had those in New Cross) and toe-curlingly expensive. A starter equated to the pedal bin they needed for the ground-floor loo, while a main course might buy them blinds for one of the spare bedrooms, and yet there Joe was, ordering champagne, the bottle opened when she joined him and two glasses already poured.

'I know what this is about,' she said, smiling. She was damned if she was going to spoil the lovely gesture. And what a beautiful restaurant it was! No wonder every table was taken, the atmosphere one of unbridled jubilation:

everywhere you looked there was vivid colour, from the fresh-lime shade of the sculpted vinyl chairs to the sparkling fuchsia of the teardrop glass chandeliers and the garden greens and ocean blues of the canvases that crowded the walls. Each table had a tangle of wild flowers for its centrepiece, and Christy reached to touch the petals to check that they were real, to check that *this* was real. 'It's about celebrating our milestones, isn't it? And I completely agree that the house is –'

'Christy,' he interrupted, and she saw how excited he was, possibly even a little drunk already. 'It's not the house. I've got some other news.' He paused in a way she recognized as being less for effect than to overcome his own disbelief. 'I've been made partner.'

She stared. Partner: the longed-for promotion he'd been warned by Marcus to not yet expect, even when two younger associates had been successful, leading Christy privately, treacherously, to interpret 'not yet' as never.

'Not equity,' he added, 'I'll be capped on what I earn, but still it's –'

Now it was she who interrupted: 'But it's *incredible*, Joe! Wow, congratulations!' And as he recounted the day's events for her, heat suffused her body, the heat of joy. Just as she'd thought they'd had their share of fortune, here was more of it – and fortune of the sort that might take the edge off their financial pressures, too.

'What are you thinking?' Joe said, their glasses refilled.

'I'm thinking we can maybe buy some furniture for all those empty rooms. And we need shelving and waste-paper baskets as a matter of urgency.'

'Those are the kind of extravagant romantic gestures I like to hear.'

They grinned at each other. 'Actually, I was thinking something else as well,' she admitted. 'You know the other day, when we moved into the house?'

'When you convinced yourself we were squatters about to be picked up by the police?'

'Yes, but after that. I was thinking I'd never seen you look so pleased with yourself.'

'Pleased with *us*,' he corrected her. 'It's all coming together, isn't it?' He raised his glass with an easy flourish, as if he'd been born to celebrate success.

'Like we're getting all our good luck in one go!'

'Well, it's supposed to come in threes, so maybe there's even more.'

'I think that only works with *bad* luck, doesn't it?' Christy said, her eyes widening in mock trepidation.

They demolished their meals. They'd chosen the same for both courses – salmon terrine followed by rack of lamb, give or take the Canvas bells and whistles – which happened almost every time; they had long ago agreed that this was absolutely fine and didn't make them in any way a boring couple. It was the first well-cooked food they'd eaten for weeks, neither of them having a reputation for culinary prowess, especially not when paired with thrift.

But anything would have tasted ambrosial that evening. When Joe's attention was stolen briefly by a phone call from Marcus, she was overcome by an urge to share his news with other diners, scanning the tables for familiar faces, though of course she hardly knew a soul in Lime

Park. That will change, she thought; in a year's time, we'll look around this room and know we belong.

'So what did you do today?' Joe asked, all hers again.

'Oh, I wasn't nearly as successful as you. Among other things, I inadvertently offended a neighbour.'

He smirked. 'Who was it? Not the hairy one you told me about yesterday?'

'No, not him. The woman from the other side. Caroline, she's called.' Christy explained what had happened, how her blunder had caused the woman to storm off.

'She sounds a bit oversensitive,' Joe said. 'She'll be one of those crazy leopard mothers, I bet.'

'*Tiger* mothers.'

'That's it. Living through her children, no sense of the wider world. They didn't have them in New Cross, but they roam freely among us in Lime Park.'

'I think you're right.' The pang Christy felt at the ease with which he aligned himself to the child-free was minimal, hardly a pang at all. Their income was about to increase, after all; the right time for a baby might come sooner than they'd planned.

Maybe that would be their third piece of luck.

'I'm back to work on Monday,' she reminded him. 'Hopefully I can make it up to Laurie for having been so useless this past month.' The uncompromising nature of Joe's job meant that it had been she who'd borne the lion's share of the phone calls and emails demanded of the expedited house-purchase process.

'I thought Ellen covered for you?'

'She did, but all it takes is one little remark from the

client. And Laurie's been a bit unpredictable since she came back from maternity leave.'

'Rather be at home being a tiger, d'you think? Well, I bet you weren't half as bad as those girls who sit at their desks planning their weddings. We've got one at JR. Photographers, dress fittings, flowers, that's all you hear her talk about. I swear she's going to get a formal warning if she doesn't lay off.'

'Easy to say when you're the groom.' Christy seemed to remember she'd organized most of *their* wedding. 'But I'm glad to hear such liberties are being taken even at Jermyn Richards.'

Joe raised his glass in salute. 'Even at Jermyn Richards.'

And with the last of the champagne they touched glasses once more.

Chapter 4

Amber, 2012

I'm not a fool. I know it must be a stretch to understand how I let it happen. It doesn't stack up, it doesn't make sense – I see that. And if I've given the impression that Jeremy and I didn't love each other, then I've done us both a disservice, because we certainly did.

So how on earth can my behaviour be explained (I would never suggest justified)? I've sought no advice, naturally, but a few theories of my own have surfaced, informed by the psychology articles I've read in magazines. One, I wanted to test Jeremy's love because even after five and a half years together my rise to affluence and security still struck me as too good to be true. Two, I was inherently self-destructive and an act like this was inevitable, a question not of if but when, and my accessory in betrayal could have been any neighbour, any colleague, any passing sucker. Three, it could have been no one but him because what we had was chemistry in its most primitive form, an unstoppable life force. I could have been married to the King of England and it would still have happened.

What I *do* know is that I didn't do it lightly. It wasn't a case of waiting for Jeremy to leave the house on Monday morning and slipping straight next door, shedding my clothes as I took the stairs, an animal in season. No, after that first encounter, I did my best to defy divine decree. Not once did I flick my eyes to the windows of 38B or take a step towards his door. I met other Lime Park residents and was democratically warm and friendly, which wasn't difficult given how welcoming the community was. I lost count of how many neighbours came by to introduce themselves those first few weeks – 'Welcome to Lime Park Road!' they'd cry, as if we'd landed on some tropical island renowned for the openheartedness of its natives – or the times I answered the doorbell to be presented with flowers or a bottle of wine.

I self-consciously applied myself to my new house, to the builders, to the deliveries that arrived several times a day. And there were constant meetings to occupy me, either formal catch-ups with Hetty or impromptu confabs with the builders about some hitch or other.

'Isn't this exciting?' Hetty said as she surveyed the deliveries stacked in the master bedroom, our designated stockroom during the build. Her eyes danced as she unpacked a shipment of hexagonal glass tiles from Italy, destined to bring iridescent magic to our en-suite shower enclosure. 'We're finally under way after all that planning!'

'Very exciting,' I agreed.

'You seem a bit shell-shocked, Amber. Don't be demoralized by the dust. People *always* get demoralized by dust.'

'I'm not demoralized,' I said.

I was, however, driven out. The ground floor was a construction site, a dirt pit, scheduled to encroach before long on the floors above when work began on the bathrooms, and the place was as insufferably noisy as we'd feared. By the beginning of the third week, I'd all but given up and started doing what I'd only joked I would: leave everything to Hetty and the team and spend my days off-site. I joined the local gym, which was a convenient walk through the park and had its own pool and spa; I familiarized myself with all the retail opportunities within walking distance and drove to adjoining neighbourhoods to do the same there; I met my old colleagues in town for lunch, keeping at bay their requests to see the new house ('It's hell. You'll need hard hats. Let's wait till the weather's better and we can sit in the garden'). I was a stay-at-home mum in a home that wasn't habitable and with no children to put in it.

A fourth theory: the illusion of homelessness, combined with my abandonment of my job, had dislocated my value system. I was unmoored, a rolling stone poised to drop into the first dark hole in its path.

And the first dark hole just happened to be next door.

I next saw him in the café in the park; it was our fourth week in Lime Park. Of course, I recalled his saying he went there sometimes to work and so I had mostly avoided it as a venue for my daylight loafing, but this was Friday and my resolve was weakening. I remember thinking, Jeremy will be home this evening and we'll be together for the weekend and that will buy me two more days of grace. I had the naive idea that the longer I was able to stave off the inevitable, the less inevitable it would become.

Rob was sitting at a quiet corner table with his laptop

in front of him, eyebrows beetled low in concentration, left hand tapping at the tabletop rather than the keyboard. As soon as I spied him I began intoning, *He hasn't seen you . . . Don't go over . . .* But of course ten seconds later I was making sure he *had* seen me, calling out 'Hello, again!' and going right on over.

He lifted a hand in greeting. 'Well, if it isn't the new kid on the block. Miss Amber.'

He'd remembered my name, of course; the 'Miss' was for his own amusement.

'That's me. Hard day at the office?'

'Certainly is.' He grinned up at me – he had good straight white teeth; I'd pictured them as stained, the teeth of a feral creature – and seeing how pleased he was to find me in front of him I felt myself ignite.

'What is it you do?'

'I'm a writer.'

'I knew it! I said to Jeremy that's what you must be.' I had said nothing of the sort, but what I had done was strike a deal with myself that if I were to meet Rob again (*if?*), I would introduce Jeremy's name into the conversation within the first two minutes.

'Jeremy's the silver fox you're married to?' he asked.

I smiled. 'He'll be pleased with that first impression.'

'What, that he's a silver fox or that you're married? Is either impression false?'

'Oh, we're definitely married,' I said, answering the question he was actually asking. My gaze was level; given how out of practice I was, I was impressively slick. 'It will be five years in July, in fact.'

'Congratulations.'

I motioned to his laptop. 'So you're working on a screenplay, right?'

This tickled him. 'Wrong. I write about education. I freelance for the papers and a couple of news sites.'

'Education?'

'No need to sound so disappointed.'

'It's not disappointment,' I said truthfully. 'It's fear of the exposure of the wasteland that was *my* education. In this conversation you'll be the only one who's disappointed.' By now I seemed to have slipped into the seat opposite him and a waitress was standing at my shoulder, ready to take an order. I had almost forgotten we were in a café, a public place. Don't order anything, I told myself, but of course when I opened my mouth I asked for a cappuccino. 'In a takeout cup,' I added, clawing back a little sanity.

'And what do *you* do?' Rob asked. He eyed my workout gear, snug and glossy as a second skin, my damp hair knotted high on my head, cheeks flushed. 'Synchronized-swimming teacher, right?'

He was mimicking my speech, mocking me, and I loved it. As a rule, educated, middle-class men treated me with politeness, even awe. Only highly confident ones teased like this, ones with an indecent number of conquests under their belt.

'Wrong,' I said. 'Until last Christmas I was a media buyer.' I named the agency, but he was as blank as anyone outside the industry would be. How pathetically our working worlds shrink the moment we depart from them. Not only did I not miss mine in the slightest but when I thought of the old gang at their desks, when I compared their continuing ten-hour-a-day graft with my new idleness, I felt merely pity. 'I'm taking a career break to oversee the works on the house. I'm an overseer.'

'You can do that from the gym, can you?'

'Sure. It's not as if I'm knocking down walls and plumbing in toilets myself. And I have a project manager who handles the day-to-day stuff.'

'The day-to-day stuff,' he echoed in parody. 'So you're not the overseer at all. You're the plantation owner.'

'The plantation owner's wife,' I admitted without a trace of apology (and quick to congratulate myself on the second reference to Jeremy too).

'Well, I've seen it all happening. Your Eastern European slaves. It's a bit like the Shard going up.'

'Oh yes. But without the vertigo.'

He considered me with unconcealed appetite, clearly impressed with the quality of my banter, not to mention the close-fitting top. Slowly, he pushed down the lid of his laptop. 'You don't seem the usual Lime Park type, Amber, if you don't mind me saying.'

'I don't mind at all. And *you* are?'

'Not any more. I'm pre-gentrification and too lazy to leave. I was here long before the private-school families and City boys. But there was a time when I *was* the type.'

'I see. Well, I'm very much post-gentrification. I had to be gentrified myself before the move to a respectable neighbourhood like this could even be considered.'

'Really?' He grew more curious still. 'You're the product of a Pygmalion project, are you?'

'I certainly am. But you can never really change a low-born. Take me to the races like Eliza and the guttersnipe will show herself soon enough.'

He nibbled at a thumb, nail in the groove between his front teeth. 'I don't see you as a guttersnipe, I must admit.'

'Not any more, sure.' My coffee arrived and I brandished the white plastic spoon that came with it. 'But I was born with one of these in my mouth, so you can imagine how chuffed I am to have switched to silver.'

He laughed. 'Not everyone's so honest about their humble beginnings.'

'I find that silly,' I said. 'After all, the less you begin with, the more reason you have to be proud of your achievements.' Quite what my achievements were, I couldn't say offhand, but I could see that with every minute I was becoming more fascinating to him and that was accomplishment enough for now.

'Well, I'm plastic spoon by choice,' he said, his gaze lingering on the sizeable diamond on my left hand. I had a disconcerting image of him sliding it off with his teeth. 'I consider it my moral duty to lower the tone of our upwardly mobile street. Neither my flat nor I are in any way modernized.'

'Unreconstructed. I like that.' This was verging on farce: I couldn't have been more flirtatious if I'd sat in his lap and unzipped my top, pressed his face into my cleavage.

'This obsession with renovation,' he went on, leaning towards me very slightly, just close enough for the edges of our breath to meet, 'I don't understand it. What is it with ripping everything out and starting again? Every time someone moves in they replace the kitchen and the bathroom and maybe the windows. Then the same happens again a couple of years later. I don't remember a time when there wasn't a skip in the street with German basins in it.'

'German?' I giggled.

'Or Italian, Swedish, wherever. And it's all completely intact, some of it in mint condition. Not exactly in tune with the recycling zeitgeist, is it?'

I thought of the worn but perfectly serviceable oak cabinets being torn out of my kitchen as we spoke to make way for the costly and high-maintenance bevelled-glass replacements that our successors might very well loathe.

'So you're our resident eco-warrior, are you?' I said.

'Not at all. I'm just not an arrogant twat.'

My eyes went very wide precisely as his narrowed, and neither of us blinked. It was an interesting moment, in which I guessed he anticipated the rebuke that he'd gone too far, but I made it clear with my gaze that he could never go too far, not with me. And that was that, the dynamic was established: we were each as bold as the other, each as damned.

I sipped my coffee as I watched him cast about for a change of subject, a half step back. 'Have you met Felicity yet?' he asked.

'Yes, she seems like a character.'

'Oh, she is. She's a big Glen Campbell fan. If the drilling gets too much, she'll blast you back with "The Wichita Lineman".'

'I don't know it,' I admitted.

62

'You've never heard any Glen Campbell?' He began murmuring a melody, presumably a line from the song he'd mentioned, and it felt like a siren call, drawing me to my death and releasing me only when it faded, which it soon did as he began chuckling at his own foolishness. 'It's too early in the day for karaoke. But gen up, if you want her onside.'

'I'll remember that.'

Together we strolled the short distance home, our stride slow to the point of reluctance. We used the main park gate; only Felicity had access to the private gate for number 38, Rob told me, and I was not yet ready for him to set foot in my house or garden. We arrived at our front gates to find the usual dust cloud billowing from my open front door, the drone of power tools beyond. Two builders leaned against the skip, smoking, and I called hello, noticed Rob clock the appreciative stares I received in return.

'You really are living in there,' he said, grimacing, 'while all of this chaos is going on.'

'Yep. Most of the rooms are sealed off, but we've set up a temporary flat at the top. The dust still gets up there but it's not nearly as bad as on the floors below. I've lived in worse conditions.'

'I imagine you have. How long is it going to take?'

'Four months and then another one for decorating.'

Five months during which I'd be displaced for most of the day, in need of refuge, consolation, distraction. And the first offer was about to be made, in broad daylight, in earshot of others.

'The builders won't be knocking off for an hour or two,' he said. 'Want another coffee at my place? It's a lot quieter on the other side of the wall.'

I looked up at the mouth that issued this invitation – or challenge, as we both knew it to be – and I wanted that mouth on my skin, kissing and sucking and grazing, making greedy contact with every part of my body. 'I would love one,' I said, at last, 'but I'm afraid I can't. There are some deliveries I need to chase up and then I'm meeting my husband in town for dinner.'

'All right,' he said, and the look he gave me was almost admiring, letting me know that he was impressed that I had the self-discipline for such gamesmanship.

'See you around,' I said, over my shoulder, casual, non-committal.

See? I tried.

As promised, I'd invited Felicity for coffee. We sat as far from the crashing and banging as we could get, in the little seating area at the top of the house where two of our smaller sofas had been set opposite one another with scarcely space between them for the coffee table. A bowl of daffodils marked the centre, dozens of them crushed into a dense hemisphere, and their yolk-yellow faces cast light on my guest's face, illuminating every pore and line and fold of her skin. I wondered how it felt to inhabit withering flesh, to be a prisoner of time. I wondered as if I would never find out myself.

I showed her Hetty's drawings.

'Goodness,' she said, 'how smart. I do like those glass

doors to the garden. I bet they won't stick when it's damp like my French windows.'

'I'll send someone round to fix that, if you like,' I offered.

'Oh no, I'm used to it. I'd miss the imperfections if they weren't there.'

Though ostensibly as easy-going and co-operative as I could have hoped for, she had eyes that missed nothing, and even without Rob's advice I like to think I would have known better than to underestimate her.

'You're a member of Lime Park Club?' I asked. She had come dressed in jogging bottoms and a fleece, which suggested we had one pastime in common. 'I've just joined myself.'

'No, no,' Felicity said. 'I can't stand those places. Full of people worshipping their own bodies, and so expensive! I like fresh air. I walk.'

She told me she had a friend on sick leave from her job with whom she undertook epic walks, the kind you had to do in stages over several weeks. Their latest was the London Loop, which stretched Lord knew how many miles around the capital. I couldn't think of anything more tedious. Who would want to end where they'd begun?

'How come your friend can walk that sort of distance when she's off work sick?'

'Depression,' Felicity said grimly. 'She was hounded from her job by a bully.'

'Poor thing,' I said. 'That happened to me too, in my job before last.' I didn't normally raise this subject, but there was no better way of accelerating trust than sharing a secret. 'Though mine was more a sexual harassment problem than bullying – what did they call it at the employment tribunal? "Inappropriate sexual conduct", that's right.'

'He was your boss, was he?'

'Yes. He was the one who did my performance evaluations and as you can imagine he had his own ideas of what my performance should entail.' It surprised me that the memory could still make me squirm.

'What a disgraceful abuse of power,' Felicity tutted. 'I'm very sorry to hear that. Vanessa's boss was a woman, but these days women are as much our enemy as men are, maybe even more so.'

'I'd agree with that.' Personally, I'd never doubted for a moment that women were the more dangerous sex; their interest in others was far sharper than men's, which made their suspicions more intelligent.

'Will you be looking for a job again soon, Amber?'

'Maybe.' No need to confide that the prospect was repellent to me. 'The idea is to have a baby.' As it happened, directly before Felicity's visit I'd had an appointment with my new GP and, still naive, had lapped up his advice about folic acid and other aids that my body could then mock for their ineffectiveness. 'Though there's no sign of one yet,' I added.

'You make it sound like the number 3 bus,' Felicity said, smiling.

'I haven't seen one of those yet either,' I joked, though I rarely bothered with public transport. 'Sod's law, I'd find a great job and then discover I'm pregnant within a week of starting.'

'Most women have the job *and* the child,' Felicity said, though she was kind enough not to condemn me for having neither. 'Not everyone is in a position to choose.'

'I know,' I said agreeably. 'One day I'll look back on this period and think how lucky I was.'

'Yes,' she said, thoughtful, even moved. 'I imagine you will.'

I'm convinced that this business of trying for a baby affected the dynamic between Jeremy and me in some crucial way. It wasn't that I disliked having sex with him, not at all, only that in changing the purpose of sex we had somehow also changed the conditions. What had once been a recreational thrill was now a necessary errand, not quite on a par with registering for council tax and shopping for cheaper car insurance but certainly closer than it should have been. Once nothing had been riding on copulation beyond pleasure, but now a great deal was, no less than our whole future. As my friend Helena had remarked the last time we met, 'The sooner the scientists take you two in hand, the better.'

But Jeremy didn't want to see any scientists, not yet.

'Is it time to make an appointment at a fertility clinic?' I asked him, when my first Lime Park period made itself known.

'No,' he said. 'It takes some couples longer than others, that's all. We have to be patient, otherwise the thinking it isn't going to happen will become a self-fulfilling prophecy.'

'I don't believe that for a moment,' I said. 'This is basic

biology, not mind over matter – at least it is for most people. If it wasn't, the human race would have died out by now.'

He glanced up at my darker-than-usual tone. 'I just mean try not to worry about it, baby. Let's give it till after the summer and then we can think about getting some advice. It might work out better that way – you don't want to be breathing in all this dust when you're pregnant, do you?'

'I suppose not.' It was unprecedented for me to be the impatient one; if either of us had an interest in hurrying the plan to fruition, it was him. 'It's just . . . well, you'll be fifty-two at the end of the year.'

'That doesn't bother me.' He reminded me that his famously spry mother was about to celebrate her seventy-eighth birthday and his still compos mentis aunt had just turned eighty.

But I didn't like to think of my husband at eighty. As I say, I was still young enough to believe that I was the exception to the universal rule of ageing, and Jeremy's enduring youthfulness and energy had to date encouraged me to persist in this delusion.

In retrospect, of course, it's clear that I was suddenly pushing for medical advice because I knew, either consciously or subconsciously, that a baby was the only thing that could save me from Rob. No pregnant woman would embark on an adulterous affair, and no man would want her – well, not the type of man that he was, anyway: the unmodernized kind.

All of a sudden, I didn't have much time to play with.

'Our finance guy and his wife just went to a specialist,' Jeremy told me. 'Apparently he has the highest success rate in the UK, so if and when the time comes we'll go to him.'

'After the summer then,' I agreed. And before I could prevent it I had conjured an image of myself lying in the garden in a bikini – a revealing black one that would pass for underwear from a distance – stretching my arms high above my head as I soaked up the sun, all too aware of dark eyes watching from the upstairs window next door.

Chapter 5

Christy, April 2013

She was inexplicably nervous about returning to work after the move, a mood only exacerbated by a puzzling episode that occurred as she left the house on Monday morning.

Locking the door behind her, she was aware of someone on the other side of the hedge in the doorway of number 38: restless feet shuffled, breath was expelled with wheezy impatience, and the word 'Unbelievable' was uttered more than once in a furious male undertone. Then came the abrupt drilling of the doorbell. After a wait of only two or three seconds, much too brief for anyone to have reasonably been expected to react, the caller rang again, holding the bell down to produce a loud, unremitting sound that made Christy wince. Inside the house, it must have been thunderous enough to wake a man from a coma. Who rang a doorbell like that at eight o'clock in the morning? Presumably not the rude shaggy guy, since he lived there – unless he'd locked himself out and had some poor flatmate he was trying to rouse?

She wondered about the woman downstairs, Felicity. Was the visitor for her, frustrated by her continued absence? She was still with her daughter in the country, judging by

70

the silence that belied the nightly and most likely timer-operated lamplight at the lower window. Christy had watched the estate agent plant a 'Sold' sign in the flower bed by the gate, but she knew the property had not yet been vacated because furniture and pictures were visible between curtains left neither closed nor open.

Reaching the pavement, she saw that it was in fact the upper flat this caller wanted, for he had moved from the doorstep and was now yelling up at the window. He was a portly, middle-aged man in a business suit and buffed shoes, his face flushed with anger.

'I know you're in there! You could at least have the decency to come down and speak to me!'

He returned to the door and stabbed the bell a third time before calling up again, tone loaded with sarcasm, 'Well, thanks for the letter, mate. Nice way to treat your friends!'

Storming up the path, thwarted and displeased, he hesitated at the sight of Christy's surprised expression before shouldering past her.

Inevitably, they were heading for the same place, the train station, and by chance boarded the same carriage. Though she sought his eye a couple of times, not so much in expectation of an explanation as an acknowledgement, he did not reciprocate.

She did, however, overhear a brief interaction between him and another commuter, a woman who evidently recognized him and initiated an exchange of Lime Park credentials. He was nodding, both voice and flesh-tone rather calmer now: 'Trinity Avenue, I know it, yes, just behind the school, isn't it? We're on the other side of the park, Lime Park Road.'

'Very nice,' the woman said approvingly and, stamping grounds established, the two returned to their newspapers.

Not just a 'friend', then, Christy thought: a neighbour.

Work re-exerted its customary hypnotic power, all thoughts suppressed beyond those billed to the client, and it took fewer than three hours for her to feel as if she'd never left her desk at the agency ten days ago, never closed the door on her rented flat that final time, never *heard* of Lime Park, much less taken up residence there. Eating a sandwich with Ellen at lunchtime, she shared photos of the new house as if it were a holiday let she'd found on the other side of the world, a trip she dreamed of taking but doubted she ever actually would.

'What are your new neighbours like?' Ellen asked.

Christy pulled a face. 'Well, I've only had contact with a few so far and, to be honest, they've all been a bit strange.'

'That's the burbs for you,' said Ellen, who lived in Shoreditch and regarded the Thames as a lethal electric demarcation line. 'It's the lower air temperature, the poorer visibility, all that tranquillizer dust in the air . . .'

Christy bore the digs about the suburbs good-naturedly. 'You know when you get the feeling you've landed in the middle of some private drama? People are being weird with you, but it's not actually to do with you?'

'Because they're zombies or Stepford wives or something? Not quite human?'

Christy giggled. 'Just not what I was expecting, that's all.' It was good to be back in the office. It put Lime Park in perspective. Of course the neighbours weren't zombies; she'd merely caught a couple of them off their game. 'Talking of not quite human, is anything going on with Laurie? She seems more fraught than ever.'

Ellen pulled a face, all at once conspiratorial. 'There were a lot of meetings behind closed doors last week, and apparently she's taking Thursday afternoon off. You know what Amy and I think?'

'What? A restructure?'

'A pregnancy.'

Christy almost choked on her ciabatta. 'Goodness, another one already?'

'I know. Twins would have been a lot more time-efficient.'

If this was correct, it would be their director's second maternity leave in two years. Christy had stood in with good grace (and mixed success) the first time around, determined not to buy into the culture of the agency that made pregnancy a Black Death, its carriers to be feared, their dwellings marked with a cross. She hoped, after all, to be doing it herself one day. But a second time so soon: the thought was exhausting. Then again, Laurie had turned a blind eye (of sorts) to Christy's month-long sideshow of mortgage-brokering and utilities comparison-shopping.

'Oh well, I've been no use to anyone these last few weeks. The least I can do is cover another maternity leave for her.'

'You are *so* honourable,' Ellen said, balling up her

sandwich wrapper and dropping it into the waste-paper basket. 'Seriously, Christy, she doesn't deserve you.'

It was the following Saturday, a still, sharp April morning, when the Davenports' neighbour Felicity moved out of number 38A. Though Christy had heard her letting herself into the flat a day earlier and had glimpsed a bowed grey head at the bay window, she did not see her properly until the hour of her departure. Watching from the bedroom window while Joe was in the shower, she saw a slight older woman in sportswear hasten down the path towards the leader of the removals team, who stood with a clipboard at the yawning doors of a large van. There was defeat in her posture – or perhaps it was simply an expression of sadness.

No amount of money could keep her here . . . That was what Felicity's friend had said when Christy had called at the flat to introduce herself. What on earth had she meant? The same friend was here this morning to assist, but given the lukewarm reception on that previous occasion Christy did not dare go down and approach her when she was genuinely occupied. In any case, Felicity was moving out, their paths would not cross again. It was more relevant to her to discover who would be moving *in*.

A surprising number of boxes were emerging from the flat, at least three times as many as Christy and Joe had brought with them, and the young removals guys hoisted the cartons with comical ease. Meanwhile, Felicity and her friend brought out a succession of fragile items, stacking them gingerly in the boot of a Honda Civic and pausing frequently to handle one object or another and comment. Among the knick-knacks was the little hourglass bottle Christy had seen on the hall table when she'd paid her call. The friend plucked this from its box and appeared to be suggesting it be discarded, but Felicity shook her head, fingered the bottle as one would an irreplaceable keepsake.

'It will all be behind you soon,' the friend said – if Christy heard her correctly – and Felicity was nodding, glancing about her with the air of a survivor.

After the removals team had pulled off – casual, without indicating, as if transporting potatoes and not the collected treasures of a woman in her dotage – Felicity's companion took the wheel of the Honda and waited with the engine running as Felicity emerged from her gate for the final time. She stood looking towards the house, pale eyes blinking, and Christy averted her gaze to allow her departing neighbour her private last moments with the home she was giving up.

When she next looked, she saw that some sort of scene was developing in the street below, one that involved the man from the upstairs flat trying to say goodbye to Felicity, or to say *something*, but whatever it was, it was upsetting her. As she held out a hand, palm flat as if to warn him off stepping closer, her friend rolled down the car window and screamed out, 'Hey! You keep away from her! Do you hear me?'

This hostility was easily loud enough for Christy to hear from behind a pane of glass, but the man ignored it, protesting instead to Felicity, 'I've tried to explain to you, why won't you listen? I didn't do anything!' His arms gesticulated frantically, even after he'd finished speaking; he was a wild creature, volatile, capable of anything.

'Please, Felicity, just talk to me!' With another explosive gesture, he turned side-on to the house, dislodging the heavy drape of hair to reveal a bruised left eye and cheek-bone. Someone must have punched him, Christy thought, and it wasn't all that hard to see how it might have happened if *this* was how he behaved.

With the implication of violence came the thought that she ought to go down there and see if there was anything she could do to keep the peace – or hustle Joe out of the shower and into action. But before she could act, the rotund man she'd seen yelling up at the window on Monday morning had appeared and begun remonstrating with the offender himself.

'Fuck you,' the bear told him, but he did at least retreat, blundering down his pathway towards the front door.

Felicity, plainly distressed, fled to her friend's car without a word to either man, leaving the second neighbour alone on the pavement as she slipped into the passenger seat and closed the door between them. As the car pulled away, with all the urgency of a getaway vehicle, her companion could be seen speaking animatedly, her features hot with outrage, and Christy could tell from Felicity's slumped shoulders that she was very shaken by what had just happened. How awful to have to leave your home in this way, to have your private goodbyes ambushed!

Who *was* this horrible man? This man who might no longer be Felicity's neighbour but was most assuredly theirs? Hearing the crashing footsteps and slammed door that signified his withdrawal to his cave, she found that she was breathing harder than usual.

At last, the second neighbour turned away, his expression troubled but weathered, almost as if he were a bouncer and skirmishes of this sort routine. Clearly there'd been some adjustment to his attitude since that display of passion earlier in the week. Christy watched him go down the path of number 42, from which she deduced he was Caroline's husband.

'They've obviously had a serious falling-out,' she told Joe, when he emerged from the shower to her breathless eyewitness account. Though she'd moved from the window, her eyes returned to it as she spoke, as if to a screen.

'Who has?'

'Felicity and the guy upstairs. Maybe that's why she decided to sell. She must really have a problem with him. He was saying, "I didn't do anything!"'

'Good for him,' Joe said mildly, and he began towelling his hair with such energy she felt beads of water sprinkle her skin. 'He probably *didn't* do anything.'

'I'm not sure he's the one whose honour we should be defending,' she said earnestly, and settled on the edge of their unmade bed, her back turned deliberately to the temptations of the window. 'The other man was obviously on her side. He's the same one I saw yelling up at the window on Monday. I think he's married to the woman I had a run-in with last week, Caroline.'

But it was clear from Joe's expression that he had no

memory of her having told him about the earlier incident and that this subsequent drama held no interest for him. 'What shall we do this weekend?' he said, dressing.

'What do *you* want to do? You're the one who's worked fourteen-hour days this week.' Joe's salary may have been capped, but his working hours appeared not to have been; rather, thanks to a merger between two pharmaceutical companies that necessitated all hands to deck, his hours had increased to encompass all waking ones.

His head emerged through the neck of a T-shirt. 'I quite fancy just hanging out in my new house. Watch the football.'

'We might have to make that a box set.' They still awaited satellite and Internet services; without them, it sometimes felt as if the house were only half alive. 'And there's some leftover chilli in the freezer. Let's challenge ourselves to not spending a bean.'

'Only eating them? I like this crazy talk.' He joined her on the bed, his arm around her waist. 'Are we allowed alcohol?'

'I believe we have stocks, yes.'

'Thank God for that. There are some things I *really* can't give up.' He sprang to his feet and she watched him return his damp towel to the rail in the en suite (the Frasers' impeccable standards were rubbing off on him, evidently), wondering if she should have encouraged the arm around the waist. There were activities that came free of charge, after all.

'I know, let's invite them all over for drinks,' she said in sudden inspiration.

'What? Who?'

'The neighbours, of course. We should have done it as soon as we moved in. They don't seem a very happy bunch, do they? It might be just what they need.'

Joe looked doubtful. 'Or just what they *don't* need.'

'Come on, let's be the sociable ones. I'll put cards through their doors this weekend. How about Friday night? Can you make sure you're back early? Or at least by seven-thirty?'

Joe sighed. 'I'll try.'

She wrote notes to the occupants of the three houses on either side of them, as well as to several across the road, inviting everyone to come at 8 p.m. on Friday; after some hesitation, she addressed one to the upper flat at number 38. Conveniently, the twin landmarks of new home and Joe's promotion had furnished them with enough gifts of sparkling wine to cater for the occasion, and glassware stocks were easily supplemented with cheap flutes from the supermarket. She spent her evenings producing her limited repertoire of baked snacks – Parmesan breadsticks and cheese straws, which were, she was the first to admit, virtually the same thing – and trying not to eat the economy caramels she'd heaped into a rather nice blue Moroccan bowl found at the back of a kitchen cupboard, presumably overlooked by the Frasers in their haste to leave.

At first no one RSVPed. Then, on the Wednesday evening, a neighbour she hadn't seen before called by and introduced herself: Liz from number 41. She was in her early forties, her dark hair worn in a pixie cut that accentuated tired eyes, the reason for which was presumably the pre-school infant who dangled from her cuff.

'I just wanted to say thank you for your invitation.' She spoke with the same self-confidence as Caroline, the same faintly defensive tone of a woman accustomed to living on high-status streets like this and not about to share the privilege with any old incomer.

'You're very welcome,' Christy beamed. Behind Liz the spring twilight glowed, birdsong wobbling on the breeze, and she felt a sudden rush of optimism, that soaring sense of a new dawn. 'Do you think you'll be able to come?'

'The thing is, we . . . I was just wondering, who else will be coming?'

'I'm not sure yet, but we've invited everyone.'

There was a pause as Liz apparently awaited names. 'Caroline and Richard?' she prompted.

Abashed still from her skirmish with Caroline, Christy answered cautiously. 'Yes, that's not a problem, is it?'

'No, of course not, we're very good friends.' Liz hesitated. 'What about the other side?'

'Well, Felicity's gone now, hasn't she, but I've posted a note to her flat in case the new people move in between now and Friday. And I've invited the guy upstairs, though we haven't actually met yet.'

And who she rather hoped *wouldn't* come if he had a habit of attracting disagreement, not to mention injury. She wasn't sure her talents as a hostess ran to dispute-resolution services.

'Mummy,' the child said. He was blond-haired, long-lashed and *very* cute. 'Rupert wants to go home now.'

'Yes, Rupe, give Mummy one minute to talk to the new lady in Amber's house.'

It took Christy aback to hear herself described in this way.

'I'm sorry,' Liz told her, 'but I don't think I'll be able to make it on Friday. You see, I've got two little ones and I'm on my own . . .'

Again, Christy was unsure how to respond: should she ask for clarification of 'on my own' (divorced single mother or just housebound on the night in question while her husband went out?) and urge Liz to find a babysitter, or should she declare small children welcome too? But at 8 p.m. wouldn't most children be in bed and their parents expecting an adults-only affair?

Why did interaction with her new neighbours already feel so political?

'Well, not to worry,' she said, finally. 'I completely understand. It's very short notice and I'm sure there'll be lots of other opportunities.'

Liz looked relieved. 'Actually, I'm glad I've caught you because I wanted to ask if you happen to have a new address for the Frasers. I've tried texting Amber but I think she must have changed her number.'

'I don't, I'm afraid,' Christy said, feeling familiar unease on the issue. She thought fleetingly of the postcard, its complaint that calls and emails had gone unanswered. Should she have phoned the sender to explain that the

Frasers had moved on? 'I need to find it out myself, in fact, so I can send on some post.' Post she'd been sitting on for weeks now, one of those chores that slid further and further down the list.

'How disappointing,' Liz said.

'I'm sorry.' Christy watched as she headed from her door directly to the Sellerses'. Oh dear, would Caroline tell her about their little misunderstanding? Would she also decide not to come to their drinks?

She soon had her answer. By the following morning, eight others, including Caroline, had RSVPed no, while the remainder – including the bear – had not responded at all.

Nor, when Friday evening came, did any of the undecideds turn up.

'All the more for us,' Joe said, a wine glass in one hand and a clutch of cheese straws in the other, and he honestly did not seem to register the disgrace of the situation. His head was probably filled with work, with the forthcoming partners' meeting that would be his first, not to mention the residual excitement of the house purchase: there was still more than enough to celebrate in his own right, and having to eat all the avocado dip himself was simply the icing on the cake.

Christy, however, struggled to share his bonhomie. Having dashed home from work, buoyed by the thought of a social triumph (or at least a few laughs), she felt dejected – *re*jected. There it was, that sudden unleashing of the trait she most disliked in herself: social insecurity, the fear that she had never quite made the leap from outsider to insider. At work, for instance, yes, she was friends with Ellen, but Ellen was also close to Amy and several others, which constituted the kind of network that Christy had never been able to build. And she had moved house enough times to know that even in London people were curious about new neighbours, about what they did for a living and where they'd come from; it was human nature. So if they wouldn't cross the road – and most of them didn't even need to do *that* – for a free drink, then it was because the hosts held no fascination for them whatsoever.

'I don't understand it,' she said. 'Everyone's at home, it's not like it's the school holidays any more.'

'They're just busy.' Joe shrugged. 'Come on, people get booked up on Friday nights, you know that.'

'*We* don't.'

'We're hostages to debt, that's why. *Willing* hostages, admittedly. And you know what everyone's like . . .'

Though he was typically vague, she *did* know. Most of their friends had new babies and it was an unwritten rule that those who remained luxuriously child-free should be the visitors, not the visited. Even the event of a major property upgrade had not proved sufficiently alluring to overturn convention. It didn't help that Christy's closest friend, Yasmin, was six months into a three-year ex-pat stretch in Kuala Lumpur with her oil-executive husband. Without the Internet, their weekly Skype catch-up had had to be put on hold.

'I should have said that woman could bring her kids,' she sighed. 'The one from across the road, Liz.'

Joe put down his glass, finally declaring allegiance to her disappointment. 'But if you'd done that then they'd be the only ones here, the kids would be wrecking the house and she would go home and tell everyone what a crap night it was. This way nothing's been damaged and only *we* know it's been a washout.'

Christy managed a smile. 'That's true. So you don't think we've been deliberately snubbed? Because I had that argument with Caroline next door?' A theory was forming that Caroline Sellers was the queen bee of Lime Park Road and had sent out the signal to shun the new arrivals; she'd dispatched Liz to the Davenports' door to reject her and then ordered her to report the newcomer's reaction.

No, that was insane.

'It must be something to do with the house,' she added, unwrapping a caramel. (Now she'd have to eat all one hundred of them herself: Joe disliked toffee and its sweet buttery relatives as much as she loved it.) 'Maybe some of the building work was done without the correct permissions, or the Frasers damaged something when they dug out the garden.'

'But why would anyone blame *us* for that?' Joe said reasonably. 'They'd know we bought the house in good faith. Come on, don't take it to heart.'

She knew he was right. But even so, as she returned the untouched glasses to the kitchen cupboard, it was with the same unsettling feeling she'd had the day she'd picked up the keys and entered the house alone, seeing in front of her those receding blank walls, that succession of pale shut doors. It was as if there was something being concealed from her, an unwelcome surprise in store.

She remembered again how Liz had referred to her: 'the new lady in Amber's house'.

As if she didn't have a name of her own.

Those first few weeks in Lime Park Road, her best stab at friendly conversation was with Dave, the guy who came to check the boiler. They'd been in residence less than a month when the hot water suddenly ceased to work. It was a brand-new heating system under warranty and the Frasers had left the business card of the engineer who fitted it. He agreed to come as a priority.

It was not ideal to leave work early on a Thursday to meet him at the house, but the notion of Joe ditching before dark was so laughable as to be not worth airing.

'Settling in all right, are you?' Dave said, having rectified the fault in the time it took Christy to make him a cup of tea. 'The house looks really different from before.'

'You mean emptier?' Christy laughed. 'The couple before had a lot more furniture than us.' She paused. 'Did you ever meet them?'

'Sure. We were here nearly two weeks installing the system.'

'What were they like?'

At once his face brightened, as if he couldn't believe his luck to be asked to speak on his specialist subject. 'Well, we didn't see him that much, but *she* was here most days. Beautiful girl, she was, a real looker. Gorgeous long red hair, fantastic figure, make-up all done like a model or a film star, you know? She was going out one afternoon and she came down in these incredible high heels, hair all piled up on her head . . .'

Christy got the feeling he might have elaborated more graphically in different company. 'Girl?'

'Well, early thirties. Seemed a bit young for round here, a bit too glamorous, if you know what I mean? More Notting Hill than Lime Park. No offence.'

At thirty-seven, and having postponed having her highlights done to save the cash, Christy was less offended than crestfallen. It didn't help that with the longer commute she also had to sacrifice crucial minutes in front of the bathroom mirror, arriving at her desk a little more tousled than she used to. And such things worked cumulatively, didn't they? You didn't suddenly go from Coco Chanel to Worzel Gummidge, you simply looked a little less polished every day until one morning people stopped taking the seat next to you on the train. OK, so she'd *never* looked polished. Polished was Amber Fraser, not Christy Davenport, and 'polished' wasn't polished enough a word either. (*Soignée*. Amber Fraser was *soignée*.)

'I'm guessing the money was the husband's,' Dave went on. 'He was older. Doted on her. Sugar daddy, we thought. Classic set-up, everyone's a winner.'

Until they'd had to give up their home, Christy thought. (*Hope you're still loving your forever home!*) 'Do you know why they moved on so quickly? They were only here a year, the agent said.'

'Haven't got a clue. Must have been something serious, though, because they weren't doing the place up to sell. She told me that herself. They'd inherited some money and had got an interior designer in, one of those posh West London types. You should have seen some of the kit that was arriving, you'd think the recession never happened. Designer furniture, everything top of the range. I said to her, "Who'd you inherit your money from, Amber? The Queen?" She goes, "The Queen isn't dead, Dave, careful with that sort of talk or they'll have your head off for treason." Great girl, she was.' He chortled, warming to his story, and Christy lapped it up like someone receiving a visit in prison after a long period in solitary confinement.

'Maybe they ended up overspending?' she suggested.

'Yeah, she might have been one of those shopaholics, wouldn't be surprised. Or he was laid off, more likely. I didn't get the impression she worked.'

'Oh well, it will have to remain a mystery.' The word stirred something in her, dislodged a remark in her short-term memory: *It will all be behind you soon*, Felicity's friend had said. *What* was behind old Felicity? And if it was behind the outgoing residents, did that mean it was in front of the *incoming* ones?

Dave scratched at his lower eyelid with the nail of a smeared thumb. 'Expensive to run, these big old houses,' he said. 'Stumping up in the first place is just the start, isn't it?'

'Yes.' Christy swallowed. She hoped he wasn't going to announce that his labour that morning fell outside the terms of the warranty. 'Speaking of which, do I owe you anything?'

'No, you're all covered.'

And she did her best to hide her relief.

Chapter 6

Amber, 2012

Well, you certainly couldn't say there was no social life to be had in the sticks. Having already enjoyed a warmth of welcome assumed out of the question for a pair of peace-wrecking incomers, we were now to have a drinks party held in our honour by our neighbours at number 42, Richard and Caroline Sellers.

'It's on Sunday afternoon,' Jeremy told me, having received the invitation on the Wednesday as he walked to the train station with Richard. 'No builders in that day, eh?'

'*This* Sunday? Will anyone be free at such short notice?'

'They all will. Richard says Caroline can mobilize the whole street with a couple of phone calls – she's the chief whip.'

'Is she indeed?' I raised an eyebrow. 'Then consider us whipped.'

It was early May by then and warm enough for us to take our drinks to the Sellerses' terrace. Weathered teak furniture had been exhumed for the occasion and a fleet of plastic cars and other toys cast to the edges in an effort to reclaim territory from the battalions of small children in attendance. Older ones clustered on the trampoline, soon a seething mosh-pit of close-combat bobbing that made me shudder slightly.

On offer for the adults were Prosecco cocktails and a tableful of canapés and nibbles Caroline had rustled up by her own fair hand: squares of pastry smeared with tapenade and crème fraiche, curls of salami stuffed with soft cheese, the sort of thing I could no longer taste even in my fantasies but that Jeremy wolfed.

'Amber, you look amazing!' she cried, when Richard led us into the throng. 'It's like you've stepped off the pages of *Vogue*.'

'I don't think so,' I protested, but soon others had joined in: 'Oh yes, you do!' 'That dress! I couldn't squeeze into that in a million years!' 'Where's it from?' 'Goodness, isn't she stunning?'

I was not used to this level of open admiration by other women; it simply did not exist in my old working world of competitive cynicism. As for our neighbours in Battersea, fifty per cent had used their apartments as occasional pieds-à-terre and the remainder had been far too self-involved to notice any sartorial success on the part of anyone but themselves. (The men were a different story. I'd soon stopped reporting to Jeremy the number of advances made to me in the lift.)

This, clearly, was a different style of community. At least twenty-five neighbours were here and every single one was demonstrably excited to meet us.

'Kenny and Joanne live a few doors down from us,' Caroline said, introducing a flushed and jolly pair, both of whom, extraordinarily, wore mud-spattered wellingtons to the event. 'You might have seen their Labradoodle?'

'I'm not sure . . .' There were numerous dogs on the street, I'd seen them being taken for walks in tangled packs; and cats, too, sitting on gateposts with an air of reserving judgement (unlike their big-hearted owners). All had names interchangeable with those of human infants: Lily, Archie, Poppy.

Jeremy and I settled in a group with Kenny, Joanne and a clutch of others keen to discuss our renovations and reassure us we were not the pariahs we feared we might be (not when we looked *this* good). They all knew the house from social occasions hosted by the Lockes and were well informed as to what our predecessors had and had not done to it over the years ('I had a shower there once when our water was turned off,' Kenny said. '*Abysmal* pressure. I don't know why they didn't just put in a pump. Total false economy'). And whatever the Lockes might think, the consensus here was that the People's Republic of China couldn't hold a candle to Lime Park.

'Did you know Rachel Locke had her third baby on your living-room floor?' Caroline told us. She had a very likeable manner, mischievous and chummy, but a rather less successful look. Her eyes were a little bulbous and the distance between nose and upper lip elongated: it was as if someone had intended making her beautiful but had abandoned the job before finishing. The main issue, however, was her personal style, which might best be described as windswept. I would need to take her in hand, I decided.

'I didn't know that, no,' I said, grateful for the pristine chevron parquet about to be laid in our living room.

'Any plans yourself in that direction?' someone asked.

This I *was* used to: the directness with which people enquired into a brand-new acquaintance's reproductive affairs. It had begun the very day Jeremy and I returned from our honeymoon, the implication being that you could only have children if you were married first. The child-free and unmarried would ask their questions with a certain dark suspicion, while those who'd already begun breeding behaved as if they'd personally proposed us as members of a golf club, our acceptance to which was a foregone conclusion. But they all asked equally brazenly.

'We *would* like kids,' Jeremy told them, his arm snaking around my waist. 'Who knows when – we thought we'd just let nature take its course, eh?'

At which everyone looked me over as if I alone represented nature and Jeremy had nothing whatever to do with the course I might take. The problem with this sort of conversation was you couldn't help suspecting that behind those enquiring eyes were images of you naked and engaged in the sexual act (or, God forbid, in childbirth itself). Perhaps Jeremy liked this more than I did: there was undisputed kudos in having a young, attractive wife as yet unburdened by motherhood. Well, enjoy it while you can, I thought, because on the evidence of this welcoming committee it was not possible to have children and get fitted for a decent bra. And did something happen to your ankles and calves too? Those I could see that were not encased in rubber

91

were uniformly stocky – did they, like hips, broaden with childbearing? I checked my own lower legs, smooth and tapered, my feet arched into elegant nude slingbacks.

'You all know each other so well,' I remarked to Caroline. 'Do you get together very often?'

'Oh, all the time. It's a very sociable street. But there are a lot of young kids and babysitters cost the earth, so we tend to do these daytime gatherings. We do have our book group, though, that's in the evening. I'll invite you to the next one.'

'Maybe I could babysit some time?' I was thinking it might be good practice for me. As a girl I'd helped my mother with her babies, but the experience seemed other-worldly now. My whole childhood did.

'I wouldn't say that too loudly if I were you,' Caroline drawled. 'Seriously, Amber, take it from a veteran: enjoy your freedom while you can. And while you're at it, remind me how it feels. No detail too insignificant, OK?'

I laughed. I could tell she and I were going to get on very well.

I sensed Rob Whalen's arrival before I saw him: a rise in oestrogen levels, perhaps, or a collective twirling of hair among the womenfolk, the sudden flicking of glances through lowered lashes. As the only unattached male in the circle, he evidently had a celebrity of his own.

'Have you met our resident enigma?' Richard said, drawing him towards us. His hair was damp from the shower and he'd shaved, presenting himself as an altogether more respectable character than the one I'd encountered before.

Jeremy seized him by the hand, his smile broad and

genuine. 'You've met my wife, I think. But I know you must already loathe us both.'

'I certainly do,' Rob said amiably. 'And a little bit more every day, I suspect, until eventually I'll snap and murder you in your beds.'

Beds. I noted the plural: wishful thinking on his part.

'Did Amber not show you the schedule?' Jeremy said, as sincere as Rob was sardonic. 'It's designed for the pain to be sharp but short. The last thing we want is to make enemies of our new neighbours.'

'She hasn't shown me, no,' Rob said, his gaze resting on my mouth. 'I'll have to invite her over and quiz her.' At this, an extremely pleasurable fluttering started up in my abdomen, the kind of sensation that can only be activated by someone new and untried. He raised his eyes to Jeremy's. 'So how are you finding the commute?'

As they chatted about signal failures and defective heaters I sipped my drink and watched. I made a point of not comparing the two men directly, their respective heights, breadths, thicknesses of hair, but I did allow myself to think that, based purely on appearances, an outsider might guess incorrectly at which of the two I was married to.

Just then a latecomer was shepherded into our huddle. Liz, she was called, a neighbour from the house across the road, who scattered two painfully loud infant boys in opposite directions as she came to a halt. Thirty seconds later they had reunited to scrap over a toy motorbike, a tussle that Jeremy stepped in to umpire while she slipped beside Rob and began discussing primary-school curriculum with him. The gist seemed to be that she felt that the teaching of spelling in England was all wrong, nay a ticking time bomb, and he had useful comparisons to make with the education systems in France and Sweden.

'That's *very* interesting,' she said with an eagerness that bordered on mania. Though pretty enough, she had the most hectic-looking haircut I'd ever seen – it was as if it had been scribbled on her head by Quentin Blake – and make-up so poorly applied I wondered if she'd handed crayons to her sons and given them free rein. 'Do you think we'll *ever* get it right here?' she asked Rob, almost in plea.

'Only by accident,' he said.

He was clearly a prized guest: Caroline brought him a selection of snacks as if he was far too important to be expected to go and help himself, and several times children came up to try to engage him in a game, as if they'd collectively discerned that he, of all the men present, might be a superhero.

'You'll be a great father, Rob,' Liz told him, with the softest of sighs. 'When the time comes,' she added.

Presently Jeremy was invited by Richard to inspect his outdoor lighting system just as Liz was summoned indoors to see what her sons had done with a twelve-pack of Andrex, and all at once there we were, Rob and I, alone under the magnolia, unsupervised.

'She's nice,' I said, nodding after Liz. 'Big on literacy, I take it.'

With an easy manoeuvre, he turned his back to the rest of the group and smirked privately at me. 'They're *all* big on literacy, Amber. They're big on everything to do with education, which is why I don't always come out to these things. I tend to get cornered.'

That explained the 'enigma' crack, I thought, *and* the VIP treatment. I had an inkling as to how he'd come to be lured on this occasion.

'They might as well be sitting in the classroom themselves,' he continued. 'You wait till the entrance exams come around, you won't believe your eyes. I swear, they'll be down on their knees, lining up to tackle the non-verbal reasoning on their kids' behalves.'

I giggled. 'I suppose it's better than not giving a damn if your child bothers turning up at school or not.'

The smirk deepened. 'Do I gather from that statement that we can add truancy to your list of former crimes?'

'What former crimes? I don't know what you're talking about.' Smiling, I glanced around the terrace. 'Isn't Felicity here?'

'No, she's out of town, visiting her daughter. She'll be back this evening.'

I liked that he knew her whereabouts; it implied a certain protectiveness of her. 'She obviously prefers city life in her old age?'

'Oh, Felicity wouldn't leave the Big Smoke if you paid her. She's been in Lime Park longer than I have.'

Over his shoulder, a neighbour I'd met once or twice before – Mel – was trying to catch my eye and I waved hello, a polite note of deterrent in my manner. I had no intention of ending this conversation. 'I must pop round soon and check we're not disturbing her too much,' I said. 'I would hate to be the one who drove her out.'

'That's not a bad idea. Maybe take a cake. She likes lemon drizzle.'

I remembered what he'd said the previous time we met, about keeping her onside. He'd not intended it purely in relation to the building works, I suspected.

'So,' he said, finished with Felicity and his attention now firmly on what he saw in front of him.

'So . . . ?' I echoed.

'Are we going to do this or not?'

I inhaled sharply.

'And don't say "Do what?" Because you know exactly what I mean.'

I have to tell you this wasn't nearly as high risk as it reads on the page, because his body language was so utterly guilt-less, his voice dipped slightly but perfectly casual in tone, as if he were proposing a trip to the garden centre. Only his eyes, which no one else could see but me, betrayed the dangerous nature of his intent, daring me, seducing me, and my excitement rose like a sudden spike in blood sugar.

'Of course I know,' I replied, the same easy tone, the same unimpeachable body language. And that was the moment that I chose to acknowledge the truth: you could reinvent yourself but you could not reinvent the wheel. Of course I would be sleeping with Rob Whalen. Accepting this, I became very calm. 'The answer is yes, we are. But there are things that must be understood beforehand.'

'Sure.' He dipped a hand in his pocket for his phone. 'Can I take your number?'

He was still tapping in the digits when Jeremy and Richard appeared behind him, Jeremy beaming with that slightly idiotic bonhomie men exhibit when they outnumber women.

'Darling,' I said, 'Rob and I were just exchanging numbers. We think it might be useful in case there's a problem with the works. But I've forgotten my phone. Could you take his details instead?'

'Why don't I just send you a text so you've got mine,' Rob said helpfully to me.

'Good idea. I'd prefer it if you addressed all complaints to my wife,' Jeremy joked. 'She's the front of house in this operation.'

'You have my word,' Rob said.

He moved away to join a different group and Richard was summoned by Caroline to circulate with drinks, so Jeremy and I held hands at the edge of the terrace, facing the flock.

'Isn't this nice of the Sellerses?' he said. 'They've made such an effort and everyone's so friendly. A different world from the Wharf, eh?'

'We're very lucky to have such sociable new neighbours,' I agreed.

'I like your Rob.'

'*My* Rob? Hardly. But me too. He's funny, kind of naughty.' I nuzzled Jeremy's shoulder a little and he squeezed me closer.

'He doesn't normally turn up to these things, Richard says, but look how the women are all over him. He could take his pick.'

'Maybe he already has?' I said. 'Liz, I reckon. *She's* certainly up for it.'

'Not with that barnet,' Jeremy said, making me laugh. 'Mind you, she's not the only one who looks like she's been dragged through a hedge backwards.'

'I know. Maybe that's why they've all got their wellies on,' I said.

He snorted and, attracted by the sound, Richard approached with a bottle of bubbly, vapour trailing like breath from a living creature's throat.

'Having fun?' he asked, replenishing our glasses.

'Oh yes!' I exclaimed. 'It's the most *wonderful* party, Richard. You must let us thank you by taking you and Caroline to lunch at Canvas next weekend.'

As Jeremy and Richard beamed at the suggestion, I happened to catch Rob's eye and we nodded with the casual recognition of new acquaintances.

It was all so effortless, so natural. You'd think I'd been born to betray.

Chapter 7

Christy, May 2013

Not quite a month after the move to Lime Park, Christy was called to Laurie's office for an unscheduled meeting. She arrived to find that her director hadn't yet finished her previous meeting: Colette, the agency's head of HR, was still sitting there, notes in front of her, mug of tea half full.

'I know this isn't the greatest timing,' Laurie said, 'you've just moved house and everything . . .'

Christy automatically glanced down at Laurie's abdomen, careful to keep her expression affable. A committed fan of the structured dress, Laurie was today loosely draped in brushed cotton, her complicated neckline nothing more than a distraction, a red herring if Ellen was right. *That* was why Colette was present: just like last time, they were going to demand extra work of Christy for no additional pay. Her noble intentions having faded somewhat in recent weeks, she wondered if she should make a stand and negotiate an increase. Even with Joe's promotion they needed every extra penny they could get.

'It's been confirmed that we have to cut staff by twenty per cent,' Laurie said, and so confident had Christy been of the lines to come that there was a delay in understanding what was in fact being said here. And now Laurie appeared to be giving her the option of taking the money and running, no humiliating consultation period to endure.

'It could be a blessing in disguise,' she said in a hopeful tone.

'In what way?' Christy enquired.

'I just meant it would give you time to sort out your new house.' Laurie looked injured, which was rich given that she was the one dishing out the painful news. 'There must still be masses to do. You can break the back of the decorating.' These were statements, not suggestions, and made with an air of victory. She was necessarily forgetting what Christy had told her about having inherited a show home; number 40 Lime Park Road was no blank canvas, but a masterpiece that had come glazed and framed and tied with a bow.

Colette said nothing; she merely witnessed.

'I have to think about this,' Christy said. 'It's so out of the blue.' But hadn't she known in some God-fearing, subterranean sense that this was *exactly* what had been going to happen?

She'd sacrificed more than a baby to get herself a house on Lime Park Road.

Pausing only to collect her bag, she fled the building and dialled Joe's number from the street. 'I have to see you,' she breathed. Approaching the entrance to the Tube station, she saw it was only a little after ten, the ticket hall still swarming with tardy commuters and early-bird tourists. Her disposal had been the first business of Laurie's day. 'Can you meet for a few minutes?'

'Only if you've got time to come here,' Joe said.

Relieved of her job and all of a sudden frighteningly, nonsensically, possessed of all the time in the world, she set off for the office where he'd worked since he was a trainee in his mid twenties. He'd been a late starter then, the oldest of the year's intake, having worked two jobs to fund the conversion course, and yet now when she pictured him it was like watching a child set out on some careless sun-drenched adventure. He – they – had had no sense of the stormy skies ahead.

She corrected herself: *his* sky was still blue, he was a partner now. Then she reminded herself that married people – best friends and fellow adventurers – stood under the same sky, if necessary sharing an umbrella . . . and she abandoned the metaphor to the roar and clatter of the Underground.

In the lobby of JR's riverside building near St Paul's, she texted her arrival to Joe and sat on one of the rigid low-backed sofas set at modishly irregular angles under grand marble pillars, surrounded by walls of 'real' art, as she thought of it (the Frasers had had real art, too). The firm, she knew, occupied only cramped space on the less prestigious side of the building, the side that overlooked the service lane, but even so, in her current mood she was as intimidated as if she'd been summoned to Buckingham Palace. As she waited for Joe to come down, she scanned the passing faces as if seeing human beings for the first time; how preoccupied everyone was, intent to the point of blankness, neutered by professionalism. She felt invisible, irrelevant, expelled.

Mostly, she felt scared. Since leaving university sixteen

years ago she had not once been out of work, starting as a secretary to her first account director, back when account directors *had* secretaries, and progressing with a steady if unspectacular momentum that had brought her to the point of being the natural choice to cover her latest director's maternity leave. Correction: it had brought her to the point of being the natural choice to be made redundant. And now what? The economy was still in recession; manifestly, jobs like hers were being eliminated, not advertised. And yet the house –

Joe appeared then from one of the noiseless mirrored lifts, face alight at the sight of her, which was a small, sweet consolation never more gratefully taken.

'I've lost my job,' she announced, standing, and saw in his eyes how startled he was.

'How much notice?'

'Three months, but they've offered payment in lieu. I might as well take it and spend the time looking for something else.' However Laurie liked to spin it, however Colette might later dress it up, she'd be leaving with very little compensation.

'Agreed.' He took her hand. 'Sit down. You're upset.'

She sank back onto the sofa. 'What are we going to do, Joe? We can't afford the mortgage without my salary. We could barely afford it *with* my salary.' She could hear the panic rising in her throat and strangling her vowels; she could feel the blunt, kneeing sensation of desperation inside her ribcage as she gazed at him. Until now, until Lime Park, *she* had been the fixed one, the supporter and soother, he the ambitious hothead whose dashed hopes required gentle resurrection, and yet here she was having the irrational – and entirely unhelpful – thought that if he were to die or leave her she would not be capable of navigating the world without him. She would be *adrift*.

'We can still just about manage it,' he said, with a decent improvisation of command.

She shook her head. 'I honestly don't think we can. I need to get another job straight away. But there's nothing in advertising, I know that for a fact. Once you're out, that's it. I'll have to retrain or start again at entry level, something completely different . . . How could I have assumed I was safe? I *knew* I went too far with the house stuff. I even left a client meeting one day to take a call from the mortgage broker – if I'd had *any* idea . . .' Any idea that they were raising a fortune they'd have no hope of repaying for a house that would soon be repossessed. 'God,' she added, remembering that their new Internet provider had yet to live up to its name, having failed to turn up on the allotted day. 'We're not even online yet and my phone barely gets a signal in the house. How will I look for a job without basic communications?'

'Don't think about any of that yet,' Joe said. Her hand was still in his and he drew it closer to him, as if to reel her ashore, the current having carried her in uncharted directions. 'You're shocked,' he added gently. 'That's completely normal. Try not to panic. Plenty of couples survive on one salary and so will we.'

'Do they have our colossal mortgage, though? Did they

lose their minds and swap their tiny affordable flat for an enormous unaffordable house on a street where everyone hates them?'

Joe just smiled. 'Nobody hates us. Now I'm really sorry, but I have to go back up before I ...' He stopped mid-sentence, eyes vague. *Before I get the chop as well*, he'd been going to say. 'You head home, go for a walk, have a bath, try to relax. We'll talk about this properly tonight.'

'OK,' she said, though she knew he most likely wouldn't be home till eleven, by which time she hoped to be unconscious — there was nothing to be gained from extending a day like today, and already the oblivion of sleep was more tempting than any of the activities he had suggested. As she watched him walk back to the lifts, the sheer complicated bewilderment of their two intersecting fortunes lanced her with a sadness that almost made her cry out. It was as if she thought she'd never see him again.

Ferreting in her bag, she found half a tube of fruit pastilles and popped one onto her tongue like a pill, enjoying the brief, fraudulent comfort of sugar.

Her phone pinged: a text from Ellen.

'Where did you go?'

Not 'What happened?' They all knew then; already, everybody knew.

She replied: 'You safe?' Unfair — and too late — to reflect that Ellen had joined the agency six months after she had.

'So far,' Ellen responded. 'Are you coming back in?'

'No. On way home.'

Disorientated, she made for the line that took her to

her old flat in New Cross, before changing trains and heading towards Lime Park.

The wisteria was out. It joined the upper bays of numbers 38 and 40 like bunting strung for a street party. The air smelled clean and cut-grass sweet, like proper countryside air from early childhood – until the bin lorry came belching along, braking right outside the Davenports' gate.

'It's just a setback,' Joe told everyone, which was exactly the word Marcus used to use when Joe had been passed over – again – for partnership. And there was some comfort in noting that that *had* been just a setback, albeit one that had lasted several years.

They had had their proper talk. As Joe had explained, he was entitled to no share of equity in his promotion, but his basic salary had increased sufficiently to cover – by a hair's breadth – their stupendous monthly mortgage payment and utility bills (it would help if they could survive till autumn without turning the heating on), and other essentials like his season ticket. Her parents had agreed to defer the private loan payments until she found another job. No one wanted them to starve.

'Now might be the time to get pregnant,' her mother said, inevitably, though she was kind enough to wait until their second conversation since the redundancy before doing so.

'I'm not sure I should be considering having a baby on the basis that I've been fired and have no income,' Christy said mildly, but right at the outset she knew she was in fact arguing against herself; the mother's role was to voice the thoughts that the daughter was duty-bound to suppress.

Thoughts such as: 'Perhaps you should have done it when Joe was keen? *Years ago*, do you remember?'

Of course she remembered. They had been in their late twenties when, influenced by nothing but instinct, Joe had briefly campaigned to start a family early and Christy, having finally made an upward job move following two sideways ones, had dissuaded him. The dynamic had not been without a certain satisfaction on her part. She'd felt strong-minded and pioneering, delighted not to be one of those women who issued ultimatums to their partners or got pregnant accidentally on purpose. Now she wondered how she could have allowed a fleeting moment of career confidence to have so defining an impact.

'You'd have all the kids in school by now,' her mother went on in her gently relentless way ('all'? How many did she have in mind?), 'and you'd just have to get on with it, redundancy or not, there'd be no choice in the matter. If you ask me, all choice does is give you more time to think of reasons *not* to get on with it.'

Christy sighed. In emotional conversations like this she could do no better than to echo Joe's rationalism. 'Mum, I've just lost my job and it really doesn't feel like I have an awful lot of choice to do anything but devote myself to finding a new one. When I do, I'll think about the next step.'

'Fine. Well, I'm sure it's not anything you haven't discussed already yourselves.'

'We discuss it all the time,' Christy lied.

Just a setback, she recited silently. She was out of work but she was not faced with the wolf at the door *quite* yet. She could sense it in the undergrowth but she had not yet caught a glimpse of its tail.

'I'm sorry, but I don't understand. I *have* got the right place, haven't I?'

'You have, yes, but the Frasers don't live here any more.'

On her doorstep stood an unknown caller, a woman with a baby, this one not a neighbour but a friend of Amber Fraser. She was about Christy's age, though Christy was faintly aware of having developed the habit of deluding herself that any new mother who crossed her path must surely be older than she was. The child was five or six months old, she judged; a chunky boyish armful with a downy head and wise eyes, he followed their conversation as if understanding every word spoken.

'But I've come all the way from north London,' the woman protested, as breathless as one who'd undertaken the voyage barefoot and scarcely made it to her destination alive, though she dangled car keys in plain sight. 'It doesn't make sense. When exactly did they leave?'

'I'm not sure of the date,' Christy said, 'but they'd already gone when the house came on the market.'

'But why? Amber said nothing to me about moving. They'd just moved *in*. They were going to raise a family here.' She sent a narrow gaze over Christy's shoulder as if expecting to see the Frasers chained to a radiator, gagged and helpless.

Christy nodded in patient agreement. She decided not to air her and Joe's speculation about financial overreaching and terminal illness. 'I'm afraid I don't know why. I didn't ever meet them. When did *you* last see them?'

There was a heavy sigh, as if the woman could not possibly be expected to recall such complicated information. 'January, it must have been. They came up for lunch one Sunday. And now it's May. It's been at the back of my mind that I haven't heard from her in ages. We normally text and I thought she must have lost her phone, but now I've discovered she's closed her email account as well.'

'What about Facebook?'

'She isn't on it. Nothing like that.'

'That's unusual,' Christy remarked. Having come to imagine Amber Fraser as the model on the *Vogue* postcard ('more Notting Hill than Lime Park'), she considered her exactly the type to post frequent visual evidence of her superior genes and enviable lifestyle. Indeed, Christy had planned, when back online, to google it.

'She joked there were too many undesirables in her past and she wanted to cut them loose,' said the friend, then, as if regretting this indiscretion, hastened on: 'Anyway, I've asked the rest of the girls and they haven't heard from her either. We thought she must be holed up with the flu or something.' She stood for a moment, puzzling. 'Was that Rob from next door I saw when I was pulling up? Heading to the park gates? *He* might know where she's gone.'

'I don't know who you saw,' Christy said, stating the obvious, 'but the man who lives next door is a big guy, dark hair. Mid thirties.'

'That's him. Rob.'

So that was what he was called. Though she'd had no further sightings of him since the morning of Felicity's departure, Christy had heard movements on the other side of her bedroom wall, the murmurs and sudden crescendos of television, sporadic bursts of music. The main door was seldom used more than once a day. She supposed he must be some sort of recluse.

'He looks dreadful,' said her visitor. 'I didn't recognize him at first and when I called his name he didn't react, but it *was* him and he *definitely* knows me. We've met two or three times.'

'He's quite rude,' Christy agreed. She wasn't sure if she should be alarmed – or ashamed – by how eagerly she had set about gossiping, stockpiling the snippets this woman was supplying for analysis later.

'Well, he didn't used to be rude.' The woman's face creased in fresh bewilderment. 'He used to be really good fun. What's going on around here? Where on earth is Amber? Why hasn't she told us her new address?' With each unanswered question she was becoming increasingly distressed, her little boy looking on in fascination.

'Why don't you try one of the other neighbours,' Christy suggested. 'Did you ever meet Caroline or Liz?'

'Yes, both of them! Which are their houses?'

Out of curiosity, Christy accompanied her to their doors, but neither woman was at home. 'They must be picking up their kids from school,' she said, noticing the time. She had quickly become versed in the rhythms of Lime Park Road, the brief frenzies of the school runs, the staggered departures and returns of the commuting adults.

'I remember there was a retired lady Amber was chummy with,' said the friend, straining for a name. 'Lived downstairs from Rob?'

'That must be Felicity,' Christy said. 'But she's moved as well, I'm afraid.'

'She has? She'd been here for donkey's years. God, this is really starting to freak me out!'

'Aren't there any family members you can get in touch with?' Christy asked, aware that she was making it sound as if the Frasers were dead. 'Or colleagues?'

'I wouldn't know how to get in touch with Amber's family. And she left work a year and a half ago, months before I did. That's how we became friends, you see, through work.'

'What about her husband? Might he be in the same job?'

At last the frown lifted. '*That's* a good idea. Right, yes, I'll try Jeremy's office.' Thus resolved, she smiled at Christy for the first time and turned to her car, a sky-blue Fiat 500 with a 'Baby Onboard' sticker. Christy imagined nursery rhymes playing on the stereo as they drove home, or perhaps an early-learning CD of times tables or Mandarin. 'If you hear from her, would you tell her Imogen and Frankie came to visit?'

'Of course.'

Christy watched from the gate as Imogen buckled Frankie into his car seat and started the engine, craning over her shoulder as she pulled away, as if not quite trusting that she'd got the right house.

As if not quite believing a word Christy had said to her.

Chapter 8

Amber, 2012

'You look very nice,' Hetty said, in that faintly accusatory way women of similar rank and attractiveness pay one another compliments. She'd noticed my blow-dry and make-up, incongruously glamorous in our chaotic encampment upstairs but much too time-consuming to have been left till after the meeting. The scheduling, while inconvenient, was deliberate: it would give me something to report to Jeremy later, something other than my primary activity of the day.

'I hope you're not distracting the team too much,' Hetty added, only half playfully.

'Oh, I'm keeping out of everyone's way, don't worry.' I pretended to study the spreadsheets she offered, updated meticulously for our meetings, and to listen when she said important things like, 'That bloody company in Milan, you know, the console for the main bathroom? I must have mailed them twenty times and they *still* haven't given me a delivery date' or 'There's a problem with the cloak-room towel rail. It's out of stock, with an *eight-week wait.*'

I couldn't have given a monkey's about consoles and towel rails, but made notes nonetheless. I couldn't rely on my memory today.

'Want to get a sandwich when we're finished?' Hetty asked. 'I'm not meeting my Richmond client till three.'

'I'm sorry, I can't. I've been invited next door for lunch.'

It was quite touching how delighted she was by this. 'You're really settling in, aren't you? How long have you been here now? Silly question! Six weeks, the same as the works. Well, I'm not surprised you're already so popular. You and Jeremy must be great neighbours, all that wine you keep handing out; it's more than most would do, believe me. And I have to say you're my easiest clients by far.'

I imagined we were: a husband who had yet to attend a meeting, and a wife with a consuming new interest that dated from the very day she might have started to get under everyone's feet.

'This is my number,' that first text had said, sent in front of Jeremy's eyes at the Sellerses' party. A second followed later in the evening, containing one word: 'When?'

And I'd responded, Jeremy at the other end of the sofa, massaging my bare feet with his thumbs as he watched a third successive episode of *Nurse Jackie*:

'Tuesday at 1?'

'Yes.'

How thrillingly fast it had come around. It was five to when Hetty left; after a typically uncompromising examination of progress downstairs, she packed up her files and fired up her red Beetle convertible at the kerb, gamely driving into the damp spring day with the roof down. When living in Battersea and absorbed in the planning stages of the project, I'd looked forward to our meetings, to the rush of each new idea, the elation of green-lighting another lavish selection. But now I couldn't wait to see her indicate left at the junction and disappear from view.

There was no lunch. Wine, yes. In the neighbourly spirit so praised by Hetty, I took a bottle with me in case he had none – though he didn't seem the type to run a dry home. I'm not a sociopath: I couldn't do this sober.

We stood at the counter of his unmodernized open-plan kitchen and took our first complicit sips. The blinds to the street were pulled low, sheer enough to create an artificial twilight in the room. I had never in my life been more conscious of two bodies: the pulses and twitches and shrugs and blinks, the beginnings of sweat on skin and saliva on lips.

'I'm glad the drone isn't too bad in here,' I said, thinking how far away my house seemed from this side of the wall. It was going to be easier than I'd anticipated to cast it from my mind – and the marriage it contained.

'Nice try, but we both know they're on their lunch break,' Rob said. 'You can't trick me, Miss Amber.'

'No, I can only distract you from the pain.'

I'd wondered if I'd be bashful when it came to it, perhaps even shocked into retreat, but it transpired I was neither.

'What about these rules,' he reminded me, turning serious.

'They're not rules, just conditions. And pretty obvious ones.'

'OK, pretty obvious conditions. Tell me.'

If he was serious, then I was severe, as severe as I'd

ever been in my life before, because this was not a joke to me and could at no point be allowed to become one. 'This must be totally secret,' I began. 'If you think there's any possibility whatsoever that you might confide in someone, especially a neighbour, then tell me now and I'll leave before there's anything worth confiding.'

He snorted, already prepared to mock. 'Men don't confide. Don't you know anything about us? I rather got the impression you did.'

'Not confide then. Brag, after a few drinks. Make claims, indulge in innuendo.'

'I see you've studied your thesaurus.'

I raised my eyebrows, stared him down. 'Just give me a yes or no, for God's sake.'

'Fine, I promise not to brag after a few drinks or make claims or indulge in innuendo.' He grimaced. 'I feel like I'm swearing an oath here.'

'You are,' I told him. 'If either of us is ever accused, we must deny it categorically. Even if someone says they've seen us with their own eyes, we have to convince them they were hallucinating. No wavering, no hints, no telling just one person and swearing them to secrecy, only to have them do exactly the same with the next person.'

'We just covered confidentiality,' he said, impatient to get these preliminaries over with. 'That's all understood.'

'When we see each other outside, we need to act the same as before, as if the friendship is progressing naturally. Like at Caroline's drinks. That's the first giveaway, suddenly ignoring each other, not mentioning that we've seen each other.'

'So we mention we see each other, just not what we choose to do together.'

'Exactly.' *What we choose to do together* . . . But it was more imperative than choice, it was an elemental command. 'You need to be friendly with Jeremy too. He knows you work from home, and I'll tell him we have lunch or coffee sometimes, you're my new chum. We *will* have lunch occasionally, and when we do I'll invite Caroline to witness how normal we are together. We'll have a house-warming at some point, too, and you'll need to attend, even if we hate each other by then.'

'We won't hate each other.' The fingers of his left hand, resting on the worktop, jerked suddenly and my skin quivered as if to their touch.

'No phone calls,' I said, speeding through my mental list. I had spent hours on it, applying myself to it as if my life depended on it. (My life, as I knew it, as I valued it, *did*.) 'No emails. No notes through the letter box.'

'How –?'

'Texts. But only dates and times, deleted as soon as they've been read. Nothing suggestive. Definitely no images.'

'You're extremely thorough,' Rob said. 'Like a barrister prepping a witness for trial.'

But a barrister would not begin to unbutton her top, as I did now. 'If either of us wants to stop, the other accepts without question. No tears, no emotions, no love.'

'Agreed.' He was watching my fingers, transfixed. 'I've never had to submit to this transactional bit before.'

'I wouldn't call it a transaction.'

'What is it then?'

'I don't know.' I took his glass from his hand and placed it out of reach. 'Maybe a blow to the head?'

We kissed, at first savagely as if the wait had been in years, not weeks, him pressing me against the worktop until I cried out that it hurt, and then in a longer and more painstaking style on the sofa. Being kissed by him was like being liquidized, being prepared by a chef for consumption; whenever I caught sight of any of my limbs I was amazed to see them in their original solid form. And then, indecently quickly, entirely without romance, we had sex, the first of what would be many times, and he was exactly as I had intuited he would be: forceful, demanding, unstoppable. You wouldn't want to change your mind midway, I thought, as he locked my wrists together above my head, his grip painful, unyielding, but then I *didn't* want to change my mind. My mind had been set the day we met, in the first ten seconds.

As our groans became less easy to control, the builders resumed their crashing next door and we were saved.

'Do you have a girlfriend?' I asked him, later. We were in the bedroom by then, window closed on birdsong, curtains drawn on the brightening afternoon, both flushed from our exertions: the very picture of daytime adultery. I was not sure how I preferred him to answer the question. On the one hand it made us even and reduced the likelihood of him demanding more from me than I could offer, but on the other it introduced another variable into the equation that I could live without.

'Nope,' he said. 'No one in particular, anyway.'

I touched his face, fingers curious rather than tender, sorry only in the most remote way for those girls of no 'particular' appeal. 'But you do see people?'

'Of course I do.' He yawned. 'You're not the only one who finds me overpoweringly attractive. I have a date tonight, actually.'

'Who is she?'

'The cousin of a mate. Fresh to these parts from Gloucestershire. She's going to teach in a secondary school in Tower Hamlets, poor sod. She won't last five minutes.'

'In the job or with you?'

'Both, probably.'

I giggled. 'And that's why your friend thought of you? Because you know about education?'

'People like a literal connection when they fix you up.'

'Do they? Aren't opposites allowed to attract any more?'

'Oh, I think it's better that they don't,' he said.

There was no need to pretend *we* were opposites: we were cut from the same cloth all right.

'How did you and Jeremy meet?' he asked.

'Through work. I was invited to a summer party thrown by his company.'

'He was married to someone else at the time, was he?'

I prodded his chest in protest. 'You see me as a husband stealer?'

He raised his eyebrows.

'He was single,' I said. 'A legitimate candidate.'

'A middle-aged bachelor,' Rob said, 'aka a sitting duck.'

'Yes, just like you'll be one day soon.'

He seized my hand, nibbled at the fingertips, bringing

his teeth together just far enough to avoid causing pain. 'I bet he couldn't believe his luck when you walked in. Not only unbelievably hot, but a stand-up comedian as well.'

I smiled, retrieved my fingers from his mouth and forked the damp tips through his hair, mapping the bones of his skull. 'You'd have to ask him that. But he did propose very quickly, it's true.'

'And what about you? What did you think when *he* walked in?'

'I thought he was great,' I said. 'I still do.'

'But?'

'But nothing.' I said this with a certainty that did not have to be simulated, naked though I was in the clutch of a man I hardly knew. 'I knew what I wanted and I was delighted that I'd found it so quickly.'

'What was "it"?'

'A committed relationship with a proper grown-up. I'd done the crazy passion thing too often – you know, meet someone in a bar and tear each other's clothes off. Only realize afterwards that they're a drunk or a lunatic or married. All three on one memorable occasion.' As I paused to register his amusement, I had the distinct sense that he was testing me. A less experienced lover would be all too easily outplayed by this man, I thought; for him, artlessness was a purely female failing. 'It was time to be sensible and think about the future,' I added.

'Did you ever wonder if you might have sold yourself a bit short?'

I frowned.

'No offence to the silver fox,' he said, 'but a girl who looks like you do, barely thirty then, you could have had anyone. One photo online and they would have been queuing up.'

'Maybe they would, but I didn't want them, I wanted him. I *still* want him.' I stretched my arms and flexed my elbows, easing aching shoulders, and Rob brought his face very close to mine. His breath was hot and short, in close rhythm with my own.

'Why this then?' he murmured. 'You missed the crazy passion.'

It wasn't a question and I could hardly deny the truth of it. 'I didn't know I did,' I said. 'I'm surprised to discover that I do. This is the first time I've done this.'

'You've never been tempted before?'

'Never.'

He didn't need to ask why he was different, why *we* were; he accepted our coupling exactly as I did, as being animal, primordial. For us, the suffering was never going to be in the complications it caused; the suffering could only ever have been in its denial.

He drew away from me, head next to mine on the pillow, and we both gazed up at the ceiling. 'Is it true you two are trying to have a baby?'

So news in Lime Park travelled fast, door to door, ear to ear, and efficiently enough to remain accurate. That was worth keeping in mind.

'Yes,' I said. 'And that's the most important condition of all.'

'Condoms?'

'Don't run out. I can hardly be found to have any in my possession when they're strictly contraband next door.'

'No, I suppose not.' He paused, turned to look at me. 'How often are we going to meet?'

'I suppose it will depend on how busy we are.'

'I'm not that busy at the moment. Work's dried up a bit lately, to be honest.'

'And I haven't got a job at all, as you know. So I may be texting you quite frequently. Keep your phone charged.'

Rob chuckled, eyeing me with admiration. 'You're very cool about all of this.'

I didn't blink, immobilized for a second or two by the euphoria of being the object of his desire. 'I have to be,' I said.

And to myself: *If I lose my head, I'll lose everything.*

When Jeremy came home that first time, I braced myself for the haemorrhages of guilt, steadying myself on the door frame as I welcomed him home in case I trembled. Don't cry, I thought. Don't blurt. Instinctively I understood that if I could survive this first occasion I would be safe.

'Let's see the latest damage, then,' he said, passing me by to enter the building site.

'Oh, there's been progress today,' I said. 'Hetty was here this morning and put a rocket up them. They fixed that fault in the folding doors, the spotlights are in, and some of the kitchen cabinets are in position.'

My voice had a rough-grained tone, a rawness to it that was not usual, but he didn't notice, too busy running his hands over the new fittings, caressing the glazing, questioning counter height, voicing new doubts about tap swivel. It was a ready-made smokescreen, this renovation project; a dust screen.

When he'd finished his hands were black. 'You mustn't stay in the house all day,' he said. 'All this dirt. The builders probably wear masks.'

'Don't worry, I'm not here most of the time. I was out all day today. I went to the gym and had a coffee with Rob next door.'

'The dust hasn't got through there, has it?'

'No, not that I noticed. Anyway, I thought that as long as I stay local and can get back quickly if something goes wrong, then I can go missing for hours.'

'You like the idea of going missing, don't you?' Jeremy smiled. 'Of being a woman of mystery?'

'Who doesn't? Besides, I need to keep you on your toes, darling.'

As his indulgent expression turned all too quickly to a frown, I held my breath. 'Hang on, nothing *has* gone wrong so far, has it? The builders know what they're doing? There's nothing I should be worried about?'

'No, that's the point,' I exhaled. 'We only worry when it *does* go wrong.'

'Good.' He checked his phone for the time. 'Let me change and we'll go out for dinner. Which of our four options shall we go for?'

On Lime Park Parade there was an Indian, a Mexican, a pizza place and, best of all, Canvas, the proper West End-style restaurant on the ground floor of the old art school. We'd been eating in them virtually in rotation, uninspired by our temporary kitchen quarters at the top of the house.

'Canvas?' I said.

Physically exhausted though I was, I got myself ready to go out. I'd already showered, of course, in the generous intermission between the builders leaving and Jeremy returning, my hair dried for the second time that day. As I put make-up on I noticed a faint grazing on my chin. I was going to have to demand that Rob shaved.

Another condition.

The next day, having extracted from my gift stocks one of my favourite room scents and selected from the patisserie on the Parade their finest lemon drizzle cake, I presented myself uninvited at Felicity's door. I told her I was there because I wanted to know how affected she was by the noise, but really I wanted to know how good the sound-proofing was between her flat and Rob's.

'I haven't seen you for a while,' I said. 'I thought it was time for a fresh offering.' As the sudden screech of the tile cutter made us both wince, I added ruefully, 'Perhaps a blank cheque might work better?'

'Let's start with this and see how we get on,' she said, taking the cake box from me. 'Ooh, my favourite! How did you know?'

'I had inside information – your neighbour upstairs. The next part of my evil plan is to get you to tell me *his* favourite.'

'Well, I'm not sure it would be cake,' she said. 'Rob doesn't have a sweet tooth.'

That, I could easily believe. I followed her in, liking that her flat was clean and tidy just for herself and not because she'd been expecting a guest. She had framed photographs of Glen Campbell on her walls, and when I admired them she showed me a video clip of him performing at the Hollywood Bowl.

'I had lunch with Rob yesterday,' I told her, in the casual way of acquaintances passing the time. We were settled by then at the coffee table with tea and cake. She had yet to open the room scent, but I knew she would love the addition of its rich, woody notes to her home.

'Yes, I heard you on the stairs,' she said.

I wasn't sure what to make of that, didn't think there was anything particularly distinctive about my approach to a staircase, up or down. I made a mental note neither to skip on arrival nor drag my feet on departure.

'It's hard to imagine he's much of a cook,' she added.

'That makes two of us,' I said, shrugging. I knew better than to fabricate details that could later be disproved. 'You should join us when you're not circumnavigating the city with your pedometer. We'll go out somewhere. I'm always looking for new places to escape the dust.' I smiled my most winning smile. 'That's the real reason I'm here now, to escape. I'm only pretending to keep you sweet, Felicity.'

'Well, keep up the pretence for as long as you like if the cake's always this good,' she said, finishing her first slice. I had pushed mine around the plate, having forsaken such treats years ago.

I glanced about the room. 'So you've got your rooms the other way around to his? Your bedroom is at the front?'

And the living room in which we were sitting was

directly under his bedroom, which was not ideal. I imagined her tucked up on the sofa with her Glen Campbell biography, her concentration disturbed as squeaks and groans leaked from above.

'Yes, he likes the bigger room for the living room, because he works from home, but I wanted my living room here, at the back, so I can see the garden. The Californian lilac should be flowering soon. You've got one as well, of course.'

'Have I?'

Felicity laughed. 'You're not a gardener, then?'

'No, to be honest I'm not sure where my talents lie in the domestic realm.'

I imagined Rob smirking at that. I imagined Jeremy smirking at that, too. I blinked their twin smirks from view.

'Better that way, if you ask me,' Felicity said. 'If you're too good at housework, they think you're no good for anything else.'

'I couldn't agree more. Were you ever married, Felicity?'

'Yes, once. So I know the pitfalls first hand. Those sacred vows people find so hard to keep.'

I looked carefully at her then, but there was nothing insinuating in her tone, nor anything in her expression to suggest disapproval. 'Well, I think I like your arrangement better than Rob's,' I said, deciding I'd fish one last time before dropping the rod. 'But I hope he doesn't keep you awake with his parties when you've gone to bed.'

'Oh, he's fine,' she said. 'I'm the noisy neighbour, with my music. I have it on all day long.'

I was pleased then, because I hadn't been aware of her music when I was upstairs, which meant she'd likely not noticed the sort we were making either. 'Well you're both model citizens compared to me,' I said, motioning to the dividing wall. 'I know it must feel like it's taking forever, but we *are* making progress. It won't be one of those situations that keeps overrunning and overrunning until you wake up one day and realize it's been three years.'

Rather like the affair I'd embarked on. Ablaze now, it would surely lose its rampant heat in a few months, or even weeks, blowing itself out naturally perhaps at about the time building work was finished. *That* could suit all concerned.

Agreeing she would not suffer in silence, Felicity cut herself a second slice of cake, while I rose to have a look at her CD collection.

'Is it only Glen you listen to or do you like others as well?'

'Johnny Cash,' she allowed. 'And Elvis, of course.'

'Everyone likes Elvis,' I agreed. 'He must have been irresistible when he was young, don't you think?'

Morsel of cake poised at the end of her fork, she looked at me with interest. 'No man is irresistible,' she said.

Chapter 9

Christy, May 2013

Well, *that* was interesting, she thought, as a couple she had not yet met but who she suspected might live at number 46 (and in which case had declined her drinks invitation with neither apology nor explanation) crossed the street outside the Davenports' house just moments after having crossed *towards* it. Their dog, a long-legged creature with a coat like lambswool, pulled at the lead in resistance before tripping after them to nose the base of a cherry tree on the opposite kerb. Though it was drizzling and hardly the weather for lingering, the pair stood in obviously contrived conference, heads down, lips moving like those of extras on a film set, mouthing but not speaking. The man had his hands in his pockets and the woman reached suddenly to grip his right forearm, as if restraining it – restraining him.

Very curious behaviour.

It was 11 a.m., the time of day when the street was at its most peaceful, the only sounds those of pre-school children in the playground in the park, the commuters long gone. Since this man was usually among them, he must have a day off or be working from home.

She imagined Joe hearing her thoughts and laughing:

Who cares who works from home? It's *his* business, not yours. She reddened, but did not move from the window.

It was then that she saw a figure hove into view from the opposite direction, passing the gates of numbers 48, 46, 44 . . . it was the churl from the flat next door, Rob – it seemed too approachable a name for one so abrasive – presumably returning home from some rare public appearance (frightening small children, perhaps, though he hardly need leave the street to do *that*). As he neared his own gate he slowed sooner than Christy was expecting – he'd noticed the couple crossing in front of him, perhaps; would he heckle them as he had Felicity that time? – and came to a halt by the Davenports' wall. To her great horror he lifted his big bushy chin and stared up at the very window where she stood spying. Even allowing for the helpful dazzle of sunlight on glass, she knew he had seen her: there was no mistaking that glare – stark, hostile, menacing. Pointlessly, too late, she slid aside, fingering the curtain fabric for comfort, relieved by the peripheral sight of him on the move again, pacing past her gate and into his own.

Returning to her original position, she was in time to watch the couple from number 46 re-cross the road and head towards their own gate. To her surprise, it was now this other man who turned to glower – in Rob's direction – before his wife scurried back to take his arm and usher him towards home. Though he exclaimed angrily, it was clear from his wife's consoling demeanour that the expletive was not directed at her.

Goodness. What had that been about? There had been genuine loathing in number 46's expression.

It was only when all parties were safely indoors and the pavements clear once more that Christy registered a detail that had been staring her in the face. The hands of the man from number 46, they had no longer been stuffed in his pockets as he stood at his gate, they'd been free, his arms hanging stiffly at his sides. And the right one, if she remembered rightly, had been bandaged across the knuckles, as it would be if sprained or badly cut. The kind of injury you might get, perhaps, from punching someone in the face.

'What do you think it *meant*?' she asked Joe that night. Admittedly, this was possibly not the first subject he wished to discuss on coming home exhausted at 11 p.m., but it was hands-down the most remarkable thing that had happened to her that day.

'I don't know, but I think you might be becoming a bit obsessed,' he said, as amused by her indignation at this suggestion as by the idea that she should be so curious in the first place. He, by contrast, was detached, just as she doubtless would have been had she still been working, the hours spent at home dwarfed by those in the office and too scarce and precious to be squandered on an audit of the neighbours' comings and goings. He had considerably more attention for the large glass of wine he'd poured himself before even uttering a greeting.

'How can I be obsessed? I've never mentioned this couple before. I've never even met them.'

'I mean with the street generally. It's like *Rear Window* or something. You'll be telling me you've witnessed a murder next.'

Christy laughed. 'I suppose I'm bored. Job-hunting when there aren't actually any jobs doesn't take up a lot of my day. My mind must be looking for some other occupation.'

'You're not in plaster like James Stewart,' Joe pointed out. 'You do have the use of your legs. You're allowed to leave the house, you know.'

Thanks to the adrenalin of shock following her redundancy, she'd been filled at first with extraordinary energy, cramming her days with meetings with old contacts and headhunters and choosing to overlook the terms they used to describe the job market – '*very* quiet', 'a bit dead', 'not as buoyant as we'd like' – until one consultant, confiding that she feared for her own job, had actually begun crying in front of her. *Then* she believed them. She'd quickly resolved that this universal pessimism would need to be counteracted short term by domestic accomplishment if she was not to succumb to it and, though there was no DIY to be done, she could clean. The Frasers had made countless improvements but they had not had the power to repel dust and the parquet flooring showed every last mote. And then there was the immense kitchen and the three bathrooms (two of which they had not yet used) and the downstairs cloakroom . . . Yes, this could be a full-time job if she applied herself to it conscientiously.

And didn't allow herself to get too distracted every time she passed a window.

'I wish I could afford a gym membership,' she said. Fitness was the saviour of many an unemployed white-collar worker, everyone knew that, but even with Joe's promotion she was not about to dive deeper into debt for the joining fee required by Lime Park Club, a luxurious facility next to the primary school with a tantalizing olive-green pool you could glimpse through the glass. (*Even with Joe's promotion* . . . She was using that phrase more and more, his accomplishment somehow recast as not quite enough to save their skin. He didn't deserve that.)

'You could go running?' he suggested. 'That costs nothing.'

'You know I hate running. It hurts and I give up.'

'That's not much of a motto,' Joe said, grinning. '"It hurts and I give up"?'

She tugged at the drawstring of her pyjama bottoms, as if to tighten them was to remove an inch from her waistline. (In the first week of her redundancy she had imposed the rule that she should remain dressed for Joe's return from work, but she had soon abandoned this wifely discipline and now asked of herself only that she remain awake.) 'OK, so I'm not going to be hired as an ambassador for British Athletics. I just want to be hired, Joe. By *anyone.*'

'Something will come up soon. You've got an interview lined up for the week after next, haven't you?'

'Yes, but according to the headhunter that agency has a reputation for pulling budgets just when they're about to make an offer.' That was how it was now, the consultants had told her, cutting short the joy she'd felt on hearing she'd made her first shortlist, albeit for a role junior to the one she'd just lost. Multiple interview rounds seemed to be standard now, and it took companies months to get through the process and make a decision.

But at least she was online again. Having given up the ghost of the cut-price supplier, she'd called the market leader and within hours was making use of the fibre-optic cables installed in the Frasers' day. She didn't need to phone her mother to be told that false economy was never a good idea.

'It's a numbers game,' Joe said, refilling his glass (*already?*). 'Eventually, your number will be up.'

She raised her eyebrows, amused. 'Would you like to rephrase that?'

'Enjoy the break while you can, that's what I say.' Though he was claiming to envy her, she could tell that he would rather jump off a bridge than be at a loss as she was. He had developed a subtle new gravitas since being promoted, she noticed; he'd leave in the morning as if eager to make his mark on the world and he'd return in the evening with the air of having made it. It was very attractive.

She, on the other hand, was reduced to what was starting to tip alarmingly close to being a nosy neighbour. Just as well she hadn't confessed that the first thing she'd done when dusting down her laptop was not to job-search but to google the Frasers. She wanted to find out who they were and where they were now; she wanted to see if they still existed.

Well, Jeremy Fraser did, she had established that at once. Amber Fraser's friend Imogen would not have found it hard to locate him, for he was a founding partner of a digital branding firm called Identico.UK, its Kingsway address given on the company website. His biography in the 'Our People' section was crammed with business achievements and yet it felt featureless, devoid of personal details, as if he himself, in spite of his expertise, defied branding. The photograph showed a man of about fifty with cropped grey hair, his expression one of self-important vexation, as though the photographer had interrupted him in conference with the prime minister.

Of Amber Fraser there was only an archived biography of a junior media-buyer role she'd held years ago, along with a list of clients she had looked after; she'd had 'special responsibility' for projects co-partnered with Identico.UK, which if nothing else at least hinted at how she and her future husband had met. Christy supposed that her marriage could have been relatively recent, any earlier references presumably involving her maiden name, which Christy did not know.

Just as Imogen had said, she had no Facebook or Twitter presence. How had she put it? *She wanted to cut loose undesirables from the past* . . . It was an interesting choice of words.

To Christy's great disappointment, there was no photograph.

Well, at least they had ended their inauspicious reign as new kids on the block, for the couple who'd bought Felicity's flat had now moved in. Having learned from her mistakes, Christy did not knock at their door and introduce herself, but posted a 'New Home' card through the letter box and left it at that.

Soon after, on the first day of spring to contain the promise of summer, a voice called to her over the garden wall (gardening being this week's activity to promote mindfulness) and when she climbed onto a tree stump to peer over she found a woman of approximately her own age, raven-haired, olive-skinned and – inevitably – pregnant, radiantly so.

'Hi there, are you Christy? Thank you for your card!' She introduced herself as Steph, distinguishing herself at once from the rest of the Lime Park Road population by making eye contact and smiling broadly. 'Oh, and we found your note about the drinks party as well, but we hadn't moved in then. Did you have a good time?'

'Yes, thank you,' Christy said, flashing to an image of Joe and her standing on either side of a tray of unused champagne flutes.

'You'll have to tell us what everyone's like around here.'

Christy hesitated. 'I'm not sure I know myself yet. They keep themselves to themselves a bit.'

'I know what you mean,' Steph said. 'I've been getting around that by accosting people in the street.'

Given the tensions she'd observed, Christy wondered if this was the best strategy.

'So far I've waylaid Joanne and Kenny at number 46' – Christy made a mental note of the names of the couple she'd spied in that cryptic interaction with Rob – 'and Caroline and Richard next to you. Caroline seems to be the unofficial social secretary of the street, doesn't she?'

So Caroline did preside, just as she'd suspected. 'You've talked to her?'

'Yes, I bumped into her with her kids in the park yesterday. She was really helpful.'

'She was?' Christy tried to keep the incredulity from her voice.

'Even before I told her where I lived, she'd already filled me in on the local nurseries, primary school admissions, the lot. She said if it weren't for the great schools, they'd have moved on by now. Liz was there as well. Her boys are *so* gorgeous. You know she's a single mother?'

'Ah.' Christy *knew* she'd made a mistake with Liz in not welcoming the offspring with open arms. As Steph chattered on, it became clear that in a matter of days she had had far greater success in engaging the natives than Christy had in several weeks, which rather contradicted her suspicion that it was the street that was at fault. Christy could only put Steph's advantage down to the fact of her pregnancy; I'm being punished for my lack of breeding, she thought, pleased with the joke if not the situation. *That*, well, it could only grow more painful by the day – if she allowed it to.

'I find that no one turns down a pregnant woman,' Steph continued. 'We naturally attract advice givers, if you know what I mean.'

'I think I do.'

'*You're* not . . . ?'

'No.' Christy chose to interpret the question as the standard one of whether she had any children rather than whether she was expecting a baby, not as outrageous a suggestion as it sounded in light of the shapeless clothing she'd taken to wearing for her long days of domesticity. 'It's just me and my husband.'

'In *that* big place?'

'I know.' All that square footage so marvelled at by their families as a luxury for two had come to be an uneasy abstraction for one woman (lugging a vacuum cleaner, generally), the rooms beyond recognition from the Frasers' day. When they'd first viewed the house, she and Joe had admired item after item, the elegant little tables with jugs of fresh flowers, clusters of quirky, mismatching chairs, beautiful woven rugs at every step; by the time of their second viewing, most had been removed, but there had remained in the air itself the stamp of the Frasers, the scent of their wealth and style. Now, under the Davenports, there was no stamp, no scent, and Christy knew that if Steph asked for a tour she would be embarrassed to give it.

Steph turned to survey her new territory. 'Obviously we'd have loved to buy a whole house, but not with the prices on this street. You have to compromise on something, don't you?'

'You do.' Staring her own compromise in the face, Christy tried to judge how many months pregnant Steph was; the bump looked solid and established. Soon there was going to be a tiny baby next door. How easy would it be then to suppress her desires?

'Garden flats on this road hardly ever come on the market,' Steph continued. 'We'd been looking for months and months.'

'I think it's only our two properties that have been up for sale recently.' Christy paused. 'Did you happen to ask Felicity why she was moving out?'

'Felicity?'

'The woman who owned your flat before you.'

'Oh, yes, of course. No, we never met, but the agent said she was getting too old to live on her own and was moving to the country to be closer to her daughter.'

It sounded reasonable enough, though Christy remembered a perfectly sprightly woman manoeuvring with ease into her friend's car; she'd looked to be in her early seventies, which was not elderly these days.

'I wish I *had* met her, though,' said Steph. 'We've got a couple of questions about the boiler and the solicitor doesn't have her new address or phone number.'

Christy frowned. The fact of the Frasers and Felicity having put their houses up for sale at the same time was a plausible enough coincidence, but for neither to have left a forwarding address when they went, was that not remarkable? And what was more, both parties had moved out weeks earlier than they were legally required to, well in advance of their completion dates; having first-hand experience of the time-sensitive juggling act demanded of most Londoners vacating one property and installing themselves in another, Christy knew this to be a highly unusual luxury.

Steph tugged half-heartedly at a dried twig in her privet. 'I have a horrible feeling the garden might end up being my department – when I can bend over again properly, that is. Felix is about as far from green-fingered as you can get, but kids need outside space, don't they? And Rob's offered to mow the grass, which I'll definitely take him up on.'

'Rob upstairs?' Christy said doubtfully.

'Yes, have you met him yet?'

'Well, I've *seen* him.' She decided to leave it at that. 'Do you share the garden then?'

'No, it belongs to the lower flat. But he's always mowed the lawn, he says.'

He must have done it as a favour to Felicity, Christy thought; before their dispute. The grass now was calf-height.

'I should invite you all for a drink one evening, but to be honest, I'm in bed most nights by nine-thirty.' She and Felix were both accountants, Steph said, working for the same Blackfriars-based firm. She asked Christy what she did and, when presented with the information, offered the standard platitudes, while Christy, in turn, felt the already-familiar sadness of having been dispossessed by the working world.

'Well, if you're still off when I go on maternity leave, we'll have to have a coffee,' Steph said.

'That would be great,' Christy said, meaning it. Steph was by anyone's standards bright and friendly, exactly the sort of neighbour she'd hoped for. 'Or if I'm back at work, one weekend, perhaps?'

Another two months, she thought. I'll be working again by July, surely. And maybe, by then, Rob will be cutting *my* lawn.

The next time she saw him she astonished herself with a childlike explosion of indignation. Approaching each other at the park gates, they would have collided had she not scuttled aside at the last minute.

'Excuse me!' she cried, but he did not acknowledge her,

let alone apologize, and she turned on her heel to hurry after him, damned if she wasn't going to be treated civilly as Steph had been. That amiable exchange over the garden wall had reminded her she had every right to expect common courtesy from those who inhabited rooms just metres from hers. 'Excuse me? It's Rob, isn't it?'

He spun abruptly, causing her to come to an immediate standstill if she was to avoid a clash a second time, and bore down on her with an unnerving glower. All that hair created a barrier, which was, she could only assume, the purpose for its having been grown in the first place. His eyes, however, were easy enough to read: bleak, wary, expectant of irritation. And there *was* a bruise, at least the last faded remnants of one. She wondered what he would say if she mentioned Kenny's name, that bandaged hand she'd noticed, and felt a shiver of fear.

'What?' He took a step closer and she caught his smell, earthy, damp, male.

She swallowed, grappling for the right key. 'I wanted to introduce myself properly. Christy Davenport. I've just moved into the house next door. Did you ever get our note? We invited you for drinks, but we didn't hear back from you.'

'Don't know anything about it.' Though his voice was soft, no more than an undertone, it was sullen, unrepentant.

'I posted the card myself. We're at number 40, the Frasers' old house? I don't know if you knew them very well?'

'Is there a particular reason you'd like to know?' He scowled now, wariness replaced by naked antipathy.

Though taken aback, Christy did not show it. She knew a bully when she met one and had no intention of serving herself up as his victim. 'No, of course not, it's just a friendly question.'

The scowl deepened. 'Well, you've picked the wrong man. I've got no interest in "friendly questions", especially when I'm the subject of them.'

'You're not the subject of any questions,' she protested.

'Yeah, right.' He spat the words at her in disdain. 'That's fucking credible.'

'Credible?' (*Fucking* credible?)

There was a tense silence, during which she had the idea he might actually strike her. She wished her chest were not heaving so visibly. 'Look, whatever your problem is, it's nothing to do with me and it would be nice if you could speak to me with a little more respect since we're new neighbours.'

'Take it easy,' he said, as if it were she who was out of order – more than that, deranged, causing him to calculate the most effective means of withdrawal from a dangerous situation. 'I think you're getting yourself a bit worked up, love.'

Love? Though his face rearranged itself more favourably, there was a subtle attitude of cruelty to his expression, as if it entertained him to toy with her.

Courtesy and respect forgotten, she cried, 'Oh, screw you!' and turned from him in indignation, marching past her own house and down the Sellerses' path, her pulse throbbing painfully. Rob did not pursue her, of course, he couldn't have cared less; by the time she'd reached the door of number 42 he'd doubtless already cast her from his mind.

At the second ring, Caroline Sellers came to the door, one hand dangling a scorched Cath Kidston double oven glove. 'Hello?' She looked doubtful that the interruption was going to be worth her dereliction of domestic duties.

'I won't keep you long, Caroline, I know you're very busy, but I have a question, one question, and I'd be very grateful if you would answer it.'

'OK,' Caroline said.

'Is there something I should know?'

Caroline just stared at her in mild horror.

'I mean, about my house? Is there something wrong with it, something our search didn't pick up on that's caused bad feeling? Did the Frasers drive everyone mad with their building works? Because there *has* to be a reason why people are being so weird with us.'

It was necessary, that plural, though she was under no illusions as to its dishonesty, for Joe remained untroubled by the Lime Parkers' lacklustre welcome; he said he had no desire to socialize with a whole new group when he barely had the time (or the finances) for the old one.

'There's nothing wrong with your house,' Caroline said at last, her energy as contained as Christy's was unstable. 'And everyone was perfectly civilized about the renovations. The Frasers handled it very sensitively.'

There was a child's cry from inside the house, followed by the sudden appearance of a sticky-faced boy at Caroline's side, his hands groping her clothing as he pleaded to get back to the chocolate crispy cakes they were making.

As if to signal the end of the exchange, Caroline slipped her free hand into the other pocket of the oven glove and crossed her arms, giving the appearance of having been put in a straitjacket. 'Look, maybe we can talk another time, but right this minute I'm a bit . . .' She was being tugged backwards; there were three children now, Christy saw, possibly four. One was Rupert; did that mean Liz was here too?

'Sure,' she said, 'you don't have time. Future taxpayers and all that.' And having apparently lost all sense of the decorum she demanded of others, she turned from her neighbour and left the premises without saying goodbye.

As soon as she got home she went to her laptop and typed 'land registry' into the search bar. An easy succession of pages later and there it was, the price paid data for 40 Lime Park Road. The Frasers' purchase had been registered in April 2012, their own in March 2013; the Frasers had been in residence for three weeks short of a year. Not only that, but they had paid more for the house than they'd sold it for. Percentage-wise, their loss was tiny, but given the six-figure sum they must have invested in the refurbishment, it did not, as Amber's friend Imogen had so starkly pointed out, make any sense at all.

'You *still* have no blinds on the windows? After six months?'

In a welcome reunion Skype with Yasmin, Christy couldn't help noticing similarities between her friend's temporary apartment in a high rise of ex-pat apartments in the Far East and her own permanent 'dream' home.

The general effect was of luxury – immaculately finished walls, lakes of pristine flooring, door after door promising spacious zones beyond – but the details were missing. The bits that made the space home; the soul.

'No,' Yasmin said, laughing. 'There's nothing to hide behind when I'm spying on *my* neighbours.'

To Christy's great relief and pleasure, Yasmin had responded to her speculation about her new neighbours with all the sympathy – and keenness to pry – that Joe preferred not to demonstrate.

'It all sounds *very* suspicious. If I were you, I'd go straight to the horse's mouth and phone this Fraser guy at his office. I can't believe you haven't done that already.'

'But what would I say? "I'm incurably nosy and demand to know why you sold your house at a loss and disappeared off the face of the earth"? It's none of my business.'

'So what? Explain that you're struggling to settle in. Ask him what you asked oven-glove lady: is there anything wrong with the house?'

'He'll think I'm mad,' Christy said.

'Then let him!'

Ending the call, she sat at the kitchen table for all of sixty seconds before pulling up the Identico.UK website and locating the contact details. Her fingers tapped in the number for the main switchboard.

'Identico.UK?'

She inhaled, throat as dry as if she'd breathed in sand. 'Jeremy Fraser, please.'

There was a moment of terrified anticipation as the call was put through – should she really be doing this without having consulted Joe? – but the sensation dissolved in an instant when a second female voice came on the line. For this was one of those discreet, apologetic women who tended to be used for acts of diplomacy, such as the breaking of bad news: 'You're looking for Jeremy, I hear? Can *I* help?'

'Er, no, I need to speak to him directly,' Christy said.

'I'm afraid that won't be possible. He's on a sabbatical at the moment.'

She hadn't expected *that*. 'What sort of a sabbatical?' she asked boldly.

The woman paused. 'It's a long-service award. Can I take your name? I'm sure someone else here will be happy to look after you.'

'No, it's Jeremy I wanted. How long will he be away for?'

'I don't know for sure, but a little while longer, certainly. Who shall I say called?'

'No one. Thank you.' Christy rang off, fingers already emailing Yasmin with an update.

And though she couldn't say why, she was faintly relieved to have ended the exchange none the wiser.

Caroline Sellers had been mistaken: there *was* something wrong with the house, as a subsequent spell of wet weather soon revealed. A leak in the roof had saturated the wall of the front room at the top and the plasterboard was bowing. Joe poked a hole into it and collected the dripping water in a bucket, which Christy was responsible for emptying twice daily (at last, structure to her day!). Roofers came and quoted sums the Davenports couldn't possibly afford, while the insurance company declined to have any involvement, which came as no surprise since they'd scrimped on their policy.

In a fit of exasperation, she phoned to complain to the solicitor who'd handled their conveyancing, but he as good as told her the house had been a bargain and she'd be well advised to quit while she was ahead.

'But shouldn't the Frasers have declared it on the forms if there was something structurally wrong?'

'Not if they didn't know about it. It would have been for your surveyor to pick up on and if he didn't draw it to your attention then he can't have thought it significant. Perhaps the damage is new?'

Christy seemed to remember that the surveyor had not had access to the roof the day he called. She and Joe had galloped on with the purchase regardless. 'The roofers say it's old storm damage,' she said stubbornly.

'Well, be that as it may, I'm afraid your options are limited. All I can do is contact the vendors' solicitor and express your concerns.'

'Don't get cross,' Joe told her, later. 'We'll work something out. Dad said he'd ask around for a cheap roofer who might come south.'

'I just feel so *frustrated*, Joe.'

'It's all part of having a house and not a flat. There's no management company to do this boring stuff for us. No need to stress out.'

She sighed. 'Yasmin says it's part of the emotional process of redundancy. There are stages, like grief. This stage is anger. Next comes paralysis, apparently – I'm looking forward to that.'

'I see.' Joe looked at her with interest, perhaps the faintest tinge of caution. 'Who is it you're angry with? Me?'

'Of course not!' she exclaimed. 'Never think *that*.'

'Who then? Laurie, I suppose?'

There was a pause. 'I think myself,' Christy said.

Awed by its elemental power, she sought to exhaust her anger by the simplest means at her disposal: cleaning. The master en suite was the latest to succumb to her furious scrubbing, though Lord knew how you were supposed to clean copper. (After pricing the tub online and finding it had cost not hundreds of pounds but thousands, she had seriously contemplated removing and selling it: *that* would pay for the bloody roof repairs.) The position of the tub under the window made it awkward to reach the strip of floor tile behind it, but such was her mood she refused to be beaten, and on her knees, at full stretch, she poked a damp cloth at the last elusive patch. There was a sudden scratching sensation, a hard object lodged against the skirting board, and with some effort she managed to hook it and slide it towards her.

It was a bangle. She took off her rubber gloves and turned it over in her palm, rubbing away the dust to find a beautiful narrow silver band with a clasp made of two interlocking pieces of amber. There was no engraving, but it was not hard to guess its owner.

After trying it on, first on one wrist and then the other, Christy took it into the bedroom and placed it in her small jewellery box, covering it with a skein of beads so Joe wouldn't notice it.

Two days later, the solicitor rang her back. 'I'm happy to report that the Frasers' solicitor has been authorized by his client to pay for your roof repairs. If you would email me the invoice, I'll pass it on.'

'Really?' Christy was amazed. She had never for a moment expected such a fortunate outcome.

'Evidently Mr Fraser wishes to pre-empt any sort of dispute. But his goodwill is on the condition that any issues that arise from now on are agreed to be your responsibility.'

'Of course.' Christy said, humbled. 'Can I have his new address so I can write to thank him?'

'I'm told he prefers not to make direct contact on the matter.'

'But I have some mail for him and his office says he's taken a sabbatical.'

'Then I suggest you post any items to this office and I'll forward them to his representative.' With this the solicitor ended the call.

When she reported their windfall to Joe, he was reserved in his praise. Maybe it was her guilty conscience, but it was almost as if he thought she'd done something dishonourable, that she'd deliberately conned the Frasers.

'I'll send a nice thank you with the redirected mail,' she promised.

'You mean we've still got that?' He frowned at her. The lines on his forehead were scored deeper these days. 'I thought you'd sent it on ages ago? There could be something important in there, Christy.'

She had no excuse; certainly not that she'd been too busy.

'I'll send it from the office if you like. I know you might be too angry or paralysed to remember.' The frown was gone and he was smiling at her now, even reaching for a hug. Somehow she had had the luck to marry the world's most forgiving man.

'Thank you.' Bundling the mail into a package for him, along with a note of grateful thanks to the Frasers, she noticed the letter to Amber Fraser in the white envelope with the stamp of 'Private & Confidential'. Seeing it again, she felt a surge of desire to keep it, just as she had the key ring and now the amber bangle. She laid it aside for a moment, filled with a kleptomaniac's elation. Then, at last, she slipped it with the others into Joe's work bag.

The cheque for the roof came not long after, signed by Jeremy Fraser. Ashamed by then, Christy wished she were in a position to rip it up and forget it.

But she was not. And the roof, at least, would be fixed.

Chapter 10

Amber, 2012

I know I've made it sound like I used to be some sort of junkie slut, crawling home on my hands and knees, living by my wits, but it wasn't nearly as squalid as that. I held down a job, I paid my rent. At the risk of coming off like one of Felicity's country music legends, I had a heart and I trusted its truth. But I'd left home for London soon after my eighteenth birthday and by the time I was in my late twenties I'd been partying pretty much uninterrupted for over a decade. I'd reached the point where I was becoming less discerning about who I drank with, who I slept with, whose unlicensed taxi I clambered into on the rare occasions I went home alone at the end of the night.

And I was in danger of wrecking my appearance. Twenty-nine was young on paper but it was starting to look old in the mirror. Another year of hard living and I'd lose my shine altogether.

The end of the era came in sadly predictable form: an office affair turned sour. I won't go into it in detail – there's no space here for *that* story – but the bones are that I'd had a one-night stand with my line manager, Matt, and had decided it should remain just that, one night, best forgotten, naively believing that I would be able to carry on in my job without interference (after all, he wasn't the first man I'd dallied with in that team). But Matt wanted an encore and turned vindictive, issuing a series of warnings before dismissing me and forcing me to take the matter to a tribunal. It was expensive and humiliating and even before I arrived for the hearing I knew that, regardless of the panel's decision, I was not going to have the stomach to return to work and spend another minute in his company.

'You should have gone back,' Jeremy told me later, 'even if it was just for a few weeks. It's the principle of the thing. It sends a message to other men who think it's acceptable to harass their female colleagues.'

'Maybe I would have if I'd known you then,' I sighed. But I'd been alone, I had lacked the support of a man like him, of any man frankly, and so I'd made the decision to walk away.

In any case, I was ready to make my life over. It is an exhilarating thing to change your industry, your friends, your wardrobe, your *ways*. I would have liked to have changed my address too, but a move from the studio flat I rented in Old Street proved too complicated and so I simply stopped answering the doorbell. I got a new mobile phone line, which put paid to the calls that came when the doorbell went unanswered, and I closed my Facebook and email accounts, truly a liberating exercise in itself. Three months passed without my drinking or smoking, which broke the back of the latter habit if not the former. I eliminated illegal substances, with no exceptions.

No sooner was I settled in my new media-buyer job than I'd met Jeremy at the Identico.UK summer party. That same night I went home and sobbed tears of gratitude at the memory of his gentleness and his certainty – qualities not combined in my previous beaus of choice – and at the prospect of having those qualities in my future life. For, unlike his predecessors, Jeremy was not in thrall to experience but a beneficiary of it; he'd stepped off the ride long ago. His idea of a good night was to stretch out on his sleek grey-wool Ligne Roset sofa with a box set and a decent bottle of wine.

And soon it was mine too, along with civilized outings with a new set of workmates, outings that involved cocktails in smart hotel bars and taxis booked in advance. No one smoked, no one did drugs, no one screamed in the street or wept on the night bus or took home the last man she'd laid eyes on – bewildered, unfocused 3 a.m. eyes.

We were nice girls.

It was this particular set of girlfriends who'd been clamouring to visit us in our new house in Lime Park from the moment we'd moved in. We'd invited very few guests, preferring to meet in central London until the house could be officially unveiled.

'It's in a complete state, why don't you wait till there's something worth seeing,' I pleaded, but they persisted and insisted and I eventually relented. Since the kitchen was still off-limits, I tore off the tape around the sitting-room door, freed the sofas of their dust sheets and set up drinks in there. Having sealed the room off since the first day of the build, I'd forgotten how lovely it was with its grand bay, high ceilings and pale marble fireplace. When the new flooring went down and the decorating was done – Hetty had ordered limited-edition Ralph Lauren fabric from the States to upholster the window seat – it would be a beautiful and tranquil place to sit, but for now I made do with a jug of lilacs on the mantelpiece and a trio of my favourite Diptyque candles, the ones that Jeremy dropped into my lap every so often like tributes.

First, I showed them the garden.

'Oh my God, it's like a wood down at the bottom!' Helena exclaimed. 'It's enormous!'

'Only compared to the little courtyards in London,' Gemma told her.

I didn't bother to point out that Lime Park *was* London. This expression of awe at the space one could buy for the same money as a shoebox somewhere central (the subtext being that any stylish urbanite would prefer the shoebox), it was all part of the ritual enjoyed by those who'd lived their whole lives with the luxury of choice. They didn't know they were born, these girls. 'We've got our own little access gate to the park, look.'

'You could let in secret admirers that way,' Imogen giggled, not knowing she'd made a genuinely helpful suggestion.

'How did you even find out about this area?' Gemma

said, speaking as if we'd chanced upon a remote hamlet not yet known to the folks at Ordnance Survey.

'Jeremy's always liked it around here,' I said. 'He knew it when there was an art school here, when he was at the LSE. He used to come to student parties here.' My thoughts drifted to the girl he'd got pregnant at college, the nearest he'd come to being a father: perhaps she'd been one of the friends based down here, a long-haired art student with a fateful artlessness regarding contraception. Strange how life brought you full circle like that.

'Will he be home this evening?' Imogen asked. 'You know how much we love our Distinguished Older Gent.' This was their nickname for Jeremy and another tiresomely persistent part of the ritual: to remark on how attractive he was for his age – as if he were knocking on the door of seventy.

'No, he has a partners' dinner this evening. He sends his love.'

'Is he always late?' Helena asked. 'Do you get lonely then, all the way out here?'

I couldn't help laughing. 'Listen to your questions! It's not the middle of the moors, you know, it's still the city. And I have new friends on the street if I'm bored.'

'Talking of which, someone's waving at us,' Imogen said. It was, naturally, Rob's window she indicated, his bedroom window, the mirror image of the first-floor room Hetty and I had earmarked for Jeremy's study. (Actually, it was earmarked for the baby's room, but I wasn't about to tempt fate with pastels.)

'That's Rob,' I said equably. I was so in control of

myself you could have taken my blood pressure and found not the slightest deviation from the norm. 'He works from home, so I see him a lot. We've become quite good chums.'

'Straight or gay?' Helena wanted to know.

'Straight.'

'Then what are you waiting for, get him to come and have a drink with us!'

'I thought this was a girls' night,' I objected. But a pair of single women in their thirties who had not been heavily sedated were not about to pass up the opportunity to tussle over an unattached male, and when Rob drew up the sash and leaned out to call hello, I obligingly invited him to join us.

'I can only stay for one,' he said when he arrived. 'I'm going out tonight.' We were in the sitting room with our drinks, Rob positioned snugly between Helena and Gemma on the smaller of the two sofas. It entertained me hugely to see the predator turned prey, trapped between two competing hunters.

'Doing anything special?' Helena asked him, with an artificial, over-familiar charm that would have made me want to draw her aside and advise more successful strategies – had I not been using them on him myself.

'Not if the first time we went out was anything to go by,' Rob said with a wicked look, and they began playfully to scold him, demanding to know what kind of girl stirred so little spirit in a man – and, more importantly, what kind stirred more. I wondered if he was feigning indifference to his date for my benefit. There'd been several, I knew, since the trainee teacher; he was a womanizer all right, albeit one who didn't have to try very hard. Did he sleep with other women on the days he slept with me? I tended to put Jeremy off on the nights following an assignation next door, though it wasn't going to be possible to maintain that discipline long term. (Long term? Hadn't I assumed we would last – at most – as long as the building works? Building works that motored along on schedule and, according to Hetty, were about to hit the pain barrier before easing downhill towards the home straight.)

We'd last met two days ago, our fourth liaison, as frantic and delicious as the others, as aerobic a session as any I'd get at the gym. 'I went with Rob for a coffee in the café in the park,' I'd told Jeremy in the evening, when he asked if I'd had a good day; I knew I would need to vary this to avoid coffee becoming a euphemism for fuck. 'We're going for lunch with Caroline next week and I have a feeling we might become a little trio.'

'I'm glad you've got some local friends,' he said, and now the girls were glad too.

'He's *fantastic*,' Helena said, after he'd gone. 'Don't you just *know* he'd be great in bed?'

I joined Imogen in her protestations. 'How can you possibly tell that after ten minutes?' I said, with perfect primness, as if the thought had never crossed my mind. It was becoming clear to me that deception was purely a matter of confidence; one did not even need imagination.

'Oh, he just has that vibe,' Helena said.

He certainly did.

Left restless by him (weren't we all?), she got to her feet to appraise the dimensions of the room, the huge bay window and glamorous fireplace, and then fixed me with good-natured accusation. 'Trust you, Amber.'

'Trust me what?'

'To land on your feet like this. You deserve it, of course.' It wasn't cool to spell out what she meant: that when the four of us had first shared a corner of the office, we'd all been — at least for a brief period — single, each unsure of what the future held, and now I alone had everything, right down to the eye candy for a neighbour. If they only knew just how extensive my everything was.

'We need a proper shot at him,' she said, returning to the sofa and the indentation of our departed guest. 'Can't you have a house-warming and invite us all?'

'I will, just as soon as the house is finished.'

'When will *that* be?'

'Soon. Late August probably.' And for the second time in a matter of minutes the prospect struck me as undesirably close.

'I didn't think there'd be anyone like that down *here*,' Gemma said.

'Lucky I'm so thick-skinned or I could be offended by that,' I said, pulling a face. I'd forgotten how by the end of the working week I'd used to tire of Gemma's slyly critical commentary; meeting in this new context somehow accelerated that. While the others accepted the received wisdom that the beautiful bird catches the worm (early *or* late), she harboured ideas that it just wasn't fair.

She looked at me with her signature half malice. 'Rob

reminds me a bit of that guy we ran into once. Obviously he's *much* more attractive, but they have a similar look.'

I frowned. 'Which guy?'

'You know, in that bar.' She sighed, casually forgetful. 'You said you'd had a thing with him?'

There was a time when this could have applied to *any* man in *any* bar, but my social life had been genteel enough since I'd known this group for me to be able to identify the match in seconds. 'Oh, you must mean Matt.'

I'd forgotten they'd met. It must have been a couple of years ago now. Gemma and I had been in a bar in Covent Garden together when a shambling figure passed by our table, turning abruptly back and gesturing towards me with an unlit Marlboro.

'Amber, is it you?' His thickened voice betrayed the thousands of cigarettes he'd smoked before this one.

'Matt,' I said. I introduced him to Gemma. 'He used to be my team leader when I worked in customer service,' I told her.

She looked as if she knew exactly what sort of euphemisms *they* were.

Matt, meanwhile, was agog at my physical transformation. 'I can't believe it, you look so . . .' But no adjective could be found to describe me adequately ('clean', I wanted to supply; 'fully clothed'). 'What are you doing these days?'

I gave him a breezy summary, lightly running French-manicured nails over the printed silk of my shirt. 'Being fired by you turned out to be the best thing that could have happened to me,' I finished, beaming.

He looked not so much crestfallen at this remark as

physically diminished by it. I'd heard a year or two after the hearing that his own career had not flourished in the aftermath.

'How about you, Matt? You're looking well, too.' I was aware of Gemma's incredulous expression and it made me want to giggle. The truth was he looked rough as hell. Though my age, he had not yet drawn the conclusion that there were only so many hundreds of times you could extend a night with drugs before it began to damage your skin, your hair, your youth. His clothes gave off that nauseating blend of stale cigarette smoke, human sweat and city grime, as if they hadn't been changed after half a dozen nights out. He must still be tumbling straight from bed to work, then off to the pubs and clubs, and back to bed again in the small hours. Judging by his grey neck, regular showers were one of the many elements of a wholesome life he'd sacrificed. I had two a day now, one at the gym before work and one before sliding into bed with Jeremy in our Battersea bedroom high above the river.

'Are you still in the same job?' I asked.

'No, I do bar work now. A place out in Walthamstow.'

Though Gemma recoiled fractionally at the words 'bar work' and 'Walthamstow', I smiled on. 'And are *you* married yet?'

He put the cigarette to his lips, needing its touch, though of course he would have to wait until he was outside to light up. 'Divorced. I married Lesley, but it didn't last – obviously.'

I tilted my head, eyes blank. 'Remind me who Lesley was?'

He stared. 'Remember, she transferred from the Bristol call centre?'

'That's right. You were *her* team leader too, weren't you? Well, good to see you again,' I said, thinking just the opposite.

'Who was *that*?' Gemma asked, with fearful contempt, the moment he was out of earshot. 'He *smelled*.'

'An old manager of mine. We had a fling. He was slightly more fragrant then.'

'Well, he's not *at all* like Jeremy.'

The way she said this, prurient, almost thrilled, implied that Jeremy must surely be unaware of my previous life-style choices, whereas in fact I'd told him my story as soon as we'd met – or certainly enough of it for any romanticization on his part to be as much a kindness to me as to him. Between us we'd settled on the notion that I'd been some kind of wild child, a free spirit whom no one had been able to domesticate until he came along and stopped the rot.

Now, in my lofty sitting room in Lime Park, the scent of lilacs sweetening our nostrils, the others rushed to atone for Gemma's latest slur. 'Oh, she doesn't mean everyone down here must be boring, Amber, especially not you! You could *never* be boring, you'll *totally* make this the place to be . . .'

But I was far too pleased with myself to really care what Gemma thought. 'I love it here,' I told them. 'And to be honest, when we moved in I thought myself it might be a bit dull, but it turns out I haven't met a single dud.' This was in fact quite true; yes, one resident had claimed

158

the greater part of my attention, but the others were an agreeable bunch too. Among other dates in my diary was one to take Caroline and Liz shopping. (I had a plan to divert them to my hairdresser's while we were at it, see if I couldn't do something about those farmers' wives' haircuts.)

'Have you noticed anything about Imogen?' Gemma said, and all at once I became aware of an air of concealment, subterfuge in the group.

'No, what?'

'Look at her properly, go on!'

'OK.' But Imogen seemed exactly the same to my eye. Weight loss would be the usual cause for excitement of this pitch, but I couldn't cite this when she looked, if anything, a little heavier than the last time I'd seen her; women tended to be intolerant of disingenuousness or bluff on this, if no other, subject. What then? We were too young for Botox, and news of anything surgical, like Helena's breast enlargement, would have been aired long before the event, not after.

'Is your hair shorter?' I asked her. 'You're growing out your highlights?'

'No, not that,' Gemma said, answering for her, then offered a clue: 'She hasn't drunk any of her wine, have you noticed?'

'Sadly,' Imogen conceded.

'Not sadly, Imogen! It's awesome news!'

'She's pregnant!' They sang it out, a chorus of hallelujahs, and I understood then something I hadn't understood before: they all saw having a baby as the summit of female ambition, the solution to the puzzle of life, the cure for all disappointment. Did I? Well, apparently not, since I'd just been luxuriating in the notion that I had everything and yet had not included a baby in that reckoning. If I was honest, recently it felt as if I was using the idea of starting a family to justify my idleness; I'd said I wanted to so often it felt like a line in a play, uttered with perfect conviction every night and twice a week in matinees, but, in the end, the author's thoughts, not mine. Was that the missing link in my otherwise seamless reinvention of myself? Was that the trapdoor by which Rob Whalen had entered?

Did I actually *want* a family?

I hugged Imogen. 'That's wonderful news, I'm so happy for you and Nick.'

'And how about you and Jeremy?' she said warmly. She was a really nice girl, far too sweet to preen or gloat. 'Any luck yet?'

'No, not yet. Maybe soon.' And I glanced at Gemma as if to say, *See, I haven't got it all.* And she looked back with a half smile as if to say, *I already knew* that.

That invitation to the Identico.UK summer party, the one at which Jeremy and I met: it had in fact been sent to her, the more senior contact, but she had passed it on to me in favour of a more promising function. She'd spent years imagining that if she *had* turned up that evening, she would now be me.

Poor Gemma. I almost felt sorry for her.

I'm aware how ridiculous I must have sounded, reporting all those conditions I made to Rob – no emails or phone calls, texts to be deleted immediately after being read – when the reality was there were none of the mousetraps of affairs between working people, none of the snatched lunch hours and self-consciously separate arrivals and exits. Schedules like ours were tailor-made for adultery: he was at home most of the time, free to work in the middle of the night for all it mattered to anyone else, while my day was unhampered by employment of any kind, my hours alone long and unmonitored. Hetty was in charge of the works, the builders accepted that my involvement was limited, if not purely decorative; in any case, they had my phone number should there be an explosion on the other side of the wall that I managed to miss. Jeremy didn't get home till seven-thirty if he was lucky, and any change of plan was more likely to involve a delay thanks to an eleventh-hour pitch or some tedious client whim. Yes, I was having sex with another man a room away from our home, but it could just as easily have been a hotel room, a flat on the other side of town. The miracle was we weren't doing it every day. We paced ourselves.

'This is great,' Rob said one afternoon in June as I slipped lazily back into my underwear, wondering if I'd have time for a snooze in the relaxation room at the gym. He liked to watch me dress, which felt as erotic as undressing, an insolent scrutiny that might at any time lead to the suggestion that I stay a little longer. 'Everything I want from a relationship with a woman, without having to have the relationship itself.'

I laughed, reaching for my dress. 'If this is all you want from a relationship, then I pity your girlfriends.'

'Do you now? That's interesting.' He thought about this, eyebrows drawn together, and I sensed a deepening of interest. Our conversation, conducted mostly in bed, had to date comprised detached, ironic banter between two determinedly dispassionate personae. 'So what is it they want? What is it *you* want? I mean, what are the elements you get from Jeremy, apart from the obvious?'

I glanced up from strapping on my heels. 'The obvious?'

'Yes, the money. And don't pretend you'd like him just the same if he was a bus driver living in a bedsit in Stonebridge Park.'

'I might.' I shrugged. 'If I knew where Stonebridge Park was.'

He reached to tug at the hem of my dress – a prim-necked black shift with a less-than-prim mid-thigh skirt – and draw me back to the bed. 'Come on, tell me what you get out of being married.' He was genuinely fascinated, intent on discovery. Perhaps he wondered how he might win someone like me in full, I thought, and allowed myself a moment of thrilled arrogance.

'OK.' I perched on the edge of the bed, swung my legs up to get comfortable, thinking about his question seriously. 'Security: that's the cliché, but it happens to be true. Also, sharing things, making joint decisions, supporting each other when things aren't going well, and celebrating together when they are.' I looked away, embarrassed to sound sentimental, though not embarrassed to feel it. 'Having someone to go home to or to come home to you. Not being alone in the dead of night, not being alone inside your own head.'

'Why don't you want to be alone inside your head?' Rob asked, a certain slyness to his tone. 'You don't like your memories of the bad old days?'

I gave him a blithe smile. 'Oh, the good thing about the bad old days is they killed enough of my brain cells for me to not *have* any memories.'

He sniggered, went on sniggering.

'What?' I said, prodding him.

'You really *don't* remember, do you?' And he laughed proper delighted laughter. 'All this time, I thought you were just messing with me.'

Turning cold, I rubbed the bare skin of my upper arms, feeling the goosebumps. 'Remember what?'

'We met before. We had a one-night stand.'

'No we didn't,' I said. 'I would have remembered that.'

'You can name every man you've slept with?' He was watching me closely, his eyes full of mischief – or was it malice? Mischief, I decided.

'Maybe not,' I said, pouting; after all, I'd had my 'One night, best forgotten' motto (if you could call it that). 'But I know I would remember *you*.'

'I would have hoped so, but apparently not. Mind you, you had a big bag of coke with you – not a wrap, a fucking sandwich bag full. God knows where you'd got it.'

I uncrossed my arms and held up a hand. 'Don't. I don't want to hear any more. Nothing you say could surprise me, but I have a feeling it might depress me.' I sighed, stretched, mourned just a little that first Sunday when I'd stood at his door and thought we were strangers. 'Well, at least you're not trying to blackmail me, which is something.'

Rob looked at me in wonder. 'Blackmail you? Why would I do that?'

'One of my exes did.'

Not long after that accidental meeting in the bar in Covent Garden, I'd had an email from Matt. Though I was fairly sure I'd mentioned neither my married name nor the name of the agency I worked for, he'd found me easily enough. He was strapped for cash, he said (no shit), adding, none too subtly: *Does your new husband know? Does your new boss?*

At the time, Jeremy had been so consumed by a demanding new client I hardly saw him myself from one day to the next and, not liking to bother him with my upset, I found myself a lawyer. A woman after my own heart, or at least a woman after the same cash Matt hoped to extort, she promptly sent him a letter alleging attempted blackmail and threatening to contact the police if any further approach was made.

'That's the way to do it,' Rob said approvingly. 'What did he think he was going to get from you? It's not like you're a public figure, is it?'

I settled onto the pillows. 'I think he thought Jeremy was some kind of dotcom millionaire and that I had passed myself off as a virgin on our wedding night.'

'What a moron. No one would believe *that*.'

I smiled, head growing heavy, eyes drooping. I couldn't let myself fall asleep: it was against adulterers' rules. 'We didn't spend the night *here*, did we?' I murmured, turning my face to his.

'No. It was your place.'

'In Old Street?'

'That's the one.' His fingers were on me now, pushing between my knees and up my thighs, making the skin shiver. 'Do you remember—?' he began.

'No,' I insisted. 'I honestly don't want to know, Rob.'

'OK.' His mouth hovered over mine. 'Then all I'll say about that night is that you let me do whatever I wanted.'

'Which is different from now *how*, exactly?'

I closed my eyes, apparently not yet leaving after all.

'You look amazing, Liz,' Caroline said.

'Perfect,' I agreed. '*Exactly* to brief.'

'Thank you,' Liz said. Spots of colour bloomed on her cheeks as she registered our thrilled reaction.

We were at my hairdresser's in Chelsea, Caroline and I standing with a hand each on the back of Liz's chair, our heads tilted identically in consideration of our third. Though we wore radiant chemical haloes of our own, haloes that would do necessary damage to our credit cards, it was Liz who was the undisputed archangel, her formerly disgraceful thatch having been shorn by a genius to a chic, gamine crop.

'You look like Mia Farrow in *Rosemary's Baby*,' Caroline said.

'I'd rather not be likened to a character in a horror movie, if you don't mind,' Liz laughed. 'There was enough of that during the divorce.'

'Jean Seberg then. Or Leslie Caron.'

'Kate Moss, when she had her pixie cut,' I said, settling

it. I checked my watch. 'We ought to get back for the school run, ladies.'

For the purposes of my affair, I had made it my business to know these women's schedules inside out. It wasn't complicated; with children involved, their day ran like clockwork and I could easily avoid arriving at or leaving Rob's house when I knew they'd be passing his gate on the way to Lime Park Primary (handily, the kindergarten their younger offspring attended was based at the school and the half-hour staggering of pick-up times meant they were away from the street for at least a full hour).

'This has been the most amazing day, Amber,' Caroline sighed, as we tumbled into the taxi, our heads turning in vain little impulses to catch our reflections in the window. 'I can't wait to see if Richard notices my highlights.'

'I think he will,' I said. She had confided to me earlier in the day that she and Richard had let a whole year pass without sleeping together, which had given us a no-brainer of a goal towards which to work. 'Keep your hair loose over your shoulders, OK? No ponytail.'

'No ponytail,' she agreed, touching her butter-pale strands as if not quite believing that the head they were attached to was hers.

I turned to Liz. 'I think it's only a matter of time now before you're back in the saddle, too. Remember, the diet we discussed doesn't apply to sex.'

They both giggled.

'What about Rob, Amber?' Caroline exclaimed. 'Do you think *he* could be a possibility for Liz?'

'We shall have to see if he likes women with short hair,' I said, safe in the knowledge that he in fact liked long, thick tresses that he could grip in tight handfuls and bury his groaning face into.

I winked at Caroline. I was particularly keen to keep the street's chief whip close, which was why I'd selected her as the third wheel I'd advertised to Jeremy, every so often suggesting coffee at the patisserie on the Parade. An unexpected fringe benefit was that I was enjoying curating the friendship between the two of them – unlikely enough for it never to have germinated in the decade they'd already been neighbours.

'All this time we've lived a couple of doors apart,' she said to him on one of those early dates *à trois*, 'and we've not once had a coffee together before.'

'Before the bad influence of Amber,' he answered, his manner smooth, oh-so-amused.

'I feel like I'm a student again. Just lazing around without a care in the world.'

'That's because she encourages everyone to ditch what they're supposed to be doing so they can hang out with her instead. This is what it is to be the idle rich, Caroline.'

'Hello? I *am* here,' I said, laughing. 'And feel free to get on with your more pressing tasks, both of you. I haven't handcuffed you to your seats, you know.'

'More's the pity,' Rob said, with just the proper trace of lasciviousness. He was an absolute master of tone, a born actor. 'We'd like that, wouldn't we, Caroline? A little bit of discipline in Lime Park.'

She gave a snort of laughter. 'I was only supposed to be getting Amelia's cello tuned. The world won't stop turning, will it?'

'Exactly,' Rob said. 'It's not as if you're using it for firewood to barbecue her pet guinea pig. Enjoy the cello holiday while it lasts, that's what I say. She could always practise that piece that's complete silence. What was the composer called? John Cage, that's it.'

I loved how Rob knew these things.

'I used to have a bit of a crush on him,' Caroline confessed when we were alone.

'On Rob? Well, he *is* very attractive, I don't blame you.'

'This was years ago, when we first moved in. I remember calling round to invite him to our house-warming and just standing there gawping at him – so embarrassing, like I'd never seen a man before! Actually, maybe I hadn't for a while, not a *young* one. But he didn't come if I remember rightly, and he's been a bit of an unknown quantity ever since. It's very exciting that you've managed to tempt him out so much.'

Little did she know that I mostly tempted him *in*.

She sighed. 'Anyway, he would *never* have considered me, even without Amelia hanging off my boob. Then Rosie. Then Lucas.'

I smiled at her. 'Just as well, since you already have a husband – and a very nice one too.'

'Oh, sure. It's not the same, though, *nice*, is it? I know you and Jeremy have only been together a few years, but, I hate to say it, Amber, as soon as kids come along, everything changes.'

I wondered what she would say if I confessed that things already *had* changed and in such a way that would make her hair curl. There was no doubt in my mind that she had no suspicion whatsoever of what was going on under her nose.

'Anyway, who would want to shit on their own doorstep?' she said, as if she still might be persuaded to bed Rob, all things considered. 'It would be an insane risk.'

'I agree,' I said. 'I would prefer to conduct my first extramarital affair from an apartment in Paris.'

She took my hand in mock urgency. 'Do it while you can, Amber, because I'm not sure the Eurostar is fast enough to get you there and back between school drop-off and pick-up.'

'I might just take your advice,' I said, winking.

'Richard says Caroline's telling everyone you're a breath of fresh air,' Jeremy said one evening at Canvas. He frowned at the menu, which did not alter frequently enough for us, constant customers that we were. He would probably have the Black Angus rib-eye again, and I would have the scallop starter as a main.

'That's sweet,' I said over the top of my Bellini. 'Are you having the steak again, darling?'

I liked to see a man eat red meat.

'I think I am, yes. Seriously though, Richard says you're just what they need round here, someone with a bit of spark. You're a real hit, baby.' And he looked at me in that way he still did, as if I were always candlelit, always accompanied by the smoothest jazz melodies, and not just when

169

we were in chichi restaurants. I watched as gentle emotions crossed his face – admiration, pride, a fleeting sense of wonder that he had ever had the luck to win me – chased by the more familiar ones of self-assurance and entitlement.

'Glad to be of service,' I said.

Chapter 11

Christy, June 2013

Just when she should have been emerging from her post-redundancy fugue (and there'd been, she had to admit, a certain perverse pleasure in being in it), just when she was finally on the cusp of doing what she should have done weeks ago and begun supplementing her job hunt with regular scourings for volunteer work locally – anything to occupy her hours, to expand her activities beyond the stalking of empty rooms – she was struck down afresh.

For the flu made no exceptions of the unemployed. It probably singled them out. Certainly it pardoned Joe.

Now the torment *really* began. All the demons of Hades visited her at once: her glands swelled, her sinuses became blocked, her head ached and her skin burned. She sneezed, coughed, sweated, vomited, shivered and sobbed. When she dared look in the bathroom mirror she saw a woman a hundred years old, born an invalid, raised in confinement. She could remember no life before that of lying in bed and wishing either for a general anaesthetic or death itself, whichever could be administered the faster.

'See if you can get someone from Dignitas to come and put me out of my misery,' she told Joe one morning.

'I'd forgotten what a terrible patient you are,' he said, amused. 'Come on, sit up. Here's your lemon and ginger drink . . .'

He was as devoted as any man absent sixteen hours a day could be. Their principle waking overlap being in the early morning, when he would bring her the 'special' hot drink his mother swore by and that she now swore *at*, she would dutifully prop herself up, overheated and malodorous, for his brief bedside visit. From her zone of flattened pillows and tangled sheets, the large bedroom looked too big for its few sticks of furniture, as if someone had burgled it as they slept.

'Oh, I spoke to your grizzly bear last night,' he said.

'Rob?' Even in her stupor, this was news enough to rouse her. 'He's not *mine*, urgh, what a grotesque thought.'

'"Grotesque"? That's a bit strong. Anyway, you'll be pleased to hear he's a perfectly respectable citizen. He's a freelance journalist, works from home.'

'I know *that*,' Christy said. 'I hear his music all day long.'

'Oh dear. What kind is it?'

'Blues.'

Joe grinned. 'Perfect for the prevailing mood, I would have thought.'

'Did you ask him why he was so mean to me in the street?' Christy demanded, but Joe seemed surprised by the question.

'I very much doubt he was being deliberately mean.'

'You didn't hear the way he spoke to me! He swore at me, Joe. It was bordering on harassment.'

Still cheerful, Joe lowered his voice as if they were in danger of being overheard: 'I'm not sure you should go around accusing people of harassment.'

'Why are you on his side? *I'm* your wife, you should be defending *me*!' She set down the drink to blow her nose and use the nasal spray the pharmacist had recommended.

Joe tried to straighten his face but his lips twitched and gave him away. 'I'm just saying he seemed perfectly normal.'

'Of course he was normal with *you*, you're a man. He's obviously some sort of misogynist bully.' She paused, recalling Steph's report of civility, before continuing unabashed. 'I hate him. I wish we'd never moved next door to him.'

Joe just patted her leg through the duvet as if to pacify an anxious pet; though gentler, fonder, it was fundamentally the same reaction as the beast's (*Take it easy*, he'd said. Patronizing bastard). 'Come on, so he's not that sociable,' he said reasonably. 'What difference does it make to us? I don't know why you care so much about him, or any of the neighbours – we've got plenty of friends of our own.'

None of whom had visited her while she'd been ill. Yasmin was in KL, Ellen was on holiday, and other friends were either routinely working late or unwilling to risk debilitation from the lurgy themselves and earn a demerit from bosses who were, in this economic climate, universally feared. The other faction, the new parents, quite understandably had enough on their plate without worrying about a bout of flu in Lime Park. Only her mother had come. She was thirty-seven years old and only her mother had come. She began to feel very upset.

'Remember what I told you Felicity's friend said? I bet that was to do with him. I bet he drove her out with his antisocial behaviour.' Her theories had had the perfect conditions in which to ulcerate during her days in bed. '*And* the Frasers. All three of them disappear off the face of the earth at the same time – it's like they were abducted by aliens!'

'Or by Rob, perhaps? Maybe he's got them imprisoned in the attic!'

Christy ignored his facetiousness. 'And I told you about Caroline's husband shouting up at his window, didn't I? We've moved next door to a psycho, you wait!'

But the lawyer in Joe rejected this wholesale. 'Come on, this woman you're quoting, what did she actually say? "This will all be behind you soon"? That could be to do with anything at all, a medical scare or a tragedy in the family. And if Caroline's husband was screaming up at his window, doesn't that suggest *he's* the antisocial one, not Rob?'

'Well, what about Kenny punching him? He had to cross the road to stop himself doing it again! I saw it with my own eyes, he had to keep his hands in his pockets. Joanne had to restrain him!'

Joe gazed at her, amazed. 'I have no idea who Kenny

and Joanne are, let alone why they should choose to cross the road and punch a third party. Seriously, Christy, you've never even talked to these people, have you? You don't know the first thing about Rob or Felicity *or* the Frasers. Finish the drink and go back to sleep.'

But sleep brought no respite during this period: she dreamed of pain, or continued to experience it as she dreamed, waking frequently, every inch of her sore and aching. Unless wedged upright, her nose would glue up and she'd have to breathe through her mouth, making it agonizingly dry, which would lead to nightmares about roaming post-apocalyptic wastelands in search of fresh water until she would wheeze and gasp herself awake.

One night, half concious, she heard voices close by and thought at first that Joe had left the television on downstairs. Disorientated, it took a moment to realize the voices were coming from the other side of the wall, from Rob's flat: a man and a woman were talking, arguing, judging by the sudden bursts of volume, and the woman sounded very distressed.

'Joe!' she hissed to him, asleep in the bed beside her. 'Joe, listen! Something's going on next door. I can hear someone crying.'

Joe did not stir – he slept enviably heavily – and Christy shook him awake, rough with urgency. 'Joe, I think we need to call the police!'

'What?'

Then, just as he was reluctantly surfacing, her own brain cleared and she realized she'd misunderstood: what she was hearing was in fact a couple making love. The woman was pleading in torment of a different kind. There was the low grumble of a male voice asking questions, overlapped by her saying, 'Yes', imploring him repeatedly, begging him to go on doing whatever it was he was doing.

'I know it's been a while, but are you really telling me you can't recognize the sound of two people having sex?' Joe said, voice slow with sleep.

'But that's his living room, isn't it?' She didn't say how she knew this, that in the weeks prior to her confinement she'd sometimes lingered on the pavement across the street and noted the flickering of a TV screen or the closing of blinds in bright afternoon sunshine.

'I haven't got a clue what room it is,' Joe muttered, 'I don't have a floor plan of his home. But he can use any one he likes, can't he?'

Christy said nothing. Now that the begging had ceased, the effects of pleasure sounded perfectly conventional, whimpers and groans rather than screams, until the inevitable crescendo that made her flinch with embarrassment.

'Stop being a pervert,' Joe said, admirably easy-going given the circumstances. 'Go back to sleep.' And he moved away from her, right to the edge of his side of the bed, burrowing easily back into his own sleep and leaving her to fester. What had he just said, *I know it's been a while*? He was right. Since they'd moved into the new house and he'd been promoted, there'd been less time, less energy. Was this . . . was this going to become an *issue*?

There was laughter now from next door, and the faint

insistent beat of music. She reached for the radio alarm on the cabinet next to her, anything to return her mind to this room, this house, this life, but in pressing a series of wrong buttons she managed only to disable it. Heaving herself from bed, she tried to locate her iPod on the chest of drawers, her fingers prodding at objects in the dark. They rested on her wooden jewellery box, the lid half open thanks to a muddle of beads spilling over the sides. Remembering the hidden bangle, she extracted it and returned to bed with it in her hand. Lying there, hot and tangled in the damp sheet, she ran her fingers over the clasp, over and over, as if comfort, or even remedy, were to be found in it.

Back on her feet, she was seized by the first desire for action she'd felt in weeks – more than desire: compulsion, an irresistible sense of urgent mission. Obeying with single-minded zeal, she set about transferring the contents of their bedroom, item by item, to the room at the back, until at last the master bedroom stood empty and the modest spare at the rear had been reconstructed in its image. She was still very weak and it took most of the day to accomplish the switch.

'What on earth have you done?' Joe asked, when he came home – for the first time in a while before 10 p.m. – and found her slumped on the bed, curtains open to the lightless park, the low dark skies.

She beamed at him, excited. 'I've moved things around. I thought we'd sleep in here now.'

Joe looked neither convinced nor impressed by this

reconfiguration. 'But the master bedroom's got Amber Baby's million-dollar en suite.'

'You can still use it, if you prefer,' she told him. 'I thought I'd just use the main bathroom. It's got a bigger shower. Anyway, I've moved all the toiletries and towels, so you don't have to do anything.'

Still he gazed about the room, as if puzzling over an optical illusion. 'How did you manage to move the bed on your own? It's solid wood.'

'I turned it on its side and inched it along the carpet.' This had been the feat of which Christy was most proud; her muscles atrophied following her ten days in bed, she'd had to rest frequently during the bed's voyage down the passageway. 'You should have seen it, it was like towing a cruise ship through the Panama Canal,' she added. It was a relief to have rediscovered her sense of fun, even if Joe appeared to be having trouble connecting with it.

For when he retraced her route he was genuinely displeased. 'You've wrecked the walls, Christy, look at all these marks!'

'No I haven't. And if I have it will give me something to do to repaint them.'

'Better not to have damaged them in the first place, don't you think? I bet this paint is some high-end heritage stuff that costs a bomb. Maybe you could check in the shed to see if the Frasers left a pot.' He squinted at her as if suddenly uncertain of her psychological health. 'This is crazy,' he said, at last. 'I honestly don't understand why you've done this. The bedroom at the front is easily

178

the nicest and now it's just going to be a useless empty space.'

'I thought we could make it into an extra living room,' Christy said. 'I'll put that armchair from downstairs by the window. This room is much cosier and it's private, it overlooks the garden and the park. And there's no traffic noise.'

'There's no traffic noise at the front either. We're on a residential road with a speed bump every ten metres.' He remained standing by the door, as if to step into the room would be to yield to her madness. 'Seriously!'

Waiting for his exasperation to run its course, Christy wondered if he'd made the connection to the noise that *had* disturbed her, in which case he might reasonably point out that if Rob's living room was at the front, then logically his bedroom must be at the back, right alongside where she'd now moved theirs. What was the sense in that when presumably the majority of his sexual activities took place in there? The answer was that at the rear they were separated by the twin cavities of staircase and landing on either side of the dividing wall, surely enough to deaden the most enthusiastic cries. And it worked both ways: she didn't want *him* hearing *them* (though – here was that thought again – there had been precious little so far for him to have overheard).

'Fine,' Joe said at last. 'If it makes you happy. It's just somewhere to sleep.' For him, he meant, passing through the room as he did between leaving the office in the late evening and returning to it first thing in the morning.

'Yes, sleep – and other things,' she said, in a new, lighter tone, and he looked at her with a marked absence of desire that was both dismaying and a relief. She had not changed out of her pyjamas for her removals antics, though he might have given her the benefit of the doubt and assumed she'd been in regular clothes for most of the day before getting ready for bed early. Neither was an especially alluring conclusion.

'Are we eating anything tonight?' he said. 'I'm starving. Did you have a chance to go to the supermarket?'

'No. I'll go tomorrow. We can cobble something together for dinner.' And she could see very well that it might look odd for her to have exhausted herself with furniture removals and yet overlooked their empty fridge. Did other partners at JR have meals cobbled together by a spouse dressed in greying pyjamas?

Possibly not.

To celebrate being back in the land of the living, she decided to go to the café in the park for the rare pleasure of decent coffee made by someone else and drunk in the company of fellow human beings as opposed to cushions. As she accessed the park by their private gate and looked back at the rear aspect of their house – high and solid, its windows shining – she felt her natural joie de vivre rise once more. It may have been by the skin of her teeth, but she still owned this house. She wondered if the astonishment of it would ever fade.

She chose a table with a view of the meadow, the long grass painted with pale feathery strokes, vivid yellow buttercups dotted atop; in the foreground rose a bank of papery dark orange poppies, shivering in the breeze. She felt as if she'd been released from a kidnapping. Seeing friends gathered at tables in twos and threes reminded her how keenly she missed colleagues, colleagues and friends, and she texted Ellen and two friends who'd gone to ground since having babies: 'Missing you, come and see our new house!'

When one replied at once, promising a visit the following week, Christy felt her mood lift once more. It would have been better to have a proper house-warming, she thought, but the expense was prohibitive and in any case their abortive drinks party made her fear another shunning. Once was disappointing; twice might break her spirit.

She took out her book. She'd rediscovered in recent weeks the pleasure of reading, and had brought with her *Rebecca* from the library. However, she'd barely finished a page when she became aware of a familiar figure at the counter: Rob. Typical! She allowed herself a treat for the first time in weeks and here was her nemesis to spoil it. Clearly he was not quite the recluse she'd thought. She couldn't hope to concentrate on her book now, only on him, monitoring his movements peripherally as he fished for change and nodded thanks for the coffee (like him, tall and unsweetened). Well, at least he was just getting takeout.

She had of course by now googled him. Stymied previously by her lack of basic information – 'Rob' and 'Lime Park' had unsurprisingly produced nothing – she found that the addition of a surname and an occupation to her keywords generated an image straight away. There he was, in clean-shaven form, but wearing the all-too-familiar arrogant sneer: Robert Whalen, freelance journalist. He appeared to be an education specialist, not what she had expected, but then you didn't need a *Blue Peter* personality to write about the broader context of schooling. There were pieces in the broadsheets about school league tables and private tutors, a report on the recent NUT conference, a profile of a former education secretary who was making himself unpopular with the present one by being a cult hero of trainee teachers. His style was dry and precise, with very little allowance for humour. No surprise there, she thought.

He had no website and his social media accounts were restricted. Odd for a journalist; you'd have thought he'd want to be readily contactable.

All at once, so suddenly it caused her to start, he was approaching her table, stopping at the sight of her and moving past only with an audible exhalation of irritation. He was staying then, and this was his regular spot – well, tough luck, she thought, *she* had it today. About to return to her page, she was aware of him suddenly doubling back and bearing down on her a second time, standing over her without uttering a word, and, to her great confusion, *joining* her. Not even gesturing for permission, he simply placed his cup on the table, waiting for her to look up and acknowledge him. This she did unsmilingly, eyebrows raised. As silence stretched between them, a flush began to creep through her cheeks. He, however, was perfectly at ease, tilting himself backwards on the rear legs of his seat as if he had all the time in the world.

'Can I help you?' she said at last, and made a point of not closing her book.

He ignored her question to ask one of his own in the same mildly sinister undertone he'd used in the street: 'So *you* don't work either, I take it?'

'"Either?"' she repeated coldly, supposing he must mean Caroline and the other stay-at-home mums on Lime Park Road. 'I was made redundant, if you must know. I'm job-hunting. I've been up for several positions, but . . .' She stopped, not wanting to detail her losses to this man; her failings.

But he passed over this information in any case, utterly careless of her circumstances. There was another silence, strained on her part, openly provocative on his if his sneer was anything to go by. She reminded herself that it was *he* who had imposed himself on *her*; she was not duty-bound to lead the conversation.

His bruised eye appeared to have healed.

'So you obviously know,' he said presently, his gaze now so intense it was causing her stomach to knot.

'Know what?'

'You know exactly what.'

Her brain, yet to be restored to full capacity, struggled with this. Had he somehow sensed her that night she'd overheard him having sex? Might he even have heard that wild accusation she'd made to Joe that he had influenced Felicity's and the Frasers' decisions to sell up? In spite of her guilt and embarrassment, she felt a flare of triumph.

So there *was* something to know; her new neighbours *did* have something to hide – at least this one did. She said nothing, but looked steadily back at him, seeing in his eyes a heightened sense of the previous belligerence: a malignant kind of pride, a resolute superiority.

At her failure to respond, his gaze narrowed. 'Oh, come on, Christy.' The way he said her name was deeply unpleasant, the way someone might identify a household pest before selecting the right poison to kill it, and she felt the last of her cool leave her.

'Look, I don't know what and I don't want to know.' She did want to know, of course she did, but she could not bear to have him staring at her a moment longer, dominating her.

'I saw you with her friend,' he said, as if she had not spoken.

'Whose friend? You mean Felicity's?'

Giving a mean little laugh, he brought the front legs of his seat back to the ground in a sudden motion that made her jump. 'Well, if you really don't know, then I'm certainly not going to be the one to tell you.'

'Fine,' Christy said, adding eventually and in as steadfast a tone as she could muster, 'I don't remember asking you to join me. Please leave me alone.'

'With pleasure.' He leaned in, clenching his takeaway cup so tightly she feared the lid would pop off and send an eruption of scalding coffee into her face. 'But let me just say this: if I hear you've been spreading false information . . .'

'About what?' Christy gulped.

'I repeat: if I hear you've been spreading false information, I *will* deal with it.' He did not elaborate and the threat felt all the more menacing for being unspecified.

He got to his feet, apparently unperturbed by this exchange, and as he strolled away she thought, Who do you think you are? How dare you threaten me? What is your problem?

And, most pressingly: *What do you not want me to know?*

The following Monday, long after Joe had left for work and the postman had dropped his latest round of bills and statements she dared not open, she heard the rattle of the letter box a second time, followed by the soundlessness that denoted a flyer dropping to the doormat. Engrossed in her new daytime TV favourite – a property show in which neighbours purged one another's junk, not a problem *she* suffered from – she forgot about it until she was leaving for the library later in the day. That was when she saw the folded paper on the doormat. Opening it, she gasped at the sight and smell of dried excrement, smears of which did not quite obscure a message, written in black ink in capitals.

SCUM. WE DON'T WANT YOUR TYPE IN LIME PARK. FUCK OFF BEFORE WE MAKE YOU.

Legs going soft, breath coming quickly, she dropped the note and made her way into the sitting room and onto the sofa. She'd known they hadn't exactly made the best impression on their neighbours, but they didn't deserve *this* vitriol. And anonymous, too. Then it dawned on her: it had to be from Rob. He was the only one who hated her, had as good as said he perceived her as some sort of threat to his privacy. And it made sense of what Richard Sellers had yelled up at the window: 'Thanks for the letter, mate. Nice way to treat your friends!' Did he make a habit of this then, delivering poison to his neighbours? What kind of a person smeared excrement on his correspondence? He must be unhinged. She'd been right to fear him – and Joe had been wrong.

She wanted to ring Joe and tell him so, but thought she might be sick if she stood up. In any case, there was no satisfaction in being right, not when it meant you were in danger.

Only when she advanced on wobbly legs to bolt the front door and saw the offending item still lying there on the doormat did she think to look at the other side of the paper. Retrieving it, careful not to touch the brown stains, she turned it over.

There was a name scribbled across the paper on the half that must have landed face down. The name was not hers or Joe's. It was Rob's.

Rob Whalen.

Not *from* him, then, but *to* him.

Evidently, it had been shoved through the wrong door. Had there been others like it that had gone through the right one? Her thoughts turned first to Felicity, who'd shared a front door with Rob and who'd left in a hurry, unable to bring herself to speak to him even to say goodbye. Had she too picked up notes like this? If so, they had to have been terrifying to an older woman living on her own.

Only then did she think of Rob himself. Much as she happened to dislike the man, this was one piece of mail she had no intention of forwarding.

Chapter 12

Amber, 2012

'Tell me more about how you grew up,' Rob said, one July afternoon. Such was the emphasis on other aspects of our friendship, we had reached this juncture knowing almost nothing of each other's early lives. Assuming, of course, I hadn't shared my life story with him when we'd first met years ago. (It seemed unlikely.)

'I'm not sure there's much to tell,' I said, not meeting his eye – owing to a lack of interest in the subject rather than any desire to conceal the truth. But there wasn't a great deal to look at in his bedroom, with its workaday bachelor's furnishings and near-absent decoration; by then I knew its corners and contours by heart, its tricks of light and shadow – everything but the view from the window, for I could not risk Felicity or another neighbour looking up from the garden and seeing me there. 'It was a typical broken home, I suppose. Not much money, not much mercy.'

'Mercy?' He repeated the word with wonder. 'That's an interesting quality for a child to care about. Do you mean you were hurt? Physically?'

I looked at him then, searching for a trace of compassion in his face and grateful to find it. 'Not me, no.'

'Who then?'

'My mother. By my father, and then by one of her next partners as well. She certainly knew how to pick 'em. I've had no contact with him for years. Jeremy's never met him.'

'How old were you when he left?' Rob asked.

'Seven or eight by the time he went for good. He came and went for years. He was an idiot, but violent, which made him a scary idiot. And he was very tall, so he seemed like an ogre to me.' I flashed then to the old sensation of seeing him looming in the doorway; not fright so much as sadness that a good day had turned bad – again. 'You know, it's awful but when I think about him now I can't think of a single thing to admire about him.' I gazed at Rob, aware that my lower lip had begun to tremble. 'No doubt that's affected how I deal with men.'

'You seem to deal with them with consummate ease,' he said.

'Now, sure, but there've been a few years of trial and error.'

He smiled. He was pleased, I guessed, to consider himself outside that category and yet surely he represented both trial and error by anyone's standards.

'So you had a stepfather after that?'

'Two. Mum never got married again, but there was a baby with the first one and another two with the second, all boys. I've got three half-brothers. They still live close together, all have kids of their own even though they barely pass as adults themselves, and they still rely totally on her. Their girlfriends do too.'

(For the record, my mother keeps occasional contact by phone, but is apt to get hysterical when we meet and I have found the best solution has been for *me* to visit *her*, that way I have control of exit arrangements. Recently, for reasons I will get to shortly, I've seen more of her and, mellowing in my old age perhaps, have enjoyed her company and appreciated her advice.)

'The last time I checked, there were six grandchildren and five girlfriends or ex-girlfriends involved,' I told Rob. 'If you set foot in that flat I guarantee that within five minutes you will be clutching a baby and listening to my mother complain about how exhausted she is. It's the free-breeding underclass. There's never enough thinking through of consequences.'

He laughed, eyebrows raised. '"Free-breeding underclass"? I'm not sure you're allowed to say things like that!'

'You are if you come from it, and I do.'

He considered this. His own background, I gathered, was solidly, unremarkably middle class and I assumed that his aversion to a committed relationship was through choice, not parental example. Looking at his complacent expression, I wondered for the hundredth time why it was that some people were set a gruelling and relentless steeplechase through life even before they'd learned how to walk while others got to coast around the track in glorious sunshine with a lackey running alongside to keep them fanned and watered.

'Do you help them out?' he asked.

'You mean financially? Sure. But funds get gobbled up

very quickly in that clan and you soon learn not to send good money after bad.'

'So you wouldn't ever go back into the fold?'

'I'd rather die,' I said truthfully.

'That bad.' He regarded me as if in a new light; he was thinking, I guessed, how my humble origins 'explained' me, but I could see that he was puzzled, too, by the illogical nature of it. For shouldn't I be protecting the fruits of my ascendancy with a zealot's single-mindedness, not imperilling it with a roll in the hay with him?

But he was nothing if not arrogant, and his interpretation, I could tell, was that my recklessness was the ultimate form of flattery – and no less than his due.

Maybe he was right. Maybe, like Elvis, he was irresistible.

'I noticed you didn't mention kids that time,' he said.

'When?'

'In your list of things you want from marriage.'

'Oh, children go without saying. You know we're trying.' I paused. Whatever else he drew from me that afternoon, I wasn't letting him within a mile of *that* vulnerability. 'But when I have them I don't want their childhood to be . . .' I fished for the word. 'I don't want it to be *ordinary*.'

'In my experience, most people who grow up with everything say they would rather have had ordinary.'

I grimaced. 'They *think* they would, but they don't mean real ordinary, they mean snuggling up in matching onesies to watch their favourite Disney movie, cute little puppy for a hot water bottle. Real ordinary is your mother struggling and striving and falling asleep every night in an exhausted stupor. Or staying awake worrying if the eviction order's on its way or whether the man coming home drunk is going to slap her around. Real ordinary is no money, no privacy, no education, no future.'

'What an idyllic picture you paint of family life,' he said, but mildly, no longer amused. 'Well, you needn't worry, because it won't be like that for your kids. The silver fox will see to that. And *you* couldn't be ordinary if you tried.'

'You just mean how I look.' It scared me sometimes to think what would have happened to me if I hadn't been born pretty – a freak beneficiary of the cherry-picked highlights of two average sets of genes, making me considerably more appealing looking in conventional terms than either of my parents in their prime, and a different species, frankly, from my half-brothers. I might not have had the opportunity to escape, or I might have escaped, failed and been forced to return, which would have been far worse than not having left at all.

When I turned, I saw Rob had taken my remark seriously and had raised himself onto a bent elbow to study me. 'No, much more than that. I don't know how you've reinvented yourself, but you've done a superb job. You're a one-off.'

'I'll take that as a compliment.' I smiled then, rolling from his grip, covers pushed away, subconsciously giving him the opportunity to admire me.

'You should. You're one of those women you read about in novels but who don't usually exist in real life. Just when you think she's a sociopath she opens the lid on a well of feminine vulnerability.'

I laughed, delighted enough to do it properly, loudly, heedless of Felicity or whoever else might hear through walls or ceilings (there was no crime in laughing, was there?). 'Did you really just make that up on the spot?'

'Of course I did. I *am* a writer. A bad one, admittedly, and with no plans to venture into romantic fiction.'

'Well, thank you. It's a great relief to know I only *seem* like a sociopath.'

'That's only to me,' he admitted. 'You're considered sweet and unaffected by everyone else. The whole of Lime Park Road is in love with you, from what I can gather: Caroline, Liz, Joanne, Mel, *all* the men . . .'

His observation was correct. If the women had taken remarkably little effort to win over, the men had required none. Joanne's husband Kenny was becoming a particular fan. One recent weekend I'd strolled past his house with Liz, both in the short summer kaftans I'd picked out for us in the boutique on the Parade, surprising him as he worked in his front garden. He'd been practically stuttering with excitement at the sight of our bare legs and it was all we could do not to howl with laughter.

'All the men except you,' I pointed out.

'I'm subject to restrictions, remember?'

'You certainly are.'

We smiled at one another in easy silence.

'You'll end this, won't you,' he said, at last, 'the moment you get pregnant?'

And I remember the question particularly for the response it elicited, definitive and startling: *Yes, but hopefully that isn't going to happen* . . . Those were the words that sprang immediately, treacherously, to mind, blindsiding me with their violence.

'Of course I will,' I told him, betraying not a flicker of this and even raising an eyebrow, as gleeful and wicked as he expected. 'And if *I* don't, Jeremy will.'

'Ha ha.'

But something had been said that afternoon, and we exchanged a look that was unusually tender for us before we put our clothes back on and went our separate ways.

Normally, when I was in Rob's flat, I turned my phone to silent, just in case one of the builders called and, hearing it through the wall, got it into his head to come and find me. The kitchen complete by then, they'd moved upstairs to the bathrooms, their tools and voices more audible than ever to my first-floor neighbour, which presumably meant *we* were also more audible to them. (If the workmen ever had any suspicions of impropriety, they certainly didn't share them with me and, thankfully, they never saw Jeremy to get the chance to share them with him.)

Later, I would continue the habit of silencing my phone; the house was rarely empty, what with decorators, cleaners, people hired to do all the things I had neither the skill nor the will to do myself, but could continue to 'oversee' from elsewhere.

But we all make mistakes, which meant, inevitably, there came cause to regret an oversight of my own. One Thursday in July, Rob and I were in his bedroom as usual, windows closed and music on to camouflage any errant moans, but I'd left my phone in his kitchen and failed to turn off the ring. It was a proper summer's day, the London heat brash and insistent, and his living-room windows werc open to the street. When I finally recovered it I found I'd missed three calls from Gemma.

As soon as I was home I called her back.

'I came to visit you,' she said, 'but you weren't in.'

I halted mid-step. 'Oh, I'm sorry. I was at the gym all afternoon.'

She made a noise of contemptuous dismissal that I chose to ignore.

'Didn't the guys let you in so you could wait?'

'No, no one answered the door, which was why I was calling you.'

'They must have turned off the electricity so the bell didn't work. What a shame. Are you still in the area?' I asked, pleasantly.

'No, I'm back at my place now.'

'Not working today?'

'Of course I'm working, Amber, I work every day. That's what a full-time job is, remember?' She gave a snort of dissatisfaction. Gemma belonged to that tribe of women who liked to make those who didn't work for a living feel morally inferior while at the same time secretly craving just such a sabbatical for themselves. I supposed the two behaviours must be linked.

'I remember only too well,' I said easily. 'So how did you happen to be down here?'

'I was in Wimbledon for a meeting and it wasn't worth going back to the office, so I thought I'd hop on a bus and swing by your place, see how the house is going.'

'It's really coming on.' I started to report in fastidious detail guaranteed to bore less long-suffering (or envious) types than her off the phone, but she was having none of it and had soon interrupted me.

'It was weird, but when I rang your number I could hear your phone going.'

'Well, it can't have been mine.' I pictured my phone on Rob's kitchen counter, mere feet from the yawning windows. 'It must have been someone else's.'

'No, I tried three times and I heard it each time. It was like it was coming from the house next door, Rob's place. I even called up to the window, but no one heard me. I went to ring the bell, but the old woman downstairs came out and told me he wasn't in.'

The hairs on my arms rose at this first warning of proper danger: I'd already said I'd been at the gym, I couldn't now change my mind and say I'd been next door. Nor could I make up a story about losing the phone since I was speaking into it now. As for Felicity covering for us, had she been fortuitously mistaken or had she known what she was doing? It didn't bear thinking about.

'How peculiar.' Only then did my brain fully engage. Remembering Gemma's interest in Rob (she'd had no problem recalling his name, she'd casually 'hopped' on a bus from Wimbledon, which was quite a distance away and not a direct route), I put two and two together: she'd come not to see me so much as in the hope of seeing *him*.

Comfortable now, I set about handling this misunderstanding. 'Well, never mind, we've managed to connect now. Listen, talking of Rob, I'll be sending invitations to our party soon. You'll definitely come, won't you, Gem? He'll be there, and he was still single last time I checked . . .'

She agreed she was looking forward to it, and at last I was able to guide the conversation to the safer ground of Imogen's pregnancy, the news that she was expecting a boy. All proceeded predictably after that and the incident was never mentioned again, but it alarmed me immensely to think of her standing under Rob's window while he and I caroused in his bedroom twenty feet away. And how easily the scene might have differed: what if she *had* rung the doorbell and, not getting a response, decided to wait? Or what if Felicity had let her pass, saying, 'I heard Amber on the stairs earlier, why don't you go on up and try the door?'

Or, worse, what if Jeremy *did* come home early one of these days and heard my phone, hunted it down like a malfunctioning smoke alarm. Finding himself at Rob's door, hearing sounds of life inside – hearing my laugh – noting how long it took Rob to answer and that he was only half dressed when he did, what would he think?

And where was I in this catastrophized tableau? Hiding in the wardrobe or under the bed, my clothes clutched to my naked body, a high-heeled shoe left behind, just visible from the door?

As I say, it didn't bear thinking about.

'*Another* cake?' exclaimed Felicity, standing at her open door. 'You're spoiling me.'

All those names Rob had listed, the names of the neighbours who adored me: hers had not been included.

'It's the least I can do,' I said. 'Victoria sponge, this time – I took a chance.'

'You *do* have a guilty conscience, don't you?'

'Not that guilty,' I said with a giggle, 'otherwise I'd have baked it myself.'

'But you don't have a kitchen yet,' she said kindly.

'I do, actually. That's what I came to say: downstairs is all finished now, so it's just the bathrooms to go. I probably don't need to tell you what a relief it is to see light at the end of the tunnel.'

'That *is* good news.' Felicity urged me towards the living room, saying, 'I have my friend Vanessa here. Go and say hello while I fetch you a cup of tea.'

The friend was in her late fifties, heavy enough for her smile to be engulfed by the flesh of her face, and dressed from head to toe in an ill-advised putty-grey. Rising from her seat, she eyed me with the air of having been sidelined by her own kind, stirring in me the instinct to take her in hand and transform her future. (Wouldn't *that* be a worthier use of my time than deceiving my husband?) I wondered if she might be the depressed one with whom Felicity went walking; perhaps I should go with them one of these days, be their little cheerleader.

'Amber lives next door,' Felicity explained to Vanessa, joining us. By now, she knew not to cut any cake for me, but automatically planted a plate with a large slice on her friend's lap. The cream oozed over the line of jam, the sponge springy and yellow; it put me in mind of an open wound.

Her gaze still fixed on me, Vanessa moved her fingers

blindly towards the cake as she spoke. 'So you're the one who . . . ?'

'Who keeps bringing me these delicious offerings,' Felicity finished for her. 'Can you believe my luck, Nessy?'

Though my brow remained smooth, I frowned internally: what had Vanessa been about to say before Felicity interrupted her? *You're the one who sneaks upstairs twice a week to have sex with your neighbour* . . . But I knew better than to put the words into their mouths (that was what the cake was for). I knew better than to let paranoia take hold.

'I'm the one they all hate,' I said amiably. 'They have voodoo dolls of me they stick pins into every morning at eight o'clock when the drilling starts up again. And I don't blame them, either. *I* would hate me too.'

'Oh, you know that's not true,' Felicity said. 'I've never known anyone so popular; she has adoring fans coming out of her ears, Nessy, just look at her!'

'I can see,' Vanessa exclaimed, as if in the presence of Angelina Jolie. She scooped the overflowing cream with her finger before noticing the fork Felicity had supplied. As she gripped it, coincidentally at exactly the moment Felicity picked up hers, I had the peculiar image of the two of them coming at me with their tiny weapons, jabbing at my arms and legs, forcing a confession from me.

'And what about that enormous bouquet of flowers I saw being delivered to your house a few days ago?' Felicity continued. 'There must have been two or three dozen red roses – the poor deliveryman could hardly stand up under their weight.'

'They were from Jeremy. My husband,' I added, for

Vanessa's benefit. 'It was our wedding anniversary.' There'd been other lavish gifts, too; jewellery, shoes, another brace of my favourite candles, as well as indulgent praise over a champagne dinner for my medal-deserving fortitude during the building works. ('I must admit, I'd thought you'd be tearing your hair out by now,' he'd said. 'But you've been quite stoic.' Stoic? The poor darling.)

'How many years have you been married?' Vanessa asked.

'Five. We had a whirlwind romance so I can't remember us *not* being married.'

'He's a very nice man, your husband,' Felicity remarked. 'Strikes me as a one in a million.'

'I'm glad you think so,' I said.

'I'm glad *you* think so.'

I stared at Felicity. Had she actually said that? She couldn't possibly have, could she? I checked Vanessa's expression – unruffled, lips dusted with icing sugar, eyes on her plate – and decided that I must have hallucinated.

'I hear you met my friend Gemma the other day.'

'Oh yes,' Felicity said. 'A very cross sort of girl, isn't she?'

'Was she rude to you? I'm sorry. She'd come out of her way to see me and was probably frustrated I wasn't in.'

'She was insisting she'd heard your phone in my flat or Rob's, but I told her you were probably at the gym.'

'Yes, I was,' I said. 'Thank you for being so helpful, Felicity.'

'You're very welcome. I would have invited her in to wait but, as I say, she was a bit bad-tempered.'

Well, praise the Lord for Gemma's surliness, I thought.

There was still hope that Felicity had missed any clues to impropriety on the day in question, but Gemma, were she to have been granted access to number 38, most certainly would not.

Felicity had been right about the guilty conscience. I drank my tea much too quickly, almost scalding the roof of my mouth, before pleading a lunch date with a friend in town.

'She's everywhere, this one,' Felicity told Vanessa, as I left.

Indeed I was, a social butterfly no less – I had nothing better to do, after all – and during those summer months Jeremy and I were constantly at soirées on the street. Other than at large gatherings it was rare that we overlapped with Rob, but whenever we did I sensed that he relished seeing me out of context rather more than I did him.

One Saturday evening in July, Kenny and Joanne invited us to dinner and it was there that a curious episode took place, one that I should perhaps have paid closer attention to at the time. Rob had been invited, alongside the usual suspects – Caroline and Richard, Mel and Simon – and among the ageing, Conservative-leaning husbands he cut a youthful, louche figure. Moving of their own accord, my fingers played with the tips of my hair whenever he looked my way.

Clearly Joanne regarded him as her guest of honour. 'Now you're in circulation, Rob, you do realize the temptation is too great to resist, don't you?' she told him wickedly.

Seated at her side in a wicker tub chair in a conservatory so charming it had wisteria growing *inside*, he looked momentarily tamed. 'What temptation?'

I got it before he did and smiled to myself. He'd been set up. In the kitchen, the farmhouse table was laid for ten.

'Great,' he drawled, 'I look forward to meeting my match,' and his gaze came to rest on my left hand, my long pearl-white nails tapping gently on Jeremy's thigh, diamond glinting in the pink evening light. On the low table between us, already unboxed and lit, was the Diptyque candle I'd given Joanne on arrival ('Ambre', naturally. It sounded so sexy in French, but not nearly as sexy as in English, when Rob said it, into my open mouth, his breath pouring down my throat like liquid).

His date was the last to arrive, a little late after getting confused about directions. A colleague of Kenny's called Caitlin, she was perfectly pretty but artfully low-key in her appearance, presumably in case Rob turned out to be a dud. I had no doubt that she'd be straight to the bathroom to make some adjustments once she'd identified the quality of the offering.

Instead, she took one look at him and went pale.

'We've met before,' he told the group in explanation, and the phrasing caused me to colour under my make-up. *You let me do whatever I wanted . . .* Well, evidently this girl had a better memory than I did. And since she'd surely have had no trouble finding the street had she been here before, I deduced that the venue for their one-night stand had been her place, not his. I appeared to be unusual in having been allowed into his bedroom, a logistical necessity of our affair and yet a distinction that pleased me.

'You already know each other?' Joanne said, disappointed.

'We only met once,' Caitlin said, and her neutral tone was belied by the anxious look in her eyes. She gulped at the Martini pressed upon her by Kenny and recoiled a little at its potency.

'Years ago, wasn't it?' Rob said, nonplussed by the coincidence. Clearly, he was not a man whose girlfriends remained in his life once discharged from duty. Well, I could hardly condemn him for that: there was not a single man I'd been with whose number still darkened my phone contacts. 'I'm not sure I would have recognized you, Caitlin.'

With your clothes on! thought the happily marrieds, exchanging significant glances.

Sadly, a repeat performance seemed unlikely that night, for the poor girl couldn't handle the pace of suburban drinking: huge balloons of red wine followed the Martinis (Simon, known for his alcoholic capacity even in this company, managed the two in parallel), and she began complaining of feeling unwell almost straight away. No sooner had Joanne served the main course, a gargantuan fish pie swimming in cream and flecked, to my horror, with disintegrating boiled egg, than Caitlin had fled the table, Kenny in pursuit. It crossed my mind that he might be having an affair with her – it was of just this younger-co-worker cliché that Liz's marriage had fallen foul – perhaps using the event as some sort of perverted game (it took one to know one). Glancing at Rob and noting his enthusiasm as he advised Richard on the expansion of his blues collection, I excused myself and headed to the cloakroom in the hall. I left the door ajar so I could hear Kenny and Caitlin talking by the front door.

My suspicion had been fanciful, it appeared. Though Caitlin was preparing to leave, plainly distraught, Kenny's solicitations were nothing but comradely. 'No, no, I understand. Of course I'll say goodbye to everyone for you. This is awful, Caitlin, I can't tell you how sorry I am.'

'You couldn't have known. But you see why I can't stay? I don't want to ruin your evening . . .'

'Don't give it another thought. Let's talk about it on Monday, shall we?'

He turned from closing the door as I emerged from the loo, lipstick refreshed. His expression was troubled.

'Are we one down?' I said brightly.

'So it seems.'

'But it's only ten-thirty, the party's hardly started! Are you all right, Kenny?'

'I'm fine.' He smiled, gazing at me fondly. 'How old are you, Amber, if I'm allowed to ask?'

'Of course you are. I'm thirty-five.'

'Exactly the same as Caitlin, then, but she's a mess. I'm not saying it's her fault, but she hasn't made your choices, let's put it that way.'

'You mean in men? Oh, believe me, I've kissed plenty of frogs in my time, Kenny.'

'Lucky frogs,' he said, and his eyes dipped from my face to my breasts; he was a lovely guy, but he was only human.

'Maybe Liz would be a safer bet if you're making up the numbers,' I suggested, linking my arm through his as we walked back to the kitchen. As one of my special cases, I liked her to be included.

'Maybe,' Kenny said.

At the table, which now resembled a frat party bar, loaded as it was with the spirits and liqueurs assembled to accompany Joanne's Eton Mess, he said merely that Caitlin was ill and had decided to go home early to spare us her groans.

'Oh God,' Joanne said, 'I hope it wasn't the Parma ham.'

Rob said nothing, but he was the next to leave, which surprised me, given his constitution. I didn't follow him out as I longed to and urge him to thrust me against the wall, tell me exactly what he thought of me.

'What was all that about?' Caroline asked, when just the eight of us remained. 'I feel like I'm missing something here.'

'I didn't want to say in front of Rob, but Caitlin got very upset,' Kenny said. 'Whatever their fling was, it ended badly.'

'What are the chances that they'd got together before?' Mel exclaimed.

'Pretty good if you ask me,' I said. 'That man goes through women like water. He's forever telling me how he loves 'em and leaves 'em.'

It was true that I'd lost count of the dates Rob had mentioned during our months together; some he'd met through work, others locally, more still thanks to introductions made by friends and family. He didn't bother with Internet dating because he didn't need to: he was attractive, unmarried and solvent, hunted rather than hunter. It amused me – and flattered me, I admit – that I had outlasted so many of them, though of course I knew the psychology: he could relax with me because I made no emotional demands of him. With the others, he gave rein to what was a pretty standard phobia of commitment: the moment a woman wanted more, he remembered to tell her he wanted rather less. (The problem – and one that I had not adequately anticipated, certainly not at that stage – was that by enjoying my special privileges I exposed myself to the risk of developing proprietary feelings towards him.)

Kenny was frowning, drinking deeply from his wine glass. By the recycling bin there'd already grown an impressive forest of empties. 'It wasn't just that he ditched her a bit carelessly or anything like that. She seemed to be hinting that he got rough with her.'

'Rough,' Jeremy exclaimed. 'You mean he hit her?'

'Well, not –' Kenny began, but I interrupted him.

'Of course he didn't.' I spoke very firmly. 'That's ridiculous. Rob wouldn't do that. Don't you agree, Caroline?'

Caroline looked pained to have to disagree not only with her new best friend but also with the stylist responsible for putting her in the partially unbuttoned cheesecloth shirt-dress that had been drawing her husband's eye all evening. It was a spectacular upgrade from the flared jeans and shapeless Breton tops she'd favoured when we moved to the street, a pairing altered so rarely I'd taken it as official uniform. 'You have to admit we don't know him that well,' she said to me, then, appealing to the group as a whole, 'I mean, we've never met a girlfriend of his, have we? In *years*.'

'I've always thought there was something slightly *dark* about him,' Joanne said.

'Nonsense,' I told them all. 'Quite apart from the fact that this took place a hundred years ago, he's our friend and we should give him the benefit of the doubt. I know him as well as I know you, Caroline, and that's good enough for me.'

As Caroline nodded, shame-faced, the others murmured their approval, impressed by my show of loyalty.

'What exactly did Caitlin say, Kenny?' I demanded.

'Well, nothing specific,' he admitted. 'It was just implied.'

'There you go. God, when I think of all the things old lovers might "imply" about me at a dinner party! I'd hope no one takes *them* seriously.'

That ignited the atmosphere again and soon spouses were freely repeating their other halves' most unrepeatable moments. Mel, a discontented spouse if ever there was one, gravitated centre stage, her descriptions of Simon's drunken buffoonery becoming subtly more vindictive and ending with the somewhat sinister line: 'And that was when I decided just to leave him there to get third-degree burns.'

The party didn't break up until the early hours. Jeremy and I left with Mel and Simon, their low-level squabbling as they staggered up the street soon obscured by the scream of a police siren in the distance. Across the road, a fox tore at one of Liz's recycling bags and extracted a soup carton. I thought of all the children of Lime Park Road, asleep in their beds upstairs as the adults and lower mammals ran amok below.

'It was good of you to defend Rob,' Jeremy said, as we strolled down our path. 'I've always found that unnerving, the way someone leaves the party and is immediately ripped to shreds.'

'I guess we like to make little soap operas for ourselves. It doesn't mean anything, you know.' This last statement I made with a dangerously confessional sincerity, almost an apology. I had allowed myself to get very drunk this evening, not identifying my witching hour as I normally did, and had almost certainly been saved from potential trouble by Rob's early departure.

Happily, Jeremy was three sheets to the wind himself. 'It just makes me wonder what they say about *me*,' he said.

'Only wonderful things,' I assured him. As he struggled to locate his key, I used mine, feeling the satisfying weight of the dragonfly charm as it knocked against my wrist bone. 'I know what you mean, though, and to be honest I think I'd rather not know.'

Jeremy followed me through the open door. 'Me neither,' he said.

Chapter 13

Christy, June 2013

Joe had observed well when he'd joked about *Rear Window*, had they not been on skid row she would have ordered the film and studied it for tips. For Christy had found that, two further job interviews having to date yielded no offer and all new initiatives disposed of in a hectic show of efficiency each morning, she had a full-time job on her hands, after all – albeit one for which she did not get paid. She was a curtain-twitcher, a peeping Tom, a voyeur. She was going the extra mile every day without setting foot outside the house.

In her case, the stake-out was a fraying and sun-damaged armchair in the bay window of their old bedroom (the room was otherwise empty now, the footprint of their bed still visible in the pile of the Frasers' plush vanilla carpet), but the fundamental situation was the same as Jimmy Stewart's: she was interested in all her neighbours, but suspicious of just one.

Of course, Rob had not murdered anyone – not to her knowledge, not to date – but there *had* been another questionable incident since his threatening display in the café and it *did* involve a well-groomed blonde. She was his girlfriend, Christy gathered, or at least an established squeeze, since she arrived in the evening twice a week and departed in the morning just after the school-run mums had left the street (it just so happened that Christy took to her chair at about this time).

On the occasion in question, the blonde had been leaving the gate of number 38, her head bowed, when Rob had loomed up silently behind her and seized her roughly by the arm, spinning her forcibly to face him and causing her to shriek in alarm. At this suggestion of violence, Christy sprang to her feet and moved closer to the window, her breath coming quickly enough to mist the glass. But there was no real fear in the girl's face, only query, even a note of exhilaration; evidently, she found his caveman handling to her taste. Indeed, there was no forgetting the way she – assuming it had been this same woman – had beseeched him in the dead of night that time, pleaded for satisfaction with an intensity Christy couldn't be at all certain any lover had ever drawn from *her*.

Rob's reasons for pursuing the blonde into the street were unclear, but the episode concluded with a long kiss, the first time Christy had witnessed any public affection between the couple.

As Joe had noted, she was not in plaster, she had the use of her legs, but when the kiss was over and the blonde at last permitted to walk on, Christy returned nonetheless to her seat.

Her curiosity about Rob Whalen was only stirred by a visit from Caroline Sellers. Though quite well again, Christy was still spending whole days indoors, and so it was that she padded to the door in leggings, a threadbare Slytherin T-shirt of Joe's and her bunny slippers, the kind that not so long ago she wouldn't have been seen dead in by her Lime Park neighbours (the kind that she shouldn't have been wearing in the house at all, frankly, if she hoped to salvage her sex life). There on the doorstep stood Caroline, bearing a Tupperware container filled with dark lumps, and, extraordinarily, at the sight of Christy she smiled.

'I bumped into your husband on his way to the station this morning,' she said in her well-spoken, self-assured tones, 'and he said you'd been very ill.'

'Yes, but I'm much better now, thank you.' Christy waited for Caroline to explain what it was she wanted. In spite of the smile, she knew better than to hope.

'Can I come in?' Caroline asked.

'Sure.' The monitoring of Rob's movements had been suspended an hour earlier when he'd driven off in his car with the laptop and files that spoke of a work appointment. He'd sworn angrily to himself when his ten-year-old Peugeot didn't start first time, which proved only that he could behave as unpleasantly to inanimate objects as he did to humans. She had not seen the blonde in three days, but that was not unusual.

She led Caroline into the kitchen, put the kettle on and gathered clean mugs, aware of her guest circling cautiously before she touched down on one of the Frasers' steel-and-leather stools; marooned in a hard and glossy landscape with only her Tupperware to clutch to, she looked unexpectedly fragile.

'I'm sorry if I offended you the first time we met,'

Christy said, bringing over the tea. 'I was thinking aloud, got carried away. I shouldn't have said what I said.'

Caroline considered this. 'You're sorry you offended me or you're sorry if I was offended?'

'I don't understand.'

'The implication of "if" being that you're only sorry because I was offended, rather than sorry for what you actually said.'

Christy suppressed the urge to scream by taking a gulp of tea. Honestly, why were communications on this street so painful? To think that she'd expected greater sophistication than in New Cross! Now it seemed that she'd not appreciated simplicity in her neighbours when she'd had it.

'Oh, forget it,' Caroline said to her surprise. 'Look, I know I haven't been as friendly as I could have been since you moved in. I wouldn't like to come to a new street and get into a row straight away. That day in the street, to be honest you caught me at a bad time. I had something on my mind. So I'd like to apologize as well. And it was rude of us not to accept your invitation for drinks, I felt really bad about that.'

'Oh, it wasn't just you,' Christy told her. 'No one turned up.'

Caroline lowered her mug. In her other hand she still kept contact with the Tupperware – talisman, safety blanket, *something* – and, remembering the circling, Christy grasped at last that she was nervous.

'It was too short notice, I guess,' she added.

'That wasn't the reason,' Caroline said quietly.

Christy looked up, the muscles between her eyebrows contracting. 'What was it then?'

'It was because we thought there might be someone else there who we didn't want to see.'

Intuiting that 'we' meant a group larger than the Sellers family unit, Christy recalled Liz standing on her doorstep and asking, *Who else will be coming?* It was only after Christy had shared her guest list that she had declined her own invitation and gone immediately to Caroline's door. Well, given all Christy had observed in the interim, it wasn't hard to guess who the 'who else' was.

'Rob,' she said and, when Caroline nodded, 'Why?'

Caroline gave a regretful smile. 'I hope you'll understand that it's not possible for me to get into the details, but I can say that distressing stuff went on before your time and we're all still a bit preoccupied with it. I'm really sorry if it's made us come across as stand-offish. It hasn't been anything personal towards you and your husband.'

'What distressing stuff?' Was it too simplistic to assume that this was also the information that Rob sought to protect? *You obviously know*, he'd said. She didn't, but Caroline evidently *did*.

'As I say, I can't discuss it. I really can't.' It was clear by the way she raised her chin that she meant what she said; she was the type to pride herself on keeping her word.

'Well, if it makes any difference to you, I loathe him anyway,' Christy said, 'and I have no problem saying why.'

Caroline's eyes widened.

'He's horrible and rude and he tries to play with my mind.' Aware that this did not sound entirely rational, Christy continued in any case: 'He harassed me in the park café last week. It was awful.'

'Harassed you?' Caroline looked alarmed. 'I don't like the sound of that.'

'Well, maybe not harassed, exactly. But he plonked himself down at my table as if he owned the place, just glaring at me, really trying to intimidate me. Then he accused me of gossiping, said he would "deal with it" if I did it again. I didn't know what he was on about. Honestly, it would have been funny if he weren't so . . . malevolent.'

'Malevolent,' Caroline repeated, frowning. 'That's an interesting word.'

Christy watched her. 'All of you, you said. *All of you* said no to our invitation just in case *he* said yes? Did you put it to the vote or something?'

Caroline sighed. 'Not quite, but we co-ordinated.'

And to think Joe had mocked her for conspiracy theories!

'And some people did genuinely have other plans,' Caroline added, with a glimmer of humour.

'Well, he didn't come,' Christy said, 'so you could have "co-ordinated" to come here. It might have been fun.'

Caroline nodded, contrite. 'I really am sorry, but we couldn't take the risk.'

Christy was at a loss as to what to make of this strange exchange. Doubtless the collective antipathy towards Rob had also been the cause of Caroline's husband having rung his doorbell so hard he would have raised the dead, the issue he'd been so impatient to discuss the same one Caroline was now determined to evade. What had Rob done? Clearly something more quantifiable than the general churlishness *she* had been subjected to. She imagined drug-fuelled parties with ear-splitting music or one of those burglary rings she'd read about in the papers where an insider would rent a flat in an affluent area and then tip off his accomplices the moment one of his neighbours drove off for the weekend.

'I thought it must have been something to do with the house,' she said, 'something the Frasers did that upset you all. Planning permission or problems with the renovations. You must have thought I was mad turning up that time and demanding to know what the problem was.'

Caroline kindly chose not to answer this directly. 'There's never been a problem with the house. It's the nicest on the street now, look at it . . .' She at last relinquished her Tupperware box to run her fingers over the sparkling quartz worktop; she touched it gingerly, as if it had diamonds set in it.

'Please tell me what this is about,' Christy said, not to be sidetracked by compliments to an eye for interior design that was not even her own.

But Caroline was standing firm. 'I honestly can't. I shouldn't even have said as much as I have. But I feel terrible that you might have taken this whole' – she paused to find the word that would give the least away – '*atmosphere* personally.'

Christy suddenly remembered Steph's report of Caroline and Liz being friendly and helpful. *Even before I told her where I lived* . . . 'So you're saying you'd have done the same with Steph and Felix if it had been their party?'

'I think we would have had to, yes.'

Even with their new membership to the parents' club, Christy thought. This *was* serious. 'The thing is, Caroline, there've been other things to do with Rob besides the way he treats me. Hate mail came through our door by mistake. It wasn't signed, but it was addressed to him. Should I be worried for our safety?'

'No,' Caroline said firmly. 'The best thing you can do is not give it another thought. Let's have our tea and talk about something else, shall we? Here . . .' She snapped open the lid of the box. 'I brought you some brownies. They're a family speciality. Can you taste properly again? When Richard had the flu he said everything tasted of metal. It went on for *months*. I thought he'd never overeat again.'

Having seen Richard Sellers' apple-shaped build for herself, Christy did not comment, but reached dutifully for a brownie to work on her own. They'd plainly been made by infants and God only knew what bodily fluids had been rubbed by young fingers into the mixture, but she ate it anyway to show willing. After all, sugar had been her trusted friend long before Caroline Sellers decided to have a change of heart. Munching, she thought how nice it was to feel liked (or at least not disliked) and to be included again (or at least not excluded), and it wasn't just because she was unexpectedly based at home, as Joe thought, it was because she was human and, these last dislocated weeks, she had been nothing so much as *lonely*. Lonely like she'd been before she went to college and met Yasmin in her first year, and then Joe the next. She reached for a second brownie.

'Well,' Caroline said, watching with approval as she chewed, '*this* is a first within these four walls.'

'What do you mean?' said Christy. Surely this couldn't be the first time the street's 'unofficial social secretary' had set foot in number 40.

'The woman of the house eating my baked offerings, I never thought I'd see the day! Rachel certainly never did.'

'Rachel?'

'Rachel Locke – she lived here before the Frasers. She had a gluten intolerance. And then Amber, well, she didn't have any allergies or anything like that, but she *never* ate cake. The kids were always baking her cupcakes, they *loved* her, but she just used to nibble a bit of the icing and keep them for Jeremy.'

'Why didn't she eat them herself?'

'Of course, you never met her, did you?' Caroline said, smiling.

'No.'

'Well, if you had you'd know she had an *amazing* figure, the best you've ever seen. Jaw-dropping, men-walking-into-lampposts sexy. And she was *very* disciplined about it. She and Jeremy used to go to Canvas for dinner all the time and she told me she only ever ate a starter. And she drank of course, so she needed to save calories for that. Do you know what she said to me once? She said she would eat when she was old, and sleep when she was dead, but she would never knowingly turn down a cocktail.'

'Goodness,' Christy said.

Caroline sipped her tea, duly warming up. 'She used to hint at all kinds of depravities in her past, like there was *nothing* she hadn't tried, no taboos, do you know what I mean?'

'I think so.' Amber Fraser sounded like a remarkable character, which was perhaps why Caroline was as eager to discuss *her* as she was reluctant to talk about Rob. 'The two of you were friends?' she asked doubtfully.

'Yes, we got quite close, actually. Oh, she was *so* great, a breath of fresh air on this street. We all had a bit of a crush on her, men *and* women. She was naughty and sweet at the same time, you know? *So* generous to everyone, always giving lovely presents, really kind-hearted. I remember Liz was at a low ebb after her divorce and Amber took us shopping one day, got her a new haircut. She *saved* her in that one day and she wasn't even aware she was doing it. She was just being Amber. It was exciting to know her, like having a celebrity next door, but without the paparazzi – or the ego. She was actually quite humble, I thought, considering how she looked. Or maybe *democratic* is the word. She treated everyone just the same.'

Christy was agape. The expression on Caroline's face during this astonishing eulogy was almost romantic. How perfect Amber sounded, plainly the Lime Park beauty to Rob's beast. She had an unwelcome image of Joe dining at Canvas with the scrupulously democratic bombshell, mesmerized by her reduced portions and *bons mots*.

'You must all wish she hadn't moved.' This sounded childishly jealous even to her own ears.

Caroline nodded. 'We just wish it hadn't been so sudden. I would have liked to have said a proper goodbye.'

'Why *was* it so sudden? We were never actually told. And Felicity as well – was it to do with this problem with Rob?'

'Really, it's not for me to say.'

That meant yes, thought Christy. Her habit of evidence-gathering was already ingrained. A shame it had to be so piecemeal. 'The Frasers weren't here very long, were they?' she persisted. 'Were they getting divorced?'

'God, no.' Caroline seemed personally offended by the idea. 'They were together forever – if it's ever possible to say that. Jeremy was a wonderful husband. Amber could have taken her pick, but she wanted him. He was older than her, you know, a bit of a father figure, I suppose. She didn't have the greatest childhood, from what she hinted to us; it wasn't like she'd led a charmed life. And then it looked like they were having trouble conceiving, though that may have changed by now, of course. I do hope it has.'

Christy's eyes widened at this further gush of personal detail. 'Are you not in contact with her any more then?'

Caroline looked down at her hands, at the large conch-shell ring that seemed an odd choice for so conservative a dresser and that Christy imagined her having bought at Amber's instruction on one of their sprees. Her sadness was plain. 'No.'

'Why not?'

She shook her head. 'To be honest, I don't even know where they went.'

'Nor do her friends,' Christy said. 'One of them sent a postcard and another knocked at the door a few weeks ago, looking for her. Imogen, she was called.'

'I remember Imogen. She was an old work friend.'

'She said she hadn't heard from Amber since January.'

'Well, I'm not sure that's good news. I thought it was just us she'd cut herself off from.' With this, Caroline grew even more despondent and Christy, almost feeling sorry for her loss, had to remind herself that Amber had not died but was probably busy eschewing cupcakes as they spoke in her new neighbourhood somewhere on the other side of time.

'She was going to try Jeremy at his office, but –' She stopped mid-sentence, on the brink of admitting that she had done the same herself, but Caroline came to her rescue.

'Oh, we tried that ages ago, but it's no use. He's taken a sabbatical.'

'Some sort of long-service thing?' Christy suggested, her face innocent.

'If you believe *that*,' Caroline said.

'You don't?'

But, bar the raised eyebrows, the conversation was over. Caroline slid from her seat, preparing to leave. 'Anyway, I just wanted to say hi, see how you are, and bury the hatchet. Enjoy the rest of the brownies.'

'Thank you. It was very kind of you to think of me.'

After exchanging numbers and email addresses, Christy saw her to the door before resettling at the bedroom window to turn over what she'd just been told – or not told, as the case may have been – and consider the rather friendlier Caroline Sellers she'd been allowed to meet. She was in good time to see Rob return alone from wherever he had spent the afternoon, his expression typically stormy.

So it was official: he was the neighbourhood pariah, disreputable and disliked.

And the question still remained: *why?*

When Joe came home, late as ever and emitting the now-familiar odour of a herd of intensively farmed corporate lawyers, she could scarcely resist launching into her account of the conversation with Caroline – until she saw his face in the full beam of the kitchen spotlights. Ashen and downcast, it was the face of a man who'd been roundly trounced.

'What is it? How was work?'

'Oh, as terrifying as ever,' he said bleakly.

She was taken aback. 'Terrifying? But in an exciting way?'

'No, in a terrifying way.'

'But why?' Christy asked. He'd never spoken like this before, though the truth was he was home so late she wasn't always awake to ask.

He grimaced, mouth sour, not a trace of characteristic humour in his tone. 'A hundred reasons.'

'Tell me them.'

'I get no air cover from Marcus any more, for one thing. At first he was on holiday, so I didn't realize.'

'Realize what?'

'That I'm not in his team any more. I'm not in anyone's team, I'm *completely on my own.*' He said this as if he'd been left naked and alone in a derelict building, a serial killer hurtling towards him. 'The only business I get is the business *I* get. Once this pharmaceutical deal is out the door . . .' he shrugged, helpless.

'But you always knew you'd have to bring in the clients when you were a partner.'

'Sure.' Joe drank from the glass of wine she'd handed him – or rather discharged the liquid into an open throat – and looked at the empty glass as if he'd been tricked. 'It's not just that, it's the lack of any kind of human decency. I went to the partners' meeting today and everyone was jockeying for position and challenging each other, there wasn't a scrap of camaraderie. Honestly, it was no different from how it was when I was a trainee trying to get noticed. If anything it's worse because now I'm in competition with the people I used to get support from.'

Not having any better idea, Christy poured him more wine. 'How long have you been feeling like this? A month ago you were still on a high.' Wasn't he? How could it have escaped her notice that he had plunged so low? 'It doesn't suddenly kick in, this sort of stuff, does it?' She knew she should do better than this to console and encourage, but she could not find the words, could not remember the psychology. The effort was perhaps visible in her face as she passed back his glass, because he dispatched the second as rapidly as the first before declaring himself sick of thinking about it.

'Enough about JR. How was your day? How goes the one-woman Lime Park Road charm offensive?'

Christy felt her heart rate pick up. 'Well, I have some news, since you ask. It's quite mysterious stuff.'

Boosted by his uncharacteristic interest, she told him all she'd learned from Caroline Sellers and how she had, following Caroline's departure, taken again to the Internet. What was it that Caroline was so intent on concealing? On a hunch, she'd googled 'Trouble Lime Park' and then added 'Controversy' and 'Mystery', but all she'd found were forums about speed bumps and news of improvements to the junction at Lime Park Parade. All local intrigue seemed to involve road traffic. (Perhaps Rob had injured someone when driving, she'd thought wildly, thinking of his anger at the wheel that time.) Taking things to their Hitchcockian conclusion, she'd tried 'Lime Park killer', which yielded a story about a teenager from a neighbouring area who'd stabbed someone on a bus bound for Lime Park and had now been jailed.

To her surprise, Joe responded to her report with a surge of hilarity.

'I get it,' he said. 'It's obvious! We must have infiltrated some kind of suburban swinging set. Amber Baby ran it and now she's gone no one's getting any.'

Christy stared. Could he really be dismissing Caroline's opaque apologies and dark hints so lightly? The news that they had moved next door to a man so disliked by the rest of the street that they worked collectively to avoid being in the same room as him? A man who had as good as threatened Christy with violence and had received poisonous notes from unnamed enemies? But before she could protest she heard the edge of hysteria to Joe's jollity and understood that he needed to laugh, he needed to make a joke of this, however unlikely the material. The ostracism of Rob was inconsequential compared to his growing anxiety about work.

He felt *completely on his own* – and for him Lime Park Road was his refuge, not a place he needed to hear contained risk and scandal.

'Why haven't *we* been asked to join?' she said, producing a plausible chuckle. 'We're not good-looking enough, d'you think?'

'You have to have a black Lab and a Range Rover to qualify? Or maybe they *have* tried to recruit us but we've been too dense to notice?' Joe grinned. 'That's why this Caroline came round, to see if you're ready to be initiated. And the reason Rob is so bad-tempered is because he hasn't made the cut. He's too hairy.'

'Well, I suppose that's *one* theory,' Christy said.

Underscored though the merriment was by the wrongness of ignoring Joe's wretchedness about work, it was good to be laughing together; it felt like the old days – before they'd moved into the new house. These were the new days now, the Lime Park future on which they'd staked everything. Ironic, then, that it had come to feel so troubled. Ironic, too, that when she pictured herself in the cramped rooms of their old flat, the street light yellow and stark even through dark curtains, traffic noise absent only on those occasions you happened to wake in the night, the loneliest hours, it was as a much happier woman.

And Joe – not yet a partner – a less terrified man.

Chapter 14

Amber, 2012

I don't like to boast, but the neighbours said there had never been such a good party on the street as the one we gave on the bank holiday weekend in late August. 'Let's throw some money at this,' Jeremy said – and I needed no second invitation.

In my opinion, a successful party serves functions beyond the giving of a good time and in this case there were several: to show off the renovations, which were a magnificent tribute to Hetty's bold taste and Jeremy's deep pockets (even Gemma admitted to being impressed); to thank our neighbours for their suffering and goodwill during the works; and, possibly most importantly, to provide the hostess with a new opportunity to observe her husband and her lover together and reassure herself – again – that the former knew nothing of the latter. Call it essential maintenance.

To this end, I suggested Rob bring a date. 'I know you don't like to at these things, but it will look more realistic.'

'That's because it *is* realistic,' he said in mock objection. He was far too self-assured ever to take real offence; this was a man who thought he was God's gift – and if I'd believed in the Lord I'd probably have agreed. 'Much as you like to think I exist purely to service your insatiable sexual needs, I do have a private life of my own.'

'All right, keep your hair on,' I said. We were in bed, of course, my phone (turned to silent) on the cabinet next to me. 'You really don't need to remind me of your prodigious hit rate. So who will you bring? Not that girl from Joanne and Kenny's dinner party?'

'God, no, she hates me.'

'Why? What happened that night, anyway? She went to pieces the minute she saw you and then she left without a word.'

He gave a shrug, enough to confirm to me his interpretation of the encounter, if not hers: at some unspecified time in the past, he'd used her for the night and she'd resented her morning dismissal. 'Some people *say* "No hard feelings" but then they go and have them anyway.'

It was clearly a pattern of behaviour he'd observed in his women.

'When was this?' I asked.

'A couple of years ago, maybe. I'm a bit hazy on the details, but you of all people can't give me a hard time about *that.*'

'Wouldn't dream of it,' I said. 'It's a small world when you're a man of easy virtue.'

'Or woman.' His palm glanced carelessly over my left breast. 'Anyway, she's given Kenny some sob story because he's been off with me ever since that night.'

'Sweet Kenny,' I sighed. 'He's like Jeremy, he can't resist a damsel in distress.'

'That's his excuse, is it?' Rob murmured.

'What do you mean?'

'I'm just saying, I'm not sure his wife thinks he's so sweet – or she certainly *shouldn't*.'

I smiled, intrigued. 'Why, what's he been up to?'

He kissed my shoulder, ran his tongue along my collarbone until I dropped my shoulders and arched my back. 'You can be hilariously dense for someone so clever.'

'Oh, I know he's got a bit of a thing about me,' I laughed. 'But nothing's going to happen, don't worry.'

Rob returned his head to the pillow. 'I'm not remotely worried.'

'So who then?' I said.

'Who's Kenny –?'

'No, who are *you* bringing to the party – stop changing the subject!'

'I think Pippa,' he said, as if plucking her name from an extensive list of hopefuls. 'We've been getting on pretty well.'

'You mean there's someone you've seen more than once?' This was the first time I'd heard Pippa's name.

'More than twice. Three times, four maybe.'

'Four, wow, that's practically an engagement for you, Robbie boy,' I said mockingly. 'I'll have to dust off my wedding hat.' If I was honest (which I was not, not then), I preferred the idea of him bringing a one-off date to the party, a Caitlin he'd dispose of after the event, not a genuine candidate whom the whole street would welcome into the fold.

'I'm surprised you haven't heard us,' he said, idly twisting a length of my hair around his fingers.

'Heard you?'

'Yes, Pippa and me. *I've* heard *you.*'

'I don't see how.'

The strand of hair pulled a little at my scalp. 'Your bedroom is directly next door to my living room, Amber, there's just a layer of bricks between us.'

'You've drilled a peephole, have you?'

'I haven't needed to. You and the silver fox go to bed earlier than I do and I'm guessing your bed is up against the inner wall, opposite the fireplace.'

'God, you *have* drilled a hole. Have you got a camera rigged up as well?'

He smirked. 'Oh, it's easy enough to visualize, believe me. I know your moves better than anyone. I'm pleased to hear that the quest for procreation continues apace, though, admittedly, he sounds more enthusiastic than you do.'

'That's sick,' I told him. 'I'm going to forget you ever shared that pathetic little insight.'

He chuckled, thrilled to get a rise out of me. '"Pathetic little insight"? You really know how to put a man down, don't you?'

He was so delighted, I couldn't help laughing with him. 'Just bring your little playmate to the party and shut up.'

And soon we were tangled up again, kissing and pressing and rolling and pitching, thrilled by how well matched we were in this hot, breathless rectangular realm, all third parties, spouses or otherwise, temporarily forgotten.

Jeremy and I invited everyone within a fifteen-door radius, both those we'd got to know and those we had not, as well as a smattering of friends. Every single person RSVPed yes, some even rescheduling return dates from holidays to be back in time, for it was customary among the families here to decamp for the whole of August to their second homes in France (already there was talk of Jeremy and me joining the Sellerses at theirs on the Ile de Ré the following summer). There were caterers and a DJ, flowers and fairy lights and lanterns and balloons. I'd even rented a small fairground carousel and candy-floss stand for the younger children and paid local teenagers to man them. At the last minute, I added a magician to the bill.

'If this is a house-warming, I can't wait to see what your children's parties are like,' Caroline said, as her own kids climbed onto the ride, squealing like monkeys for her to watch. She often spoke as if I were already pregnant, which would cause us to exchange a significant look. Naturally, I didn't let her suspect that she was far keener for me to join the club than I was myself.

'The dress looks good,' I told her. It was a gorgeous style, a midnight-blue maxi, daringly low cut, and bought of course at my advice. While not wishing to give the impression of being a marital miracle-worker, I will say that since I'd become involved in her wardrobe marital improvements had been noted. Meanwhile, Liz, my other charge, was unrecognizable from the wild-haired lunatic I'd first seen on the Sellerses' terrace. The cropped haircut had been the first of many gratifying improvements and this evening I'd supervised the sliding of her diet-shrunken figure into a vintage-inspired pink sundress with a full pleated skirt.

Both women had been taken for pedicures and bullied into the highest heels of their lives.

Not normally competitive about desirability, I had pulled out the stops this time with my own appearance and I knew very well that the object of my rivalry was neither Caroline nor Liz. No, that strapless ivy-green macramé-lace dress and those red peep-toe high-heeled pumps, that silky pin-curled hair falling on shoulders polished smooth in a Mayfair spa – it was all conceived to put one woman in the shade: Pippa.

Maybe it was that flippant little comment of Rob's – 'I'm surprised you haven't heard us,' as if their enjoyment of one another could not be contained, and which, turning it over in my mind with unhealthy frequency, had assumed the form of a taunt – but she had somehow gained a right of way to my thoughts that shouldn't reasonably have been granted. Why had she been chosen over the others? What did she have that Caitlin and her ilk did not? Did she have something in common with *me*? I wished now I'd dug deeper.

She was, it transpired, a typical London girl working a mid-level marketing job: late twenties or early thirties, long blonde hair that had been teased straight when it would have suited her better to allow a natural wave, a mask of make-up that spoke of professional trickery and yet served only to conceal her true attractiveness, a summer tan and towering wedged heels: all the standard ingredients of glamour. She had charm too, was gushingly appreciative of the invitation and offered help several times; soon she had everyone eating out of her hand.

She deserved better than Rob, but I was unique in this circle in having insider knowledge of him and of course everyone else judged them to be perfectly matched.

'How long have you been together?' people kept asking, and, on ambushing Rob alone, 'She's *really* nice, could be the one, eh?'

My ear was tuned to the frequency of every last one of those happy exclamations. Liz, after one too many glasses of Pimm's, even said she'd always thought how nice it would be for someone to stage a wedding in one of the gardens backing onto the park, in springtime, when the cherry blossom would supply the confetti.

'Sounds charming. I look forward to an invitation to yours,' Rob replied, which threw her slightly (her confidence had not quite caught up with the external improvements) and perhaps explained the sudden punch she landed on his arm. It was a rather heavier blow than she intended, I gathered, seeing Pippa scurry to comfort him, while Liz fussed about in apology.

'It's all right,' Rob groaned. 'I really don't think there'll be extensive bruising.'

'Everything OK here, ladies?' Kenny had appeared, his expression absurdly protective.

'Of course,' I giggled. 'Liz was just beating up Rob – no less than he deserves, if you ask me.'

Still rubbing his arm, Rob winked at Kenny. 'I do like an empowered female, don't you, Kenny?'

Kenny smiled weakly.

I had made a point that evening of watching for evidence of ill feeling between the two men, but could detect nothing more than this unremarkable exchange. Either Caitlin had not substantiated her accusations or the two-week break in Provence Kenny had just returned from had mellowed him on the issue.

As for the only other neighbour I knew to credit with a suspicious mind – wise old bird and feminist Felicity – she also proved nicely gullible that evening, hovering proudly over Rob and Pippa like the mother of the bride.

'I take my hat off to you, Amber,' she said. 'Of all the parties I've been to on this street over the years, I've *never* known him bring a girlfriend. And that's if he decides to turn up in the first place. What's your secret?'

Recalling that strange paranoid moment in her flat when I'd delivered the Victoria sponge, I studied her face for signs of ambivalence – to no avail. Like everyone else here, she was genuinely thrilled to see Rob so prettily paired. Whatever she'd intended in forestalling Gemma that afternoon, it had not been to protect the double lives of adulterers.

'Oh, just call me Cupid,' I told her, laughing. I was regretting my strategy, however: I'd intended some sort of beard, not a people's princess – that was *my* job. And yet I couldn't help liking Pippa myself, too.

'Your house is the most beautiful I've ever set foot in,' she told me, with adorable earnestness. 'Your husband is so charming and funny.' There could be no mistake that *she* was paying court to *me*.

No, there was no contest between us. And nor was there any between her and Gemma or Helena, both of whom had arrived dressed to seduce and both of whom understood immediately that they were too late. They surrendered unconditionally.

'I can't believe Rob's off the market already,' Helena complained, raising her voice above the jangle of the carousel. She was smoking, always a sign of defeat. 'It's only a few weeks since he said there was no one serious.'

'Oh, they're not serious,' I said, refusing to admit to myself that I spoke for my own benefit, not theirs. 'I'd never heard him mention her until about a week ago. You've still got a shot, girls, get to work!'

'Amber, she's a complete leech,' Gemma said, bearing her imperfect teeth to tear at a stick of candyfloss. 'There's no chance for anyone else. Look how she keeps helping with the carousel to show what a brilliant mother she'd be! It's so *obvious*. You watch, she'll already be plotting to move in with him and get pregnant.'

I sincerely hoped not. I took a pinch of her candyfloss and let it melt in a gritty pool on my tongue.

Just as everyone was nicely inebriated, Jeremy made a little speech to say how lucky we were to have such tolerant and forgiving neighbours. 'This marks a new tradition: every last Saturday in August we will hold a party, come rain or shine.'

'Come rain or shine' struck me as one of his old people's turns of phrase, a thought I cast from my head as he went on to thank me for creating such a glamorous home for him, praise I gallantly deflected by pulling Hetty into the spotlight.

'Really,' I said, 'I've done nothing.'

And Rob heckled, 'No, really, she hasn't!' and in just the

right tone for a neighbour and friend, as opposed to a lover who had only two days earlier immobilized me on the floor of his bathroom and torn my underwear so badly I'd had to throw it away.

Hetty was laughing, Pippa was laughing, Caroline was laughing, Felicity was laughing, everyone was laughing, and then there were cheers and whistles as the music was turned up and dancing broke out in earnest (and with some of the fifty-pluses, believe me, it *was* earnest). As I wove among my guests, beaming, I told myself I was not monitoring Rob's whereabouts out of the corner of my eye; I told myself I did not yearn to separate him from his new mate and lure him out of sight for *my* turn. No, I knew better than to take risks of any kind at a function like this; they inevitably led to exposure. You hear about it all the time, the stolen kiss witnessed by a child who later tells his mother ('The pretty lady with red hair was kissing the tall man with dark hair, it was yucky!'), or that crops up in the corner of someone's photo, slightly out of focus but unmistakably criminal. With iPhones being brandished even by infants, there was as much surveillance as if we'd fixed a camera to a tripod and made a fly-on-the-wall documentary of the event. (How much easier infidelity must have been in the pre-digital age!)

Instead, it was the back of Pippa's head that Rob steadied with his left palm as he leaned to kiss her hard on the lips, Pippa's hips his fingers kept straying to, Pippa's arched feet and tensed calves on which his eyes lingered.

My only private exchange with him that evening was anticlimactic, to say the least.

'I can't do next week,' he told me, as I refilled his glass at exactly the moment someone had caught Pippa's eye and bombarded her with more breathless questions about where she had 'popped up' from. I misjudged and the champagne foamed onto his hand; as I watched him splash the drips to the ground before bringing his fingers to his lips to lick them, I felt a lurch of lust at my deepest core.

'That's a pity,' I said. 'Why not?'

'I'm out of town for a few days.'

'Then we'll have to debrief another time.'

He looked directly at me then and that, at least, was a personal look – as if his definition of debrief was to strip you of your clothes and burn off the top layer of your skin – and a source of consolation I only realized I craved as badly as I did once I'd been given it.

All this considered, and not to mention what came after, I was admirably in control of myself that night. I refused on principle to be ambushed by unseemly emotions. With the carousel still turning and ridden now to illegal weight levels by the adults (Liz was, indeed, back in the saddle), the laughter growing louder, the late night and bottomless wine bottles drawing confidences from all directions, I remained, on the surface, measured, gracious, discreet. I was as deserving of Jeremy's devoted gaze as I was the flow of compliments about my beautiful dress, accepting of the knowledge that it was he, my legal mate, my original choice, who would later remove it.

Chapter 15

Christy, July 2013

She'd finally made it to the second round for a job, a buying position at a media agency, not her established area but a junior enough role for that not to worry her. The woman who conducted the interview and would be her manager was younger than Christy and had a suppressed indignation about her, as if she'd expected to be doing something rather better at this stage in the game but understood that such desires were best masked. Especially when an ageing candidate who would have killed for her job sat in front of her, trying to remould her unrelated experience into something highly relevant.

That was life, Christy thought: you didn't appreciate the value of a decent mid-level job until it was suddenly impossible to get one. But she knew she shouldn't use words like 'impossible'; that was not can-do, that was can't-do. With nervous fingers she touched the silver bangle on her wrist, ran her thumb over the clasp. She couldn't explain why she was wearing Amber Fraser's jewellery to this interview; for the same reason that she'd appropriated the dragonfly key ring, she supposed, because it was costly and beautiful and she wanted such things to belong to her.

'The salary is a *lot* less than you earned in your previous job,' her interviewer said matter-of-factly. It was commonplace for candidates to be casually demeaned like this – to expect anything more would be to arouse suspicion.

Christy agreed, it *was* less. All she could think of was the column of debits she saw when she pulled up her and Joe's bank details online, that mortgage payment jumping out so horrifyingly it might have been scrawled across the screen in blood.

'I don't mind taking a cut in the short term,' she began, but that sounded wrong. She feared that these occasional forays into the real world exposed her as slow-witted, a relic from a lost generation. In a matter of months the world had got younger, its cultural references a puzzle. To combat the effects of isolation, she'd begun walking to the train station most days for her copy of the free titles commuters read on the train, the daily bibles of office managers like this one. 'I mean, I'm more interested in finding the right company than the right salary.' That was a little better, if somewhat uninspired. 'It's lucky for me you had someone leave.'

'Yes, well, babies will be born, won't they?' her interviewer said. 'And in this case she's decided not to come back.'

Something in her expression suggested that it was she who would have liked to have left and not come back, and Christy thought, How awful, all of these people wanting to live each other's lives. Was it only women, or did men do it, too? Look how Joe had chased and chased his partnership; he'd seen it as a one-way ticket to Arcadia, only to

238

suddenly declare his disillusionment because it did not resemble the destination of his dreams. And this was *Joe*, the man who never admitted defeat, Jermyn Richards' ebullient 'cheeky chappie'. If *he* was disenchanted, then what chance did the rest of them have? Overwhelmed for a moment with the insoluble sorrow of it all, she felt her features droop.

Evidently suspecting pitying thoughts in *her* direction, her interviewer flung her an insulted look and Christy knew then she wouldn't get the job.

'We'll be in touch via the recruitment agency,' the woman said, checking as they said their goodbyes that she had the contact details she needed to dispatch her rejection in all available formats. All of a sudden her interest was rekindled: 'You live on Lime Park Road, do you?'

'That's right.'

'How funny. I know someone who used to live there. She worked here, in the same team, in fact, but she left about eighteen months ago.'

'Who?' Christy asked, though she was already making the connection herself – media buyer, a husband she'd met through this agency's branding partner: who else?

'Amber Fraser.'

'I live in her old house,' Christy said, smiling. 'Small world, eh?'

'Not a small house though. I went there a couple of times. It's stunning.'

Salvation beckoned: might Amber be useful in the form of a little reflected glory? For she would undoubtedly have worked the same magic over colleagues as she plainly had neighbours. 'I'm not sure it looks so stunning now,' Christy said truthfully. 'I don't have Amber's taste.'

'I'm not sure *Amber* had Amber's taste,' the other woman said, and Christy thought she detected the faintest of sneers in her tone. As unobtrusively as she could, she pulled her sleeve over her wrist: it would look weird if this woman saw the bangle and recognized it as her friend's – almost as if Christy had looted her dead body. 'You know she used an interior designer, right?'

'I heard that . . .' Christy tailed off, having been about to add 'from the plumber' and deciding against it. Tittle-tattling about Lime Park when she was supposed to be interviewing for a job: she must be, as Joe had said, *obsessed* – obsessed enough to hear herself continue, 'Where does she live now? No one in Lime Park seems to know.'

'Me neither. I haven't seen her since before Christmas; she's totally dropped off the scene.' Though this acquaintance expressed neither Caroline's melancholy nor Imogen's anxiety at the Frasers' removal, she was nonetheless considerably more engaged than she had been at any time during their formal interview, her eyes alight with interest, her skin gently flushed. 'If you see her, tell her Gemma said hello.'

'Of course.' Encouraged, Christy went on, 'You don't think . . . ? No, that's silly.'

'I don't think what?'

'Well . . . you don't think something bad has happened to her, do you? It's just that there seems to be such a mystery about her and her husband leaving. Even our solicitor doesn't know where they've gone. It's like they've vanished into thin air.'

To her surprise, this was met with unrestrained laughter – and not in an altogether pleasant spirit.

'Oh, believe me,' Gemma said, 'bad things don't happen to Amber.'

'Really?'

'Really. If that's what you think, then don't waste your energy.' And she shook her head to show how foolish that would be. 'Wherever she is now, it will be because she wants to be there.'

And when they parted company at the reception doors, Christy saw that her eyes had gone quite cold.

Two days later she heard officially of her rejection. The successful applicant was younger and cheaper, said the consultant; no doubt she'd said the right things because they were true as opposed to creating a false impression out of desperation.

'It's not desperation,' her mother said on the phone. 'It's necessity.'

'Same thing,' Christy sighed. However positive she succeeded in remaining, she found that each rejection brought a short period of negative thinking, even apathy.

'You need to find a voluntary job, get a sense of purpose from something else. Don't let this plunge you into a gloom.'

'I won't.' We can't both be in one, Christy thought, Joe's stricken face and slumped shoulders in mind.

And then there was the ultimate voluntary work, of

course, the most vocal advocate of which now continued in her ear with what was starting to sound like the right-eousness of a crusade. 'You *really* should think about a baby, you know. Dad and I were just saying this morning, with this career break you're having, the timing is ideal.'

'We've already had this conversation, Mum,' Christy protested, but with sympathy because she was well aware how 'ideal' her situation looked. And how seamlessly redundancy had become 'career break', as if it were a life-style choice of her own making.

'I know we have, but the longer it goes on, the more it makes sense to use the time constructively.'

'The longer it goes on the less we can afford to start a family. Not on one salary.'

'But Joe's a partner now,' her mother said, and Christy could clearly picture her baffled frown. 'If a partner in a law firm can't afford to have a baby then I'd like to know who can.'

'He's not with one of the big firms,' she said patiently, because, as ever, her mother's questions only echoed her own. 'You know that, Mum. They're really struggling in Mergers & Acquisitions and he's just a salaried partner, he doesn't get a share of the pot. Anyway, he'd need to be a partner in the Saudi royal family to afford this bloody house.'

'Christy!' her mother exclaimed, sounding personally offended (she had, after all, lent her daughter and son-in-law money to buy it). 'I thought the house was your pride and joy?'

That took Christy aback because she hadn't realized

quite the extent to which that pride and joy had been eroded. Perhaps that was why she still sometimes thought of it as belonging to the Frasers, in spirit if not in name. The Frasers' en suite, the Frasers' garden shed, the Frasers' quartz worktop. The Frasers' social panache. Her memory of their first Sunday in the house, when their families had descended and she and Joe had been as besotted as new parents, seemed to exist now in a glass jar, miniaturized and fragile, utterly inaccessible.

She pulled herself together. 'Of course it is. I didn't mean to sound ungrateful. But the fact is, Mum, it's expensive to run, and starting a family would push us to the brink. I need to be earning again before we can take a step like that.'

'Well, if the financial situation is really so bad that it's stopping you from having a family, perhaps you should think about selling up. No house is worth that sacrifice.'

Christy's recognition of the truth of this took her breath away and it was a long moment before she could reply. 'It's not stopping us, it's *delaying* us. It has to be me – Joe and me – who want a baby, not you.'

But it frightened her how her mother's words had stirred her. It *was* the right time to have a baby, it was the right time in every respect but financial, and yet that was the concern that overrode all others. They were defined by their crippling debt. Emotions, desires, instincts: they couldn't be allowed to come into it.

On Saturday morning, alone in the kitchen – lately, Joe had established the habit of sleeping till noon at the weekend – and settled with her laptop and coffee, she found that Caroline Sellers had reached out to her a second time:

> Hi Christy, it was good to meet properly the other day. I wondered if you would like to come to our book group on Thursday the 18th? 8 p.m. at my place. We're doing 'Madame Bovary'.

Only when Christy saw a further email from Caroline sent soon after and requesting she ignore the previous one while containing exactly the same message did she understand that the first included a long trail of correspondence between the regular members of the book group – correspondence that Caroline evidently preferred not to share. Christy probably wouldn't have noticed it had she not been asked to disregard it, but of course she read it now with relish.

It began with suggestions for the month's choice of title, *Madame Bovary* having been proposed by the girl in the bookshop on the Parade and an offer of discounted copies accepted (amazing how these wealthy women rejoiced at a saving of £1). Then came a message to all from Caroline:

> I think the new owner of the Frasers' house has been quite upset by how unwelcoming we've all seemed and so if everyone agrees I thought we could invite her to our next gathering. She knows nothing and I suggest we keep it that way – for her sake. It's a good opportunity for us to avoid a certain subject and try to move on.

For her sake? What did *that* mean? Judging by the replies, everyone else knew what the certain subject was, just as Caroline had admitted in their conversation in Christy's kitchen ('we co-ordinated').

'Good idea, we got a bit out of control last time,' Liz wrote, and someone called Mel added, 'It was starting to feel like a witch hunt, not very healthy!'

'At least it was behind closed doors, eh?'

'Can't fault us on that.'

What *was* going on in this street? The witch being hunted was Rob, she was clear on that, but what he had done to offend the women remained the $64,000 question. Scrolling down, Christy could find not the scantest suggestion as to the nature of his transgression, which somehow made it both more tantalizing and more threatening. It crossed her mind – indecently briefly, shamefully rare – that it was none of her business, none whatsoever, and she should respect the group's desire to 'move on', not to mention heed Rob's personal warning.

Then her eye was caught by another familiar name:

'No one's heard from Amber, I assume?'

A host of negatives followed. She remembered what the woman at the agency had said: *Wherever she is now, it will be because she wants to be there.* Well, this was certainly not the position of the group.

'If she doesn't want to keep in touch, that's fine,' Sophie wrote. 'I respect that. But if we just had news she's safe I'd feel a lot happier.'

'I know,' Liz replied. 'Just one text or email would be such a relief.'

Then it was Caroline again: 'Richard's going to call Jeremy's office and talk to one of the other partners, try and find out exactly when he's due back. It's his company, he can't stay away forever.'

'Look at this,' Christy said, taking the laptop up to the bedroom, where Joe still languished under the duvet.

But he had no interest in trawling through the thread. 'I hate it when people do that, just tag you onto a group conversation. This is why we all feel so totally crushed: no one can get through this stuff.'

'*I* did.'

'Yeah, but you don't get thousands of work mails. You've got the time.'

'Thanks for reminding me,' said Christy, but not crossly. Plainly he had woken in the doldrums (*totally crushed*?). Any minute now he'd be rummaging for his BlackBerry so he could begin checking emails of his own. 'The point is, Caroline sent it by mistake. She didn't *want* me to read it. Look what she says about a witch hunt.'

Joe gave the email a cursory glance. 'It could be anything, Christy. It'll be about schools, I bet. One of them had a go at the lollipop lady and now they feel a bit bad. Or something to do with the council – the new recycling bins, maybe.'

'Bins! Come on, isn't it obvious it's about the big secret everyone knows except us? The one that Caroline said was the reason they boycotted our party – to do with Rob? Don't forget we had a note for him through our door smeared with shit, Joe!'

Joe's brow knitted with irritation. 'It was anonymous

and I refuse to take an anonymous letter seriously. That kind of thing is outside the rules of society.'

'Maybe *he's* the one outside the rules of society?' Christy suggested, her exasperation growing. 'It's clear to me that he must have done something illegal.'

'Illegal? Why would you think that? This email, it's just a load of neighbours gossiping, by the look of it. What did you say was the book they've chosen? *Madame Bovary*, the most famous bored-housewife story of all time! You're not actually going to this thing, are you?'

'Of course I am! This is the first time I've been invited to anything. And just because they're women and based at home doesn't mean they're bored housewives and a bunch of gossiping crones. "One of them had a go at the lollipop lady"! What kind of patronizing, misogynistic rubbish is that?'

Christy was starting to feel distressed. She was certain the old Joe would have been as curious – and as worried – as she was by this trail of clues regarding a neighbour. He would have been worried *because* she was worried. In a film plot, such perverse refusal to be interested would be evidence of guilt of some sort, but in the plot of their lives it was because he was exhausted. Seeing him shield his eyes, as if from some atrocity, she could tell he was thinking it would just be easier to go into the office (and that was saying something).

'Maybe I am getting a bit overinvolved,' she conceded. They rowed infrequently enough for the flare-up to have shaken her.

'More than a bit,' Joe said. 'This stuff isn't important, believe me.'

'Why not believe *me*?' she asked, her voice catching. 'I'm the one in a position to know, I'm living here twenty-four-seven.'

'Yes and it's turning you into a crazy woman!'

She blinked, hurt.

'I wish you could just find a job and put us all out of our misery,' he added.

There was a taut silence, alarmingly reminiscent of the one that had fallen between Rob and her at the café table that time. But this was *Joe*, the venue their *marital bedroom*. She'd just caught herself thinking in terms of 'the old Joe'; doubtless, he referenced 'the old Christy', too. Incredible to think that only a few months ago they'd been trading beams of disbelief over the top of champagne glasses about how wonderful life was, how it was too good to be true. How had they reached this impasse, this cliff edge?

She scurried back from it without a moment's dilemma. 'I want that as much as you do,' she said, sitting on the bed. 'I'm going for everything any of the recruitment guys suggest, I promise you. I'm not being fussy. After the summer, I'll consider anything – literally: deep-sea oil driller, prison warden, whatever.'

Joe managed a half smile before sighing heavily. 'It won't come to that. Look, I think we need a change of scene. This is all getting a bit intense. How about we get out of town for the night?'

Immediately, Christy had an image of that tree-house hotel in the brochure sent to the Frasers: in the photographs there'd been a huge white bed and fluttering organza drapes, a log burner and clusters of tea-lights. It was just a phone call away, but might as well have been a visiting land at the top of the Faraway Tree, so far beyond their means was it. Having during the past weeks experienced countless highs and lows, she now felt the lowest yet: desolation, deep and raw.

'We can't afford a night away,' she said. 'Not unless we borrow a tent.' Which wasn't so bad an idea if the decent weather held.

'We'll go to Mum and Dad's. They're around this weekend. Or your folks'?'

'No thanks,' Christy said, her smile rueful. 'I can do without being quizzed on how soon we're going to breed.'

'What?' Joe looked at her in a new way then, as if to say, *Ah, now I see what this is all about,* and then, *I don't have time for this, not now.*

Bored housewives, broody women, Madame Bovary, he didn't have time for any of them, and she was not so egocentric as to not be able to admit a certain sympathy for his position.

'Let's do a day trip,' she suggested. 'Get the train down to those woods near Chislehurst and go for a big walk.'

His feet poked from beneath the duvet, followed by an arm. 'OK. But can we please not spend the whole time talking about your bonkers *Rear Window* plots?'

She swallowed her protests. 'Fine.'

But if she was prepared to give up discussing them with him, she was not prepared to give them up altogether.

She had Yasmin, of course, but there was only so much a co-conspirator 6,500 miles away could contribute. She had the sudden inspiration that she could recruit Steph, who of all her new Lime Park acquaintances had struck her as the most like-minded (she was also, presumably, as in the dark as Christy). She must be about to go on maternity leave by now, so would be at home all day and in an excellent position to keep tabs on her upstairs neighbour.

But that was unfair: Steph was about to have a baby and would not be interested in the petty secrets of the street (even less so anything that might prove genuinely sinister). Besides, Caroline had confirmed that Rob was at the centre of the unnamed bad feeling, and Steph liked him, didn't she – just as Joe claimed to.

No, the fact of the matter was that the old guard would not confess their secrets and the new guard had made up its mind that he was 'one of the good guys', a man whose only crime was to have forgotten to shave.

She was on her own.

Chapter 16

Amber, 2012

September was a low time – and all the lower for the plunge not having been anticipated. At first I put my mood down to anticlimax, to the hangover after the party, not so much a Sunday slump as a restless ache that persisted day after day after day. I didn't know then that it was in fact the beginning of an extended period of torment for me, its cause, I was slow to acknowledge, Rob.

Looking back, I see that the signs were present at our first liaison after the party.

'So what were you up to last week?' I asked, referring to his unprecedented time off from our arrangement (I was still arrogant then; it was fine for me, the married one, to disappear with my husband without a word of explanation, but *his* absences were different).

'Oh, nothing much,' he said.

'You're suddenly very mysterious.'

He shrugged. 'Come on, you don't *actually* want to know what I do when I'm not entertaining you, do you?'

'Who said anything about entertaining me?' I teased. 'Maybe you bore me senseless.'

'Oh I do, do I?'

'As a matter of fact, you do – in one sense of the word, anyway.'

It was our standard patter but it was flat, had a going-through-the-motions ennui to it. And though the assignations that followed this one were as physically pleasurable as ever, there were strikingly fewer of them. The established protocol of our affair was that I would send a text to suggest a day (usually the next) and time to meet and he would, invariably, respond yes; suddenly he was responding no as often, pleading work out of town or urgent deadlines, evasive when I asked for specifics.

'What is this,' he'd say, 'do you want a copy of my schedule?'

Good-humoured and yet offhand, it was how I imagined he would speak to his disposable dates, not *me*.

Naturally, I suspected Pippa's hand in this new unavailability and blamed myself for having inadvertently given their romance the public blessing that had very likely helped him break the relationship pain barrier. Not that he ever mentioned her. He left that to me.

'I hear we almost booked ourselves a double date,' I said.

'Oh yeah?'

'Caroline and Richard's dinner party on Friday.'

'You and Jeremy are invited as well?' And he was not quite quick enough to hide the flicker of excitement the suggestion aroused.

'Don't worry,' I said. 'We're not free. Dinner with clients.'

'A shame. That would have been fun.'

I begged to differ. Seeing him ignore Kenny's hapless colleague might have passed for sport, but watching him paw Pippa as he had at our party certainly would not.

A week or so after this exchange Jeremy and I ran into the two of them one evening on the Parade, stopping of course to say hello, and I was shaken by just how violently I disliked seeing them together again. Pippa was visibly in the process of falling in love with him (a truly ghastly thing to witness even when the object of desire is not your own lover), and he, if not reciprocating with quite the same depth of emotion, was plainly enjoying himself in a real way, as opposed to indulging in a fit of method acting for my benefit. As she chattered carelessly on about that dinner at Caroline's, his fingers kept reaching to pet her: idle, territorial, just as they did me when we were in his bedroom, post-coital and relaxed.

'Rob warned me about the swinging scene in this area, so I was a bit worried,' she said, deadpan, and it was only when she began hooting like a demented owl that I was aware of my own shocked reaction.

'Oh, I think you can be confident we all sleep with the right people,' Jeremy told her, keen to participate in the fun, and when I glanced at Rob it was only to meet his profile as his face turned to Pippa's, full of private mocking. Enraged, I lowered my head, concealing my displeasure from Jeremy, from *him*.

'You can see what stage *they're* still at,' Jeremy said, when they'd strolled off hand in hand, not a backward glance between them. '*Swinging?* Can you imagine? Fine for some other lucky bloke, but what about me?'

Even flattery could not raise my spirits; it took every working neuron in my brain to direct the required smile to my lips.

I'm ashamed to admit I spent an indecent number of hours analysing this casual encounter. All of a sudden I was experiencing exactly the feelings I'd declared contraband in the first place, exactly the feelings Rob had never appeared to feel about Jeremy and me. I persuaded myself that the true cause for agitation was not jealousy per se but a fear that our arrangement could not continue for long if his new girlfriend was to go where others had been denied and be established as serious. (*She'll already be plotting to move in with him* . . . : those words of Gemma's revisited me time and again; if anyone had a good instinct for a bad turn of events, it was she.) The number of variables would double, spontaneity would enter the equation as she became more confident about coming and going (what if he gave her a set of keys?), and as soon as they had any kind of pow-wow regarding relationship status she would understandably demand fidelity and he would inevitably be obliged to co-operate.

No, deceiving a contented husband was one thing, deceiving a brand-new girlfriend was quite another.

As September slithered into October, Jeremy and I had at last arrived at those once-faraway landmarks 'after the summer' and 'when the house is finished'. And it *was* finished, to all intents and purposes: where once there'd been a large team in occupation, there remained only two decorators whose names never quite stuck but who'd been hired by Hetty for their reputation for phenomenal speed. She herself had all but withdrawn from the project, needed only for a last visit or two to check the paintwork and to assess snagging, and I began slightly to fear the day when the nameless decorators would rinse their last paintbrushes and leave me too. I'd rarely been in the house on my own, and I had the sense that I didn't know it well enough to be left alone with it. I suppose the Rob distraction had prevented me from bonding with my new home, from earning its protection.

As agreed, the subject of the baby was resurrected.

'You haven't mentioned it for a while,' Jeremy said. 'You haven't gone off the idea?'

'No, of course not,' I lied. 'I just thought not discussing it constantly might help make it happen. Like you said, let nature take its course.'

'Looks like the course nature wants to take is not the one *we* want it to. Do you still want to see a specialist?'

'Sure,' I said, 'if you do.'

'I do.' Jeremy was typically resolute. 'I'll make an appointment then.'

I knew from every conversation I'd had on the subject that it was exceptional for the man to drive a project of this sort, but our dynamic differed from other couples'. Perhaps it was the age difference, perhaps the enduring perception that I was a free spirit and he my earthbound guide, but in our relationship it was Jeremy who pressed and I who yielded. He had pressed for marriage, he had pressed for the move to suburbia, and now it was he who would take on the task of pressing for a baby. I listened with unexpected nervousness as he phoned the Harley Street clinic of choice and gave his details as the primary contact. I felt squeamish, suddenly, as if defined purely by my sexual activities; the thought of all that prodding and scraping and squeezing, the needles and the pills and God knew what else, made me cross my legs and wince.

Did I want to be a parent enough to sign up for all of that? Did I want to be a parent at all? The last time I'd cared to listen, my maternal instinct had been all but extinguished by rather more self-serving ones, and to chronicle my evolving position on the issue was only to confront horrible truths about myself. In the beginning I'd been agreeable to Jeremy's suggestion, especially since it came with the side benefit of not having to work for a living; then, when the clear and present danger of Rob had reared its head, I'd been briefly keen, recognizing pregnancy as a cure for temporary insanity; but once we were under way, enmeshed, and I was used to living with the lunacy, I'd begun to have those thoughts of evasion and delay, thoughts that had only grown more appealing.

Now it was time to acknowledge my current position (and my sense that Rob was detaching from me in favour of Pippa made not a jot of difference to it): a baby meant the end of the affair, and I wanted the affair more than I wanted a baby.

Which I know sounds terrible, truly terrible.

'Right, all set.' Jeremy was off the line, phone still in hand. 'Nine o'clock next Wednesday morning. We'll meet with the consultant and do some tests.' He reached to hug me and I surrendered willingly, enjoying the protective strength of him, the knowledge that these decisions at least – if not any others – were going to be made for me.

'OK?' he asked, glimpsing my stricken expression.

'The thing is, Jeremy, I know I said I was sure, but now that we're doing this, I feel as if I don't know what I want any more. I feel confused.' It was as close as I would ever get to betraying myself to him.

'I think that's totally natural,' he soothed. 'It *is* confusing. It's not what we thought was going to happen. But if we do start IVF or something like that, you have to remember that it won't be forever. It's only the means to an end. And whatever happens, whether we have six kids or none, we're still *us*. We're in it together.'

His tenderness made me want to cry. Jealousy was not the only emotion I'd granted entry of late; there was, too, the beginnings of guilt.

And about time too.

In fact, the consultation was as painless as it could be. The consulting rooms were opulent, the consultant, Mr Atherton, a man of about Jeremy's age who possessed the same air of determined self-preservation (I supposed it followed that someone who could conjure life from thin air might also believe he had a stab at eluding death). He was matter-of-fact, candid on the subject of success rates, not least in respect of our ages: unsurprisingly, mine was still in the range that yielded high success, Jeremy's more problematic, though 'by no means disastrous'. The medical terms and acronyms were familiar to us from our investigations online – IUI, IVF, ICSI, donor eggs and so on – the key word being one we both knew and under-stood well: *strategy*. There was no set of circumstances that could not be tackled with the right strategy, Mr Ather-ton assured us. It was a good line, I thought: 'tackle' was a very different word from 'solve', and the strategy could be, after all, to give up and get a dog.

I wondered what he would say if he knew I led a paral-lel sex life to the one I was detailing for the medical record.

'So let's get these tests out of the way and then meet again in a couple of weeks to look at the options,' he said, handing us over to his worker bees. There were blood tests to establish hormone levels, a sperm sample from Jeremy, consent forms to sign and health histories to fill in. We left the clinic feeling optimistic, the issue unbur-dened rather than exposed.

Within days, Jeremy had heard from them and phoned me from the office to relay the news: 'They're sending full results in an email, but it's basically good news: there's nothing wrong technically. They suggest we keep on try-ing for another six months and then if it's still not happening, report for our first cycle of IVF.'

'Another six months?' Having identified an unwilling-ness of my own to get the science under way, this nonetheless seemed a longer stretch than I would reason-ably have expected Jeremy to allow. 'We've already been trying for a year.'

'I agree it's frustrating, but Atherton knows our history and he suggests six months to be sure. You can see his point, especially given your age: better to take a bit longer and conceive naturally. You heard what he said: IVF is stressful and exhausting and very expensive. This is a private consultant speaking, Amber. Think how easy it would be for him to take our money straight away and get on with it, with or without results. Instead he's telling us *not* to have treatment – at least not yet.'

'What about Clomid? I don't need to take it?'

'No, not necessary. You're absolutely fine, there's no need to stimulate egg production. Oh, but we do have to do all the healthy lifestyle stuff he talked about. Cut down on drinking, especially.'

'Hmm, I don't like the sound of that.' I pictured the bottle of wine Rob and I drank as a matter of course during our afternoon rendezvous: that would be hard to forgo. Instead I would have to give up the glasses shared with Jeremy.

'The nurse is emailing me some stuff about optimizing. I'll print it out and bring it home with me.' He'd become both the expert and the administrator, as if he didn't have a demanding enough job already. Meanwhile, I drifted about my perfect castle and admired my beauty in the mirror like the wicked queen, in a perpetual state of dread of the news that someone more beautiful had been sighted in the kingdom. I hung my head in shame to think how little I deserved Jeremy's devotion.

'Thank you for doing all of that,' I said. 'Handling all the phone calls and everything. I know I've got more time, but . . .'

'It's all right. I know you don't like the way all of this makes you feel. You know, constantly trying.'

It was the first time he'd referred to the fact that I'd

enjoyed sex less in the last few months, and I was grateful he was not in the room to see my reaction face to face. Even *I* didn't know if my fading ardour was owing to the chore of trying to conceive or to the fact that I was also sleeping with someone else, someone with a style that suited me better.

'Let's just relax for a bit, try and forget about it. What about going somewhere hot for Christmas and New Year? The Caribbean, maybe? Somewhere totally relaxing. I'll see if I can take ten days.'

Not so long ago this suggestion would have thrilled me, especially as Jeremy demanded of his accommodation nothing less than complete luxury, but now I feared it would be utter torment for me to be away from Rob for this long, however exotic the location.

Imagine if you were going away with him, not Jeremy, whispered the wicked queen.

'I'll look at some options,' I said.

In the meantime the progression of Imogen's pregnancy – she was only a few weeks from her due date when the group next met – struck me as a visual representation of the time Jeremy and I had already indulged in 'relaxing'. Fresh confusion assailed me: was I *really* pleased it was taking us so much longer than we'd expected?

Certainly the girls perceived the delay as an out-and-out tragedy.

'Shouldn't you at least have your name down already?' Imogen asked when we gathered at her flat in Islington, depot now to an array of baby-related deliveries. Seeing all the boxes stacked up and half opened reminded me of the weekend we'd moved into Lime Park Road, and it seemed now like an ancient, unspoiled time. Pre-Rob; prelapsarian indeed.

'She's right, Amber, aren't there long waiting lists for IVF?' Helena said.

'Not where *they'll* be doing it,' Gemma said, smilingly snide, and for once I turned on her, tired of her begrudging brand of friendship.

'Have a bit of sympathy, can't you? Who cares who's paying and who isn't, who's waited ten minutes and who ten years? The end result is the same for all of us – at least I hope it will be. Or don't you think Jeremy and I deserve a baby for some reason?' I was breathing hard, red mist rising fast, obscuring all sense. 'Go on, Gemma, why don't you tell me what's *really* on your mind? Are you annoyed I didn't set you up with Rob? It's not *my* fault he seems to have chosen this Pippa woman! Don't you think I –' I stopped, gasping, right on the precipice of saying too much and giving myself away.

To a woman they looked utterly shocked. Gemma flushed deeply and stammered an apology, unprecedented in the years of our acquaintance. As I sat on my hands to stop myself from fidgeting, I saw Helena and Imogen exchange an anxious glance.

It was the first public sign that I was starting to fray.

Chapter 17

Christy, July 2013

Arriving at number 42, Flaubert in hand, just before eight on the evening of the book group, Christy found herself in the eye of the storm that was the Sellers children's bedtimes. As Caroline ushered her into the hallway a small girl slid down the stairs on her bottom and announced that she wasn't at all sleepy and should therefore be allowed to put the light back on and get out her Sylvanian Families collection. A second girl had complaints to make about a sleeping brother's heavy breathing, and these she foghorned from the top of the stairs, causing the first girl to object, the boy to awaken and start crying, and Caroline to yell for everyone to shut up and bloody well get back into bed or they'd be late for school the next morning and the teacher would call the police. There was no one else there yet, not even Richard Sellers back from the office.

'Did I get the time wrong?' Christy asked.

'Oh, no one ever makes the actual start time,' Caroline said, tossing a wet towel up the stairs with impressive aim. 'You can see how hard it is to get these evil goblins into the land of Nod, especially when school's about to break up. It's not even dark yet, how can it possibly be night-time, it's illogical – that's what you're dealing with, Christy. The same thing'll be happening in every house on the street.'

Except number 40.

'Would it be better if I went home and came back later?'

'God, no, stay now you're here, you can help me with the nibbles. Let's go and have a glass of wine. I'm officially off duty, whether the other residents of this house choose to acccpt it or not.'

Christy followed her into the kitchen. It was the first time she'd been inside the Sellerses' home (or any of her new neighbours', for that matter) and it almost broke her heart to see the child-centric chaos of it, the items of school uniform draped over the chairs, the infantile draw-ings pinned on the walls, including an enormous framed portrait entitled 'My Mummy by Rosie Sellers, 2F' in which Caroline was missing nose, ears and eyebrows. A large notice asked 'Have You Cleaned Your Teeth and Washed Your Face?' while a chart displayed the merits attained in a bid for a puppy.

Christy drank deeply of it, a travellcr unaware of the life-threatening acuteness of her thirst until presented with a freshwater lake. How clinical her own house by comparison; there was no escaping the worst word of all: soulless. We should have stayed in our flat, she thought, feeling sudden and actual panic. We weren't ready for this. We should have realized the child is more important than the square footage. Her mother was right, no house was worth the sacrifice. What did Steph say that time? *You have to compromise on something, don't you?* Well, she thought, we've

263

compromised on the wrong thing, any fool can see that. I'll talk to Joe tonight, I'll tell him what I want.

'Any luck on the job front?' Caroline said as she tackled 'nibbles' by tearing open small bags of what looked like infants' packed-lunch snacks and mixing them together in a large bowl. ('I used to make more of an effort,' she shrugged by way of explanation.)

'Not yet,' Christy said, 'and it'll be completely dead over August. I've decided to look for something voluntary just to keep busy. I've set aside tomorrow to sort it out.' ('Set aside' from what? Her long days of advising the Treasury on economic policy?) 'I thought I'd start at the library, look at the noticeboard there and find out what the local forums are.'

Caroline crushed the packaging into an overflowing bin. 'What about getting in touch with those people who run the local literacy initiative?'

'What's that?'

'It's a voluntary programme where you help out at one of your local primary schools –' There was an interruption as one of the Sellers girls could be heard at the kitchen door, asking in a bold, accusing tone, 'Are there *crisps*?'

'Back to bed!' Caroline screamed, startling Christy and causing her to slop wine over her wrist, before continuing seamlessly with their conversation: 'Just a couple of mornings a week, supporting kids who've fallen behind with their reading and need a bit of extra encouragement. But it wouldn't be till the new school year, I'm guessing.'

'I could still give them a call,' Christy said, applying kitchen roll patterned with cherries to the spillage, for September was not so far away.

'And if you did have a new job by then, you could always negotiate the hours off. I think you have to commit for at least half a term. I've probably got the details somewhere, I'll dig them out and drop them round tomorrow if you like.'

'That would be perfect.' Thanks to this – and the fishbowl of wine – her epiphany was receding to a more manageable size. 'All these lovely photos,' she remarked, standing before a radiator cover stacked with framed school portraits of the Sellerses' smiling children in various stages of dental development.

'Yes,' Caroline said. 'Just when you think you're sick of the sight of them, you can come in here and see their faces a thousand times over. It's like Room 101.'

Among the school photos there were a few family ones, including one of the Sellerses at a beach café somewhere exotic, Richard looking as if he'd just escaped a house fire, Caroline vividly draped and accessorized; the look did not quite gel with her disordered appearance this evening. In another, a group of mostly middle-aged adults clustered before the camera in a garden strung with fairy lights, glasses raised. In the corner was what appeared to be an oversized swan; closer inspection revealed it to be part of a fairground ride.

'Why's there a carousel in someone's garden?' she asked. 'Hang on, is that *our* garden?'

Caroline peered over her shoulder. 'It is, actually. The Frasers had a party when they'd finished their renovations. There were all sorts of entertainments, including the ride. I was never entirely clear how they got it in and out of the garden, but no doubt Amber charmed some-one on the park committee into risking life and limb with a fork-lift truck.' She smiled. 'I hope you don't think it's a bit creepy to see your own home in a photo in someone else's house?'

'Of course not, it's nice,' Christy said, chasing off any deflating thoughts of her own guestless get-together.

'It was going to be an annual thing,' Caroline said, 'every August bank holiday, but of course it turned out to be the first and last. Richard and I talked about hosting it instead this year, but it wouldn't be the same without Amber. She made things special. Look, that's her there, in the middle. See what I mean about her figure?'

Christy inspected the picture with fascinated interest. At last, an image of her famously alluring predecessor. And it was all she could do not to gasp, for it was true, Amber had all the components of outstanding beauty: a body that was both toned and curvaceous, a shining mane of flame-red hair, glowing skin, an immaculately fitted designer dress and high heels. Her cheekbones were high, her nose straight, her eyes wide and her smile broad: all the right adjectives went with all the right features, not a mix-up among them. Such was her youth and glamour compared to the others in the group it looked as if a Hollywood actress had put in an appearance at her par-ents' small-town barbecue. All at once, the idea of her having removed herself from Lime Park made complete sense to Christy. An exotic creature like this, a bird of paradise, didn't belong in a suburban garden.

'So who is everyone else? I can recognize you and Richard, and that's Felicity, isn't it?'

'That's right. She was lovely, Felicity, quite *political*, always lecturing my girls on financial independence – as if they have a clue at their age – and there's me, standing right next to them, an unwaged wastrel!'

Christy could not help but contrast this display of easy humour with the indignation unleashed on her the first time they'd met. She very much liked this new, droll Caroline.

'And on the left is Kenny, then his wife Joanne – you've probably seen them with their Labradoodle, Poppy. She'll be here tonight. Not the Labradoodle, I mean, the human.'

As she pointed out others half-recognizable from her daily surveillance, Christy's eye settled on a male figure she'd seen in another photograph: cropped greying hair and angular, intelligent face. He was in excellent shape for his age.

'Is that Jeremy Fraser?'

'That's right. Wonderful man.' Caroline paused. 'That's why I don't worry, not really.'

'Worry about what? Amber?'

'About both of them. If they're together, then wherever they are I know they're OK.'

Christy wondered if she should report what Gemma at the media agency had said about Amber only being where she wanted to be; would that put Caroline's mind at ease a little? But the last time she'd mentioned one of Amber's other friends, she'd only succeeded in disheartening her.

'Who's the younger guy?' Christy indicated the smiling black-haired man standing directly behind Amber. He, too, was familiar to her.

'You don't recognize him? He's your neighbour on the other side.'

'Rob?' It occurred to Christy that Caroline never directly used his name. Did her loathing run so deep? 'He looks so different without his beard.' She thought of the photo she'd seen on the Internet, coloured slightly at the memory of her snooping.

'Yes, he's put on weight since then as well.' Caroline spoke as if it were a decade ago, not eleven months.

'He's like a bear, we think,' said Christy (again, that fraudulent 'we'). 'One of those ones that can decapitate a human with a swipe of its paw.'

Caroline laughed. 'Well, in those days he was more the lithe panther type, quite the heart-throb in fact – I think I'm allowed to say that.'

'Why wouldn't you be?' For Christy, Rob's presence in the photo only made more of a riddle of him. Seeing him in this new context jarred her assumptions, made a mockery of her speculation about formal illegalities ('Lime Park killer'!). *He didn't used to be rude*, Imogen had said, and on this evidence he'd been in fact very popular, right in the centre of the throng, smiling happily, certainly not someone you'd be warned to avoid or want to anonymously call 'scum'. How could a 'heart-throb' have become *persona non grata* in so brief a time? 'Distressing stuff' Caroline had called it before, which could apply to a multitude of sins. Might his fall from grace, for instance, be the result of something more prosaic, a case of the oldest story in the book – and indeed in the book to be discussed that evening – an extramarital affair? A romantic skirmish that had caused the closing of ranks and reprisals that included fists flying and people yelling up at windows?

If so, with whom had he had the skirmish? Looking once again at the photograph, she was quite clear that Amber Fraser was the one you'd pick out of a line-up, the one with mythical levels of desirability, the one who had left in mysterious circumstances. And yet Caroline had vouched for the Frasers' marital devotion as if in a court of law (*They're together forever . . .*), her words having struck Christy as entirely truthful and authentic. So if not Amber, who? Caroline herself? It would certainly make sense of her ambivalence towards Rob, for what woman was not ambivalent about past passion, even the legitimate sort?

But no, that didn't make sense either, for Caroline had approved the choice of *Madame Bovary* for the book group: a guilty woman, especially one who appeared to be the leader of the group, would surely have used her power of veto to avoid such an awkward discussion. In any case, adultery did not explain that repulsive note. A raging husband or established opponent would surely sign his name; he'd certainly not make the mistake of posting it through the wrong door.

'Well, he can't be as awful as we think, because his girlfriend keeps coming back for more,' Christy said.

'His girlfriend?' Caroline turned sharply. 'Who's that? What does she look like?'

'She's small and blonde and tanned. Very pretty. Early thirties, maybe?'

'That sounds like Pippa,' Caroline exclaimed, amazement overriding discretion. 'She must be *crazy* if she's still hanging around! I thought she moved out months ago.'

'Oh, she doesn't live there,' Christy said. It was out of the question for formal removals to have escaped her surveillance. 'So she used to, did she?'

'Yes, earlier in the year, but not for long.'

'Strange.' Who would move in with a boyfriend, leave again, and then continue to visit regularly immediately afterwards? 'Maybe they've got one of those relationships that thrives on drama and insecurity?'

'If that's the case then I worry for her.' Caroline sucked in her lips, her vow of silence reclaiming her, as her eyes drifted once more to the photograph. The way she looked at it was as if she longed for the glory days, for that golden age when Queen Amber presided. Like a deposed aristocrat dreaming of the last days of Versailles.

By the time the doorbell signalled the arrival of other book lovers, Christy had almost forgotten why she was here. A group of four, including Liz and Joanne, had come together; Christy imagined them calling on one another as they walked down the street, like kids knocking on doors to see who was coming out to play. Sophie and Mel were the other two, their faces now familiar both from her stints at the window and the photo in Caroline's kitchen. They were a friendly enough group, if disappointingly eager to resume a conversation begun en route, which had to do with Lime Park Primary and the resignation of the deputy head, the content of which was recapped as a matter of priority for Caroline's benefit. It appeared that discussion of the book would wait until the subject had been dissected to its smallest particles.

Christy glanced around the sitting room, where Caroline had arranged refreshments and hooked up an iPod that shuffled disconcertingly between eighties heavy metal and noughties Disney. It bore signs of a hasty tidy: in one corner a tennis racket, a tangle of chargers, a collapsed tower of magazines, three odd trainers – as if someone had used the racket to sweep the rest out of sight. On one of the bookshelves was a familiar object, the hourglass bottle of scent she'd seen in Felicity's hallway. Christy reached for it, raised it to her nose. It smelled warm and smoky and dark.

Rejoining the conversation, she found it had progressed: one of the women's husbands was being discussed and found wanting. 'I suppose I just have to accept that I'm married to a fucking moron,' Mel said, and Christy couldn't imagine speaking of Joe in this way; even if they had begun to argue a little lately, it was nothing like *that*.

'Aren't we all,' Liz said with bitterness. 'That's why some of us decided *not* to be any more.'

Joanne pulled a consolatory face. 'I'm lucky with Kenny. He's no trouble.' This caused a quick glance between Caroline and Liz, which Christy guessed had to do with the hand injury. Was the scuffle with Rob not common knowledge then? (If indeed there had been any scuffle; sometimes she forgot what she knew and what she only thought she knew.)

As faint praise failed to save Mel's husband from his damning, the one called Sophie remembered the newcomer by her side and broke away to say, 'So you're in the Frasers' place, right?' And she reached to touch Christy's wrist, exclaiming, 'What a beautiful bangle! Is that amber?'

'Yes, I think so.' Christy gave a guilty start, twisting the bangle so the clasp was not visible, the narrow silver band sliding innocently over her wrist bones onto her hand. She'd meant to take it off before spending the evening with Amber's friends.

'I *love* amber. Where did you get it?' Sophie asked, speaking into a sudden hush, for the others had allowed their conversation to lapse, Mel and her maligned spouse evidently forgotten. It was because the word 'amber' had been mentioned, Christy realized.

'I don't remember,' she said. 'On holiday somewhere, I think.' Self-conscious now she had everyone's attention, she resorted to the more comfortable role of questioner: 'So did Amber Fraser ever come to your book group?'

To her surprise, at this the women broke into a delighted uproar. Exactly as she'd found with Caroline, the subject of Amber-in-residence was not only fair game but also everyone's decided preference. Glasses were drained, wine replenished and the atmosphere became almost festive.

'Yes and no,' Caroline explained to Christy. 'The first few times we invited her she pretended she was busy, and then when she finally did agree to come, do you know what she did? She insisted we do it at her place, *your* place, but when we all turned up she'd hired this guy to make cocktails for us. She said, "Why read when we can carouse?" That was such an Amber word, wasn't it? "Carouse".'

'It was,' Liz agreed. 'I'd completely forgotten she used to say that!'

'Oh my God, it was *carnage* that night,' said Sophie. 'Like a hen night.'

'I couldn't get my key in the door when I got home,' Joanne confessed. 'I had to shout through the letter box to wake Kenny up to let me in. The dog was going berserk.'

'Her copy of the book was still in the bag from the shop, do you remember?' Caroline said. 'She hadn't even opened it.'

'That's right,' Mel said, 'it was the new Ian McEwan. She said she'd got the low-down on the plot from Jeremy.'

'And when he came home he was annoyed because she was supposed to be following some clean-living programme to help with getting pregnant. And there she was, knocking back these lethal mojitos.'

'I don't think he minded *really*, do you? She could get away with *murder*, he was so besotted.'

'Any man would have been. Anyway, ridiculous, don't you think? If you had to be sober to get pregnant there'd be a population crisis!'

'There would in Lime Park, anyway.'

With this the conversation took a feverish turn: the conceptions of the women's own babies, the shortcomings – or absences – of their sex lives since, the galling way attractive younger men now looked straight through them in the street or, worse, treated them with scrupulous respect, as if reminded of their own mothers. Having longed to be accepted, Christy now felt rather relieved to be outside of their shared realm of experience.

'I'd almost prefer to be ignored,' Sophie said, becoming angry, 'than patronized in my own street.'

'I totally agree.'

'Me too.'

'I didn't know there *were* any young men on Lime Park Road,' Christy interjected, a sly attempt to get one of them to mention Rob, but she was too late because Liz had become tearful at their talk of waning desirability (her ex-husband had just become engaged again, Mel whispered; to someone much younger from Sales).

'Why are the decent ones *always* married?' Liz asked, with tipsy theatricality. 'Why can't *I* meet a Jeremy Fraser?'

In the absence of a satisfactory answer to this (Jeremy Fraser was, after all, married too), the group decided instead that it should turn its attention at last to the book.

'Did anyone manage to finish it?' Caroline asked brightly. 'The print was really small, wasn't it?'

But they'd all been far too busy to read more than the first few chapters. All except Christy, who opened the discussion with a rather faltering precis of Flaubert's plot, all too aware that the minds of the women in the room remained on the dramas of their own lives.

Chapter 18

Amber, 2012

Well, what can I say? It was my mistake and mine alone to believe that honeymoons could last forever – and I don't mean only with Rob, I mean with *everyone* on Lime Park Road. That glorious giddying sensation of being at the centre of everyone's attention, the sunshine in which they queued to bask: it passed that autumn as garden gates were closed, curtains drawn and folk began to hibernate.

Just as Rob had once warned, school concerns dominated the community. Even Caroline became distracted by applications, her elder daughter Amelia now preparing for senior school entrance exams. Out for the campaign came the old jeans and nautical tops, though she did at least grasp the importance of getting her highlights refreshed. As for Joanne, who had a son in the same class as Amelia, so all-consuming was *her* obsession that she was temporarily to be avoided. Once I even saw Felicity cross the road to elude her, while Kenny could be seen to roll his eyes as his wife paused at their gate to exchange war stories about private tutors with yet another antsy parent.

Ironically, the only neighbour who could be prised from the subject of education was the education journalist himself – if I was lucky enough to get an audience with him, that was.

For Rob continued to give me the runaround. Oh, it was classic stuff, I see that now, unworthy of Amber Speed, much less Mrs Fraser, but the unedifying truth was that the more he waned the more I waxed. I waxed *because* he waned. And the fact that this was no deliberate strategy on his part, that he was oblivious to the effects of his casual neglect, just strung me out all the more.

I began to have anxiety dreams. Not for me the mutant monsters and slasher-film plots of normal nightmares, but the real players in my life, the actual backdrops, distorted and dangerous: Rob with Pippa at our party, making love on the carousel, faces strained in rapture; Jeremy ninety years old and emaciated, tottering towards me with a newborn baby in his fragile grasp; Gemma on the screen of every computer and television in the land, announcing my guilt, mocking my beginnings.

It was *grotesque*.

'You've got a lot on your mind,' Caroline said, which was kind of her since as far as she and the rest of the outside world were concerned I had precious little to worry about. Not only were there no school-related preoccupations to trouble me but there were also – that they knew of – no double life to schedule, no dual emotions to manage, no lines to keep from crossing. 'I've got Richard's mother here helping me for half-term, so why don't we go and have lunch at Canvas? Shall we see if Rob wants to come?'

I tried not to look glum. 'He's still away in Hull, I think, at some conference.'

'Really?' Caroline looked doubtful. 'He's been away for ages. Conferences can't last that long, can they? Maybe he's back and holed up with Pippa?'

'Maybe.'

'It's always a bore when a chum falls in love, isn't it?' she sighed, and it was all I could do not to scream out my knee-jerk protest: *He's not in love, not with her!* Then I remembered the faces of Imogen, Helena and Gemma, their horror when I – the charmed one, the beautiful one – had lost my cool in front of them, betrayed the existence of an ugly impulse they'd never before been permitted to glimpse.

'Maybe that's it,' I said, mustering a smile. 'Let's go without him. Now tell me all about this school you want for Amelia. It's the one on the bus route, right, so she can do the journey on her own?'

It was not long after this, when over a week had passed without his replying to a single one of my texts, that my frustrations regrettably got the better of me and I marched to the door of number 38 to confront him. I pressed my thumb down so hard that the flesh behind the nail turned white – as if relief could be found in the discordant grind of it, audible even through two solid timber doors. Audible to Felicity too, for it was she who eventually answered, luring me in for a cup of tea.

'You know he's not at home?' she said, in that way she had of seeming to know both everything and nothing at once. 'I've hardly seen him at all since the summer.' And it was her words, rather than his silence, that gave me the strong sense that my days were numbered.

That night in bed, for the first time in a while, I put Jeremy off. Jeremy being Jeremy, he accepted this with a good grace.

'All right, baby? Has someone upset you?'

'I'm just tired,' I said, furious with myself for wanting to cry.

'It's not to do with Imogen?'

In fact, my last meeting with her *had* distressed me, but not for the reason Jeremy thought. As I had been chalking up the days that separated me from my last contact with Rob, she had been counting the same ones down to the birth of her baby, and at last he arrived, a boy she and Nick named Frankie. Visiting, I had found the family settled in a nest of flowers and cards and balloons, puddles of cashmere at every turn, early learning apps flashing on every gadget: a nativity for twenty-first-century north London. The baby was pink and placid, Imogen besotted with him, and Nick in raptures with both of them, leaving me no choice but to coo and cluck exactly as etiquette demanded.

'You are so lucky,' I told them, beaming.

'We know,' they said, beaming back.

It was only when driving home that I had found myself in trouble, my thoughts having turned to the subject that had consumed me, coincidentally, for the same length of time as Imogen's pregnancy – and in direct substitution for the bid for parenthood that I *should* have been prioritizing: my affair with Rob. Crossing the river into south London, I was torn limb from limb by dilemma, one minute rigid with the sudden clarity of what I'd been risking, of the imperative to safeguard my marriage without delay and make my current estrangement (as I characterized it) from Rob permanent; the next slumped in my seat with the despair of knowing he had only to snap his fingers and I would extend this 'fling' of ours, would go on extending it, craving it, as long as he allowed me to.

Because I had *never* been more obsessed than I was now.

The city streets spun by, navigated on autopilot, dark to human eyes.

I was lucky to get home without causing a collision.

Finally, after twelve days of silence, there was word. My phone suddenly signalled the arrival of several texts at once and one of them, to my delight, was from him:

'Back in one hour. Be ready for me?'

It was 5 p.m., which meant a 6 p.m. rendezvous, a certain risk. Rob and I normally spent two hours together, but by 7 p.m. it would be cutting it fine for me to return and shower the scent of him off me before Jeremy arrived home from work with plans for dinner. But I was desperate (an overused word, but I think the right one here) and I decided I would do it. I would leave a note for Jeremy saying I was at the gym, then I'd break convention by showering at Rob's and slipping back home later when I knew Jeremy was safely indoors.

I dressed with an unusual lack of refinement, taking no prisoners: stockings, high heels, a tiny black dress that was the sole remnant of my bachelorette wardrobe, unworn to date in my marriage and featuring the kind of neckline you could not wear on public transport without being molested (Matt's favourite, if I remembered). Glancing down at my cleavage I experienced a moment's doubt, for it was obscenely prominent and, while I might not be catching the bus, I did need to get from my door to Rob's without attracting the eye of any neighbour. I decided I would cover myself with a dark coat buttoned up to the neck (he'd like that) and limit exposure by slipping through the hedge between our paths. If I were unlucky enough to encounter Felicity I'd tell her I was on my way out and simply follow through by walking to the station.

In the bathroom I leaned towards the mirror, out-lining my lips and shading my eyelids, fanning my hair extravagantly over my shoulders. Beautification complete, I closed my eyes in anticipation, almost as seduced by myself as I was certain he would be in ten minutes' time . . .

And then the unthinkable happened: I felt a stranger's fingers on my hips, a thick arm scooping me roughly backwards, palms sliding crudely over the exposed skin of my breasts, lips on my bare shoulders and teeth nibbling, a tongue prodding . . .

'Get off me!' I screamed, my whole body clenched in terror, eyes screwed shut in shock and revulsion. My attacker must have come in through the garden gate and entered the house noiseless and deadly, and it struck me then with an instant, brutal lucidity that *no one would have seen him*, no one would know to rescue me. I was going to be raped, perhaps murdered too; I was thirty-five years old and I was going to die, no child to be remembered by, no professional accomplishment to leave to the world, no goodbye words, nothing!

Just a slut dead on a bathroom floor.

Amid a great tide of nausea, it occurred to me that this might not be random, I might know my assailant, and, hardly daring, I squinted at our reflections in the mirror.

'Darling,' Jeremy said, my scream having startled him into releasing me, his head jerking back as if struck with a fist. 'I gave you a surprise, I'm sorry.'

'Jeremy! I thought you were . . .' I turned and fell against him, tears blurring my vision. 'I didn't hear you come in. I always hear you, you call out hello . . .'

'I sneaked in. I wanted to catch you unawares.' He took my wrist in his hand. 'My God, your pulse is going crazy.'

'You almost gave me a heart attack. I thought someone had broken in and attacked me.'

'I'm so sorry, sweetheart.'

I felt the gulp in his throat as he recovered his composure.

'Not a secret fantasy of yours then, clearly,' he added.

'No. I was really scared.'

Now I can't see Rob: that was my first thought, and I could have beaten Jeremy's chest with my fists in disappointment.

'I'm sorry,' he repeated. 'You poor baby. But you obviously got my message . . .' Eyeing the provocative outfit, he allowed his hands to begin roaming once more, tentative now, their muscles remembering the first rebuke, fearful of a second. 'I thought we needed something new . . .'

'What?' My brain tangled and turned; it took a full thirty

seconds for me to process the misunderstanding, the whole while submitting to his groping. *He* had sent the text, not Rob. I'd been so determined to see what I wanted to see that I'd selected the wrong one and made Jeremy's words Rob's. 'Yes,' I said miserably. 'I got your message. I was just getting ready.'

'You look fantastic, darling.' He swivelled me gently and pressed against me from behind, his excitement unavoidable. 'I don't think I've seen this dress before, is it new? It's incredibly sexy.'

'I thought you'd like it,' I murmured.

'I certainly do. Do you think you've recovered from the shock yet . . . ?'

I didn't want this with Jeremy. My body protested, though I knew I had to force it to comply. 'I think so,' I said.

I checked my phone afterwards, terrified that I'd imagined Rob's name, willed it into being having plunged into the abyss that was hallucination, madness. But there it was, sitting in the inbox directly below the one from Jeremy:

'Take it easy, Miss Amber. Lay off with the texts. Back tomorrow, can meet afternoon.'

I re-read Jeremy's message. *Be ready for me?* It was not his usual style, certainly, but had I stopped to think about it then that question mark should have been a clue. Rob would not have used one. His would have been a command.

Chapter 19

Christy, August 2013

'See? Not one, but two invitations,' Joe told Christy, when one Saturday afternoon in early August the Davenports were invited to meet Felix and Steph's new baby daughter. 'I *knew* they would love you once they got to know you a bit better.'

He gave every impression of believing that her happiness was purely a matter of being greeted on the street with plausible cheer by an interchangeable cast of female neighbours – was this her status now?

Well, it had been good enough for Amber Fraser, she supposed.

It was a limpid, sun-drenched day as they closed the front door behind them, and she thought what a fundamental pleasure it was to feel the sun on her skin. A gentle silence had descended on Lime Park Road now that most of the families were away for the school holidays. Caroline and her children were among the escapees, spending a month at their second home in France; Richard flew over for weekends, apparently. She could only dream of such a leisured lifestyle, though she was the first to admit that sitting in an armchair and watching her neighbours

283

from the window was 'leisured' by most people's standards.

Her principal subject, Rob Whalen, had gone to ground in recent weeks (though she was fairly sure he wasn't holidaying with the Sellerses), which at least spared her any further fracas of the kind that had occurred in the park café. She imagined herself ditching her sleuthing and spending the rest of the month sunbathing. The Frasers had left a rather nice pair of teak loungers in the garden shed; she should have had them out weeks ago, not moped about indoors, staging profitless stake-outs at the bedroom window. Still, better late than never, she thought, and took Joe's hand in hers.

The main door to number 38 had been left ajar, and to their surprise Steph met them at the flat door before they could knock.

'You must have good hearing,' Joe laughed.

'Come on in.' Her voice was breathy, hardly audible, and Christy thought she must have a sore throat – until she remembered the same stage whisper from the times she'd visited friends with first babies, the underlying tension in a house where the survival of the collective hinged on the tiniest of its number not being woken from her nap.

'Shhh,' Steph added, finger to her lips.

Christy was keen to see the layout of the space that twinned their own ground floor. The kitchen, just across the hall from the front door, was tiny and to be converted later in the year into a second bedroom, Steph said sotto voce. Felicity's old gold had been obliterated with matt white. The living room was at the rear, French doors opening onto a cracked concrete terrace with terracotta tubs of pink dahlias. Christy rather envied the family their compact space as it currently stood, but she chided herself for falling into the trap of thinking the grass greener on the other side of the fence. (Looking out at Steph's and Felix's garden, however, she saw the grass *was* greener, for she had somehow managed to let her own lawn turn yellow.)

'We're hoping to get planning permission next year for an extension,' Steph added.

Goodness knew how she would ever cope with the noise of building works if conversation posed a threat to security. The bedroom door, closed on the resting child, drew regular sidelong glances across the hallway from the new mother, as if a direct gaze would set off air-raid sirens. Christy thought of Caroline's bedtime yells and wondered when it was that a parent made the sanity-saving leap – soon, she hoped, for poor Steph's sake.

Thankfully the situation resolved itself when the baby woke up spontaneously and Steph sprang up to tend to her.

'Sorry about that,' she said in her regular voice as she returned to display Matilda to her guests. 'I think I've gone slightly mad.'

'All in a good cause,' Joe said gamely, and with a haste that stopped just short of impoliteness began engaging Felix about work, leaving Christy to admire the baby and ask Steph questions about the birth and her early days of motherhood.

I'm *not* envious, she told herself, eyeing the soft-skinned infant in her chalk-blue cotton Babygro, and yet she *was*. She knew the exquisite scratching feeling of it, the sensation of being presented with the answer before you'd asked the question. Alcohol would help, as it had in Caroline's kitchen. She and Joe had brought with them the last remaining bottle of champagne from a case given to him in celebration of his promotion, but so far they'd been offered only tea, the making of it interrupted by Matilda waking. Now Steph seemed to have forgotten about refreshments altogether.

Just as Christy was wondering if she ought to offer to make the tea herself, there was a knock at the door.

'That'll be Rob,' Felix told the Davenports, rising. 'Steph's already trained him not to ring the bell.'

'It's just so loud,' Steph protested. 'Matilda jumps out of her skin every time it goes.'

'Poor guy,' Felix said. 'He won't be allowed to sneeze in his own home at this rate.'

Poor guy was not how Christy would have put it. She felt herself stiffen as the man she least cared to see on this happy occasion made his lumbering entry and, astonishingly, kissed Steph on the cheek and offered her both a bottle of champagne and a box of the French *macarons* they sold at the patisserie on the Parade that Christy considered too expensive to set foot in. (This, at least, prompted recollection of earlier proposals of a drink, and soon both a pot of tea and flutes of champagne were produced.) Rob shook hands with the two men and took a seat next to Joe, only acknowledging Christy very faintly, as if she were an idea of a woman rather than an actual person sitting in front of him.

'Please tell me I've missed the account of the birth,' he said to Steph, and the quip seemed to alter the whole physicality of him. He was straighter-backed and not so inflated as Christy had thought; rather, broad and solid and masculine. She allowed herself a brief recollection of the pictures she'd seen of him in his 'lithe panther' incarnation, the shape of his skull under that hood of hair, the attractive bone structure beneath that brush of a beard.

Steph was giggling. 'Yes, the grisly bit's out the way, don't worry.'

'And how's the bundle of joy? Come on, hand her over, I'd better have a go . . .' And suddenly Matilda was in Rob's arms, not setting about the wail of protest Christy privately willed, but staring in fascination at the face of her captor.

'Aren't you a natural?' Steph cooed, delighted. 'You haven't got kids yourself, have you?'

'Not to my knowledge,' Rob grinned.

Grinned? Bundle of joy? It beggared belief. To have offended his other neighbours to the point of being an outcast, to have attracted vile letters, to have been so antagonistic towards Christy that she had come to regard him as her nemesis – and yet to be so unthreatening with the others in this room as to be invited to cuddle a newborn baby . . . where were his opaque statements about knowing or not knowing, his threats to punish gossiping harpies, his slurs on other people's employment status?

Psycho, Christy thought, gulping her champagne.

'Work going all right?' Joe asked him, eyes skimming the baby's downy head. It had not escaped her notice that he wanted no turn in holding Matilda.

'Well, it's not going *entirely* wrong,' Rob said. 'You?'

Joe grimaced. 'Wish I could say the same, mate . . .'

As phrases like 'baptism of fire' and 'sold down the river' were bandied about, Christy tuned out from this tribal exchange, her attention muddied. She couldn't relax now *he* was here, but was already rehearsing the complaint she'd be making to Joe when they returned home, already allowing indignation to rise for the denial he'd be sure to make that there'd been anything different in Rob's treatment of her. *You're imagining it*, he would say. *It's all in your mind. He's a great bloke.* And he would remind her that he for one had no truck with a vendetta.

Breaking presently from this fictional dialogue, she became aware that she was being discussed. 'We had no idea it would be so tough,' Joe was telling Rob. 'The whole market's dried up in the space of four months. Once you're out, there's no way back in. She's tearing her hair out being at home. I thought she'd love the chance to be a domestic goddess, but she hates it.'

This was all rather franker on her behalf than Christy had ever allowed herself to be publicly, and she was both relieved to hear it and faintly offended by it. 'I can't hate something that doesn't exist. There's no such thing as a domestic goddess,' she said in a level tone, thinking inevitably of Amber Fraser, the nearest to a deity Lime Park Road had produced to her knowledge.

288

'There certainly isn't,' said Steph, who'd bolted a glass of champagne and now spoke with a fire Christy hadn't seen in her before. 'They should outlaw that ridiculous term. It's horrible being in a state of suspension, isn't it? If you just had a date when you'd start again, you'd be able to relax and enjoy the time off.'

'That's just it,' Christy said, grateful for the insight that she'd somehow been unable to articulate these last months. 'No matter how positive I try to be, there's always this fear that no one will ever want me again.' She stopped short of revealing any deeper deficiency, not only because *he* was listening but also because of the reason she was linked to these people in the first place: the valuable pile of bricks next door that bore her name. Who could reasonably complain of hard times when known to be the owner of such a large and beautiful house? 'Anyway, I've found some voluntary work – helping in a local primary school with reading. I start next month.'

Finding a way to occupy herself, gaining a purpose beyond the domestic, it had been so easy in the end. Caroline had supplied the contact name and number, a meeting had taken place in the organization's HQ and, police checks permitting, she would begin at St Luke's Primary the first week of term. It was walking distance – just – and so would incur no travel expenses.

To her great surprise, it was Rob who responded first to her news, turning to her in a convincingly avuncular manner and saying, 'I volunteered on that programme myself for a while. It's very rewarding, more than paid work in a way. Primary-age kids are great.'

Christy felt the look Joe slid her way: how can he be the monster you say he is when he teaches underprivileged children to read?

'Sounds like a good move, Christy,' Rob added. 'Best of luck with it.'

She almost fell off her seat to hear him speak her name, over the top of a baby's head, no less, and with no trace of contempt.

'Yes, I think I'll enjoy it. I love kids. And it's just short term,' she said.

'Oh, terms *are* short,' he drawled. 'At least they feel that way to the parents. The teachers and kids aren't quite so sure.'

As the others laughed, Christy gaped. This was not simply an advance on their previous hostilities but a repudiation of them; it was as if their set-to in the café had never taken place, nor the argument in the street. Miracles will never cease, she thought.

'Hey, Christy, you could get your pupils reading *Madame Bovary*,' Joe suggested, joining in the fun. It was weeks since she'd seen him this chipper.

'I think they might be a bit young for that,' she said. 'It will be *Harry Potter*, presumably.' But she'd relaxed sufficiently to allow herself to reach for one of Rob's *macarons* – the yellow one that she hoped would be lemon and not banana.

Rob turned to Joe, a trace of the old distrust in his face. 'Why *Madame Bovary*, out of interest?'

'That's what the ladies of the Lime Park Road book

group have been reading,' Joe told him. 'Christy's just joined their august circle.'

'I've only been to one,' she said, chewing (it *was* lemon). 'They've stopped now for the school holidays.'

'I never did read that,' Steph said. 'She's unfaithful to her husband and then poisons herself, right?'

Christy remembered the group's criticisms of this method of suicide; most had been able to cite their own preferred means of self-destruction, as if having given it full and uncompromising consideration.

'Turns out it's the number one adultery read in town,' Joe said, winking at Felix. 'Don't get me wrong, I'm not saying the wives of Lime Park would ever think of playing away themselves.'

That was for her benefit, Christy thought, as had been 'august circle'; he knew better than to trot out the bored-housewife cliché a second time. As Steph offered her another turn with Matilda, she felt again that forbidden hunger.

To her relief Rob left soon after. She noticed he had hardly started his glass of champagne and would have marked it as evidence of unsociability had he not been so manifestly sociable otherwise.

'I feel terrible he might be being kept awake by Matilda's crying,' Steph told the Davenports.

'I wouldn't worry, the soundproofing's much better from floor to floor than it is side to side,' Joe said, and Christy knew at once the occasion he was thinking about.

'Oh, I'm sure he'll get his own back sooner or later,'

Felix said, beaming at them. 'And you two will as well, I imagine.'

And Joe laughed uproariously, as if the idea were quite farcical.

'You need a break,' Christy told him later. Having extracted him from Felix's and Steph's before the baby's bedtime could become an issue, she was perplexed to see him go straight to the fridge in search of alcohol, finishing a bottle of white wine before it was even eight o'clock. She hadn't been keeping count, but she guessed he'd had at least three glasses of champagne next door by the time they'd left.

'We can't afford to go away anywhere,' he said as he opened a second bottle with the carefree air of someone who had no need of further excursion, not when he'd discovered paradise in liquid form. 'We both know that. It would be cruel even to dream.'

Having not even been out together for dinner since the night at Canvas to celebrate his partnership, they had of course not discussed the possibility of a summer holiday, a week by the pool somewhere hot, a pile of paperbacks between them, their preferred getaway of old. But *something* was needed – an extra day off, a decent night's sleep, a change of scene. Slow season it may have been for other industries, but Joe was working the same gruelling hours as ever, the cumulative exhaustion causing him to function at a whole new level of chaos.

Earlier in the week, in search of personal documents needed by the administrator of the literacy programme,

Christy had entered their makeshift office at the top of the house to find a mound of old newspapers and documents on the desk; it was as if some vandal had just emptied a dustbin onto it and walked away. Picking through the drifts she gathered that Joe had opened his work bag and dumped the contents, in need of a document or his phone but too frantic to search methodically.

Among the discarded material was the package of letters for the Frasers that he'd assured her he would post to their solicitor all those weeks ago; it must have been weighing him down on every walk to and from the train station and yet he'd evidently not noticed.

Well, it was far too late to forward it now, she thought, reopening the package and looking once more at the items. It was embarrassing to send it on so late in the day and expose their utter hopelessness (after all, they'd been efficient enough in getting in touch about the roof and extorting money for it, hadn't they?). In any case, it was mostly junk mail. She looked a final time at the brochure for the tree-house hotel, symbol of the summer holiday they could never afford, and was able now to picture the Frasers' faces in place of the models' in the image, Amber stretched out on the deck, feline and contented in the deep green shade, Jeremy alight with adoration as he watched her from the open doors.

In the end, she disposed of it all, even the postcard ('Sorry, Hetty, whoever you are . . .') – with the exception of one item: the 'Private & Confidential' letter in the plain white envelope. This she separated and slipped into the desk drawer. I won't open it, she thought, as if that

justified the crime of keeping someone else's mail –
deliberately now, as opposed to absent-mindedly as Joe
had been guilty of.

'I'll see if we can go to my gran's,' she told Joe now,
inspiration striking. 'Her place might be free for the bank
holiday weekend because she usually goes up to Mum's
for her birthday.'

And so it was arranged that they would spend the
August long weekend in Christy's grandmother's bungalow in East Sussex, a bus ride from the coast. In the event,
swimming things were dusted down in vain, for the sun
was blotted by a persistent dense grey that transformed
before long into a great British downpour.

'I don't think anyone's going to be admiring our
tans,' Joe said, as they huddled on the sofa under a cro-
cheted blanket and watched a wildlife documentary on
television. He had spent the first day asleep, the second
letting off steam about Jermyn Richards, and the third
insisting he couldn't bear to hear himself complain a
moment longer. Only by the Monday was he good company again.

'I wonder what our Lime Park friends would say about
our holiday accommodation,' Christy laughed. There was
a certain irony in having left a grand house with
state-of-the-art heating to huddle together in a bungalow
with ancient radiators they didn't like to turn on for fear
of boosting a pensioner's gas bill. This time last year the
Frasers had opened their house to their neighbours, held
a summer party that they'd planned to repeat this very
weekend. Instead, the house stood empty, the street's

residents scattered around rural France. 'I'd far rather be here than where they are,' she added defiantly.

'Me too,' Joe said. 'I had a text from Rob yesterday and he says it's as silent as the grave on Lime Park Road this weekend. They're all still in the Dordogne or wherever they go to eat their body weight in cheese.'

In spite of having just had identical thoughts herself, Christy started. 'You had a text from *Rob*?'

'Yes. Why?'

'I didn't know you had his number!'

'Why shouldn't I?' Joe looked at her with amusement. 'Come on, don't tell me you still suspect him of criminal activities?'

Christy flushed. Away from home, her various speculations about Rob – and indeed the entirely unexplained hostility on the part of Caroline and her circle – struck her as being as melodramatic as they must have been to Joe all along (it seemed the change of scene had been as crucial for her psychological health as for his). And she had to concede that if there'd been a crime, an actual illegality, it would surely be in the public domain, and yet search after search had yielded nothing.

'I never said that,' she muttered.

Joe laughed at her discomfort. 'Oh, that's right, he just stands accused of sleeping with his attractive blonde girlfriend.'

'Joe!'

'You know, I bet that's who sent that ridiculous note, some ex-boyfriend of hers? These things are always to do with sexual humiliation.' Joe watched the rainwater

295

sheeting down the windowpane in pleasing rhythm, like a water feature fed by a pipe. 'God, I take it back. I *would* rather be in the Dordogne. Burning to a crisp, swimming in the river. There is a river there, right?'

Christy ignored the question. 'What else did he say?'

'Who?'

'Rob, of course.'

'Oh, Christy!'

'I want to know. Did he mention me?'

'Of course not, why would he? It was just about the football, I think.' He sighed. 'He's just a normal bloke, when are you going to admit it?'

In the interests of marital harmony, she met him half-way. 'I admit he was less satanic last time.'

'Fine. Less satanic will do for now.' Joe stretched and flung off the throw. 'Shall we go out for dinner tonight?'

'I don't think we should,' she said, their constantly swelling overdraft never too far from her thoughts.

'The pub and fish and chips, then? Seriously, if we can't afford a pint, we might as well kill ourselves now.'

'Spoken like a true Brit,' she said, casting Lime Park and its residents from her mind. For now, at least.

On Tuesday morning Joe returned to London on the early commuter train, but it made sense for Christy, who had no office to commute to, to follow on a cheaper service. Unsure whether or not she had intended to do so all along, she filled her spare hours by taking a bus to the edge of Ashdown Forest, to a village whose name she had memorized long ago. As she entered the reception of Treetops

Suites, any sense of her own unravelling sanity was purely fleeting.

'I wondered if I might be able to look around one of the tree houses? I'm researching possible hotels for my honeymoon.' She had slipped her wedding band into her purse in anticipation of this lie. On her left wrist, Amber Fraser's bangle felt like more than the adornment it was; it was the wristband that admitted Christy to the club she'd always dreamed of joining.

'Of course.' The receptionist beamed in that way people did when weddings were mentioned; a cynic would say it was the prospect of overcharging, an idealist that love brought out the best in all of us. 'I'll see if anyone's free to give you a tour.'

Five minutes later, clutching the rate card you'd be forgiven for thinking had been misprinted, Christy followed the duty manager through the paved woodland trail from which steep stairways led to the tree houses. They climbed the one named 'Silver Birch'.

It was remarkable how high it felt up there – almost like having taken flight – the world and its weight no longer her concern (*that* was a welcome feeling). The suite itself caused her to draw breath. The furniture and fabrics were luxurious, all Egyptian cottons and Thai silks, she'd known that from the brochure, but what the photographs had not evoked was the smell, of wood freshly felled and of the forest itself, green and fresh and alive. On the other side of the vast picture window, the leaves rippled, tens of thousands of them in that framed square, fragmenting the world. It seemed to Christy this was that rare sort of place that comforted and cleansed, where you could hide not only from other people but also from your worst self.

Again, she touched the amber bangle.

Her waiting guide sought to move her on. 'Let me show you the outdoor hot tub, Miss Davenport.'

Clearly the romantic centrepiece, the large tub was on a raised portion of the rear terrace, encircled by potted trees, an outdoor lantern evidently the only illumination. It was like a sacrificial dais. As her guide murmured about al fresco massage treatments, Christy turned to rest against the glass barrier, closing her eyes as the cloud broke and light poured between the branches onto her skin. For several seconds she stood in perfect stillness, sun-kissed, spotlit, special.

'So what did you think?' the receptionist asked when Christy returned to thank her.

'I think it's a real possibility,' she said.

Only on the bus to the train station did it occur to her that not once during her tour had she imagined Joe and herself in the tree house, on the big white bed, in the bubbling hot tub, wrapped in robes as they sipped their bespoke cocktails on the veranda. She'd imagined only the Frasers.

It was almost as if she'd expected to find them there.

Chapter 20

Amber, 2012

Come November, I could avoid the truth no longer: for whatever reason, Pippa or otherwise, Rob had marginalized me. I needed to redress the balance of power as a matter of urgency and my only choice as I saw it was to upgrade my package, to offer him an enticement that had been previously out of bounds.

Thus resolved, I told him that Jeremy would be away for work in early December and proposed we use the opportunity to go away together for the night. 'Twenty-four hours together, doing whatever you like.'

'Sounds interesting,' he said, which was neither the biting-my-arm-off enthusiasm I would have liked nor the outright rebuff I had dreaded.

'I'll book somewhere suitable.'

'I'm not sure you know the meaning of the word,' he chuckled, and I ignored the suspicion that his mockery lacked its old inflection of admiration. I would arrive at the hotel early, I decided, to prepare myself, set the scene; he would soon be reminded that this was a mutual enthrallment.

'But, hang on, isn't this an infringement of the terms

and conditions,' he teased. 'Going away, being seen together?'

'The terms and conditions are different off-site,' I said. 'And no one will see us, don't worry about that.'

This last was literally the case, for I booked a hotel with tree-house suites where room service was delivered by dumb waiter, eliminating the usual eyewitnesses in such situations; if we arrived and left separately we would not be seen together by a soul – except maybe an owl or some other passing woodland creature. As an additional precaution, I insisted the booking must be in my name only, telling the hotel it was a surprise for my partner. I booked treatments for myself in the morning and instructed Rob to arrive in the afternoon.

As for Jeremy, I told him I craved a change of scene and planned to go alone to a spa. Worried by my recent low spirits, he agreed it would be a nice treat after living in a building site all those months and an excellent way to revive my flagging commitment to healthy living (there had recently been a cocktail night with the Lime Park Road book group that had sorely tested his indulgence of my not-so-occasional flouting of Atherton's rules). He kindly resisted pointing out that it might have been more logical for me to go while the works were actually in progress, since we now had a house that resembled a hotel, with bathrooms as glossy as any my five-star facility was likely to offer.

'You've had a tough time, baby,' he said. 'You go off and relax.'

I gave him the hotel's details in the full knowledge that he wouldn't bother making a note of the name, much less think to phone me there on any line but my mobile.

Poor Jeremy. The Amber he'd married would have wept to look into the future and see him as a cuckold, a patsy, a chump – and herself as a heartless deceiver.

Only obsession stopped me from weeping now.

It did not begin well. When Rob arrived, overnight bag slung over his shoulder, he appeared reluctant to set it down, muttering about the lane closures and temporary lights encountered on his journey, all but announcing to me that he wished he hadn't come. Soft-footed and cautious, he assessed the dimensions of the place like an animal scanning for predators.

A waiting game, then. Fine. I sighed to myself, admiring my blood-red manicure as I let the suite work its magic on him, just as it had me when I'd checked in, skittish and uncertain for my own reasons. Nestled forty feet aloft in the oaks, the windows overlooked by no one, it was a hideaway that might have been conceived expressly for adulterers: wood burner and acacia-scented candles, ice-cold champagne and gleaming glassware, a hot tub both discreetly screened and exhilaratingly open to the elements. But wherever you were in the place, all roads led to the huge bed, the morning view from which would be of the rising sun.

'Must be costing a packet,' Rob said. (*That* was his only comment?)

'Well, you don't have to worry about that,' I said smoothly. 'Why don't you open the champagne?'

'You do it.'

I obliged, refusing to be irritated by the thought that he might have Pippa on his mind, that he might be having misgivings about this, about me. As confident of my allure as I'd ever been, I had prepared as if for a wedding night, getting massaged with perfumed oils and perfecting my hair and make-up before dressing in a silk robe to await him, and yet he'd hardly bothered to glance at me.

'It's all right,' I said, 'you really don't need to sweep for hazards. It's just us. No one knows where we are. No one knows what we'll be doing.'

As I eased the bottle back into the ice bucket, he at last flung down the bag and turned his scrutiny to me. 'Just as well, I would've thought,' he growled.

That was more like it. The way he looked at me was as he had in the beginning – there was insolence and lust, that unconcealed taste for debasement combined with recognition of a match well met – and I knew this had been an inspired idea.

I placed the champagne glasses to the side.

'You're all oily,' he said, investigating under my robe.

'I've just had a massage.'

'It's going to get on my clothes.'

'Take them off then. Anyway, there's no one to notice, is there? It's not like she's doing your laundry, whatser-name?'

'You know her name, Amber.'

Undressed, he smelled different from usual. The scent

of his hair, his skin, his sweat, I was familiar with, but I caught also traces of female. I grasped a handful of his hair, turned him roughly to look me in the eye. 'You were with her this morning? You haven't even *showered?*'

'So what?'

It should have revolted me, it should have insulted me, but being with him like this, here in this secret den, had tipped me into some animal derangement and I liked it, I liked that he was dirty and used, that he pretended not to care. Because it was *my* name he spoke now. Soon he'd sacrifice all thoughts of *her*, just as I would all thoughts of clinically prescribed abstinence as I rang for vodka and more champagne. As promised, the order was sent up in the dumb waiter: no staff, no observers, no complicating third parties. We had complete privacy.

Naked, we wandered outside and filled the tub, lowered ourselves into the water and faced one another as if in ritual. The hot water released mists of steam into the winter air and I dipped lower and lower, up to my chin, scented bubbles popping in my eyes.

'I could get used to this,' Rob said. 'You clearly already have.'

'I love it,' I said. 'It's my natural habitat.'

He looked out at the treetops, the last vestiges of autumnal red and ochre touching the dusk sky. 'Which? The eye-wateringly expensive luxury or the wild woods?'

'Both, maybe.'

'Both definitely.' And he gazed at me in abject admiration, which was precisely my preference as gazes went – and a long time coming.

I didn't like to think how close I'd come to having lost it forever.

'You're unbelievable, do you know that?' he said. 'I honestly don't know how you get away with it. You're like my dream female of the species.'

'Only *like*?' But this was getting better by the syllable, and I could feel the euphoria radiating from me. How blissful it was to have him back, the old Rob, my kindred soul and sinner. 'You haven't been around much lately,' I said, careful not to make a question of it.

'Busy with work,' he said, shrugging. 'Some of us do have bills to pay, you know.'

He enjoyed the notion that I was wealthy and he struggling, but we both knew that the truth was he'd never suffered a moment's financial anxiety in his life. I alone understood what it was to have nothing, to look into the greedy, heartless future and have no idea how you were going to survive. In this crime of ours, the risk was all mine.

'Unless your husband wants to take care of mine as well . . . ?' he added, casually impudent.

'He'll pay this one,' I said. We'd drained our glasses, drinking fast, recklessly, and I poured more, plying him, plying us.

'You'll have to thank him for me. In your own special way, of course.'

And I knew he would want to know what that special way would be, for me to demonstrate on him. It was only then, you see, that I began to intuit that he was excited by

Jeremy's role in this; our relationship was more triangular than I'd believed. I had not told him about the misunderstanding with the texts, but I knew now that I would: I would save it for when I needed it.

He eyed me with his laziest smile. 'I'd love to know how it feels to do what you're doing.'

'Well, since you're doing exactly the same, I'm guessing it *feels* exactly the same.'

'I doubt it. You're the only one of us cheating on a legal mate.'

I spread out my arms and splayed my fingers over the soft bubbles, feeling that freeing weightless sensation of flotation. 'I agree it's not my finest hour, but I'm not sure it's the worst thing I've ever done to someone.'

'No?' His gaze settled brazenly on my nipples as they popped above the water line into the chill of December. 'Go on then, tell me your worst.'

I wondered which one to choose, frankly. Matt's face surfaced, and so did Phil's. But who was I kidding, the victims who mattered were those I'd never pictured, the wives and girlfriends (and, occasionally, children) whose feelings I'd never dignified with a thought, much less an action. 'OK, let's see ... I once slept with someone on his honeymoon.'

He whistled. 'I assume you don't mean your own?'

'No. On my own I only slept with the person I was supposed to sleep with. I have *some* standards.'

'So we're talking pre-Jeremy?'

'Of course, when I was still a bit wild.'

'A *bit* wild?' Rob smirked, delighted. 'Unlike now, eh? Because you're completely domesticated now, aren't you? Totally under the thumb.'

Under yours, I thought, closing my eyes to a psychedelic blaze of light and colour, for the combination of Rob and alcohol was the best high of my life, exhilarating, consciousness-expanding, addictive. And to open my eyes again and find him watching me, it was pure rapture. As we ogled each other across the surface of the water a forbidden thought came in an unstoppable explosion: *I love you.* Shocked enough for my face to redden, I extinguished the words before they could be recorded – or repeated.

And Rob, mercifully, noticed nothing. 'So this other bridegroom you seduced, didn't you feel guilty when you saw his new wife wandering about the hotel in an oblivious romantic haze?'

'I suppose I would have felt guilty if she'd known, but she didn't. She was having a facial at the time. It didn't affect her enjoyment of her honeymoon at all.'

He grinned. 'That's your defence, is it? Unless the victim discovers he or she has been wronged, then it isn't a crime?'

'No, it *is* a crime, it just doesn't hurt anybody. I think a lot of people operate that way. Little white lies, big white lies: in the end, they're all the same colour. Blurting the truth just to relieve your own guilt, I think that can do more harm than good.'

Fascinated, Rob slid towards me, his voice low and conspiratorial, even though we were completely alone.

'That's the classic justification of the deceiver, do you realize that?' Under the water his fingers were between my legs. 'Making yourself feel like a hero by telling yourself you're doing the right thing by being discreet.'

'Discretion *is* a good thing,' I said.

'No, a good thing is to not commit the deception in the first place. They call it self-control, Mrs Fraser.'

'Oh, self-control.' I gasped. 'You'd know all about that, wouldn't you?'

After he'd shown me what he knew, right there in the tub, we moved back indoors, closed up the cabin to the thick and silent wood and climbed into bed. Maybe it was the setting, as remote and romantic as you could wish for, with the warm sweet scent of wood burner, the flickering candlelight reflected on every polished surface, or maybe it was that leaked sentiment I hadn't *quite* managed to banish, but I felt very close to him, as close as I ever had with Jeremy. To me it was not only a return to old intimacy but also a progression of it; in spite of circumstances that pointed to the very opposite, it felt like the very wedding night for which I'd beautified myself.

Our sweet nothings, though, were rather different from those of newlyweds, as you might imagine.

'Your turn now,' I said. 'Come on, tell me your worst crime.'

'That's easy,' Rob said. '*This.*'

'This doesn't count, I already know about your misdeeds with *me*. Tell me something else.' In retrospect, I think I was daring him to say he loved me, that his infraction concerned the violation of my original rules. I think

I was hoping that if *he* said it then I could say it too and with its release everything might change once more.

Our faces were pressed together and I was aware of an intake of breath, a decision being made; I felt the feeling of free fall as my heart opened, ready to receive.

Then he said, 'Why don't I tell you the worst thing I've been *accused* of doing?'

'OK.' Wrong-footed, I adjusted.

'I was once accused of rape,' he said.

Now it was I who sucked in my breath, holding it painfully in my lungs until I feared they might rupture. I'd hoped for love and I'd got . . .

'*Rape?*'

As I drew back, I saw in the candlelight that his eyes had darkened. He was not looking at me; his focal point was a different time and place, a different woman.

'That's what I said. A whole different league from lying to your husband, isn't it?'

'But you didn't do it?'

He recoiled. 'Of course I didn't. Do you even need to ask?'

I frowned, but gently. 'I'd be crazy not to.'

'It was a malicious allegation,' he said grimly.

'Who by?'

'An ex-girlfriend. At university.'

I could feel his pulse quickening and sense his skin firing as he related the details, the first time I'd ever known him to become angry. He'd ended their relationship when he'd met someone else, he said, she'd sworn revenge, and the next thing he knew the police had turned up at his door and were taking him into custody. Just as his parents were arranging legal representation, their family's harmony devastated overnight, the claim had been withdrawn.

'That must have been horrendous,' I said.

'To put it mildly.'

I placed my fingertips at the pulse in his neck, felt its livid beat. 'Thank God it didn't go anywhere. There can't have been any physical evidence, presumably? You can tell if there's been force, right? Bruising, that kind of thing.'

'I suppose she could have done that to herself if she wanted,' Rob said, and I sensed the power she still had over him; it was quite clear that, unknown to me till now, this girl had been — and remained — his Achilles heel. 'But she admitted she'd made it up. I think she got scared when the police started interviewing our friends and she knew she might have to be cross-examined in court, which is frightening enough if you're telling the truth. I was lucky, though, in the end. Some people would go through with the false claim rather than admit they lied. As it was, she ended up being cautioned.'

'Wow.' Between us the air felt thin and deoxygenated, burned hotter than five minutes ago. 'You hear of women doing that, but why? I know you said revenge, but if what she actually wanted was to get you back, then it's a terrible tactic.' I didn't add that all this girl had needed was a hotel room, an oiled body, an insistence on victory. 'Who would forgive something like that?' I asked. 'You'd never trust her again.'

'It's not a rational strategy. It's spite and cruelty and

they're not rational things. Lashing out when you're wounded, it's a kind of self-preservation.' His voice was hard, splintering the tender silence of the cabin. 'Accuse someone you know of rape or abuse and it's your word against theirs. It's one of the best ways to destroy an innocent person's life. People think there's no smoke without fire. Often there isn't.'

I considered this. 'Maybe when you make an accusation like that you start to believe it yourself.'

Rob narrowed his eyes, the lashes almost meeting, and yet the intensity was undimmed. 'I imagine you do. Which makes it even worse, because if *you* believe it you're so much more likely to be able to convince others.'

'Were you thrown out of college?'

'I was suspended for those few weeks, but reinstated as soon as I was in the clear. She decided to transfer to another university for her final year.'

'And there's no police record? It didn't affect your finding work or anything like that?'

'No.'

I suppose I could have felt threatened, up in an isolated tree house with a man who'd once been accused of rape, but for someone who'd often made poor choices in her men I'd always had keen instincts about my own safety – and I knew I was safe with him. Not only did I believe he was telling the truth, but I was also moved by it, by his unprecedented display of vulnerability, which may sound distasteful given the subject matter, yet – I feel the need to repeat this – I was utterly convinced of his honesty. He was hardly a noble man, but he was certainly not a vicious one. As far as I was concerned, he was no more capable of rape than Jeremy was.

A thought occurred, a loose end that needed tying: 'She's not that girl who turned up at Kenny and Joanne's? The one who got upset and left?'

'What on earth makes you think that?'

Because there'd been that implication of brutality, of a full story best left untold. 'It's just that there was obviously history between you,' I said evenly.

'I told you,' he said, irritated, 'she was just a one-night thing from a few years ago. She was embarrassed to see me, I think, not very good at forgiving and forgetting.'

'Right.' I burrowed into him, hoping that my demonstration of unconstrained trust might be a source of comfort to him. 'After this college girl, it must have been a while before you could get close to someone again?'

Did he get close? I thought. Was this the reason for his keeping women at arm's length, for his hot and cold handling of them, for his not feeling towards Jeremy the jealousy I had felt towards Pippa?

'I suppose it was,' he said, finally. 'But it's a long time ago now, and since then I've been a lot clearer about asking.'

'Asking? You mean you ask permission?'

'Every girl, every time.'

'What do you say, exactly?'

'I don't know. "Do you want it?" Something like that.'

'Even if it's someone you've been seeing for a while?'

'*Especially* if it is,' Rob said. 'Given the history.'

'So you'll still say, every time, "Do you want it?"'

'Or words to that effect. It's not that hard to work into the scenario.'

I was fascinated by the idea of formally asking permission to take someone to bed. 'And when you ask, do you record the "yes"?' I was relaxing into our more usual playful repartee, but he resisted the gear change, answering me quite curtly.

'No, that wouldn't be permissible in court – unless I get her consent for the recording, as well. Let's not joke about this, Amber. I hate being thought of as a rapist, however falsely, however briefly.'

'No one thinks that,' I assured him. 'I'm sure no one ever did. You need to forget it ever happened.'

'I thought I had. Until your stupid game.'

'Hey, don't be cross with me.' I pressed against him, pliant, ingratiating. 'Or only a little bit, anyway.'

'A little bit?' He began caressing me with the backs of his fingers, a feather-light skimming contact that produced an unbearable sensation just short of tickling, but every time I shifted from them, the fingers tracked me.

'You don't ask *me* every time,' I pointed out.

'Because you're different. You're exempt. You've never felt a split second of uncertainty in your life.'

'Haven't I?' Not the uncertainty *he* meant, no.

His fingers continued to toy with me in their slow, indifferent way, making my breath come faster, my thoughts draw closer to my tongue. But even as I missed my chance I knew I had always been going to miss it; some unnameable emotion held me from exposing myself, something between self-pity and melancholy. Did he *really* not feel an inkling of what I did that night? This simulation of the connection between a man and a woman when they have forsaken all others – this counterfeit that was so convincing it was impossible to tell it from the original? Who but true soulmates exchanged confidences like ours?

'Ask me anyway,' I said, at last. 'Ask me if I want it.'

And so he did ask me, to his credit waiting for me to say yes before he began. 'Do you remember this from before, Amber?' he murmured, and kept on murmuring that night. 'Do you remember?'

'I remember,' I lied.

In the morning, breakfast was delivered by dumb waiter, the empty bottles and other detritus of our night's debauchery dispatched by the same method. We lounged in front of the polished picture window, drank coffee, picked at the papers. Sunlight filtered through the leaves, patterning Rob's torso as if with a giant stencil. I sat in the shade, sated and content.

'You have an uncharacteristically romantic expression on your face,' he said. After last night's intensities, he was back to his wry best, it seemed. I wondered if he regretted his confession. 'Don't forget your rules,' he added. 'No love.'

Taken off guard, I impressed myself by not even flinching. An expectant moment passed between us that I told myself meant nothing, gave nothing away. 'Don't flatter yourself,' I told him.

Looking back, I think we should have ended it then, that morning, when we were up in the tree house in that secret suite, immune from earthly promises. When we were as high as we were ever going to go.

For there was only one way to go now.

Chapter 21

Christy, August 2013

'You've got one as well,' Christy said.

It was the first thing her eye went to when she stepped into the room, a small square space with painted panelling and a shuttered sash overlooking the side return.

'My sanctuary,' Liz had said, explaining that it was the only downstairs territory her sons had not 'marked'. Indeed, there was an air of feminine defiance about its contents, all pink glass bowls and decorative silver knick-knacks. On a vintage sideboard, next to a jug of sweet-smelling stocks, stood the hourglass bottle.

'What, the room scent? Pretty, isn't it?' Liz said, sipping her Lady Grey. She'd served the tea in bone china painted with polka dots and daisies, the first time Christy had used a cup and saucer in about a decade. Having seated her guest on a rose-coloured velvet chaise longue under the window, Liz perched on an adjacent armchair upholstered in a gold fabric printed with butterflies and birds. Of the Lime Park Road women, she was the first to have returned from her August break. Lacking a husband and therefore the holiday home that apparently came with one, she had instead taken the boys to her parents' place in Cheshire, where they remained to give her 'a few days' grace', as she put it.

'Caroline has one,' Christy said, tracing the curved glass with her fingers, 'and I remember seeing one in Felicity's flat before she moved.'

'I should think the whole street has one,' Liz said. 'Amber gave us them. It was her signature gift when she came over for dinner or, I imagine in the case of Felicity, when she wanted to say sorry for the building noise. You can only get them from Liberty, apparently.'

Of course Amber Fraser would have a signature gift that you could only get from Liberty. Christy could not imagine what *hers* was: supermarket tulips, perhaps, the Sainsbury's stickers removed in an attempt to make them look like she'd bought them from the florist on the Parade; or some sort of biscuit offered less out of consideration for her hostess than for herself (unless their children had baked, the women of Lime Park Road *never* offered sweet treats).

'She had a few things she liked to give. There was a particular candle, as well – amber-scented, of course – and a little book from the fifties, I've got it somewhere . . .' Liz put down her cup and extracted from the bookshelf a small pink hardback with curved corners; the title, in silver lettering, was *The Art of Being a Well Dressed Wife*. 'Of course, I told her that as far as *that* was concerned it was a case of closing the stable doors after the horse had bolted, but she said to me, "No, Liz. We're thinking ahead."' Liz chuckled. 'We used to call her little gifts "Amberbilia".'

Christy thought of her own Amberbilia, not just the bangle and the key ring and the blue Moroccan bowl, but also the sun-loungers and other objects she'd liberated from the garden shed: a French grey enamel watering can that now took pride of place in the Davenports' hallway; a pale green linen sunhat that Christy had taken to wearing in the garden.

'She was obviously very generous,' she said.

'Oh, she was. I guess it helps to have plenty of cash. But then again I've known wealthy people who are shockingly tight-fisted – my ex-husband, for one.'

Remembering Liz's tears at the book group, Christy did not pursue this. Besides, she had not finished with their previous subject. 'The way Caroline talks about Amber, it's like she was some sort of divine being.'

Liz smiled. 'She certainly had her worshippers. I was happy to be one myself, in fact.'

Christy waited for the customary gush of compliments, the established phrases of glorification, but instead Liz narrowed her gaze with revisionist care: 'You know, I always thought there was something not quite right about Amber, charismatic though she was.'

Christy's eyes flew open in astonishment. 'How do you mean?'

'Well, she had this recklessness about her. She kept it under control of course, everyone took it to be nothing more than a delightful free spirit, but I sensed it sometimes and it was almost a self-destructive force.'

'Caroline said she had a bad-girl past,' said Christy, by nature wary of those who spoke of sensing others' forces.

'Yes, she told us a bit about that. She'd done a lot of drugs. She still drank, but that's pretty much compulsory on this street. She was certainly not the worst on that score.'

Christy thought briefly of Joe, of the wine that was demanded almost faster than it could be supplied.

'Jeremy was very good for her,' Liz continued. 'She'd made an excellent choice there. In other hands, she might have missed her chance for rehabilitation.'

Drugs, self-destructive, rehabilitation: these were not terms Christy had heard applied to Amber Fraser before.

But Liz's thoughts had moved on. 'You know, I'm going back to work when the school term starts. With Rupert going into Reception, it's the right time.' She placed her polka-dot cup aside, as if formally renouncing such domestic baubles.

'What will you be doing?' asked Christy.

'I used to be a management consultant,' Liz said, to Christy's surprise. (Somehow, she had expected holistic ther- apy or soap-making.) 'But I need flexible hours now, so I've taken a part-time role in the finance department at the coun- cil. I'll be earning about a tenth of my salary before I had the boys. Seriously, Christy, take my advice and make as much money as you can before you start a family.'

'I'll try.' Christy thought of the mounting number of bank statements in which the 'Income' column failed to contain a single penny's contribution from her.

'You're covered in dog hair,' Liz exclaimed as her guest stood to leave, and she used her hand briskly to dust the back of Christy's trousers as if she were a child.

'You don't have a dog,' Christy said stupidly.

'I know, but I always invite the neighbours' in, and even

the dogs that aren't supposed to moult still do, don't you find?'

Dogs: another Lime Park specialism in which Christy found herself utterly ignorant. She had no idea which were moulters and which not, let alone which defied the conventions of their breed. It amused her to think of some Lime Park mutt luxuriating in the very sanctuary where Liz's own sons were forbidden to tread.

As she departed, Liz made her farewells with a certain remorse. 'What I said about Amber, I don't want you to think that I was in any way suggesting that she –' Inevitably, she stopped herself before the 'suggestion' could be stated. 'Oh, it doesn't matter,' she said in resignation. 'She's gone now.'

'Gone but not forgotten,' Christy joked.

'Oh, never that,' said Liz.

How peculiar it was to be back in the classroom, that same scuffed, scruffy zone of juvenile odours and images, its staff the all-too-familiar double-edged symbols of safety and ennui. The children, seated in groups of four or five, seemed as easy to label as if they had badges pinned on their pullovers: the restless one who wouldn't be able to hold down a job; the evasive one who wouldn't be able to *get* a job; the pretty one who would breed early; the watchful one who'd go far . . . and so on.

Which had she been? Christy wondered. She liked to think she'd been the watchful one who'd go far, but that looked ambitious at this moment in time. A mile and a half east, that was how far she'd gone of late, to the

borders of Lime Park and its more downmarket neighbour, where the junior school that wasn't Lime Park
Primary was situated. Lime Park Primary, it transpired,
had an outstanding rating and more than its share of volunteers among the well-educated community, including
her neighbours and fellow book group members Joanne
and Sophie. St Luke's was not so well supplied, its rating
the rather less desirable 'requires improvement'.

'Are you sure you should be influencing young minds?'
Joe had teased that morning. 'You are a bit of a conspiracy theorist these days.'

'Oh, shut up and go to work,' she'd said, markedly better humoured now that she had a destination of her own,
a role. And better rested, too, unlike Joe, who was now
working so late she no longer heard his taxi pull up in the
dead of night, only to have him complain in the morning
that he hadn't slept a wink. What was the point in dropping off, he said, when he was only going to have to be
awake again in an hour or two? It was as if their long
weekend by the sea had never happened or, worse, had
been counterproductive, its contentments serving only to
accentuate the woes he'd met on his return.

The literacy programme co-ordinator had asked only
for a commitment till half-term and Christy had given this
willingly, fairly certain that no fairy godmother would be
appearing with her magic wand any time sooner than that.
Her only interview the previous month had gone encour-
agingly, only for the role to have been eliminated before
any offer could be made, and there had not been, as yet,
the stampede she'd been promised the moment August

gave way to September, and she knew she had to ease her anxiety down a gear. Yes, she and Joe had less cash at their disposal than at any time before, but they were not – yet – homeless. They'd survived for nearly six months on their tightrope; they could survive a couple more.

'Right, let's start,' she told her first designated child, Sam (the restless one), who was nervous of meeting her eye. They were alone at a desk in the corridor outside the classroom, all other spaces in the school fully occupied. 'Do you like reading?'

'Not really.' Sam beheld the page in front of him as if it were an open fire that would singe his eyelashes if he leaned too close.

'But do you like stories?'

'I don't know.' He looked suspicious of a trap: was she going to reveal that 'story' was another way of saying Spelling Test?

'Stories can be in a book, a film, a play, even a song,' said Christy. 'People tell them to each other all the time. I bet your mum tells you stories about things her friends have done.'

'She talks about people behind their backs,' Sam said hopefully.

Christy giggled. 'Well, that's a kind of story. I'm sure you *do* like them. So how about I start and then you join in when the action gets going?'

A cautious nod.

Guided reading: it was simple enough. (Guided *living*, that was what adults needed.) The child read aloud and she corrected any mistakes, noting difficult words in a little book and trying to get a discussion going about characters and plot. She'd been pleased to be allocated older children, Year 5, nine- and ten-years-olds, rather than the very young ones who stirred the reproductive urge in her most strongly.

'Brilliant,' she told Sam, at the close of the chapter. 'You're going to be the best reader in the class soon! Who's your favourite character so far?'

'I like the yak,' he said shyly.

'What would you name him if you were the author?'

'Jack,' he said at once, 'Jack the Yak,' and they were still laughing when the teacher came out with the next pupil.

'Have you worked with children before?' Mrs Spencer asked her at the end of the morning. 'You're very enthusiastic, exactly what we need.'

Christy waited for the inevitable question of whether she had a family of her own, fearing what she might hear herself divulge in the sheer relief of having been useful when she had not been useful in so long. He wanted a baby when I didn't, and now he doesn't I do, and we never see each other because he works so late, and anyway we seem to be on the verge of bankruptcy so the last thing we need is another mouth to feed, perhaps? But Mrs Spencer's attention was seized by an outbreak of cries in the corner of the classroom – 'Amy's crying!' 'Jess won't be her partner even though she promised!' – and she went off to investigate before Christy had the chance to embarrass herself.

As she left the premises, she felt the opposite of embarrassment, she felt an emotion she had sorely missed these last months: pride.

*

So filled was she with a sense of reward that by the time she reached Lime Park Road she'd fantasized herself through teacher training and up the career ladder to Secretary of State for Education. How susceptible she was these days to wild dreams, and lengthy ones too, inviting them to fill whatever time she had to spare (which was plenty); she supposed their false pleasures replaced the smaller exhilarations of day-to-day accomplishment you had at work.

Whatever their purpose, this one filled her with a euphoria so overpowering it caused her to forget everything she thought she knew about Lime Park Road and accept an invitation to have a coffee with Rob Whalen. Or – it would require some reflection that evening to be clear on this – *might she have invited herself?* Deep in that ecstatic reverie, when she'd seen him at his window, hand raised in acknowledgement, had she not reacted mistakenly, as if he'd gestured for her to come up, pacing to the door and ringing his bell, her mouth hovering over the intercom in readiness to announce her name? This must be how it felt to be dosed up on happy pills, she thought; to be emboldened, uninhibited, to misread signs in *favour* of your own popularity and desirability. Was this how it felt to be one of the Amber Frasers of the world? Well, if so it was marvellous.

Rob's voice came promptly down the line: 'Yep?'

'It's Christy. Can I come up?'

He buzzed her in and she bounced noisily up the stairs. 'I thought I'd drop by and tell you how my first session at the school went,' she blurted, even as the door was opening. 'But only if you're not in the middle of something.'

Surprised, but commendably quick to adapt, Rob ushered her in. 'No, I'm interested to hear,' he said, and he led her into his living room, returning to close the door, which in her haste she had left wide open.

'Please, sit.'

The flat was more recognizably the pair to number 40 than Steph's and Felix's, the proportions and features of the living room – which doubled as an office, judging by the desk of disarrayed documents and electronics – identical to those in her abandoned master bedroom. It struck her that getting from her side of the wall to his, from scourge to casual caller, was a journey far more incredible than any daydreamed career rise.

'I was just making coffee,' Rob said. 'Want one?'

As she watched him operate a gleaming red machine, she wondered what was different about him and decided it was that he looked *clean*. Though dressed in his customary slovenly casual, he had just showered and had swept his damp hair from his forehead, exposing more skin than usual and making the planes of his face clearer. He *was* good-looking: at last she could see it.

Shortly, she received a richly aromatic espresso and did not dare insult its purity by requesting milk. She felt herself smiling foolishly at him as he settled in a chair in the window that was uncomfortably similar to her own stake-out seat, though this one was turned inward, his legs stretched out towards her own spot on the sofa.

'So which school have you been allocated?' he asked. His mien was just as it had been in Felix's and Steph's flat, when he'd said, *Sounds like a good move, Christy* (tragic that

324

she remembered the exact words). So it hadn't been an act for the benefit of the others, he had changed his position about her; for whatever reason, he'd decided now that he could trust her.

'St Luke's,' she said.

'St Luke's?' He paused, something of his old darkness revisiting his expression, before his face cleared. 'It didn't do very well in the latest round of inspections, I'm afraid. It's all about staff morale, you know. The contrast with the Lime Park Primary experience is iniquitous.'

'How do you mean?'

'It's a vicious circle. Families on roads like this – including Steph and Felix when the time comes – will do everything in their power to avoid sending their children there, and yet a handful like theirs at St Luke's is all it would take to make the difference.'

As he continued, evidently well versed in the assets and liabilities of her new workplace, he spoke so passionately that Christy decided that if she had a child she would pledge then and there to send it to St Luke's. What am I doing? she thought, as he quoted figures to do with Ofsted. Am I really sitting here offering up a child who doesn't yet exist as a sacrifice to a man I distrusted on sight? The caffeine was reviving her, and she had a sudden unsettling sense of the exoticism of being alone with him, the sheer bizarreness of it.

'You look tired,' he said, surprising her with the note of kindness in his voice. 'Children are harder work than you'd think. I'd far rather write about teachers than be one.'

'Who do you write for?' she asked, as if she had not

already scrutinized samples of his work online, and when he mentioned a new regular column he was writing for a news site she promised she would read it. 'I'll look it up when I get home. Are you Rob or Robert?'

'Actually, I'm writing this under a different name,' Rob said, freely giving her the pseudonym.

'Why's that?'

'Oh, you know, a fresh voice. Different angle. It's common practice.' He glanced at the wall clock above his desk, drained his coffee.

'Just say if you need to get on with it,' Christy said, though he was not exactly the type to suffer in silence.

'No, I'm done for the day, but I am expecting my girlfriend any minute.'

'Oh yes. Pippa, isn't it?'

'You've met her?' Rob said, surprised. 'She didn't mention that.'

'We haven't been introduced, but Caroline told me her name.'

'Caroline Sellers?' All of a sudden the storm cloud was above his head again and Christy understood she'd made a serious misstep in this conversation. 'What else did she tell you?' he growled.

'Nothing,' she said mildly. 'If anything, she's been very secretive about you.'

'I doubt that.' Clearly struggling to control himself, Rob now spoke in the low deliberate tone of someone who'd been trained in anger management: 'I think you'd better tell me *exactly* what Caroline Sellers has been saying to you.'

'Nothing,' Christy insisted. 'Really.'

He eyed her very intently, somehow creating the illusion that he'd moved physically closer, though she was fairly certain he had not. 'But you just said she told you Pippa's name?'

'Yes, but what's the harm in that? It's just a name.'

'Oh, believe me, there's plenty of harm if she's been spreading lies.'

Christy frowned. 'Because she's *not* your girlfriend? Is that what you mean?' She felt about fourteen saying this, but there was nothing teenage about the way Rob glared at her, the stark animosity of it. He was a climate in himself, she thought; he could foster growth or cause shrinkage and there was nothing you could do about it.

'Don't believe what she tells you just because she believes it: *that's* what I'm saying.'

'Are we still talking about Pippa?' Christy said. 'I'm genuinely confused here.'

He gave a long sigh, long enough to become a groan, and she could tell he wished this little social call of hers had never taken place, was cursing himself for having caught her eye from his window. 'No, we are not,' he said.

'Who then?' And she recalled that snarled accusation in the park café, *I saw you with her friend,* his dismissal of her assumption that he was referring to Felicity. Not *her* friend then, but someone else's. The young mother at the door, perhaps, Imogen. 'Is this something to do with Amber Fraser?' she said.

Rob became supremely still then, his expression closed, mouth taut, but the lack of rebuttal was a confirmation in itself.

'Does Caroline . . . ?' Christy faltered. She had been cautioned plenty of times, she knew she should not poke an animal like this with a stick, and, besides, why would someone repeat a falsehood about themselves when they were indisposed even to share the truth, but she had lost her mind that afternoon and in spite of all the warnings she went ahead: 'Does Caroline think something was going on between you? You know . . . ?'

Rob exhaled very slowly, a smoker expelling a long plume of grey and watching it hang in the air. 'I told you before, I don't like to be the object of gossip, and if you want us to get on you'll have to accept that. It's non-negotiable.'

It surprised Christy how badly she wanted to be on better terms with him. Of course a part of it was simply to be rid once and for all of that fear she'd developed that he was in some form or another dangerous, but a different – newer – part of it was because he had a magnetism that drew her, just as it plainly had Steph, Felix and Joe before her. She wanted to be liked by him. 'OK,' she said. 'I accept it.'

'That's Amber's bracelet you're wearing, isn't it?' He changed the subject abruptly, causing her to flush guiltily.

'Yes, at least I think it is. I found it behind the bath. I know I ought to return it, but I don't have a new address for her.' Another convenient fudging of the truth: not only did she have an established route to the Frasers via the couples' respective solicitors, but she also had the option of posting the item to Jeremy Fraser's office. (Even if it did not immediately reach his hands, at least it left hers.) She could not begin to explain to Rob that she kept the bangle – kept on wearing it – out of some growing sense of connection to Amber Fraser. It was almost an act of protection, though what it was she was protecting she did not know.

'I worry it might have sentimental value,' she added.

Rob's expression grew grim. 'Oh, there's no fear of that. She's not the sentimental type. You can take my word for it.'

At the sound of the doorbell, Christy rose gratefully to her feet. 'Well, thank you for the coffee and the advice.'

'You're very welcome.'

On the landing she passed Pippa, a fragrant blonde blur, and caught the astonishment in the other woman's face at the sight of her departing Rob's flat.

'Hi you,' Rob said behind her, and Christy was staggered by the change in his voice when he spoke to someone he desired. Rough-grained and seductive, it raised the hairs on her arms.

'Hi you,' Pippa said, and then the door closed on the two of them.

Chapter 22

Amber, 2012

Christmas was approaching, that celebrator of the domestic status quo, savage separator of adulterous lovers, and Rob and I made the most of each other in the weeks that preceded the break.

Appetites rekindled since our night in the tree house, we had, it seemed, entered a new phase sexually. I wasn't sure if it was conscious or not, but I knew now to use his taste for risk to keep him interested. All at once it was clear that the idea of exposure to either of our partners aroused him. He began to make direct comparisons between Pippa and me – or maybe it was I who made them; I'd grown crass, desperate (that word again), no longer content to pretend she did not exist but determined to cast her in a poorer light than my own.

'Does she let you do this?' I'd ask, where once I'd been satisfied with simply doing it.

'"Let"?' Rob questioned. 'You make it sound as if I'm harassing her, wearing her down with my depraved demands.'

Now that I knew his history I was able to notice his sensitivity to the language of sex.

'All right, I'll rephrase: is she as bad as me?'

'Oh, I don't suppose I've scratched the surface of *you* yet,' he said with that trademark air of challenge, and it delighted me to hear the inference that we had a further stretch of intimacy ahead of us.

Deceiving Jeremy appeared to be at the heart of his enjoyment (though, please believe me, not mine): he was obsessed with my telling – and retelling – of the incident involving the mistaken texts, encouraging me to wear the same clothing I'd worn that evening, the same dress and make-up. I created other fantasies for him too, talked of us meeting at night in the park, letting ourselves in and out through my garden gate, making love in the long grass. It was far too risky to execute (not to mention too damp), but he was excited by my descriptions of it.

Then, one afternoon just before Christmas, with my holiday with Jeremy imminent, I was insane enough to act on a risk that *could* be undertaken.

Jeremy had been feeling run-down, partly from over-working and partly from his stewardship of our fertility quest. We were by then almost three months into our six-month extension and, a born problem-solver, he had forged a path through it by following to the letter the clinic's programme for optimizing fertility (since when were words like 'programme' and 'optimize' supposed to be applied to sex?). Trying had been honed; now we made love only during the fertile window ('fertile window'?).

No further attempts had been made to surprise me.

He was told by the GP he had flu; he needed to stay in bed for at least a week and allow himself to be looked after by me. Mindful of the forthcoming holiday, he monitored his email from his pillows and even croaked his way through a few conference calls, summoning me frequently to bring the things he was too weak to fetch.

By the end of the first week, I was suffering from cabin fever. Being in the house was not the problem; not being able to slip next door *was*. Not usually in my own bedroom during the day, I was aware for the first time of Rob's voice as he spoke on the phone in his living room next door, the disembodied laughter in the evening that signalled a visit by *her*. For she was resilient, Pippa, just like the rest of us, just as I had been with boyfriends of old, ignoring the signs, hoping her instincts were wrong, convincing herself a leopard could change its spots if it only fell into the hands of the right zookeeper. I imagined her discussing the situation with her girlfriends, asking her Imogen and her Helena if they thought she was wasting her time with him. I wouldn't have known myself how to counsel her. Run for your life or play the long game? Neither struck me as being less effective strategies than the other. Or less doomed.

But she'd get no advice from me.

'Do you mind if I go for a quick run?' I said to Jeremy one afternoon. 'I won't leave you on your own for long.'

'Of course not, you don't have to watch over me every moment of the day, darling, I'm not in intensive care. I'm going to sleep now, anyway.'

I brought up some soup for him and set up the podcast he wanted, before changing into my running gear. Then I texted Rob.

'Are you in?'

'Yes. Still playing Florence Nightingale?'

'She's on her lunch break. Can I come?'

'You tell me.'

I slipped through the gap in the hedge and made the briefest of contacts with his doorbell before being buzzed in. Felicity was at home; I could hear her footsteps behind her door as she pottered from room to room.

Upstairs, I held a finger to his lips and explained in an undertone that Jeremy was resting next door.

Rob whistled softly. 'He's actually in the house? I thought he must have gone out. You are unbelievable.'

He began pulling me towards the living room. I resisted, motioning instead to the bedroom, but he was stronger and manhandled me with ease in the direction he preferred.

'He's in bed, Rob, right there!' I whispered, pointing at the dividing wall. How many layers of bricks between us? One? Two? Rob's desk stood against the wall that had the headboard of our bed on the other side. I could hear very faintly the podcast playing by Jeremy's pillow. 'Are you mad?'

'*I'm* mad?' Even as he moved to the windows to lower the blinds, he did not release me, and I bowed my head for fear of idle eyes across the road. 'It's here or nowhere, Amber Baby.' How I regretted telling him that nickname; he used it so habitually, I feared he might let it slip in a group situation. 'Take it or leave it,' he added.

But it was not possible for me to leave it, as he clearly

appreciated. 'All right, but complete silence,' I hissed, allowing him to lower me onto the rug and lay me next to him.

'Trappist sex? There's no way in a million years you'll manage that . . .' And, tormentor that he was, he set about trying to make me squeal, restraining my hands so I could neither touch him nor prevent him from touching me, my body at his mercy as he removed my clothes with agonizing slowness, groping and stroking and grazing my body with his touch before drawing away for seconds at a time to enjoy the frustration in my face, causing me to beg in whispers that got more and more urgent. Only when I made some animal noise of distress did he put me out of my misery, his hand over my mouth to stop my moans from escaping. My newly freed hands scratched at the skin of his back to punish him (explain *that* to Pippa, I thought) and through half-closed eyes I watched the muscles in his neck strain violently under the skin, his teeth bite his lower lip to keep himself from crying out.

Ten minutes later I stood in the doorway of our bedroom, sweaty and hot-faced. 'Jeremy, you haven't touched your soup!'

His smile was weak and guilty. 'I dozed off, sorry. I'm not hungry, anyway. I feel sick and my throat hurts.'

'You poor bear.' I approached him, trying not to be repelled by the stale odour of the flu patient and yet grateful for it since it masked my own altered smell. 'Just keep sipping your water so you don't get dehydrated. I'm hopping in the shower and then I'll come and lie in bed with you for a bit.'

'That would be nice.'

I know it was cruel. I want to be clear that I didn't feel good about this; kicking a man when he's down gave me no thrill. But it had pleased Rob, and such were my skewed priorities by then that pleasing Rob mattered more than protecting Jeremy.

As hot water rained down on me, blinding my eyes and clogging my nose and ears, I shivered at the memory of the glimmer in his gaze as I'd left his flat, the glimmer that spoke of satisfaction in another boundary broken, a new experience gained.

Something dark and daring he could not get from Pippa.

Both parties left town for New Year, Jeremy and I to Jamaica, Rob to Morocco with a group of friends. By sheer and necessary bloody-mindedness, I succeeded in – mostly – devoting my thoughts to the man I was with, only once allowing myself to think of Rob when my husband was making love to me. I have to admit, it was hardly a challenge to feel happy in that beachside hotel: sworn enemies could have lost their hearts in our little horseshoe cove, the sand sugar soft and sheltered by tropical palms, the air salty-sweet and gentle as baby's breath. Jeremy called it a second honeymoon, and there were sun-drenched pockets of each day when I could delude myself into agreeing. I even convinced him to relax the rules about alcohol ('I bet Mr Atherton was drunk when he conceived *his* children'), which helped the time sail when it might otherwise have run aground.

We both made a disciplined effort not to talk about our troubles conceiving, doing so only in the most general terms.

'You know, I wouldn't mind if it was just us,' he said, as we rocked together in a hammock on our veranda at the edge of the sand, bodies as relaxed as could be without losing consciousness. Just feet away, the sea murmured its consolations.

I smiled. 'Nor would I if it were like this all the time, together on holiday, but back home I'm on my own all day long.'

'I didn't realize you felt lonely. What about your chums? Caroline and Rob?'

We were not normally in such close proximity when my lover's name was spoken between us and I prayed there'd be no detectable drumming of pulse or flushing of skin.

'They're great,' I said, sighing. 'I'd see them every day if they'd let me, but they've both got work. Rob with his writing and Caroline with the kids.'

'What about Liz and the other stay-at-homes?'

'That's just it, it turns out they never *are* at home, at least not during the day. They're all too busy chauffeuring the younger kids to activities or doing volunteer stuff. Sophie helps out at the school and Joanne walks the dog for hours on end. Liz is talking about going back to work next year when Rupert starts school. Seriously, I'm the only layabout on the street.'

'Oh dear, that's no fun.' Only Jeremy could console me for being bone idle. With his free hand he stroked my hair from my forehead, bringing his arm to rest on my chest;

the muscle on the back of his hand was slack, I saw, the skin aged and paper-dry after a few days in the sun. 'Then what about starting a business? Interiors, maybe? You did a great job with the house.'

'Hetty did,' I corrected him. 'All I did was encourage her to spend our money.'

'Well, I suppose that could be considered a valuable skill in a recession.'

'Are we *still* in a recession? I would have thought that had ended by now.'

Jeremy kissed my pretty little head. 'Have you thought about some sort of voluntary job? Just short term, while you're at a loose end? One or two afternoons a week?'

Noting with shame that this was my standard weekly commitment to infidelity, I had to agree there was an urgent need for the broadening of my horizons. 'I'll think about it,' I said, closing my eyes for another snooze.

But no sooner had the plane touched down at Gatwick than such thoughts had evaporated – all thoughts, in fact, but those of Rob and when I would next see him. As our taxi turned into the street, my eyes were as keen to find his window as they were my own front door. Perversely, I now associated my new home not with the man I shared it with but with the one who lived next door. I was frantic to see him again, terrified to find I'd been shut out as I had in that hellish period in the autumn. Try as I might to deny those words I had thought that night in the tree house, they *had* been thought, and I was fooling myself if I believed I had the strength to end our affair now.

To my satisfaction, Rob responded eagerly to my text

and a liaison was arranged for the first day that Jeremy was back in the office.

'I missed you,' I told him. 'Did you miss me?' Where once such words had had purely sexual import, now I could not deny that they meant something deeper. *I needed you*, I might have said. *Did you need me?*

'Of course I did.' Rob watched, riveted, as I peeled away my winter layers to reveal the indulgently costly underwear I'd bought that morning for our reunion. His fingers were on the lacy bra, cut low at the nipple, the fabric straining. 'Have you put on weight?'

'A couple of pounds, yes. I'm on an overeating regime, doctor's orders. He said I shouldn't get too thin in case it starts to affect fertility levels. I ate like a pig in Jamaica, it was bliss.'

'You look incredible. Keep it on.'

'The weight or the bra?'

'Both.'

Later, he surprised me. 'I know we said no gifts, but I saw this in Marrakech.' He passed me a small paper bag, the kind that might contain lollipops from the newsagent. 'I thought it would be easy enough to assimilate into your vast collection without the silver fox noticing.'

It was beautiful, his gift: a fine silver bangle with a clasp made of two interlocking pieces of amber. You and me, I thought, admiring their precise alignment.

'You have a good eye,' I told him as he fastened it for me. I was utterly elated. Here, finally, was proof that he thought of me when we were apart, that there were moments other than those directly preceding ejaculation when he was willing to admit that he'd missed me.

'I wonder if it's a bit delicate now I see it on?' He kissed the heel of my hand. 'A cuff would suit you better . . .' And his lips moved to the inside of my wrist, breaking contact only when he felt my pulse start to quicken.

As I say, utterly elated.

But using his bathroom before departure I saw an increased number of items belonging to Pippa, and that displeased me enough to make my goodbyes sulkier than they should have been, even drawing a sigh of irritation from Rob. It was clear now that there was a version of me I could not control, and who appeared to be operating as if she were in a monogamous relationship with him and not an adulterous one; a woman for whom a silver bangle was no appeasement.

For she thought she had rights to him, this character, who had either subsumed bad Amber or was functioning in parallel with her. Either way mature, reformed, dutiful Amber Fraser had been shoved unceremoniously to the back of the line.

She'd lost her voice, if not her mind.

Chapter 23

Christy, September 2013

She next saw Rob Whalen a few days later when he joined Steph and her in the queue for coffee at the patisserie on the Parade. It was the first time Christy had set foot in the place – so high-end was it that its confections were displayed behind glass like jewellery, their prices withheld – though she had dreamed of it daily. Now that two interviews had been scheduled for the coming weeks, she was becoming a little more blasé about squandering funds on treats; one of the jobs was a position identical to her old one in an agency she was fairly certain Amber Fraser had never worked. The promised September upturn was materializing at last.

Conversely, Joe had become more fretful about their finances – more fretful in general. Sporadic complaints about sleeping poorly had become constant claims of chronic insomnia, in spite of those punishing hours that would fell an ox, and he seemed able to lose consciousness only at weekends. Awake, he had the eyes of a fugitive, the scent of stress on his skin.

'If you saw my income and billings for last month, you'd never sleep again,' he'd told her that morning, and there was a tremor in his voice that was not only new but foreign to his character.

This was more than complaint, it was anguish, and no wonder: he was enduring his epic working weeks with fewer hours' rest than the new parents next door. (Every so often Christy would catch Matilda's cry on the breeze and would jerk towards it in some unstoppable primordial reflex.)

'I'm sure it must feel like that for everyone,' she soothed.

'Everyone who's fucking up, yes.'

Privately, Christy wondered if part of the problem might be that all the time Joe had been working towards making partner, he had been thinking of it as an end in itself, giving scant consideration to what came after, rather as Steph had said she'd fixated with such single-mindeness on the birth of Matilda that she'd neglected to consider the part that followed. A child's whole life. A man's whole career.

But how easy it was to spot the fatal flaw when you were the observer – and an unemployed one at that. All the months Joe had urged her to enjoy her enforced leisure, and she had not been able to; now she seemed finally capable of relaxation, *he* was suffering.

'It hasn't even been six months, Joe. I think you should give it a year before you start worrying about your billings,' she told him, careful not to betray her own distress at his needing her to hold him like a child. In her arms he felt soft-bodied, out of condition; she could not remember when he had last exercised or even strolled around the park to breathe fresh air. 'Then we'll decide what to do,' she added, with a bravery she only half felt. If they had to sell up after a year then so be it, she thought, it would be no less precipitous than the Frasers' departure. 'This isn't a prison sentence, you *can* get out.'

'Can I? How?'

But she had no answer ready and he'd left for work with the air of a condemned man.

It was a beautiful translucent early-September afternoon, a belated bolt of summer just as the city had thought itself finished with the season, and she, Steph and Rob took one of the tables on the pavement to drink their coffees. It was purely coincidence of course, but Christy couldn't help noticing that the giver of new life, Steph, sat in the sunlight while Lime Park's very own Antichrist chose a seat deep in shadow. She pulled her chair marginally closer to Steph's to share the light.

'Well, this beats the slave pits, eh?' Rob smirked.

(Slave pits! When poor Joe talked of lawyers being sent home at daybreak, a taxi waiting while they showered and changed, ready to return them to the office to start the cycle all over again.)

Far from re-entering the fugue that had led her to his door the previous week in an intrusion she now lamented, she was this time self-conscious, careful of every word that passed her lips, and happy to let Steph fill any silences with her observations about Lime Park and its denizens, her good-natured gripes about sleep deprivation and breast-feeding. She wished, however, that Steph had complimented her on her new hair *before* they ran into Rob.

Instead, Steph slid her sunglasses down her nose with

some theatricality as she demanded, 'When did you decide to turn Titian, Christy?'

'I'm not sure you can call it Titian,' Christy said. 'But it's true I dabbled in home-colouring a few nights ago. It's a russet glaze, apparently. It will wash out,' she added, almost in apology.

'It's worked really well on the highlights, hasn't it? What does Joe think?'

'Oh, he likes it.' Christy could not bring herself to admit that Joe had noticed neither the reddened hair nor the faint orange stain on her pillow. The 'glaze' she'd used was by no means the costliest on the market.

'How about you, Rob?' Steph said, her tone as teasing as a sibling's. Her easy confidence with him continued to impress Christy. 'Do *you* like a redhead? Oh, hang on, your girlfriend's blonde, isn't she?'

'She is,' Rob agreed, and Christy noticed he did not object this time to the reference to Pippa (what *were* his rules? They were unfathomable). 'I'm not so sure about redheads,' he added. 'They say Eve was one, don't they? Not to be trusted.'

'But we can trust *Christy*,' Steph giggled, and to stop herself from blushing Christy fixed her gaze on a tray of chocolate meringues visible through the window. Given the funds and five minutes of solitude, she'd eat the whole lot, she was sure of it. She'd eat the portions of every Amber Fraser in the city.

It was then that Matilda began gently to fuss, and Steph took her to the bathroom to change her, leaving Christy and Rob alone. What to talk about? Her next session at

St Luke's was not till the following day, so she couldn't fall back on that; to mention Joe's misery would be disloyal; and she dared not ask him anything about *his* life for fear of blundering once more into territory deemed off-limits. And so they sat sipping their coffee, talking mostly *of* coffee. Rob was something of a geek, it transpired, with opinions on the relative merits of Javanese- and Costa Rican-grown beans, the role of milk. (The role of milk! When Joe couldn't tell her whether he had eaten that day or not; when no matter how late he came home he couldn't go to bed before filling a wine glass large enough for a trifle; when he'd almost wept one night to discover there was no alcohol in the house.)

There was a sudden hush on the Parade as the traffic was held at a red light at exactly the moment the pavements happened to clear of pedestrians. The sun was lower in the sky, its late-season light soft and gauzy – it didn't feel at all like London – and all at once Christy was flooded with a sense of natural passing, of survival.

'I do love it here,' she told Rob, surprising herself with the confidence. 'I always thought the most important thing about a place was the people who live there, but I'm starting to think that might not be true. The place is enough.'

'The most important thing about a place is what happens there,' Rob said. 'Steph, for instance, she'll always know Lime Park as the place her children were born.'

Christy nodded, couldn't help wishing he'd given any other example but that. How would *she* remember Lime Park? Where her children could not be born because their parents had bitten off more than they could chew? 'In that case, I don't think I know this place properly yet,' she said, reconsidering. 'Because nothing has happened. Nothing at all.'

Rob was looking at her more closely, as if she'd finally said something – *thought* something – that interested him, and she felt herself take intense pleasure in this. (And her husband, the man who kept her life afloat while believing himself drowning, what would *he* make of that pleasure? It was the kind that could fracture a marriage, break a man as badly as any workload, and she knew she must never take it again.)

When Steph returned, she laughed at their solemn expressions. 'Is he complaining that I talked him into minding Matilda for five minutes the other day when I went out to pick up a package from the post office?'

'No, how did it go?' Christy asked.

Rob grinned. 'It was terrifying.'

(Terrifying: just the word Joe had used to describe his work situation.)

'But we all have to face our fears sooner or later,' he added, looking once more at Christy.

'What fears?' Steph asked, chuckling. 'Believe me, Christy, when you've looked childbirth in the eye, there's nothing left to fear.'

There was no reasonable response to this, and in any case Christy was saved from making one by the rising commotion of noise and energy on the Parade, the thickened flows of traffic and pedestrians that signalled the arrival of three-thirty and school pick-up. She realized she had missed the rhythms of it over the August holidays.

'Isn't that Caroline and her kids?' Steph said, squinting into the sun. 'I haven't seen them since they came back from France.'

She and Christy called hello to a Caroline Sellers who appeared to be both a different colour (burnt-flesh) and dress size (one, perhaps two, larger) than she'd been before the break. She waved merrily back before taking a child by each hand and striding towards them.

'Christy, Steph, it's been *ages*!' Such was the angle of her approach, she did not see the third of their group until she stood right in front of the table, but when she did, her expression hardened instantly.

'Caroline,' Rob said. His tone was not quite curt enough to alert Steph, but for Christy, his keenest of students, the hostility was plain.

'Well, if it isn't just like the old days,' Caroline said, and though she could only have been addressing him, she did not actually look directly at him. Her face was set in grim disapproval, as if she'd caught the three of them doing something so unspeakable, gesture alone was going to have to suffice.

Christy wondered how long Caroline was prepared to stand there, her dim view of their gathering palpable enough that even Steph had noticed and begun casting quizzical glances at her table-mates.

'Time for our doctor's appointment,' she said, tucking Matilda into her sling and zipping up a bag so voluminous you could emigrate with it. 'I'll see you all soon. Bye, Caroline. Welcome back.'

'Bye,' Caroline said mechanically, and at the sight of the

vacated seat her daughter immediately began agitating for a treat.

'Would you like to join us?' Christy said. 'Shall I find chairs for the kids?'

Caroline handed her purse to her daughter. 'Rosie, take Lucas inside and choose yourselves something. Remember to say please and thank you.'

Christy had a strong suspicion she was banishing the children in order to make some unpleasant announcement out of their earshot, and she braced herself accordingly.

'Take my seat,' Rob offered Caroline, draining his coffee and rising to his feet. 'I'm heading off as well.'

Caroline said nothing, expressing in mood alone that she would rather throw herself under a passing bus than allow any part of her body to enter space previously occupied by his. She pointedly took Steph's seat instead.

'Oh, and Caroline,' Rob said, his tone insolent.

She raised her eyebrows in query.

'It's *nothing* like the old days, believe me.'

And Caroline glared at him in fury, obviously longing to lash out but succeeding – just – in controlling herself.

With a last glance at Christy (was there a note of warning in it?), Rob strolled off.

'Are you all right?' she asked Caroline, who was peering through the shop window to check the length of the queue; Rosie and Lucas, at its tail, would have to wait at least five minutes to be served.

Caroline turned to face her, eyes dark with consternation. 'Did I *really* just see that? You were having coffee with *him*?'

347

And it returned then to Christy in its original intensity: the intrigue she had been so stirred by, the antipathy towards Rob that she had begun to doubt during the empty month of August, Rob's bêtes noires absent all.

'Well, with Steph really, but we bumped into each other and he joined us for a few minutes.' She tried not to sound apologetic for switching sides – after all, how could you take sides when you didn't know what the argument was?

'I thought you said you loathed him?' Caroline said, less in accusation than concern.

She'd remembered the exact verb, Christy thought. 'Maybe I overreacted. Whatever's gone on in the past, I think he deserves a second chance. We do all live side by side, and it would be a lot less awkward if we just got on, don't you think?'

Caroline plainly did *not* think. 'Well, there've obviously been some changes while we've been away.' She left Christy under no illusion that she regarded these changes as deeply unwelcome. 'Your hair, it's gone red.' She said this as if pointing out something Christy might not care to know but really ought, like having a stain down her front or toilet paper stuck to the bottom of her shoe.

'It's just a glaze,' Christy said.

'A glaze?'

'You know, like you might put on a roast chicken. Or carrots.'

'I see.' Caroline did not crack a smile at this attempt to lighten the mood, and under her continued scrutiny Christy began to sweat.

'Look, there's no need to worry, Caroline, honestly. I've

just got to know Rob a bit better, that's all. It was horrible to feel like I had an enemy next door. I'm relieved to discover this other version of him.'

'Version,' Caroline repeated, as if the word crystallized the issue, defined the fault that had previously been indefinable. 'Well, I'd be very careful about this one if I were you.'

'Careful about what, exactly? I assume this is about the mysterious thing no one will talk about. *He* doesn't want to either, you know. So that's something you agree on, at least.'

Caroline clutched at the straps of her handbag, as if it were in danger of being snatched. 'You've actually asked him . . . ?' She didn't finish the thought, adding in an urgent undertone, 'I wouldn't do that if I were you. Seriously, Christy, I can't say any more, but if you're going to be friends with him, please promise me you'll look out for yourself.'

They stared at each other.

The children returned from inside with their selections. 'Mummy,' Rosie said, edging onto Caroline's knees and slotting the coins of her change between her mother's fingers, 'I chose a cinnamon bun and Lucas has got a cookie with Smarties on it. Can we eat them now?'

'Of course you can, sweetie, but don't get any on your uniform, OK? I really need to get the kids back,' Caroline told Christy. 'Amelia will be home soon.'

'I'll walk with you,' Christy said. 'You must tell me how she's getting on in her first week at senior school. Does she walk or get the bus?' The elder Sellers girl's new school was in the same neighbourhood as St Luke's, and Christy had seen the girls the previous week in their black blazers and rolled-up skirts, their serious little confabs at the bus stop about what could only be minor scrapes next to the heart-stopping crises of adulthood.

'No,' said Caroline. 'A few of us on the street have put together a rota for driving them.'

'The bus isn't safe?' Even Christy knew that secondary-school children made their own way to and from school; surely it was overprotective to chauffeur them so short a distance? But she knew better than to voice this opinion and jeopardize the good feeling so diligently built with Caroline.

An account of the Sellerses' glorious four weeks in France sustained them for the stroll home, only the pinched skin between Caroline's brows belying her earlier chagrin. For her part, Christy told her about the bank holiday weekend in East Sussex, Joe's work stresses.

'I don't think we've ever needed a change of scene more,' she said, as they reached their houses.

'I know the feeling,' Caroline said. 'I've only been back five minutes and I already feel ready to leave again.'

It was only after they'd parted that this last remark stirred a memory in Christy, one she was aware had floated close to the surface before, but remained inaccessible. That was right: it was something Steph, in their first conversation over the garden fence, had reported Caroline as having said: *If it weren't for the great schools, they'd have moved on by now.*

That was how much Caroline Sellers 'loathed' Rob

Whalen. She loathed him as much, perhaps, as had the two sets of neighbours who *had* moved on – the two who had not shared her use for Lime Park's outstanding schools.

Caroline was not the only one to voice concern that Christy was on coffee-slurping terms with Rob Whalen: there were also, apparently, objections on the part of his girlfriend. These she discovered only by accident, or rather by eavesdropping, old habits having died hard – and in brazen disregard of those avowals she'd made to her new friend about minding her own business.

She didn't mind admitting that she'd become quite fascinated by Pippa. That seductive drape of smooth blonde hair over her bare right shoulder (always the right one, never the left); the painstaking grooming that spoke of a strict desire to please; the slowing of her step as she approached the gate to number 38, followed by a visible, almost therapeutic, bout of deep breathing: what was she preparing herself for?

Hi you, he'd said, and those words, leavened with lust, had lingered in Christy's imagination rather longer than was decent. She supposed it was because Rob and Pippa were unlike any other couple on the street: not only were they younger and electrically attracted, there was also something oddly clandestine about them. Other than the occasion when he'd chased after her and seized her arm, Christy had never seen them together in public, their meetings apparently confined to his flat. Pippa arrived and then Pippa left, a girlfriend who was not exactly kept hidden, but not exalted from the rooftops either. Rob had not even wanted her *name* known, presumably because it elicited reactions like the one from Caroline: *She must be crazy if she's still hanging around.*

One evening, passing the door of her deserted master bedroom, Christy became aware of raised voices on the other side of the wall. It was unusually humid for the time of year, and both her window and the one to Rob's living room were open, meaning she didn't have to step far into the room to be able to hear every word being said; evidently she'd learned nothing from his previous reprimands.

'I can't handle this any more!' Pippa was saying, audibly riled. Christy had not heard her voice properly before, and it came as a surprise that she was so well spoken, much more so than Rob. 'Seriously, if I find out it's happening again . . .'

'"Seriously"?' Rob echoed in a humourless tone. 'All this because I've *shaved*? That's insane.'

Shaved? Did that mean that horrible thatch of a beard had been washed down the plughole?

'Not just that, no.' Pippa's voice was sulky, her position oversensitive even to a stranger's ear, causing Christy to feel a twinge of sympathy for Rob. Was this how women sounded? Was this how *she* sounded in discussion with Joe? She had a sudden disagreeable image of him pulling the duvet over his head to blot out her unwanted complaints.

'What then?' Rob said.

'You *know* what.'

'I assume you mean the new neighbour, do you?'

Christy's nerve endings sizzled: which new neighbour? Felix, Steph, Joe . . . her?

'Come on, I thought we'd been through this the other day? You can't jump to conclusions every time a woman calls round. It's untenable.'

She gulped. That meant Steph or her, and Steph had just had a baby, which presumably exempted her from the sort of conclusions a live-out lover might have jumped to.

'I'm not jumping to conclusions,' Pippa said, 'I'm just saying *if* it happened again, then I don't think I could handle it.'

'"If"?' There was an increased sourness in Rob's irritation. 'You don't mean *if*, you mean *when*. Come on, admit it: you're fucking *willing* it to!'

Christy's jaw fell open. Quite apart from the unpleasant way Rob was addressing his girlfriend, this 'conclusion' Pippa had jumped to – and what was it if not the obvious, infidelity? – evidently had roots in some historic transgression. Here we go again, she thought; if this became any more circular she would go dizzy and fall to the ground. As a precaution, she dropped into her stake-out chair, its back to the window these days in mimicry of Rob's, but still in excellent range of the private conversation she monitored. Both shameless and ashamed, she closed her eyes, lost to the drama.

'You're putting words in my mouth,' Pippa protested.

'But you obviously don't trust me, do you?'

'I don't know what to trust any more.'

'Does it not occur to you that it might be quite nice for

me to have a coffee with a neighbour? Especially a woman? That it might be quite nice to be treated normally again?'

'*Does* she treat you normally then? Not so long ago you were saying everyone was still giving you the cold shoulder.'

'That's the point, *she* doesn't. And nor does the husband – he's a really decent guy, actually, a lawyer, I like him a lot.'

Christy swallowed.

'Seems like lawyers are the only people I can trust these days,' Rob sniggered. 'Who'd have thought?'

'We're not talking about the *husband*,' Pippa said sullenly.

'Oh, for Christ's sake, listen to yourself. Do you have any idea how unattractive this is? This petty jealousy? Fine, if you want to talk about her, then let's talk about her. She's a bit dull, to be honest, though as I say I hardly know her. I'm not sure there's that much *to* know.'

Christy flushed deeply, felt a wobble in her legs. *A bit dull, not much to know*: how humiliating (and no less than the eavesdropper deserved).

'Not so dull she wasn't trying to dig up the dirt a few weeks ago,' Pippa said.

'I don't blame her for that. It must be pretty mind-boggling to have been dropped into the atmosphere around here. It's fucking *joyless*. People dropping hints, making little remarks about what might or might not have happened. I'm amazed she hasn't been told outright by someone by now.'

'I assume none of them would dare,' Pippa said, sounding somewhat chastened (and no wonder, given his damning appraisal of her 'rival').

There was a silence. 'Yeah, well, for how long?'

'You know *I* haven't done anything like that, don't you?' Pippa's voice sang out in indignation. 'I've never discussed it with anyone.'

'Then what's this conversation about? Why are we even having it? Don't you see this is not like before? You've got nothing whatsoever to be jealous about. I've chosen *you*.'

'I'm just ... I suppose I'm still upset about the overlapping.'

'Oh, for God's sake, not that again! I've told you a thousand times, Pippa, I ended it as soon as we got serious. I asked you to move in with me, and you did. You'd still be here now if you believed me in the first place.'

'I did believe you. I do.'

'Well, it doesn't sound like it.'

There was another silence. Christy wondered if they were eyeing each other or avoiding the other's gaze. How close were they standing? Was this one of those arguments that was going to end in intense reconciliation? (*Still* she didn't move out of range; it was deplorable, pitiable. She did herself a far greater disservice than she did them.)

'I think I just need some time to think about it,' Pippa said, at last.

'Oh, for fuck's sake ...' Rob was explosive now, his fury acute enough to cause Christy – not before time – to get to her feet and shuffle a step or two away. 'Go ahead,' he sneered. 'Take all the time in the world.'

'What does that mean?'

'It means I'm sick of this crap. I'm sick of having to

plead my case over and over again, account for every move I make. Can't you understand that I want to forget all about that nightmare, not rake over it constantly? It's bad enough having to deal with the neighbours, without getting it from my own girlfriend.'

'I'm not –'

'Let's forget this, eh?' Rob's voice was receding; he must have begun walking away from the window, deeper into the flat. Christy strained to hear. 'It's obvious you can't forget a part of it, so I think we're going to have to forget the whole thing.'

'I can't believe you're willing to end it,' cried Pippa, distraught. 'You just said you chose me!'

'Well, I *un*choose you.' Rob's voice, cold and mean, was closer again; he must have returned to face her. 'Go, Pippa. I'm serious. I'm not interested any more.'

'But, Rob –'

'Just go. It's over.'

Seconds later, the door banged shut. When Pippa appeared on the path below, her back was to Christy and her head held low, so it was impossible to see if she was crying. And though she lingered for almost a full minute, Rob did not come after her.

The next day, as she left the house for her latest session at St Luke's, Christy saw a young male figure stroll along the pavement towards her house, earphones in, head nodding faintly to the rhythm.

It was only after he'd turned into number 38 and gestured vaguely in her direction that she understood who it was. The difference was truly arresting. Not only had he shaved off his beard but he'd also cut short his hair, revealing the forceful, eye-catching bone structure of a hero, a leader.

So this had been the catalyst for his row with Pippa the previous evening, and Christy could understand why. A bold unmasking like this, it said something. It sent the message that the old Rob, the Rob in Caroline's photograph, he was back.

Chapter 24

Amber, 2013

I'm sorry, but I don't think I'm psychologically prepared for the next section. Not yet. I will get to it, I promise – otherwise, there's no point in this exercise – but not straight away, not in sequence. My trauma counsellor told me that in order to truly understand what has happened you sometimes have to break the chronology in its retelling, and while I've discounted almost everything else that woman has said, I *do* think that's true.

The thing is, the aftermath is going to be hard enough to reconstruct without my first having to relive the worst day of my life (and there've been some bad ones to choose from, I think you've gathered that).

What I will say now is that I *never* expected us to finish the way we did. I'd imagined a lingering farewell, a parting no less erotic than the body of the affair itself. But when the time came, there was no kiss goodbye.

All along, I'd been the innocent one, the fool.

Because I *never* expected his anger, his malice, his cruelty. The way he behaved, it was so wholly inexplicable to me that there was even a moment that day when I wondered if he'd been holding a grudge against me since the beginning, that there might have been some unguessable slight on my part during our night together all those years before, that I'd hurt his male pride. But I know now that can't possibly have been the case.

And finish we did.

It was the 15th of January 2013 when it happened, a date I would not forget. As I say, the worst day of my life.

Chapter 25

Joe and Yasmin were in complete agreement, a position all the more infuriating for their not having had the opportunity to speak to one another in almost a year.

'I don't want to hear this,' Joe said, holding up a hand to silence her.

One look at his expression – not only derisive of her Rob-related theories but also cross with himself, as if it pained him to have to downgrade his opinion of her – and Christy took him at his word.

'Joe's right. If I were you I wouldn't give this stuff another thought,' said Yasmin's pixilated mouth on the laptop screen. The audio, however, was unbroken: 'When you're back at work, you won't believe how much time you spent thinking about it. Anyway, it's obvious to me what's been going on. This Rob guy had an earlier relationship that overlapped with the blonde and she can't forgive him. Maybe some of the others on the street were great friends with her and didn't like the way he treated her? You said she moved in and then she moved out, so she's probably embarrassed to have come back. That's why she sneaks in and out when she knows she won't be seen. We've all been there.'

I haven't, Christy thought. 'It's more than that,' she insisted. 'He called it a nightmare and whatever it was it was bad enough for half the street to refuse to be in the same room as him. And don't forget two households upped and left over it.'

'So you say.' Yasmin sighed and Christy knew she'd lost her last ally. 'I think you need to forget about the rest of the street and concentrate on you. You and Joe.'

It wasn't that Christy didn't recognize good advice when she heard it; it was just that when your advisor was in another continent, turned on and off at your own technological whim, it was all too easy to choose to ignore it.

As September surrendered to October, the leaves on the neighbourhood limes grew yellower as the cherry trees began to blush. She was going to like autumn here, she decided.

In her fifth week of volunteering at St Luke's, Christy was asked for the first time to take pupils in pairs rather than singly. The final pair of the morning, Leah and Zoë, were thrilled to escape class, and took every available opportunity to break from their reading and chatter.

'Do you read much at home?' Christy asked them, when she'd finally coaxed from them a page apiece.

'Only books we get from school,' Leah said. She was the more forthright of the two and of a more striking appearance, her hair honey-coloured and plaited to the elbow, brown eyes clear and large, almost bulbous. 'We haven't got any books at home.'

'None at all?'

'Not stories. There's a cookery book in the kitchen.'

Christy was pleased to hear that; she wanted all families to conform to the Sellers ideal, the spines of their recipe books encrusted with icing sugar, the kitchen a chaos of treats stacked higgledy-piggledy in Tupperware.

'But my mum dropped it in the sink,' Leah added. 'She never used it, anyway, not once. She doesn't like recipes. She says they take too long.'

'How about you, Zoë?' asked Christy. 'What books have you got at home?'

Zoë, shyer than her friend, glanced to Leah before responding. 'Well, we've got *some*, I think, but my mum's always too busy to read with me.'

'What about your dad?'

'I only see him once a week and he doesn't help me with my homework. My mum says he's got no brain.'

'OK. I'll help you then, and you can show your mums how well you read and really impress them.'

They liked that idea. 'You're really nice,' they said, which made Christy feel ridiculously happy.

'Who did reading with you last term?' she asked them.

'Milly's mum,' Leah said. 'But she had to go and work in Tesco's. Milly's dad lost his job and now he's depressed.'

Fathers tended to lack heroism in the children's anecdotes, and Christy allowed herself a brief, reassuring image of Joe, the intrinsic decency of him and the potential he had to be a good parent, even though he wanted nothing less in the here and now and the last words he'd said to her on the issue were: 'I don't want to hear this.'

'Now Milly can't go on the trip to Hever Castle,' Zoë added mournfully.

'What a shame.' Christy, identifying Milly as a pale-haired girl who was as quick to please as she was to flush, wished she had the spare cash to pay for her place on the trip. 'I'm sure the family will get themselves back on their feet soon and Milly will be able to go on all the trips.'

'Before Milly's mum there was a naughty man who came,' Leah said, speaking with the air of spilling a secret she could no longer reasonably be expected to keep.

Christy was startled. 'Really?'

'Don't tell her, Leah!' Zoë hissed. 'Mrs Spencer said we're not allowed to say!'

But Leah, a girl after Christy's heart, had the conspiracist's gene, right down to the surreptitious glances she was casting down the corridor and the furtive, breathless tone she now adopted to defy Zoë's advice: 'The police got him.'

'Goodness.' Christy knew she should be closing down a conversation like this, reporting it discreetly to Mrs Spencer out of the girls' earshot and putting it from her mind, but she could not. On the contrary, she was encouraging it, urging the girls to say more, asking, 'What did the naughty man do to get himself into trouble?'

'My mum won't tell me *literally*,' Leah said, 'but she said he wasn't allowed in the school any more. Not *anywhere* on the premises. They changed the code on the gate. My mum told Mrs Spencer that her and all the other mums would keep us at home if he came back.'

'*She* and all the other mums. I see.' Christy was beginning to understand the need for the references and police clearances that she, the most casual of volunteers, had been asked to supply. 'Better safe than sorry, I'm sure she did the right thing.'

'He was a writer,' Zoë said, evidently having decided if you can't beat 'em, join 'em. 'But not stories like this.' She gestured to the forgotten book on the desk between Leah and her, an innocent tale of kittens lost in the snow.

'A journ'list,' Leah said, pronouncing the word as if for the first time, and with these uncertain syllables came the initial symptoms of suspicion in Christy, an effervescence of adrenalin in the veins, a thinning of oxygen in her throat. Leah's expression intensified, a child's mimicry of adult consternation as she pronounced, 'My dad said he would find *plenty* to write about behind bars.'

'Behind bars? You mean he's in jail now?' Christy asked, shocked.

'No, he's not,' Zoë said, but Leah was insistent.

'My dad said he is. He said he can't hurt anyone there because *everyone's* bad in jail. It's more likely *he'll* get hurt.'

'In jail, you're not allowed to go for a walk or ride your bike,' Zoë agreed. 'You can't play netball or go on the trampoline or anything good.'

'You have to work in the kitchen,' Leah said, confidently, 'cooking horrible dinners for the other prisoners and mopping floors. But there wouldn't be biscuits, would there?'

'There might be *some*,' Zoë said, 'but not really good ones like gingerbread men.'

There was a brief diversion as the girls compared their preferred methods of tackling a gingerbread man, and to Christy's shame it was she who steered the discussion back towards the subject of the bad man.

'The police didn't come to the school, did they?'

'No,' Leah said. 'There was a lot of shouting one day and Mr Webber sent all the mums a letter.'

Mr Webber was the head. Christy had not yet met him but had glimpsed him once through the glass panel of his office door and been pleased to see a smiling, dynamic figure in place of the hunched, beleaguered cliché she had expected. She could just imagine his expression if he heard one of his volunteers encouraging *this* conversation.

'We should get back to our reading,' she said, and drew their attention to the open page in front of them. 'Let's see how the story ends.'

She had, however, one final question: 'Just out of interest, girls, what was the man called?'

But who was she kidding? Even as they told her – voices in unison at last – she already knew the answer.

There was no reply at Caroline's or Liz's houses and so she tried Joanne, a member of the group she knew less well but who she was confident occupied a position in the inner circle.

She was taken aback when Kenny answered the door. Lime Park Road was a traditional place where, with the exception of Rob, the only adults at home in daylight were female. Kenny was, she knew, a financial analyst, a regular on the same early train that Joe and Felix took into Blackfriars.

'I'm working from home today,' he said, and judging by his half-buttoned shirt and uncombed hair, he had not left the house all day (at least he was not in bunny slippers).

She couldn't help glancing at his right hand, but it was months since she'd noticed the bandaging and the skin was of course long healed. By his side, his tall blond dog looked excited by her visit and when she reached to stroke its ears it pushed its nose into her palm, snuffling aggressively for treats.

'*Poppy!*' he warned.

'I was hoping Joanne might be in,' Christy said.

'Sorry, she's on a school trip, not back till five. The British Museum, I think she said.'

Which was probably where Caroline was too; the two families had younger children in the same year at Lime Park Primary and were class reps together.

'Can *I* help?' Kenny offered.

She had no doubt he could, but whether or not he *would* was a different matter.

'It's about Rob,' she said, a little wildly.

Kenny's face, flushed and friendly, dropped an inch. 'That explains it then. You'd better come in.'

Having presumed she'd be led to the kitchen, she was surprised to be taken into the sitting room at the front, a space that was an exact match with her own and yet considerably more comfortable for sitting, with its deep oatmeal sofas and nests of washed-linen cushions, its tranquil seascapes and trails of potted greenery. Taking a seat opposite Kenny, she had the sense of being interviewed, until the dog hopped onto the sofa next to him, sitting upright and alert, head angled exactly like its owner's, and the sight of the two of them side by side was so comical she relaxed.

On a shelf behind Kenny, between a peace lily and a framed photograph of the kids, was Amber's room scent, being used somewhat ambitiously as a bookend. Barely a centimetre of the liquid remained, the last drops of her 'special touch'. Christy wondered if refills were available.

'So what's on your mind?' Kenny asked.

'Well, I've been volunteering at St Luke's and the kids said something today about a "naughty" man called Rob.'

The police got him.

'I'm fairly sure they meant our Rob,' she added, and saw Kenny recoil slightly at her use of the possessive, 'because I know he volunteered at a primary school in the past, he told me that himself, though he never said which one.' Which, now she thought of it, was odd, given that he'd asked her directly which she'd been allocated and she'd clearly stated St Luke's.

Kenny did not ask what the children had said, but a look of fleeting fury crossed his face before it was replaced by one of resignation. Did that mean he was willing to talk?

'They said he wasn't allowed in the school any more, had maybe even been in prison. Do you know if that's true?'

Kenny sighed, enervated, his shoulders slumping visibly. Now the dog was the taller, neck erect, eyes alert; every few seconds its head turned towards the door, ears pricking, as if it suspected someone was out in the hallway but wasn't convinced enough to go and investigate. 'Believe me, Christy, I'd like nothing better than to tell you what I know, or what I think I know, but I can't.'

'Why not?' Could this situation get any more maddening? The residents of Lime Park Road really had taken a vow of silence; they were not so much a circle as a sect. 'Caroline says the same whenever I ask about him. I don't mean to be rude, but why are you all so scared? There are a lot more of you than him. I don't see how he's been able to call the shots like this.'

There was a pause. Then Kenny surprised her by not shutting down the conversation and recommending she be on her way, but by asking a question of his own: 'How do you *think* he's been able to?' And a lift of the eyebrows implied a level of exasperation that far exceeded her own.

'He's threatened you?' she guessed. 'You think he might hurt your families?'

It sounded a bit Mafia even as she said it.

'Not the way you think, but yes. Wait here a second.' Kenny rose and left the room, the dog scrambling in pursuit, and returned with two or three A4 sheets stapled together. He and the dog settled in their previous spots as if they were permanently assigned.

Able to see only the blank reverse of the document, Christy could do nothing but await whatever summary or excerpt he was prepared to share.

'He sent us a letter,' Kenny said. 'Or rather his lawyer did.'

'His lawyer?'

'Yes. That's what this is. A cease and desist letter, essentially.'

'Cease and desist doing *what*?'

'Slandering him. We have been warned not to repeat certain opinions and conjectures. If we do, he will sue us for defamation. So you see, we really *can't* talk about it, however much we might want to. I can't even show you this letter, because it sets out in detail what we're supposed to have said and if you saw those passages then it would amount to a repetition of our alleged offence.' To prove his point, he folded the letter in three and placed it out of her reach on the arm of the sofa.

Christy stared. At last, an explanation of the curious and sustained secrecy – not to mention the naked antipathy towards Rob Whalen: he had threatened them with legal action. *I think I'm allowed to say that*, Caroline had said. *I* will *deal with it*, he'd told Christy, though she'd been clueless as to how. Well, now she knew. She had an image of Richard Sellers under Rob's window. *Thanks for the letter, mate* . . . It had been the Davenports' second Monday in the house, and only days earlier she'd had that awkward set-to with Caroline, who by her own admission had had something on her mind.

'You said "our offence"? Caroline and Richard got this letter as well, did they?'

'All of us did. Jo and me, Caroline and Richard, Mel and Simon, Liz.'

Practically everyone in the photograph – bar Felicity

and the Frasers. She and Joe really had touched down in the middle of a civil war. But why had it begun? What were the conjectures that had so offended Rob that he'd instructed a lawyer?

Just then the dog let out a single gruff bark, startling her, and tore out of the room at unnatural speed. Kenny called after her: '*Poppy! There's no one there!* Of course I don't believe for a moment he ever *would* sue,' he added, returning to Christy. 'That's the difficulty in defamation cases – they tend to spread exactly what the person is trying to suppress – but I'm sure you understand we don't want to take the risk. People lose their homes in legal costs alone, and we would be looking at damages as well if we lost.'

Rob had adopted a pseudonym, Christy thought; his career had already been affected by this, letter or not. He had a case and these people knew it.

'Just because we live in these houses, it doesn't mean we're millionaires,' Kenny added.

'No.' She of all people understood that. 'Thank you for telling me this. I wish I'd known before, I would never have put any of you in such a difficult position. Poor Caroline . . . I've been so nosy.'

'Which is understandable. She won't think any the worse of you, I'm sure. But I seriously advise you to stay out of it, Christy. Don't discuss this man with anyone, certainly not with your pupils at St Luke's. You really don't want to get one of these letters.'

'Joe's a lawyer,' she said. 'He might be able to advise you all.'

'Is he a defamation lawyer?'

'No.'

'Well, Rob's apparently managed to get one of the leading ones in the UK on a no-win no-fee basis. A friend of the family, we heard. He's been very aggressive about it and if he chooses to, he *will* take this as far as it can go.'

'So you've decided it's better just to pretend he no longer exists?'

'Not quite so extreme as that, but yes – to not provoke him further.'

Kenny and the dog returned her to the door. It was as it closed on her that a thought opened, a rare sensation of revelation: that post she had never sent on, the white envelope in the desk drawer at the top of the house . . . Maybe Amber Fraser had been sent a lawyer's letter too, a letter that 'set out in detail' what the neighbours believed Rob had done.

Well, if she had, Christy was mere minutes from discovering just what it said.

Chapter 26

It was about 4.15 p.m. when I began crying.

I cried from the moment I fled his flat, shrieking over my shoulder, 'You will never lay a finger on me again as long as you live!' and crashing the door shut before he could reply.

I cried as I thundered down the stairs, paying no heed to Felicity's face in her doorway, her calls of concern, not caring if I slammed the front door behind me and brought a shudder to the very foundations of the place.

I cried as I let myself into my own house and bolted upstairs.

I was still crying when Jeremy came home from work that evening. I simply could not stop. And the more I alarmed myself by not having the power to cease, the harder I cried.

'What are you doing up here?' he said, finding me huddled under the duvet in the guest bedroom at the top. I hadn't wanted Rob to hear me sobbing through the wall of the floor below.

'Why was the front door double-locked?'

'I locked myself in,' I whimpered.

'Why? Are you crying? What is it, darling? What's

happened?' He was becoming distraught himself, anxious to comfort me, bewildered by my hysteria. Then he saw the trace of blood on the bed sheet and of course he assumed I was upset because my period had started. I let him believe this was the cause.

'I can't bear it . . .' I vacillated between not being able to stand his presence and clinging to him like a child. 'There's no point any more . . .'

'Sweetheart, you mustn't say these things. Everything will be all right. Everything you want *will* happen.'

'No it won't. I hate myself.'

'You're not to blame for this, you haven't done anything wrong . . .'

But I only cried harder. Powerless, he lay down with me, stroking my head like a baby's.

I stayed in bed for days, emerging from the covers only to use the bathroom. Quite simply, my life had ended. Jeremy, convinced it was about our failure to conceive, was prepared to weather this collapse; it was almost as if he'd been expecting it all along. He worked from home when he could, brought me books I couldn't read, flowers and candles I couldn't smell, food I couldn't eat.

'Why don't you come back to our bedroom?' he said on the fourth day. 'There's a TV in there, or you can sit in the chair and look out of the window.'

'I sleep better here,' I lied.

'I don't like being in separate bedrooms.'

'You come up here then.'

This he did. At the top, under the eaves, it was just as it had been when we first moved in. I still remembered the contentment of those two nights. *Two nights!* That was all I'd had in Lime Park with my husband before I met *him*.

'I wish I could take time off,' he said, 'take you away somewhere . . .'

'We've just come back from holiday.' My voice was small and toneless. 'I want to stay here, anyway.'

'The thing is, I have that conference in Germany next week. I'm one of the speakers, I don't think I can cancel.'

'I don't want you to cancel.'

He gazed at me, at a loss. 'Felicity called round,' he said, finally. 'She's worried about you, said she heard you on Tuesday when you were upset and tried to check on you before I came home, but you didn't answer the door.'

'What did you tell her?' I asked.

'I said you're laid up for a few days with that bug I had.'

I seized on this with what little energy I had. 'Maybe I *have* caught your bug. That must be it.'

But Jeremy wasn't buying it. 'You seem depressed, baby, really low. Maybe we should get you to the doctor?'

'No!'

'I know it's tough on you, one of your best friends having just had a baby. You feel like it should have been you. Maybe we should go back to the clinic earlier than agreed?' But the suggestion seemed to pain him and I knew he was thinking about work. Flu had kept him away, then our holiday in the Caribbean, and now he was overloaded; the last thing he needed was a string of medical appointments he hadn't accounted for. This breakdown of mine was trouble enough, and even in my trough of wretchedness I felt sorry for him.

'It's not that,' I said. 'I'm happy for Imogen. It's . . .
I . . . I can't explain.'

'You don't *have* to explain,' Jeremy soothed. 'Not to me.
I understand everything you're feeling. I just wish I knew
how to make it better for you.'

I swallowed, failing to stem a fresh onslaught of tears.
'You can't. No one can.'

It was heartbreaking that he was so unconditionally
loving. I didn't deserve it; I didn't deserve him. And yet I
had never needed him more.

Several things happened next and in rapid succession, so
rapid it's not easy now to get the chronology exactly right.

First, I stopped crying. Any longer and the tears would
have disfigured me, eroded my skin like the tide and left
watery scars behind.

Jeremy flew off for his work trip; at the time I was too
inebriated with misery to register where, but I know now
it was Frankfurt, a digital conference of which Identico.UK
was a minor sponsor. He remained reluctant to go even as
the taxi waited outside, especially when I rejected his
scheme of having Caroline supervise me in his stead (as
with Felicity, I refused to take my friend's phone calls or
answer her pleas through the letter box), but I insisted. He
needed a break from me, whether he knew it or not.

He'd been gone two days – maybe three – when I discovered I was pregnant.

I hadn't taken a test since mid December, tired of the
repetitive disappointment, done with the incessant monitoring of the workings of my menstrual system, as if my

body existed for medical science and not to live its life. I'd had a period in early January, but that could happen; we experts knew that. I remembered Rob's remark that I'd put on weight, and guessed I must have already been pregnant then. All factors considered, I calculated that I must have conceived in late December, probably on our holiday in Jamaica — a second honeymoon indeed.

I longed to share the news with Jeremy, but knew that after everything we had endured together a revelation this sweet needed to be made face to face; however, we spoke on the phone several times a day and I could tell he was overjoyed to hear an improvement in my spirits. And what an improvement it was! It was as if a partition had been slotted between past and present — a partition made of reinforced steel, impenetrable to all known forms of pain — and all at once my skies cleared, my world was back on its correct axis. My affair and its traumatic conclusion might have taken place five years ago for all its relevance to my future, a simple paradise in which all my emotions would be redirected to my husband and child. The idea that I'd ever doubted I wanted a baby was risible, the result of some hormonal imbalance caused by obsession.

So transformative was the discovery that I was even able to watch from the bay window in the master bedroom as Rob moved Pippa into his flat, and not hurl a chair through the window at him, scream at him the terrible names he had earned. Instead, I contented myself with flinging his amber bangle across the room, tracking the metallic scrape of it across the tiled floor of the en suite before letting the partition absorb all further fury, all received injury – all common sense. Since our final meeting, I'd heard from him just once, when he'd texted the day after, asking, 'No hard feelings?' I had read the words repeatedly in disbelief and rage. It was the only message from him I kept. I did not respond.

Finally, I thought, as I heard Jeremy's taxi pull up outside the house that Tuesday night in late January, clenching my fingers to my palms with joy, warmed on that sub-zero winter's night by new blood in my body.

'Finally,' I said to him, pressing a glass of champagne into his hand as he settled on the bar stool next to me.

'Wow,' he said. His joy at having found me restored to full health was inexplicably short-lived; he drank deeply from the glass, like . . . like a man who'd been given *bad* news.

'Aren't you pleased?' I prompted, beaming. 'I know it's been tough recently, but we got there in the end, didn't we?' I shuddered slightly at what might very well have been lost before we did. 'Jeremy, what is it?'

'I'm . . . I'm surprised,' he said, at last.

'Why? You always said it would happen naturally, didn't you? As I say, it's been a bit of a slog . . .'

'A slog?' He was looking at me strangely, but awash once more with elation I misread that strangeness. I thought he must be thinking that sleeping with his beautiful wife could never be labelled so crudely; I thought that for all those months when I'd been in two minds, so too must *he*. Now we'd got what we wanted, there was a fear that we'd never wanted it enough in the first place. It was doubt, cold feet, a perfectly natural reaction. Imogen and Nick had probably felt it too.

'I know how you're feeling and I'm just the same, but it's –'

He interrupted me. 'Stop, Amber, please. You need to listen to me.'

'OK.'

That was when he told me a secret of his own.

'I'm infertile.'

'*What?*'

Immediately he looked like a different person, and I saw in his eyes that I did too. In that instant neither of us knew the other any longer. We were both imposters.

'I don't understand,' I said, my breath quickening. 'The clinic said we were in perfect health.'

'They said that *you* were, yes.' Jeremy closed his eyes, rubbed his fingers into the sockets so violently I worried he'd drive his eyeballs right into his brain. He reopened them only with reluctance, the whites startlingly blood-shot, and made fleeting contact with my gaze. 'But I lied about my results. The fact is they showed that there is no possibility of my fathering a child.'

'Then they must have made a mistake,' I said, with all the bravado I could muster. But he did not consider this, and nor had I realistically expected him to. We looked at each other, silent, stricken. 'Why didn't they bring us back in to talk about it?' I added.

Jeremy fingered the stem of his glass on the counter, eye-ing the fizzing liquid as if it had been concocted expressly to mock him. 'They tried to. They strongly recommended a consultation to discuss next steps, and I said we'd call when we had absorbed the news. I haven't called back.'

I stared. All the joy of the last few days had been lost in a catastrophic nosedive and now my thoughts were tearing away, deserting the scene of the crash. 'So they didn't say take another six months?'

'No.'

'Why didn't you tell me?' My voice cracked. For all my own sins, I still felt sinned against – and by the one person who had never done anything but adore me. But as Jeremy looked straight at me, new emotions crossed his face, dark, terminal ones never before expressed towards me. As long as I live, I never want to repeat that feeling, the feeling of watching your own fall from grace in the eyes of your most ardent champion.

And in his voice: not disappointment, nothing so mundane, but defeat, *annihilation*. 'I think that pales into insignificance compared with what *you* didn't tell *me*. You've slept with someone else, clearly.'

I didn't reply. The partition was rising once more, freeing the terrible memory of what had happened at my final meeting with *him*. In gushed the pain, as relentless and searching as liquid, until at last I bit into my lower lip and lowered my eyes in affirmation.

'Am I allowed to know who?' Jeremy asked, his tone dismal.

I gave a whimper. 'I can't tell you.'

'I think I ought to know who the father of your child will be.'

He was speaking as if I belonged to this other man now, as if I were no longer his. It frightened me, it wasn't what I wanted, it wasn't what I'd *ever* wanted, even when

379

in the grip of my fever for Rob. I imagined divorce, destitution, a rock-bottom life. I began to cry.

'I can't,' I repeated, weakly.

'Do I know him?' Jeremy asked, cold, desolate, out of reach. *Barren.* 'At least tell me that.'

'It's not what you think,' I said.

'How can it *not* be what I think, Amber?' The way he said my name, it was almost with nostalgia; he was already in mourning for the woman he'd loved.

I was sobbing hard by now, tears spilling hot on my skin, and I knew I was going to have to tell him. I took a step forward and reached for him with a feeble, shaking hand that no longer felt like my own.

'Because it's not,' I said.

Chapter 27

Christy, October 2013

She was about to commit a crime. She didn't know what the penalty was for opening a letter addressed to someone else, but whatever it was it couldn't be worse than the ceaseless, itching torment of not knowing.

As she sprinted home from number 46, tripping in her haste, her certainty that the letter she'd salted away was a replica of the one Kenny had held in his hands, *withheld* from forbidden eyes, took on an evangelical intensity and within thirty seconds of entering the house she had torn upstairs to the office and snatched it from its hiding place.

Trembling, she took a last look at the name on the envelope – *Amber Fraser* – and spoke the words aloud, caught off guard by the romantic wonder in her own voice.

Amber Fraser: one half of the couple who'd lived here before, the half who'd had beauty and charisma in such measure that she'd been worshipped when she was here and mourned now she was gone. The half who'd been a breath of fresh air in a street lauded for its fragrant breezes.

But something had happened on this street that was not so fragrant: was she *finally* going to find out what?

Christy turned the envelope and slipped a thumbnail under the flap, in one decisive motion slicing the paper like a blade. The tear was jagged, irreparable; there was no going back now.

Extracting the single A4 sheet – Kenny's had been two or three – she noticed at once the blue insignia familiar to all Londoners: *The Metropolitan Police: Working Together for a Safer London.* The assumption that it was no more than a mailshot about Neighbourhood Watch deflated her almost to the point of paralysis – until her eyes settled on the signature and she understood that this was in fact private correspondence to Amber Fraser from a named CID officer.

Detective Sergeant Marcus Graham. His signature was large and legible; you could see it had been made with deliberation, as if he had lingered over this letter for reasons he could not quite explain.

Christy's eye swept downwards to the date – 19 March 2013, six and a half months ago, evidence in black and white of the length of her hoarding – and she felt her pulse surge.

Dear Mrs Fraser,

Following your recent retraction of your witness statement, I am writing to let you know that our inquiry into the events of 15th January is closed.

Given the nature of the original allegation, please be assured that you are free to contact me at any time if you have anything additional to report or if you have any concerns about your safety.

Yours faithfully,
Marcus Graham
Detective Sergeant
CID

Christy stared at the short text, processing the phrases – witness statement, inquiry, allegation, concerns for your safety – and felt them meld in her mind with others:

Seriously, Christy, promise me you'll look out for yourself...

My mum won't tell me what he did...

I'd like nothing better than to tell you what I know...

If certain of nothing else, she was of this: Rob Whalen was the criminal in this investigation. The reason Amber Fraser feared for her personal safety was to do with the 'falsehoods' about his actions that he sought to suppress, and those actions had to have been something violent or threatening, something that had got him banned from working in a school and had inspired overprotective attitudes among Lime Park mothers towards an age group you'd reasonably expect to be given greater freedom. Something so awful it had impelled the Frasers – and Felicity – to pack their bags and flee.

She fished in her pocket for her phone, holding the letter in her shaking hand as she dialled the number for DS Graham. He was not available, but the officer who fielded the call offered to hear her enquiry.

'I've discovered that the person who used to live in my house was involved in a police investigation and I wondered if I could get details of it.'

'Can I take a name, please?'

'Amber Fraser. I know she retracted her statement and the case was closed in March. I have a case number,' Christy added with an air of confidence, and quoted it before she could be stopped.

'What is your connection with the incident?'

'Just that I live in the same house and I need to know if the investigation has any repercussions for me. If I might be in danger myself.'

'I see.' There was an unnaturally generous pause, doubtless a holding strategy deployed with more overwrought callers. 'I'm not sure I understand why you think you might be in danger.'

'Because I'm fairly certain it also involved my next-door neighbour. Robert Whalen, he's called.'

'Hold the line, please.' There passed a few moments when the officer consulted either computer or colleague, but whichever it was the result was not in Christy's favour. 'I'm afraid this information can't be given over the phone.'

'I could go into my local police station in Lime Park,' she suggested. 'They must have been involved?'

'It's not that simple. You'll need to apply in writing and prove you have a good reason to be given access to the case notes.'

Christy knew what that meant: weeks of waiting and, likely, an unfavourable verdict. 'But it's not like it's classified information,' she protested. 'Everyone around here seems to know what happened, even the children.'

'Perhaps then you might find out what you need to know from someone in the community. An adult whose advice you trust.'

Christy floundered. She could hardly explain that the adults had been gagged and she alone was foolhardy enough to pursue this. 'I could, but I want to know the proper facts from the authorities. I could be at risk here.'

'We would need to judge for ourselves that there is an imminent risk to you,' the officer said.

'What about the Freedom of Information Act?' Christy was grasping at straws now. 'Don't I have a legal right to know if there's been a criminal investigation involving people living at my address?'

But it was clear the officer was not going to change her mind. 'We have to respect the rights of everyone. When an inquiry is closed and no prosecution brought, there is a duty to the party or parties involved.'

'I don't know what that means,' Christy said, frustration making her shrill. How many more times would she have to speak to a person who knew but who would not share that knowledge with her?

'It means that if you had done nothing wrong and you'd gone through an investigation that did not raise enough evidence to prosecute you, you'd be entitled to go about your business without everyone knowing your private history.'

'But I'm not "everyone", I'm living in the same house as someone who witnessed something so serious she went into hiding! I need to know what it is so I can protect myself.'

This was starting to sound like a nuisance call even to her, but the officer remained admirably even-tempered. 'As I say, write to us here, quoting the case number and stating your reasons, and you have my word we will give your request the proper consideration.'

The discussion was over. As she ended the call, her

thumb moved at once to dial Joe, who picked up with his customary harried air: 'Christy, I'm –'

'Don't hang up,' she interrupted, her breath short. 'I know you're busy, but this is important.'

'I don't –'

'Please, Joe, just listen!' She told him first what the St Luke's pupils had said, before recounting her conversation with Kenny. Then she read the letter aloud to him, skirting the issue of how she had come to recover it and open it. 'Do you know anyone in the police? I bet this is on a database that they can all access.'

'What, the Police National Computer?'

'That'll be it, can you get into it?'

'Of course not,' Joe said. 'I'm an M&A lawyer, Christy, I never work with the police, and even if I did I wouldn't have the right clearance. I think we should follow Kenny's advice and not get involved in this. If Rob's got some defamation lawyer on their case, then he'll have no hesitation in getting him on ours as well.'

But Christy had come too far to be cowed now. 'I don't agree. Unless he's tapped this phone, I don't see how he can possibly discover that we're making our own investigations.'

'No one's tapping our phone,' Joe sighed.

'And just because the inquiry was closed, it doesn't mean he didn't do whatever it was,' she continued, 'it just means they didn't have enough evidence to prosecute him. He could strike again, couldn't he?'

'"Strike again"? He's not a serial killer in an eighties cop drama!' To her aggravation, Joe was laughing at her; after months of his refusing to take seriously her speculation about there being something dark and rotten about Rob, here he was with evidence to hand and *still* he mocked her. 'We don't even know for sure it's him who's involved. He's not mentioned in the letter from the police, is he?'

'They mustn't have released his name. But it *is* him. It's got to be. Why else would he have a lawyer send out warning letters? Joe, we *have* to find out what we're dealing with. You must know someone. What about Henry? He's a criminal barrister, isn't he?'

'That doesn't mean he's going to be happy to ask a police officer to abuse his position for the wife of a friend of a friend. We'd be better just paying some private investigator to do it.'

'Private investigator? We haven't got the money for that!'

'We haven't got any money to defend a defamation charge either, have we?'

But she could tell that he was finally taking this seriously.

'Let me ask around, OK, and find out how we can get this information. Try to avoid Rob until we know what we're dealing with.'

It was impossible to do anything else that afternoon but drift from room to room in search of clarity. They'd been Amber's rooms, were still painted in colours she'd chosen, and yet she'd never felt more elusive to Christy, so far beyond reach. Had she known when she left that the investigation had been closed? Had the police been apprised of her change of address and sent her a duplicate?

As for Felicity, she must have been receiving mail for at least a month after the Frasers' departure; had she too been a witness and received notification of the case's closure? Had she retracted *her* statement? And if it was indeed Rob's alleged crime that had caused their respective flights, hadn't both parties been duty-bound to report their concerns to their solicitors? Yet the Frasers had not disclosed a word of it and nor, presumably, had Felicity, or surely Steph and Felix, a couple expecting a baby, would not have touched the place with a bargepole.

And where did Pippa fit into all of this? How could the crime be so bad that two neighbouring households had sold up and vanished, and yet not be bad enough for his girlfriend to have left him? Yes, she had moved out, but she hadn't stopped seeing him – *he* had been the one to call time on the relationship in the end, to *her* distress.

Unable to sit still any longer, she decided to call on Steph, slipping through the hedge between their doorsteps to avoid being spotted by Rob, should he happen to be idling at his window. But there was no answer from the lower flat. Steph often decamped to her parents on weekdays for help with Matilda, and it appeared that this was one of those occasions. Christy stood on the doorstep, paralysed with indecision. Where could she turn? It was three-thirty by now. Caroline and Joanne would still be on the school trip; Liz, she knew, was working part-time and even if she happened to be free that afternoon would surely be at the school picking up the boys.

To her horror the question was answered by the least desirable turn of events imaginable: the sound of heavy footfall on the stairs inside, the sight of the door swinging inwards, a male figure materializing in front of her. In her turmoil, she'd forgotten he'd changed his appearance, and could not stop herself from gasping out loud.

Rob's fingers flew to his chin. 'Oh, yeah, the beard. I'm the plain Jane who's whipped off her glasses, eh? So what are you doing, malingering on the doorstep like this?' His tone held its customary sardonic edge, but he had an affable expression on his face that reflected their fledgling friendship – until he registered her obvious emotional commotion. 'What's wrong?'

'I . . . I was looking for Steph.' She was panicking, breath catching in her windpipe and smothering her voice.

'I think she's away for a few days. Are you feeling all right?'

'No, I'm not . . . I need to show you this.'

'Show me what?' Still he emitted only concern, a once-coveted neighbourliness that would last only seconds longer, never again to be offered. The sense of crisis was acute, almost claustrophobic.

She held out the letter to him. Right on the doorstep he took it from her, his quizzical expression hardening to a grimace as he read the words.

'You have to tell me what this is about,' she said, swallowing hard. 'I can't go on feeling like I'm in the middle of some awful drama, it's driving me out of my mind.'

Rob looked from the text in front of him to her face, his expression, as she'd expected, radically altered and utterly unambiguous on his newly exposed features: sheer dislike, rank distaste. 'This letter is addressed to Amber Fraser. What are you doing with her mail?' He gestured abruptly, stirring the air between them, and she sensed the controlled rage, the harm a man of his height and strength could do.

Instinctively, she took a step back, broadening the gap between them. 'I opened it by mistake.'

'It's dated from March. That's over six months ago.'

'I was planning to forward it, but I haven't got around to it.'

'"Haven't got around to it"? You've got to be kidding me, after half a year?' Rob's gaze was sour with displeasure. 'Fine. Whatever you say. So why are you bringing it to *me*?'

Christy felt her body start to tremble. 'Because I know you were involved. *You* were the subject of the inquiry.'

He glanced again at the body of the letter, raising his eyebrows at her. 'And how do you "know" that, exactly? I don't see my name anywhere here.'

'I overheard something at St Luke's. The kids said a few things they weren't supposed to.'

He jeered at this, a jeer that seemed to animate his whole body: 'So you're getting your information from nine-year-olds, are you? Jesus, did you not listen to a word I said when we spoke about this before?'

But Christy had too many questions of her own to reply to his. 'Why didn't you tell me you'd volunteered at St Luke's before me? You knew I'd been allocated that school, you told me all about the problems they have there, and yet you didn't say a word about having worked there yourself.'

'Well, if that doesn't sound like a guilty man, I don't know what does,' he sneered.

'They said you'd been in prison.'

'Then they lied.'

'Did they lie about you having to stop volunteering because the police were called? Was that why you changed your name for your new column?' She construed his silence as admission. 'Anyway, if the charges were dropped, it doesn't matter if I know or not, surely?'

He took a step towards her, regarded her with burning-cold fury, a glare more intimidating than any she'd been subjected to before in her life, and she shrank from him in spite of herself. 'It *does* matter, yes. Have you got no respect for other people's privacy? What gives you the right to turn up at someone's door and demand to know their business?' He was close enough now for her to feel his breath on her skin, to smell his disgust for her. 'Oh, sorry, you already said: you don't like feeling like you're in the middle of a drama. Well, join the club, love.'

'*Please*,' Christy pleaded, her agitation peaking and tip-ping back in that single syllable. 'I know you've sent Caroline and everyone a letter threatening legal action, but I'm not spreading falsehoods or anything like that, I'm just asking *you* for the truth.'

'I told you before. I have no intention of discussing this with you.'

'Why not? I'm your next-door neighbour, don't I have a right to know if I'm in danger?'

'Oh, you're not in danger – except perhaps from your own mind.' He handed the letter back to her. 'You need to stop meddling, Christy. That would be the best decision you could make.'

They stared at each other, both breathing hard.

'This is why the Frasers left, isn't it?' Her voice was fractured with fear. 'And Felicity? They left because of you.'

Rob loomed over her once more, face clenched in anger, making her acutely aware of where she was and how easy it would be for him to overpower her. She scuttled back a few steps out of his range, causing him to scoff as he retreated into the hallway, his original errand evidently abandoned.

'Don't look so terrified,' he said. 'You're not my type.'

Returning home, she locked the doors and windows as a precaution. Just as she was about to ring Joe and beg him to come home early, he phoned her.

'Listen, I've managed to get hold of the call log from the police, the first complaint of something happening on January 15th. You were right, it *was* him. Robert Whalen, date of birth: 12th of June 1978. He was arrested at the end of January.'

'I *knew* it.' Eight months ago, that was all. When they'd moved in, his brush with the law had been only weeks old, frighteningly recent. It was *still* frighteningly recent. 'Oh God, Joe, I saw him just now. I showed him the letter.'

'Why on earth did you do that?' Joe's rising stress echoed hers. 'You didn't go up to his flat, did you?'

'No, I saw him on the doorstep. I didn't think you'd be able to find anything out so I thought I'd talk to Steph but she wasn't in and . . .' Her tongue was moving too fast against her palate, swallowing the spaces between words and making her incoherent.

'Try and calm down,' Joe said. 'Are you at home now?'

'Yes. I've locked myself in.'

'Well, don't approach him again. I'm on my way.'

'Why, what did you find out? What was his crime?'

'Alleged crime,' Joe said.

'OK, alleged crime. What was it?'

'It's bloody serious, Christy.'

'Just tell me!'

And she heard the anxious suck of his breath before he spoke.

Chapter 28

Amber, January 2013

'I was raped,' I said.

Jeremy stared at me. I could see from the faint flinching of his eyes that his instinct was to repel the notion before he could absorb it. 'You were . . . ?'

'Raped,' I repeated. 'Two weeks ago.' And horrific as it was, I felt a euphoric surge of relief in releasing the words to the world.

He came to me at once and held me very close; then, a growled syllable, scarcely human: 'Who?'

'Rob,' I whispered.

'*Rob?* You mean the guy next door? Your friend Rob?'

'He's no friend.'

And then the situation was no longer mine. It was the runaway train, the kamikaze plunge towards certain death. Jeremy's anger was of the contained, implosive kind, the kind that can cause hearts to fail, blow flesh to bits, the most potent kind of all.

'He will not get away with this,' he vowed, 'not while I am living and breathing.'

'Please don't go round there,' I begged, clutching to him.

'Don't worry, I won't. This needs to be dealt with

properly. I'm not having him slapping me with a charge for assault when *he's* the criminal.'

He phoned the police, though I protested hysterically that I didn't want to report the incident. It was after ten by then, and I heard him give his assurance that we would be safe until morning, when officers would visit early to talk to me. Then he rang his assistant at home and told her he would not be coming to the office the next day. His voice was eerily steady, stripped of tone or nuance; though he gave no reason, I knew she would assume that someone had died.

I never wanted to involve the police, not knowing as I did about the baby. Looking back now, I think I hoped I'd wake up in the morning and find that time had folded and we'd missed a day, that I'd be given a choice of alternative endings and be able to select the one that could save me. But instead two uniformed constables from the local station arrived at nine o'clock, exactly as planned, to make their preliminary assessment.

I quaked as they accepted our tea and sat on the sofa opposite us in our sitting room, composed myself at first with unrelated trains of thought: Hetty would not have liked to see the mud brought in onto the vintage kilim by one of the officers . . . Should I adjust the blinds, because the light seemed awkward for them . . . ? Wasn't it funny how their expressions – mild, honourable, encouraging – were perfectly identical? Did they have to practise it in training? Sliding my hand into Jeremy's, I wondered if I could get through this without speaking, by letting him speak for me.

But there were questions and I, inescapably, was the only one who could answer them. Clearly defined roles were immediately apparent: DC Mayer did the asking, while the officer whose name I didn't catch noted my answers in a pocketbook.

'You have something to report to us, Mrs Fraser?'

'Yes.' There was a sensation of standing on the roof of a very tall building, longing for a sudden gust to take me. 'I was . . . I was assaulted by the man next door.'

They asked the name of the male in question, and when Jeremy answered they requested that I repeat it.

'He was known to you before the incident?'

'Yes, as I say, he lives next door. At number 38. Flat B. That's where it took place.'

'When was this?'

I named the date, Tuesday the 15th of January, one I knew I would never forget.

'I can confirm that,' Jeremy said. 'When I came home from work that evening she was very distressed. Hysterical, I'd say.'

'And what was the nature of the assault?' said DC Mayer.

'He made me have sex with him. He raped me.'

The officer explained that he did not want details at this stage but only to record the nature of the rape and if I had sustained any injuries. I said the rape had been vaginal and though I'd felt pain during it and for several days afterwards I had not been injured enough to need medical assistance.

'There was some blood, wasn't there?' Jeremy reminded me, his tone troubled. 'I saw it on the sheet.'

396

I closed my eyes. 'Yes, but that's been washed now.' As had I, washed and healed – physically.

'No external injuries?'

'I would have noticed if there were any,' Jeremy interjected. 'I've been away on business since last week, but I would have noticed before that.' His brow tensed as he blamed himself for his failure to read my mind in the immediate aftermath, for his unavoidable absence afterwards. I knew he felt miserable that I'd been unable to tell him sooner, and I squeezed his hand harder, just as miserable to know I was so unworthy of him.

'Would you be willing to have a medical examination, Mrs Fraser?'

'I think too much time will have passed,' I said. 'How long . . . ?'

'We usually have a window of seven days,' said DC Mayer, 'if the male ejaculated without a condom.'

He kept saying 'male', as if Rob were a different mammal, or perhaps represented *all* men. In a way, he did.

'It's been much longer than that,' I said. 'Over two weeks now.'

'CID may still consider it evidentially worthwhile,' he persisted. 'There may still be bruising.'

'He's right, darling, if you don't have a medical then the defence will be able to exploit the fact that you didn't co-operate,' Jeremy said. 'They'll use it against you.'

He was already anticipating a trial. I felt faint, gave him a beseeching look before turning back to the officers.

'The thing is, I've just found out I'm pregnant, so I'd really rather not.'

Noting Jeremy's startled reaction, I saw that he had momentarily forgotten about the pregnancy – a bombshell for sixty seconds, it had been totally vaporized by the crisis that had followed – and immediately he revised his position to support me.

'I agree with Amber. If there's only a seven-day window then I don't see any reason for her to go through the additional distress of an internal examination.'

The officers appeared to accept this for the time being, and I gave Jeremy a grateful look.

'Have you seen Mr Whalen since the incident?'

'No, I've hardly left the house.'

'She's been very low,' said Jeremy. 'I've never seen her like this and now I know why. If I'd had any idea! This man has been next door all this time, while I was away! He could have tried to get to her again . . .'

I began to snivel and Jeremy pressed me to him, kissing the side of my head, whispering that I was safe now.

In sympathy, my questioner's tone became more compassionate still. 'And you decided not to report what happened straight away?'

'Yes.' I bowed my head. 'I'm sorry now that I didn't, I know I should have. I think I was traumatized. I couldn't believe it had happened, I didn't know whether to trust my own memory of it, it was so out of character for him. He's normally . . .' I trailed off, inarticulate, lost.

'But now you're sure you'd like the police to investigate this?'

'Of course she would,' Jeremy cried, indignant. 'You

can't have a rapist roaming the neighbourhood! You need to get him under lock and key as soon as possible. This morning, ideally!'

I could tell his interruptions were worrying the officers. In a tactful effort to sideline him, they assured him that he would have the opportunity to make a statement of his own and that it was necessary to know my wishes personally regarding an investigation.

'Yes, I would like you to investigate,' I said, though the truth was I shared none of Jeremy's fervour. I'd read magazine articles about victims of violent crime who chose not to make a complaint and, as a rule, I'd scorned their cowardice. Now I understood how they felt. When you are damaged your instinct is to seek to limit that damage, not to extend it, to reopen its wounds. Revenge is no priority.

Mercifully, the assessment appeared to be at an end, because the other constable was closing his pocketbook and DC Mayer was smiling. 'In that case, we will pass this straight to CID and a specially trained officer will be in touch with you this morning to arrange the formal interview, probably for later today.' He added that owing to the nature of the allegation the interview would take place in a special unit rather than the police station, and that it would be recorded as evidence.

'Later today?' I repeated, worried.

'Yes, they move very quickly in Sexual Offences. Reports of this kind are taken with the utmost seriousness.'

And as Jeremy applauded this dedication to excellence,

I felt the beginnings of raw dread, sharp fingers throttling my natural resources of courage.

I began again to cry.

The facility was not in Lime Park or its environs but more central, closer to the river, to the casual eye a nondescript semi-detached house with an exterior that was decently maintained. Inside, the rooms were comfortably furnished and unremarkable – until you noticed the pulled blackout blinds and video equipment.

Two plain-clothed CID officers were there to meet us, as well as Wendy, the specially trained officer who had phoned earlier to arrange the interview and explain her role. She was in her forties, low key in both look and demeanour but possessing a fierceness in her eyes that was protective, almost maternal. She, the two male officers, my own husband: each of them radiated such integrity, it was overwhelming.

'As I said on the phone, Amber, I'm here to support you through the whole process,' Wendy said, 'however long it takes. I'll be interviewing you today and I'll keep you updated on the progress of the investigation. You already have my mobile number and you can contact me at any time with any questions you have. Do you have any now, before we start?'

Only one, I thought. How can I travel back to January 15th and alter the afternoon's events? Tell me, *please*, at what moment I might have withdrawn, prevented the conclusion from taking the devastating form it had.

Jeremy and I were to be kept apart. While I was formally

questioned, he would be making his statement of first complaint, and we were not allowed to be present at one another's interview. Saying goodbye, I felt overcome, as if I might never see him again.

Wendy and I sat in easy chairs angled towards one another, a table at knee height for glasses of water and, I noticed, a box of tissues, making me think of the many who'd sat in the chair before me and been in tears as they relived the suffering of their experiences. There was an odd comfort in that. The video equipment was pointed out to me, though I could hardly have missed it.

'Everything in the room is being recorded visually and audibly, and the DC will be monitoring outside the room. Are you comfortable with these arrangements, Amber?'

'Yes, fine.'

In fact, I was appalled to find myself here, at the eye of an expensive police investigation. I felt frightened, inadequate, so consumed by the magnitude of it that I could not at first begin. But Wendy was patient, almost hypnotic in her murmured encouragement, and as we began with a clarification of the logistics of Rob's flat, the date and time I'd arrived, I felt myself relax and forget the camera.

'Why were you in his flat that afternoon, Amber?'

'He'd invited me over for coffee. We're friends – we *were* friends – and we met up most weeks, maybe twice a week. It started when I had builders in my house last spring. I'd go to his flat to escape the chaos. That had all finished months ago, but we still got together regularly, often at his place.'

'Which room did you usually drink your coffee in?'

'In the living room.'

'How did you come to be in his bedroom this time?'

I'd had all night to think how to explain this, for I could not of course utter a word about having been a regular in his bedroom, about the countless liaisons we'd had in which there'd been no whisper of a possibility that the atmosphere between us could ignite so disastrously.

'I hadn't been there long when he said he wanted to show me a new shirt he'd bought, get my opinion on it because I'm quite into clothes and fashion, I've advised other neighbours. So I followed him into the bedroom. He closed the door and before I could even ask why he'd done that he was pushing me really roughly against it and was covering my mouth with his hand. I tried to wriggle free, but he was very strong and I couldn't speak through his hand and he was threatening me with violence if I didn't go along with what he wanted. He said he'd hurt me, not just physically, but he'd spread terrible lies about me, things about my past. He said he'd start a hate campaign against me on the Internet.' Hearing once more his words in my head – *The evidence just keeps on coming, Amber Baby* – I whimpered, paused to take a breath and drink from my glass of water.

'Go on, when you're ready,' Wendy said.

'I was terrified, I didn't even recognize him. He made me lie on the bed and take my underwear off. Then he raped me.'

'You were lying on your back?'

'Yes.'

'And the penetration was vaginal?'

402

'Yes. He told me not to fight him or he would hurt me even more. I couldn't scream because he had his hand over my mouth still. I was really panicking and couldn't breathe very well.'

'He would have understood that you were not consenting, would he?'

'Yes, I was saying "No" all the time, or trying to, and I was obviously objecting physically. But it was like he didn't understand what I was saying or doing, he didn't care. He was so rough the way he handled me. It was as if he hated me and wished I was dead.' I remembered then the mercilessness in his face as it hovered above mine, the intensity of his contempt, the scorn on his breath. 'It wasn't like normal sex. I could feel the pain everywhere. He wanted to hurt me *inside*.'

'Were you able to use your hands to fend him off?'

'No, he had them pinned above my head, both of them in one hand.'

'So, just to be clear, he used one of his hands to grip yours and the other one to restrain your mouth?'

'Yes, when he needed to use one of them, he pressed his mouth against mine to keep me quiet. When that happened, I tried to bite him but I couldn't get my mouth open. I was struggling to breathe. And then the hand came back.'

'He was fully dressed, so you mean that he needed to use his hand to undo his trousers?'

'Yes. And . . . and also to put himself inside me.'

'And did he remove his hand from your mouth at any other time to allow you to speak?'

'Only afterwards, when he let me go. He said to get out and remember what he'd said about destroying me. He said it wouldn't just be me who would suffer but Jeremy as well, because he would deny everything and Jeremy would think I'd been having an affair.'

'Did you call out or say anything that might have been overheard by a neighbour?'

I remembered Felicity then, standing in her doorway as I staggered past, already half-blind from the streaming tears. Extraordinarily, until then, I had forgotten she'd been there. 'He has a neighbour downstairs, Felicity Boyd she's called, and she saw me leave. When he let me go I screamed something as I ran out, "You'll never touch me again," something like that. She may have heard. I was completely hysterical,' I added. 'I'm not really sure what I said or when. I'm so sorry.'

'No need to be sorry, you're doing brilliantly, Amber.' Wendy continued to draw details from me about the sexual attack itself, the number of times penetration had taken place, whether there'd been any anal or oral assault, if I still had the underwear and clothing I'd worn that afternoon. The questions were difficult to answer, they almost broke me, but I reminded myself that there must have been women in this seat before me who'd experienced far worse than I had.

'Had you been in his bedroom before, Amber?'

Oh God. I had prepared this overnight, but now the moment had come I struggled to remember the lines. 'Yes, a few times. He showed me the view from his window once when I wondered if he overlooked my garden. I think I sat in the leather armchair once.'

I certainly had, straddling him, joined to him, sucking at his mouth, tearing at his hair. I felt nauseous at the memory, my brain still unable to reconcile the original infatuation with the final conflict.

'I've been all over the flat,' I said, thinking it best to volunteer this. In the event, it was surprising how truthful I was able to be about the logistics of my visits while withholding all information about the sexual activities themselves.

'And has he tried to see you or contact you since the incident?'

'No. I've seen him out of the window, but I've mainly stayed inside. I couldn't stop crying for ages and I didn't want anyone to see me in that state.'

'So there are no voicemails, texts or emails from him that you can show us?'

'There is one text, yes. It says, "No hard feelings?" But I know that doesn't prove anything.' Briefly, anger flared. '"No hard feelings?" That makes it sound like we just had some little disagreement! I didn't reply to it, I was too upset.'

'You did the right thing, Amber. There are no other messages from earlier in your friendship?'

'I suppose I might have one or two from before . . .' But of course I did not. Every text between us had been deleted, I was certain of that. But my relief was short-lived, for Wendy did not seem as disappointed by this as I might have expected, by which I deduced that the police would be able to access phone records, they'd have technology that allowed them to read deleted messages. Nothing was ever truly erased, was it? And though the majority of our texts had been innocent by design – 'Free tomorrow at 2?' 'Coffee as usual Thurs?' – there had been of course that period in November when I'd given rein to lunacy and bombarded Rob wildly: 'Where are you?' I'd demanded, over and over, and 'Why don't you respond?' Later, there'd been other liberties between us: *Still playing Florence Nightingale . . . ?*

It was becoming clear to me that I needed to abort this investigation before it got properly under way if I was to succeed in concealing from Jeremy my long-term infidelity. I needed to make it my priority to protect him from the truth of the affair, regardless of how catastrophically it had ended – and that did not necessarily mean doing the right thing as the police saw it.

But while I was here, a captive of my own making, I had to go through the motions of finishing this interview. 'Is that all?' I asked Wendy hopefully.

'There's just a little more, if you can manage it.' She passed me my glass of water, urging me to take another mouthful, to try to relax. Then she raised an issue that I deeply regretted having shared with Jeremy the night before, when I'd been in the full flow of emotion.

'We understand from your husband that Mr Whalen told you he had been accused of a sexual offence in the past.'

'That's right.'

'Could you tell me exactly what he told you?'

'It was when he was a student,' I said, 'but the charges were dropped. It was a girlfriend he'd just broken up with. She accused him of raping her, but she admitted it was a false claim.'

I reached for a tissue and held it to my throbbing face as she drew from me everything I could remember from Rob's treetop confidence.

'Can you say how it was that you still felt safe with him after having learned of this previous incident?'

'We confided in each other, we were friends. I believed him when he said there was nothing in it. I trusted him.' I took a sharp breath, causing pain under my ribs, and I thought for a split second of the beginnings of a baby in my abdomen. A son or a daughter in miniature human design, burgeoning, seizing precious life. I thought of the tree house, the rawness of Rob's need and my celebration of its return. That confession of his: I *had* believed it. 'I still do believe him,' I said firmly. 'On that score. I don't see that and this as being related at all.'

But *they* would, I knew, just as Jeremy had. 'I'm amazed he told you something like that,' he'd remarked in the early hours. 'They might not have found out otherwise, it's been so long. He's dug his own grave now.'

I knew, too, that Jeremy would mention that girl at Joanne and Kenny's dinner party, urge the police to question her – and others – to discover a damning pattern of abuse.

When the interview was over, Wendy and I joined Jeremy and the two CID officers in an adjoining room.

'Darling!' Jeremy leaped up straight away to embrace me and check for any adverse effects of my interrogation.

'I'm fine,' I told him. It was becoming my catchphrase.

'What happens now?' he asked the officers. He seemed positively refreshed by his own experience of making a statement, as determined to pursue justice as I was reluctant.

DI Swann cleared his throat. 'Well, based on your wife's statement, we have enough information to arrest Mr Whalen and question him about the incident.'

'Good,' Jeremy said, grim, unequivocal.

I could imagine it all too clearly, the officers on the doorstep, Rob buzzing them in, hearing the words that would infuriate him, all too soon filling him with abject terror: 'An allegation has been made against you ...' Would Pippa be there? Would she stand by him, thinking she trusted him instinctively, as I once had, convinced that he was incapable of such a crime?

'Will he be put in handcuffs?' I asked.

'Yes.'

This detail pleased Jeremy. 'When will you go there? Today?'

'Within the next twenty-four hours. Possibly this evening or first thing tomorrow before he leaves for work.'

'He works from home,' Jeremy said. 'He's usually in all day, isn't he, darling?'

I nodded. 'I didn't think things would move so fast.'

'It's an extremely serious situation, Amber,' Wendy said. 'You have our word that we'll progress as efficiently as we can.'

'Will you put him in a cell?' Jeremy demanded, focusing on the most senior officer present, DI Swann. 'How long will you hold him for?'

'He'll be held in a police cell, yes, for as long as it takes to question him and visit the scene.'

'What do you mean, "visit the scene"?' I echoed.

'Well, once we've brought him in we'll arrange access to his flat so that we can examine it. There may still be evidence that's useful if the CPS decide to bring a case.'

My hand flew out in involuntary protest. This was unravelling badly. 'The thing is . . .' It was difficult to voice my objection without making it sound as if I were protecting my attacker, but I worried, of course, about evidence in his flat of other, historical intimacy. I imagined a forensic team combing the rooms in the way I'd seen done on TV; they'd find fibres from my clothes – an extensive collection of them – as well as hair, skin, traces of bodily fluids. 'As I explained to Wendy, I've been all over the flat on previous visits. And anyway, his girlfriend has moved in since it happened. He'll have changed the bedclothes, cleaned up, surely?'

'Even so, there may still be evidence we can collect that will help build the case.' As DI Swann and his colleagues peered benignly at me for signs of approval, I felt as if I were standing on the set of a crime drama, the words being spoken by actors deep in character.

'Will you let us know when he's released again?' I asked numbly.

Wendy laid a comforting hand on my arm. 'Of course. I'll be in touch to let you know as soon as he's released, along with the decision made – charge or bail, with or without conditions.'

'I don't think he should be bailed at all,' Jeremy insisted, not only speaking now as if a member of the investigating team himself but also exuding all the authority of the highest-ranked among them. 'Not when he's been accused of the same thing before – you've made a note of that, right?'

'Rest assured we'll be checking our databases to see if this previous charge is still on record,' DS Graham told him. 'It may not be, however; you need to be aware of that.'

'Why wouldn't it be?' Jeremy asked, frowning.

'Records are sometimes removed after a period of time, partly to protect the innocent from malicious allegations.'

Malicious allegations: that was the exact phrase Rob had used in relation to the college girlfriend.

'Even if the crime report is no longer available, his arrest should still show on PNC,' DS Graham told Jeremy.

'Police National Computer,' Wendy clarified for my benefit. 'Every force has a system going back fifteen years to show the basic details of the allegation at the very least. As long as we can find out which force to ask, we'll be able to get the information.'

'So even though the charge was dropped, it'll be useful in a trial,' Jeremy said. 'It shows he's got a bad character, if nothing else.' Sure enough, he now mentioned Kenny's colleague, and a note was made of Kenny's phone number, address and employer.

'Where will you be for us to contact *you*?' Wendy asked us.

'I can't go back home,' I said. 'I can't be there when he's arrested or when he gets back from questioning. He'll come and find me.' Again I could imagine it in grotesque detail: Rob storming around, spewing details of our assignations in front of Jeremy, in front of the street, the horror of those details obliterating the effects of the single episode I had reported.

'Of course you can't,' Jeremy said. 'You can't be anywhere near this monster. I can't believe I've left you there on your own; you must have been absolutely petrified every time I left the house.' He pulled me close, my rescuer and protector, just as he'd been when we'd met years ago, when I'd falteringly confided the personal history I'd so recently shed. 'Let's go to a hotel. I'll check us in and then I'll go back to the house to get some clothes and things.'

He promised to let Wendy know of our new, temporary accommodation the moment we were installed.

Finally, as we were finishing, there was good news. DS Graham confirmed that a discussion had taken place in which it was agreed I would not be expected to undergo a medical examination. He mentioned my pregnancy and asked if I had been examined by my GP or an obstetrician in the period between the assault and my reporting the incident. I said no, but I intended visiting my GP in the next week or so.

'I'd rather no one was told about my situation,' I added. 'It's early days and I don't want it to be affected by everything that's happened.'

Wendy nodded. 'We can't say for sure if it will be relevant to the investigation or not, but we'll do everything we can to respect your privacy.'

It was then, just as we parted, that DI Swann said

something I was not expecting and could find no response to at the time, but which, ghastly as it was, did at least bring a halt to the spinning and flailing of my mind and direct it instead towards a solution.

It would need some thinking through, but it was possible I had found a way out.

Chapter 29

Christy, October 2013

The man next door was a rapist. Or he wasn't. And only a few weeks ago she'd craved his approval, *basked* in it when she'd got it.

Christy could not stop shivering – and not only because it was a cool early-October day and the Davenports' draconian household budget prohibited the turning on of the central heating before the clocks went back. She looked at Joe's scribbled notes, just a few names and dates on the back of a printed document: the date of the incident, the date the report was made, the person who made the complaint, and the person against whom it was made.

Amber Fraser and Rob Whalen: at last, the truth about how they were connected – or how their connection had been severed.

'Rape,' she said to Joe, thinking it was the bleakest, the blackest syllable she had ever uttered. 'I can't believe it.'

'Alleged,' he corrected her. 'He was only questioned. Like the letter says, the inquiry was closed.'

'Felicity must have been a witness, mustn't she? Perhaps she was the one who phoned the police.'

'No, look at the log details: Jeremy Fraser was the one

who phoned – and two weeks after the event, as well. They took their time reporting it.'

'No wonder the police didn't prosecute. There can't have been any physical evidence by then, can there?'

'Possibly.' Joe paused. 'Or perhaps there wasn't any crime.'

Christy chose to ignore this.

'So Rob was arrested on January 31st. Then the letter about the inquiry ending was sent in mid March. It probably sat in a pile of paperwork for weeks, as well, so the investigation can't have lasted very long at all. And this was all happening at the same time the house came on the market, when we first heard from the agent.

'Now we know why the Frasers sold up,' Joe said.

'Rob must have threatened her,' Christy continued, 'pressured her into withdrawing her statement. Perhaps that's why she took her time coming forward in the first place. If he's the kind of man who would commit rape, then he's the kind who would use intimidation, and we already know he sent the neighbours letters trying to browbeat them into silence, so –'

'He'll stop at nothing?' Joe finished wryly. 'I'm sorry, but the way the law works is we accept he has *not* committed rape and he has sent the letters because he has every right to defend his good reputation.'

Christy shook her head. It was inevitable that he would take a rational approach; he'd make a decent detective himself. 'I know you don't believe that, Joe, or you wouldn't have told me to stay inside and avoid him. You wouldn't have come home.'

'I was worried you might get into a row with him,' Joe said.

'Yes, because he's potentially violent!' She was already driving on, aligning clues, tidying frayed ends. 'That's why the Frasers sold at the price they did, that's why they authorized the solicitor to pay for our roof – to keep us sweet in case we found out they'd been withholding information about a police investigation and kicked up a fuss. Oh my God, Joe, *rape*. I *knew* he was evil – I told you, right from the start! It must be torture for Caroline and Liz and everyone having him still living here when they don't believe he's innocent!'

Joe remained solidly resistant to hysteria, every inch the legal professional. '*They* might not believe it, but the police obviously do. Caroline and her crew are not relevant.' He reached for her hand. 'But you're right, we do need to talk it through, find out a bit more. This is serious stuff we've unearthed.'

Calmed by his grip, Christy paused. As she looked at him now in the limpid light of the kitchen, it seemed like months since she'd seen him in the day. Perhaps it was because he was wearing work clothes at home in the middle of the afternoon, dark corporate clothing that brought an alarming pallor to his sun-deprived complexion. He looked frighteningly aged, in that accelerated way a prime minister did midterm, half broken, as if it could go either way. You certainly would not bet on him in a fight against Rob Whalen.

Don't look so terrified. You're not my type. Well, Amber Fraser had been his type and she'd fled for her life.

She gave a sudden involuntary whine.

'Hey, come on,' Joe said, 'I know you're shaken, but we don't want to be a part of any witch hunt, do we? Felix and Steph seem perfectly happy with him, don't they? You said he was left in charge of Matilda the other day.'

'Only because they don't know anything about this – if they did, there's no way they would have left their baby with him. They wouldn't have bought the flat in the first place. Living downstairs from a rapist!' Hysteria was rising once more. 'Should we tell them, Joe? I think we should. I wish someone had told *us*.'

'No. It would be slander, we'd get a letter from his lawyer, exactly like Kenny and the others did, and if you carry on like this it will be more than a letter, we'll be prosecuted, ordered to pay damages, costs, the lot. So calm down.'

Christy did not reply. As far as she was concerned the letters were an expression of Rob's bullying, his need to control what others said and thought.

'Before today, you were starting to get on well with him, remember?'

'I should have trusted my instincts,' she said.

'Instincts aren't always right,' Joe said. 'What about his girlfriend, the same one he's been with since before all of this, didn't Caroline say? Doesn't her trust in him suggest a reasonable assumption of innocence?'

'I don't see why. Even serial killers have women in love with them, it's a known phenomenon.' But at the thought of Pippa, Christy remembered the scene on which she'd eavesdropped and her conviction wavered: regardless of what she'd discovered since, the disagreement she'd over-heard had been about infidelity, sexual jealousy, not assault. If nothing else, they had been in accord about the 'nightmare'. *You know* I'd *never discuss it*, Pippa had said. Joe was right, she *hadn't* given credence to the Frasers' allega-tion, even if Christy thought she should have. But it was academic, Christy reminded herself, for she and Rob had broken up two weeks ago and she hadn't been seen in the neighbourhood since. Pippa was safe.

But was *she*? Rob was at that moment *next door*, and he would be there day after day after day. She couldn't expect Joe to take any more time off work, and yet she couldn't countenance the thought of being left in the house alone while Rob paced about *there*, on the other side of the wall, knowing she was getting close to his hidden truth. Having strived for so long to share in the street's secrets, she now felt crippled by their weight. There was no solution, no resolution. There was certainly no satisfaction.

'I'm going to ask Caroline about this,' she said, spring-ing to her feet with sudden decisiveness. 'It's five-thirty, she must be back from her school trip by now.'

'Do you think that's a good idea?' Joe said, his frown making it clear that *he* did not. 'Shall I come with you?'

'I'll be fine. You stay here. You probably need to check in with work.' And she touched his arm before she left, grateful that he was here today, at least.

Outside, the early evening shimmered as if nothing were awry; there was even birdsong. Marching down the

Sellerses' path, Christy was reminded of the previous time she'd blundered down it, back in the early days when she'd been so naive she'd thought the drama was to do with Joe and her, with *planning permission*.

'Christy, hello! Come in,' said Caroline. 'Oh dear, I can see you've got something on your mind ... .'

All the Sellers children were home from school and there was the debris of toast and fruit on the kitchen table, discarded souvenirs from the museum, including a half-eaten chocolate mummy. Blurred figures dashed in and out, and Christy wished she didn't have to destroy that easy mood by launching another fraught interrogation. She asked Caroline if it was possible to talk privately.

'We can certainly try.' Caroline pushed shut the kitchen door and placed a foot against it to bar entry to any curious youngsters.

'I know about the rape,' Christy said in an undertone.

'Oh.' At once, Caroline's face slackened. She leaned back, her full weight limp against the closed door, and for a moment Christy thought she might slide to the floor and cry.

'Kenny told me you've all been warned about spreading falsehoods, but this conversation goes no further, you have my word. You knew both of them, Rob and Amber. Do *you* think he's guilty?'

'You know I can't answer that,' Caroline said.

'Don't even speak then, just nod. He can't stop you nodding, can he?'

And with a barely perceptible bow of her head, Caroline's long period of self-censorship was over at last.

When she spoke, the words were muttered low, as if she feared microphones had been planted in the pen pots and biscuit tin; she'd lived this way for months, Christy thought, appalled at having railed against her own ignorance when she should have been appreciating its benefits. 'I can't speak for everyone, though. Richard, for one, follows the letter of the law and says if he wasn't charged then there can't have been evidence, and if there was no evidence there was no crime. Kenny says the same.'

Which was Joe's position. Gender lines were drawn here, it seemed. 'You were all friends, weren't you, before it happened? Was there ever anything strange about the way he behaved towards Amber?'

'No, not at all. I must admit I hadn't seen either of them much since before Christmas. He was away on work assignments and seeing Pippa a lot and then they were all on holiday, but the last time I saw the two of them together they seemed fine. They were being quite flirtatious with each other, actually, but Amber was like that with everyone so it didn't mean anything. She was happy, glowing from her holiday.'

'Was *he* normally flirtatious, though?'

'Sometimes, in his own way. They were quite similar characters, which I guess was part of why they got on so well. He knew the effect he had on women. Quite a few around here had a soft spot for him back then – God, I remember joking with Amber myself about having an affair with him. But we didn't really *know* him. Before the Frasers moved in and Amber got him on the social scene, he'd been very enigmatic. We used to invent histories for him, say he was an assassin, stupid stuff like that. No one ever saw him with a regular girlfriend, not until Pippa. I told you she moved in with him for only a little while, didn't I? Well, it was actually a matter of *days*. She can't have known a thing about what happened with Amber until he was arrested.'

'Maybe he moved her in to cover his tracks?' Christy suggested.

Again, Caroline dipped her head in agreement. 'I feel very sorry for her because I know she really cared for Rob. Enough to stand by him, obviously.'

'They've split up now,' Christy said.

'I think that's for the best,' Caroline said. 'If you were her, well, you could never actually be *sure*, could you?'

'Were you there when the police came?'

'Yes, I saw him being taken off. It was terrible timing, about eight-thirty in the morning, right as we were all leaving for school. The kids were excited about seeing a police car; people were looking out of their windows, coming out to watch. He was so *angry*, Christy, it was truly frightening. And then when he came back, for that whole period afterwards, he just went to ground, you never saw him. I actually felt some sympathy for him, because people were behaving appallingly; he was pretty much under siege up there. He'd been helping at St Luke's and some of the parents found out his address and turned up screaming under his window, even throwing stuff up and breaking the glass – you'd think he'd been convicted of paedophilia the way they were talking.'

Perhaps it was one of these parents who had sent the hate mail, Christy thought; someone from further afield who'd made a mistake with the house number. It made sense too of the chaperoning she'd observed, the older girls being ferried to and from school when they might easily have made their own way.

'And it wasn't just them,' Caroline continued. 'I remember Kenny thumping at his door and yelling through the letter box for him to come out and explain to us why she'd gone. He was very fond of Amber, but I'm not sure that was the best way to tackle the situation. Especially since Rob decided to come down that time.'

'They got into a fight?' Christy asked.

'Yes, they were shoving each other and Kenny lashed out. He hurt himself more than he hurt Rob – I think he broke a knuckle. That must have been just before you and Joe moved in. By then we'd discovered Amber and Jeremy had gone for good and the house was being sold. We were all in complete shock, of course.'

'Was Felicity aware of all of this?'

'Yes. She felt completely besieged, sharing a house with him. And she told me that she'd heard shouting the afternoon it happened – *allegedly* happened – and she'd seen Amber crying as she left his flat. She said she knew instinctively that Rob had hurt her.'

'Then why didn't she phone the police?' Christy asked.

'Oh, believe me, she wishes she had. But at the time she didn't trust her instinct, said she'd always thought there was something a bit deceitful about Amber, which was of course ridiculous. When it all came out, she felt terribly guilty, really blamed herself. She didn't want anything more to do with Rob.'

'What about Amber? Did you speak to her after that day?'

'No and that's my greatest regret.' Grief shadowed Caroline's face, pulled its contours downwards, ageing her. 'There was a week or so when I didn't have a clue anything had happened, I thought she was just busy with other things. But then Jeremy was going away and he asked me to keep an eye on her. He said she'd been feeling low about not being able to get pregnant, hadn't got out of bed for days. Of course I promised I would, but whenever I called round or phoned her there was no answer and I started to think she must have gone to stay with friends or maybe even flown out to join him. It's so sad to think that she must have been in the house all that time, alone and suffering. And then Jeremy came back and they left for good.'

'You still don't know where they went?' Christy said.

'No. The one time Richard managed to speak to him he said they wanted a clean break and hoped we'd all respect that. He said to forget they'd ever lived in Lime Park, because that was what *they* were trying to do. We think he's probably back in the office now, but Richard says we shouldn't make contact.' Caroline groaned, a guttural, animal sound, her fingers tearing at the ends of her hair. 'As you can imagine, I've thought about this thing till I'm blue in the face. I've tried and tried to understand why they felt they had to disappear when I'm sure everyone would have preferred *him* to go.'

'And *do* you understand?' Christy asked her.

'Not completely. But I keep coming back to the same thing. To leave like that, literally overnight, not a word to a soul, whatever happened or didn't happen she must have been scared out of her wits.'

'I agree,' said Christy. Noticing a tear rolling from Caroline's eye, she touched her arm in sympathy, in apology. 'Thank you for talking about it. It's really helped.'

'We didn't have this conversation,' Caroline said.

Not long after she returned home, darkness having finally fallen on that longest of days, the inevitable came to pass: Rob Whalen was on their doorstep. She could tell it was him by his outline behind the stained glass, the tall, broad-shouldered bulk of him, once menacing, then seductively benign, and now, all too soon, threatening once again.

Christy opened the door and planted her feet firmly apart, trying not to shrink from him even as she found herself incapable of drawing a full breath.

'You know,' he said, simply. They were the same words he'd used before, and hearing them caused a powerful sense of fatalism in her. To have convinced herself she'd had him wrong, when it now appeared she'd had him right all along: well, it pained and confused her.

This time, at least, she had Joe to speak for her. He was at her shoulder, one hand on her hip, steady and protect-ive. 'We know there was a police investigation and we know it was dropped. I for one don't think we need to know anything else.' His tone was laudably devoid of accusation or insult.

'But you've filled in the gaps for yourselves,' Rob said. 'Go on, say it, it won't be worse than anything I've already heard.'

'We're not going to say anything, mate. It's none of our business.'

Rob looked directly at Christy. 'But you, *you* think I attacked her, don't you? You probably think I terrified her into not pressing charges, forced her to leave, and now you think you live next door to a rapist and are wondering how quickly you can sell up too. It's written all over your face.'

'I don't know what I think,' Christy said flatly, though he had in fact summarized her thoughts rather accurately. She didn't *want* to think what she thought, however. And the fact that he plainly cared, well, that was not lost on her.

'That's the conventional line, anyway,' Rob said. There was a tremor in his voice, the first inkling of frailty she'd observed in him. The fire had gone from him, that devouring intensity that had moved her one way or another right from the beginning, and he looked, for the first time, beaten. 'And I can't stop them thinking it any more than I can stop you.'

'What *I* think is that you should come in,' Joe said, and he stepped back, pulling Christy with him. 'This isn't a conversation to be having on the doorstep.'

So he was nailing his colours to Rob's mast, Christy thought. He believed him and was inviting him into their home without having sought her consent, presumably because he suspected she would object; after all, she'd performed her own interrogation on the doorstep earlier that afternoon, too cowardly to take the discussion indoors. Trooping after the two men, she felt a chasm open between Joe and her – *I for one*, he'd said, not *I speak for both of us* – followed at once by a primitive instinct to close it. As long as she did not know for sure if Rob Whalen was craven and manipulative or unjustly misunderstood, he was a danger to them. She would not let him threaten their household as he had the Frasers'.

In the kitchen, Joe poured typically oversized glasses of wine, placing them on the table to draw the three of them into closer conference. It was the first time Rob had been in their house while they had been in residence.

'You've obviously had a hellish time,' Joe said, every inch the good neighbour and friend.

Rob's chin sank towards his glass. 'You could say that. Let's see, I've had hate mail in every form of media you can name, I've had to change all my numbers and email addresses, I've had people spit at me in the street and scream obscenities at my window. I've been punched and kicked. For weeks I couldn't leave the flat at all, and when I did I might as well not have existed because no one looked at me or answered when I spoke, which was almost as bad as the punches. You know they don't allow their teenage kids to walk down the street on their own? It's a real-life case of "lock up your daughters". Lime Park Mothers Against Sex Offenders: never mind that there was never a conviction.'

'But how did they all know?' Christy asked. 'It wasn't in the press. I've checked online.'

'I'm sure you have.' Rob looked at her with sorrowful resignation, as if her words had just proved his point. 'My lawyers issued warnings, so the local forums and news sites took my name down. But it was too late: enough of them had seen the arrest. And now I've lost work, I've lost my girlfriend . . .'

'So Pippa knew what you were accused of?' Christy asked, interrupting. She was determined to discover the missing pieces of her own hypotheses, even if Joe chose to distance himself from them.

'Of course she did. She didn't believe it for a second, but the tensions of it all . . .' Rob broke off, groaning. 'To be honest, I still don't know whether I can stay or not, even though I've lived on this street longer than most of the people here. And all because everyone is prepared to believe a lie. They *want* to believe it.'

None of this was uttered in self-pity.

'Maybe what they want is to believe *her*,' Joe said. 'And that automatically means disbelieving you. She was very popular, wasn't she, Amber Fraser?'

'Oh, she was popular all right,' Rob said. 'The life and soul. They all worshipped the ground she walked on. Old Felicity had her measure, but she was the only one. When I heard that even *she* had believed Amber's story, then I knew it was hopeless. I knew I was going to prison.'

'But if it's *not* true, why would she make something like that up?' Christy demanded. For all her bluster, she did not dare speak the word 'rape'; its utterance felt like an allegation in itself. 'Why would she be prepared to lose her home just after she'd bought it and spent so much money on it? They hadn't even been here a year, they

426

intended staying long term. It makes no sense to make a false claim like that and sacrifice everything.'

'She had her reasons,' Rob muttered.

'What reasons?' Joe asked, but discreetly, mindful that he was leading a conversation and not an inquisition. He poured them each more wine, though his was the only glass that was finished.

'It was to cover up what she'd really been doing,' Rob said, his expression grim.

'Which was what?'

'Having an affair.'

'With you?'

'Of course with me.'

The admission stirred a physical response in Christy that was both curious and frightening, a blend of moral vindication and sensory agitation. Caroline and the others hadn't know, she realized. No one had known.

'I'm not clear how fabricating an assault charge covered anything up,' Joe said, fingers tapping on his glass. 'Wouldn't it produce the opposite effect? Unless . . . the husband found out, did he?'

Rob nodded. 'I'm not exactly sure of the chronology myself, but I think he must have done. And she came up with the rape story to save her marriage. I know how she got the idea, as well, because it was something we talked about. A similar thing happened to someone I used to know. That case was dropped early on, as well.'

What a strange affair they must have been having, Christy thought, if *that* was their idea of pillow talk. She

427

was as sceptical of his version of events as her husband was – apparently – accepting.

'She had nothing on her own,' Rob continued. 'Jeremy was the one with the money.'

'If they were married, then all their property would have been jointly owned,' Christy pointed out stiffly.

'Sure, but he might have divorced her, screwed her over in the financial settlement. She wasn't working, she had no income of her own. They didn't have kids.'

It took a supreme effort for Christy not to note the parallels with her own marriage, to suppress afresh the memory of that sunny afternoon on the Parade, the sudden moment of understanding she and Rob had shared when left alone together. Was that how he and Amber had started? A cup of coffee, an unseasonably warm day, an unexpected shift in mood? Had all of this been born of that great suburban cliché: *boredom*?

'She was the kind of woman who needed a wealthy man,' Rob said, then corrected himself: 'Actually, not so much wealthy as adoring. A believer, an acolyte, you know? She needed him to put her on a pedestal. That was their dynamic and they were both very happy with it.'

As he spoke about his accuser, the woman who he claimed had destroyed his life, it was impossible to read his emotions; there was loathing, yes, but it did not run as deep as you might have expected. The allure of Amber Fraser endured, perhaps. Or was it that his words were weighted with the guilt of what he'd done to her? Having damned her by driving her out, he sought to praise her by appearing to understand her motives for going.

'There must have been other options open to her,' Joe persisted. 'Didn't you ask her why she did such a terrible thing?'

Catching his eye, Christy gave Joe a look that said, *Shouldn't you be asking him how* he *could do such a terrible thing?* He did not acknowledge it, however, his attention returning to their guest, alert to his answer. Quite apart from Joe's position on any other aspect of the matter, he seemed entirely unaffected by the revelation that Rob was the sort of person who slept with other men's wives.

Well, she had a mind of her own and, above all else, it was certain of one thing: Rob was not to be trusted.

Joe went on: 'If not at the time, then afterwards, when the case was closed and you were free to talk to her?'

But Rob was shaking his head, his hunched posture that of a man thunderstruck by his experiences. Whatever he had or had not done, he had not recovered. Cosmetic transformation or not, he had not been able to reclaim himself.

'No,' he said. 'By then she was gone.'

Chapter 30

Amber, January 2013

Within an hour of leaving the police suite, Jeremy had booked us into a hotel on the Southbank. It was the perfect safe house, an artificial community of the carefree, tourists and out-of-towners coming and going in high-spirited gaggles. As we checked in, carrying only the possessions we'd taken with us for the interviews, I never imagined that I'd left the house on Lime Park Road for good.

But I had. Though Jeremy returned that evening to pack a bag of clothes and toiletries, and then again later to supervise removals, I never set foot over the threshold again.

We spent many quiet hours together in our hotel room, sitting side by side on the sofa by the drizzle-stained picture window, the new glass towers beyond concealing all but a chalky sliver of Shakespeare's Globe. I imagined the actors contained within, weaving a drama as real as my own; the only difference between us was that they had the advantage of knowing their ending.

How I wish I'd known mine.

Late that first night, neither of us capable of sleep, I found myself able to revisit the subject that had been the catalyst to this crisis, this flight of ours. Without it, I was certain I would never have told Jeremy what had happened with Rob that day.

'How long have you known?' I said.

'About what?'

'You know.'

'Oh.'

'Was it really only when the test results came from the clinic?'

'Yes, of course. That's the only time I've ever been tested.'

'I suppose you've never tried for a baby with anyone else.'

His face etched with dejection, he looked for once every inch his fifty-two years. 'No, but Sarah came off the Pill without telling me, and nothing happened there.'

Sarah had been the one before me. She'd wanted marriage and children when Jeremy had not and, to be fair to her, it had been reasonable to expect them of a man in his forties. When they'd split up she'd tearfully predicted that he would 'do it all' with his next girlfriend, but I could have told her at the time that changes of heart never come purely in reaction to what went before. Whatever else you may have decided about me, trust me when I tell you that Jeremy and I, when we met, when we married, we were the real thing. Any life philosophies altered, any new dreams created, they were *for* us, not *against* other people.

'She said later it had been almost a year. She thought *she* must have been the problem. I didn't think much of it other than to consider myself lucky to have avoided that

431

kind of complication. Obviously I now know I should have thought about it a bit more.'

I watched as he blinked repeatedly, a symptom in him not of weariness but of sincerity.

'I hope you believe me when I say I've never tried to trick you, Amber.'

'Of course I believe you!' The possibility needed instant smothering; this situation was dysfunctional enough already. 'Besides, there was your girlfriend in college who got pregnant, wasn't there?'

'I've been thinking about that. It can't have been mine,' Jeremy said. 'Apparently, this isn't something that's suddenly happened to me, so the only explanation is she must have been sleeping with someone else. Maybe she didn't know whose baby it was. Maybe it didn't occur to her that it could have been anyone's but mine.'

The parallel between his present predicament and this historical one was as strong as Rob's with *his*. Both haunted by college ordeals, the two men were more alike than they could know.

'In any case, I was her boyfriend so I was the one who went with her to the hospital for the termination.'

Neither of us mentioned the embryo inside me and whether a visit to a hospital was the next step for us, too. I could only guess at Jeremy's thoughts. Perhaps he was still absorbing the news of the rape itself and had not yet turned his mind to the pregnancy; there was ample time to make a decision and act on it.

It goes without saying that I greatly feared he might wonder of the existence of a fuller story than the one given.

In the seconds between my announcement that I was pregnant and my confession that I'd been raped, there could have been only one hypothesis in his mind: an affair. And an affair-gone-wrong provided a motive for assault just as plausible as the one given on record. Inevitably he must have wondered if I had ended it and been raped in anger, my lover refusing to let me go without punishing me.

Well, even if he hadn't yet considered the possibility, he would soon because it could only be a matter of days, perhaps hours, before Rob made a statement to the police and its contents were shared with us. If I knew anything for certain it was that he would dispute my version of events and propose one of his own.

'You were so serious about us cutting down on drinking,' I remembered, 'even though you must have known it would make no difference.'

'Yes, but that was because . . .' Jeremy faltered, clearly wanting to spare my feelings.

'Because what? Please tell me.'

He gazed at me with a depth of remorse that was nothing short of heroic. 'I suppose I was getting the feeling you were partying more, needing a bit more excitement than I was giving you. I was worried you might . . .' Again, loath to insult me, he let the comment hang incomplete.

'Slip back into my old ways?'

'Yes, I'm sorry. I shouldn't have tried to restrict you. I should have told you the situation as soon as I knew myself. Please forgive me.'

'There's nothing to forgive,' I said, taking his hands in mine, squeezing until I felt the bones inside. 'We both know the truth now and that's the most important thing, don't you think?'

But looking at him in the grey winter light of our hide-away, I wasn't sure he knew *what* was important. Not yet.

'I have an idea,' I said to him the following evening. We were sitting on the bed after a room-service dinner, propped up with stacks of pillows and flanked by the soothing amber spheres of our bedside lamps.

'Oh yes?'

Wendy had by then phoned to tell us that Rob had been questioned that morning and, just as I expected, had not only claimed consensual intercourse with me on the 15th of January but also a long-term sexual relationship between us. We'd rowed, he claimed, because he'd tried to break off the affair and I had objected. He'd had a lawyer with him for the interview, after which he'd been released on police bail with conditions: he was not to leave London without consulting the police and he was not to contact Jeremy or me, either directly or through a third party. A forensic search of his flat had taken place in his absence, but not yet the search for physical evidence during which his mobile phone and computer would likely be seized. The thought of his phone and the records the network provider might be compelled to supply remained my primary source of anxiety, causing a distress that had to be buried deep if it were not to spill out and catch Jeremy's devoted eye.

And then there was my new concern: the business of the tribunal. Until then overlooked – it had been, after all, several years ago – I saw now that if anything promised to be twisted out of shape it was that. The term 'sexual harassment' was incendiary in itself, and I knew that Rob would be just as aware as I was of its potential to obscure. Wendy hadn't mentioned it in her update, but it was surely only a matter of time before the investigation found its way towards it.

'What idea?' Jeremy put down his BlackBerry. Though he'd been keeping up with work email, the moment I gave the signal that I wanted to talk he was scrupulous about putting technology aside and giving me his full attention.

'What if we sell the house and move from Lime Park –'

'Of course!' Across the covers his hand captured mine. 'I've already decided we'll be doing that. We can't go back now. We can't live next door to that man. Even if he's put away for it, he'll be out again soon enough – aren't prison sentences for rape always being said to be scandalously short? You'll be terrified in your own home. Besides, everyone will be making their own judgements, all the neighbours, even the ones we think are friends. You'll be surprised who supports you and who blames you; this kind of thing divides people, sends the gossips into overdrive. Some of them will be asked to testify, as well. It will be horrific for you. I wouldn't dream of putting you through that.'

I listened patiently as he outlined the likely consequences, all of which I'd already turned over and over for myself until it left me dizzy. But the words were powerless, even meaningless, now that I'd made up my mind. 'No, I mean move from London, or at least to the opposite side of it. Cut all ties with Lime Park. I mean have the baby.'

Jeremy stared at me, his fingers quite still, and I could see that whatever he'd been pondering these last two days it had not included this. 'But I assumed . . . You mean you want to go through with the pregnancy?'

'Yes,' I said. 'I want to have the baby and say it's yours. I want to believe it's yours.'

His astonishment increased. 'It's *not* mine, though, is it? It's *his*.'

I nodded, self-possessed, grave. '*We* know that, but no one else would, including him. It would be like an adoption,' I went on. 'There'd be no difference emotionally. From day one we'd be the family, *you'd* be the father.'

Jeremy did not answer and I knew I'd said enough for now. I got up from the bed and made us hot drinks, black coffee for him, peppermint tea for me; I had not wanted caffeine since I'd discovered I was pregnant, finally subscribing to the clean-living regime the clinic had urged of me – better late than never. Mr Atherton had had a strategy for every set of circumstances, I recalled: what would he suggest for this one? Would he back mine?

Jeremy drank his coffee in silence before turning back to me with a neutral expression. 'You mustn't think this is the only way we can have a baby, darling. There are still options, when you're ready again – *if* you're ready. I know Atherton wanted to talk to us about sperm donors . . .' He did not press this particular point for obvious reasons.

'I agree,' I said. 'There are options. But the fact is I *am* pregnant already. I may not like how it got there but there's a baby growing inside me right now. And now we know you can't be the genetic father in any scenario, we don't *need* other options. Like I say, it would be a form of adoption.'

Again there was silence. 'Could you do that?' he said, when at last he spoke again. 'Could you go through with being the parent of a child conceived by rape?'

We looked at each other, as searching, as candid, as we dared. 'If we adopted we wouldn't know the circumstances of *that* conception, would we?' I said.

'True, but we need to think about this case, these circumstances, which we obviously *do* know. And they're as bad as it gets, aren't they? Could you seriously get past that, darling?'

My eyes filled. 'Yes, I could. I know I could.' I paused. 'But could *you* do what we would have to do to make it possible?'

'What would that be?'

I pressed closer to him, taking his hand in mine in gentle appeal. I would not bully him into this. 'Support me when I withdraw the allegation. Get the police to close this investigation.'

Just as I anticipated, he went rigid with opposition. '*What?* Drop the charges against that bastard? Why on earth would we do that?'

'It's the only way, Jeremy. Think about it, if they go ahead with the prosecution it will take months to get to court, maybe a whole year. I'll either be heavily pregnant or have just had a baby, and either way we won't be able to conceal it. But if we disappear now, he'll never know.' *Never know he is a father. Never know I am the mother of his child.* 'We'll ask the police not to tell him I'm pregnant, and I'm sure they would respect that.' I'd already gained their support on the matter of the medical examination, after all.

Jeremy was frowning heavily, I could feel his body temperature rising. 'What does it matter if he knows? From his point of view it would be mine anyway, wouldn't it? He attacked you once. He couldn't possibly have imagined that he made you pregnant in the process.'

Which was, when you thought about it, precisely the scenario I'd envisaged, had we not discovered he was infertile and had I continued to suppress the memory of January 15th. I would have had what I assumed was my husband's child while my former lover lived next door, with no reason for him or anyone else to doubt the paternity. But that outcome struck me now as having been hopelessly naive, at worst a public disaster – what if the baby clearly resembled Rob? – and at best an uncomfortable compromise that could only ever have been temporary.

As I considered this, surer with every minute that my solution was the right one, Jeremy's thoughts had moved along parallel lines. 'Say we did go ahead and keep the baby, don't you think that if anything it would *help* our case for the jury to see you pregnant? If the defence let them think you were already pregnant when you were attacked, they'd have even more sympathy for you.'

438

I inhaled deeply. 'But I wasn't already pregnant, was I? That wouldn't be fair.'

'*Fair?*' Jeremy's face twisted in indignation. 'He's a violent criminal, Amber, don't worry about being fair to *him*. You trusted him and he assaulted you. Quite apart from the physical violation, who knows what the psychological damage might be?'

I closed my eyes, imagined cool, cool fingertips on them, a gentle, sweet-scented touch that would cure me of all disquiet. 'I don't think there'll be any psychological damage, Jeremy. The worst is over. I'm strong, and now I have a reason to *stay* strong.'

He did not answer.

I thought about what DS Graham had said to us in the police suite before we left, a comment dismissed as irrelevant by Jeremy but that had been useful to me, sowing as it did the seed of this idea. 'Also, I'm worried about this DNA test the police mentioned,' I said. 'If the baby is born by the time the CPS bring the case to trial, they might ask for a test on him or her.' Just for the purposes of elimination, DS Graham had said, not implying anything else. But I'd worked up the storyline for myself: if the test went ahead and the true paternity was made public, it would not only let the world know that Jeremy was not the father, it would also let Rob know he *was*. And then I'd be connected forever to a man I'd either helped send down or tried to at least, and that was no way to live the rest of my life. That was no way for my child to have to live his. Which gave me two choices: do as Jeremy had assumed I would and terminate the pregnancy, or persuade him to agree to my plan.

'We would refuse to give permission for the test,' Jeremy said, defiant.

'I don't know if we *could* refuse. And think about it, Jeremy, even if they didn't request DNA, even if Rob saw me again, in court or anywhere before then, pregnant exactly the right number of months since it happened, knowing he hadn't used contraception . . . Well, you say it wouldn't cross his mind but there *could* be doubt, couldn't there? Enough doubt that if we didn't win and he walked free, if he chose to pursue it, if he found out about your fertility test and tracked us down, he could demand a DNA test of his own? It would be a disaster, I – we – would never be rid of him our whole lives!'

'But why on earth would he go looking for fertility tests? Did you ever say anything to him about our having problems conceiving?'

I hesitated. 'Well, yes, I hinted at it.'

Jeremy blanched. 'Oh, Amber.'

'I had no idea any of this was going to happen,' I protested. 'And we were friends, good friends – all my friends knew we were trying for a baby, I was getting advice from every mother on the street. Don't you see how complicated this is? This idea will only work if we disappear now, before I start to show. We have to stop the police from pursuing this and cut off contact with everyone we've met in Lime Park. I can't even see Imogen and my other friends. We can't have anyone guessing the truth.'

'This is insane, darling.'

I could feel myself growing agitated. 'I don't want to go to a trial, Jeremy. You heard the statistics Wendy quoted. This type of case is the hardest to get a conviction for, for obvious reasons. Everyone knew I was in and out of his flat all the time. He's already claiming we were having an affair . . .' My voice strained and caught as I presented Rob's truth as a lie. 'He's insisting that I was consenting that day, and there are sure to be people who'll believe him. I don't know if I can cope with testifying, reliving it in front of him.'

Jeremy stroked my forehead very delicately, as if testing the tenderness of a bruise, and I knew then that he did not believe Rob's story about the affair, he believed mine; he believed it wholeheartedly and had allowed himself to develop no alternative theories.

'I understand your feelings about wanting to keep the baby, really I do. After all that time trying, it's completely natural, plus you're still suffering from the shock of the assault. But, as I say, there *are* other options. And what about the fact that if you *don't* go through with this and he gets away scot-free, he could do it again to someone else? What about that poor woman you said he's just moved in, Pippa? We can only hope she's moved straight out again the moment the police came calling.'

We had arrived now at the crux of the dilemma, the very trickiest of all the moral ambiguities we faced: could Jeremy continue to share his life with a woman selfish enough to put other women at risk? Could he collude in that crime?

He didn't have an answer for me, not yet. He said he

needed to think about it. 'Try to rest,' he said. 'I don't want you worrying about him any more.'

'But –'

'Whatever we do, wherever we go, I will protect you from this monster. That's a promise.'

'Thank you,' I whispered.

I imagined the monster in his flat, sitting in the dark, Pippa surely having fled by now, his life suspended as he faced the prospect of a criminal trial and possible conviction. Did he wonder if his university nightmare would be resurrected, or those blurred lines he'd navigated with Kenny's colleague – and who knew which others – damningly redrawn? I imagined his thoughts of what jail might be like, a place where perpetrators of sexual assault were shown little mercy.

Mercy, he'd said to me once, that's an interesting quality for a child to care about. Do you mean were you hurt?

Not then, I thought. *But now, yes.*

The next day Jeremy went into the office for the first time since we'd moved into the hotel. I stood at the window and watched him walk from the entrance towards the river, to anyone else just another middle-aged man in a business suit with the weight of the world on his shoulders, and I imagined him never returning. Contact with his colleagues, with normal people, would bring him to his senses and I would hear from him again only through his solicitor. I would go back to my mother with my tail between my legs and a baby in my womb, no different in the end from her.

And irrespective of my status as victim, that was, after all, no less than I deserved for my marital betrayal.

But I should have known better. When he came back that evening, he brought with him the flowers and chocolates and magazines you might take someone in hospital. He held me and kissed me and told me he'd made a decision. He would accept the baby as his own. We would not return to the house or cross paths with any of our Lime Park friends again, but would move far away. He would talk to his partners about taking a six-month sabbatical, or at least working from an office at home, and his team would be briefed to rebuff all enquiries that were not strictly business-related. He would arrange for us both to change our mobile phone numbers and email addresses.

'We'll put my name on all the medical forms and on the birth certificate. We won't discuss it with anyone else ever. That has to be our sacred vow.'

'Yes.'

'Quite apart from anything else, we don't want our child finding out he was the product of rape. We'll move heaven and earth to prevent him from finding that out.'

'Or her,' I said, pleased that he was thinking like this, like a parent.

'Agreed?' he asked.

'Agreed,' I said. 'I can convince myself, I know I can. This is a new start.'

'You're very brave,' he said.

'No, I'm not. It's you who's brave.' This was quite true. I'd made new starts before, cut off circles of friends, denied selective stretches of history; it was Jeremy who'd had no need to and knew nothing of the emotional disorientation, the mental stamina, that it entailed.

'Rubbish. I don't want you to suffer any more distress than you've already suffered. I'll phone the police first thing tomorrow morning. Leave everything to me.'

I could not obey him on this score. It was not a flawless plan even from his perspective and certainly not from mine. Rob was not the kind of man to roll over without a fight (I knew *that* to my cost). And so, having sent Jeremy out to buy me more toiletries, I did something against all official advice and without telling a soul: I made contact with the perpetrator.

'Rob?' The phone felt like a grenade I needed to hurl as far from me as possible to survive. I gripped it uncomfortably hard, forced it to my ear.

'Amber, is this you? What the *fuck* is going on?' His fury kindled instantly, the spitting heat of it causing my heart to squeeze and stutter.

'Nothing's going on,' I said, cool and steady in voice if not in body. I was shaking badly, but reminded myself that he could not see my fear, he could not intimidate me. 'Not any more. You'll be pleased to know that I'm going to withdraw my allegation tomorrow morning.'

There was a horrible pause before anger and relief combusted. 'Why the hell did you make it in the first place? What are you playing at? Is this some kind of sick game, history repeating?'

I held my nerve. 'There's no need to pretend with me, Rob. I'm not recording this phone call.'

'Pretend? I'm the only one here who *isn't* pretending.'

444

'You know that's not true. We both know what happened and nothing will change that. I'm withdrawing for reasons of my own, not to save *your* skin.'

'Reasons of your own? I'll give you reasons! Do you realize I was led from my house in handcuffs? A fucking squad car in the street outside? I'm on *bail* and all our neighbours are going wild about it!'

'What?' I was taken aback by the idea of the neighbours knowing anything – Jeremy had been right, the gossips had flourished. Well, it was no more than he deserved, I thought.

His voice came again, spitting into my ear. 'That's right, word spreads when someone is thought to be a danger to society. When they're picked up by the police at exactly the same time the kids are leaving for school. It took about two minutes for people to believe your total fiction.'

'It is *not* fiction,' I said, as forcefully as I could muster, but he seethed on, his hatred as tangible, as poisonous, as it had been that horrible afternoon.

'Pippa's left me. Doesn't fancy prison visits, d'you think? Felicity's put her flat on the market. A lot can happen in a couple of days when you're a sex offender, eh? It's only a matter of time before I get a brick through my window or a mob forcing me out.'

'Well, so be it,' I said, bravely. 'That's nothing to do with me. As I say, I'll be withdrawing my statement and you'll have to deal with your guilt however you choose.'

He gave a bitter, black-hearted laugh. I could hear the ragged sounds of shallow breathing, and his voice when it came again was ominous, almost infernal: 'Did he find out? Is that why you did this?'

'You know why I did this. You were there.'

'You had an affair, Amber. You were willing every single time. More than willing, you were fucking *avid*. How can you live with yourself, lying like this?' The words were not spoken but spewed, vented, leaving me in no doubt that he despised me and always would.

'How can *you*?' I countered, losing confidence, terrified to find that he still had power over me. This was how bullies worked, I told myself. They made you believe their truth; they rendered yours worthless.

'You know, my lawyer rang the hotel and they said there was no record of you having had a guest that night. They said you were on your own. How long have you been planning this?'

'There was no plan,' I told him, sickened by the memory of how naïve and defenceless I'd been that night. 'I don't know what you're talking about.'

'Are you clinically insane all of a sudden? Or maybe you have been all along, Jesus . . . It's evil, Amber, what you've done. Did you think he'd just forgive you, no questions asked? Did it turn out he wasn't so indulgent after all? Was he going to throw his little princess out of her interior-designed tower, back into the gutter where she came from?'

I did not respond to this storm of abuse, only grateful that we were not face-to-face when he delivered it, for if we had been he would have struck me, spat at me. Degraded me. As it was, his voice in my ear was petrifying enough. I remembered what I'd said to Jeremy – *I am*

446

strong, I have a reason to stay strong – and it gave me the courage I needed to say what I'd called to say, to bring this exchange to a close. 'I'll withdraw the allegation only on the condition that you never contact me again – or Jeremy. We're moving away and we want to put this behind us. If you try to find me, I'll contact the police immediately and ask them to reopen the investigation.'

'I wish I'd never laid eyes on you in the first place,' he hissed. 'Slut.'

Don't listen to him, I told myself. You're almost there now. He will never hurt you again. 'So you accept my condition? Will you promise not to come after us?'

He made a sound of pure revulsion, pure enmity. 'Just get the police to drop the inquiry and I swear I will never try to see you again as long as there is breath in my body.'

'Thank you. Goodbye, Rob.'

'Fuck you, Amber.'

By nine-thirty the following morning Jeremy had informed the police that I wished to retract my report of rape. He put the call on speakerphone and I listened with trepidation, fearful of being accused of wasting police time or even warranting a charge myself. There was a horrible moment when DS Graham pointed out that they might still proceed with the investigation without my co-operation. He said they'd interviewed Felicity Boyd the previous afternoon and she had confirmed my evidence about saying 'You'll never lay a finger on me again' and leaving number 38 that afternoon in extreme distress. She would be a very credible witness. There were others too in the process of being located, including the college girl-friend, now living in Newcastle, and other former partners, though it would be several days before formal interviews could take place. But with Jeremy's urging, he at last admitted that the CPS would almost certainly insist on dropping charges without my central contributing evidence.

There was nothing else, after all: no physical injuries, no forensic evidence – whatever they'd collected at the scene could only have pointed to sex, which Rob freely admitted to, and not to sexual crime, which he did not. There'd been no restraints used, no torn clothes. And Felicity's testimony might just as easily be shown to corroborate Rob's account – that he had ended our affair and I'd reacted badly – as it did mine. We all knew how crucial context was.

I was required to make an official retraction of my statement and it was agreed this could be done at the station local to the hotel, to avoid any possibility of my running into Rob in Lime Park. I had to declare that I did not wish to pursue a criminal allegation against Mr Robert Whalen of 38 Lime Park Road and that this was my own decision; I had not been persuaded by any other person.

I was asked if I would reconsider since it was so serious an allegation.

I said I would not.

'Does it remain true?'

'What do you mean?' I said.

'Is it your support you're withdrawing or the allegation itself?'

'Both. I just can't do it,' I said, my voice weak. I felt

448

faint, not myself, the strain of this – or perhaps the pregnancy – depleting me of energy.

The police said they understood my position and that a letter would follow in due course to confirm that the inquiry had been closed. I imagined the details, the names and dates and times, on that national computer database for an indeterminate period.

Next, Jeremy spoke to the estate agent and solicitor about putting the house on the market. Profit was our last priority, speed our foremost. We would not hold out for the best price or consider anyone in a chain, but would sell at a realistic figure to the first cash buyer past the post. We would rent in another part of the capital short term while we decided which area to relocate to. No contact details were shared besides Jeremy's office address and new mobile phone number.

'I can't rest until I know it's sold,' I told Jeremy. Now, in my mind, the house on Lime Park Road became a symbol of the mess I'd created, its rooms, some of which I'd hardly set foot in, the beautiful smooth shell inside which I'd allowed myself to turn bad. 'I need to know we're not linked to it legally. I need to forget we ever lived there.'

'It will be done within a month,' he promised.

All concerned agreed that whoever the buyers turned out to be, they'd be getting the bargain of their lives.

Chapter 31

Christy, October 2013

The day after she opened the letter from the police, Christy emerged from the Frasers' state-of-the-art thermostatically hypersensitive rain shower to find Joe still sleeping. She woke him in alarm.

'You're going to be late for work. Shouldn't you call in and let them know? Where's your phone?'

He flinched at the brightness of her voice, as if at the sudden application of searchlights. 'I'm not going in.'

'What do you mean? Oh. Rob.'

When Joe had come home yesterday it had been to a wife who had locked herself in the house for fear of reprisals at the hands of the predator next door. Later, the two of them had spent an hour in conversation with that predator, the upshot of which was that Christy was now expected to accept as final the excellent reasons why the criminal legal system was predicated on the presumption of innocence.

'Imagine if I were him,' Joe had said, when Rob had gone, but the fact that she could *not* imagine it only confirmed her belief that the existence of doubt worked both ways.

'Imagine if I were *her*,' she replied.

The truth was that only two people knew what had happened in Rob's flat on the afternoon of the 15th of January and Christy was not one of them.

'You don't need to stay at home on my account,' she told him now. 'I admit I was a bit hysterical yesterday, but I know he's hardly likely to do it again so soon after –'

'He didn't do it the first time,' Joe interrupted, unequivocal in his support of Rob even as he rubbed sleep from his eyes, the day hardly started. 'I think that's been established.'

'It's been *presumed*,' Christy said. 'And you know what I'm saying. If he *did* do it then he wouldn't be likely to do it again, because he'd know this one would stick.'

'I see you've continued to embrace the language of the TV cop. Maybe that could be your new line of work. A scriptwriter for a crime series.'

'Maybe it could. I'm open to ideas. But either way, you're still a lawyer at Jermyn Richards and should go to the office.'

Making no move to leave the bed, Joe was at least sitting up now. 'I didn't mean I'm not going in *today*,' he said. 'I meant I'm not going in ever.'

Christy gaped. 'What are you talking about, "ever"?' She sank onto the edge of the bed, water from her hair turning cold on her bare shoulders. 'Did something happen when you left yesterday? You told them it was an emergency, didn't you?' She'd come to imagine JR as a team of tyrants branding and whipping their slaves, Joe somehow remaining one of the latter group even when he had – nominally, at least – switched sides.

451

'Something happens every day, Christy,' he said, 'it's called fear and loathing. I'm phoning in sick, I'm getting the doctor to sign me off, and then I'm resigning.'

Christy could scarcely absorb this. It was, in its way, as shocking, as destabilizing, as yesterday's news: neither of them working, neither of them earning, a mortgage that sucked at the neck of their bank account with vampiric appetite . . . 'Shouldn't we discuss this properly before you make a decision like that?'

'We're discussing it now and I'm telling you I can't go on. Another day of that hell and I'm going to jump under a train. Resign or commit suicide: they're my choices, and I'm happy to debate them with you if you think there might be pros and cons to weigh up. Me, I'm fairly clear which way I want it to go.'

As bailiffs and bankruptcy notices began inevitably to surface in front of her eyes, she noticed, to her horror, that Joe had tears spilling from his. She clutched him to her.

'Don't be upset. Of course you must leave if it's that bad. At the very least you need time off . . .' His frame felt slighter as she held him: he must have lost weight in recent weeks without her having noticed. Nausea rose as she recognized that she had not cared for him as she should have; she had not taken his unhappiness at work seriously enough. There'd been days – weeks – when she had given the man next door more thought than she had the one in her own house. And the tragedy was that still, even at this juncture, the balance was awry.

When he stopped crying they agreed they would not talk about it for the rest of the day.

'A twenty-four-hour amnesty,' she said. 'We need to take stock. What shall we do instead? What do you feel like doing?'

'You really want to know?' Joe said.

'Of course.'

'I just want to be alone.' And he sighed with a yearning so deep it moved her, shamed her afresh. 'I can't remember the last time I was alone.' His glance moved about the bedroom as if its corners were unfamiliar to him. 'I don't think I've *ever* been on my own in this house.'

Christy swallowed and nodded simultaneously. 'OK,' she said doubtfully. 'I understand you need time, but I'm not sure it's the right thing to leave you on your own.'

He gave a half-grin. 'Don't worry, Rob won't come and get me.'

'You know what I mean. To decide to leave your job' – she didn't say career, that would be overstating it (wouldn't it?) – 'it's a traumatic thing, Joe.'

'No, it's a wonderful thing, believe me.' And it was true that he looked convincingly contented; the tears had served their purpose. But still, as mood swings went, this was a violent one by anyone's standards – it was only a matter of minutes since he'd mentioned suicide.

Seeming to follow her thoughts, he reached for her hand, his grip steady, reassuring. 'I just want to be alone in an empty house. No phones, no voices, no emails, nothing.'

'OK,' she said again, for she *did* understand. He needed the cure of silence, seclusion, sleep. 'I'll go out for the day. I'll call and check on you,' she promised.

'Thank you.' And as he slid back under the duvet, his eyes were already glued shut.

'I've got things I can do,' she added, to herself.

One such thing was to ring Identico.UK and verify Caroline's suggestion that Jeremy Fraser had returned to the office from his sabbatical. She studied once more his staff photograph on the company website before travelling into town and stationing herself, *Standard* in hand, outside his building near London Bridge station in good time for the evening office exodus.

When he appeared, thirty minutes later, it was as much of a shock as any other she'd encountered these last days; in fact, she was immobilized by a surge of adrenalin at the sight of his lean, silver-haired figure detaching itself from the clot of workers exiting the revolving doors and striding in the direction of the station. After months of embedding herself in the Frasers' mystery, she carried with her a healthy reserve of credulity, a readiness to accept anything about them, however outlandish: a change of appearance or even identity, as if they were MI6 operatives kidnapped by the enemy and not, as had emerged, an unusually popular couple of Lime Park residents who'd happened to have a neighbour from hell.

For Jeremy Fraser had re-entered the world physically unaltered by the crisis, his well-cut lightweight navy coat falling elegantly over his suit, his gait erect, almost noble, which helped keep him in view once she'd stopped gaping and started following. But as he moved with the home-bound herd towards the Underground entrance, through the barriers and down to the platform, it became clear that she was woefully out of practice in the choreography of the London rush hour, had completely forgotten her steps. Reaching the Northern Line platform in time to see him swallowed by the doors of a northbound train, she was lucky not to be trampled underfoot.

When the train slid by, she snatched a glimpse of him in profile, still and expressionless.

Returning home, there were no signs of life in the houses on either side of hers, all the windows cold and unlit. The mood on the street was reminiscent of nothing so much as the day she'd arrived, when she'd almost felt the dust settling around her – from an explosion she had not yet dreamed of. Letting herself in, she felt sudden fright at the wholeness of the quiet, and with it incredulity at herself for having taken Joe at his word and left him for hours in some post-traumatic fugue. But, dashing upstairs, blood pounding, she found him just where she'd left him, in their bed, unconscious and serene. He was breathing quite normally, even snoring a little, and she leaned to kiss him very softly on the forehead.

Downstairs, she cooked herself a plate of pasta and watched television alone, much as she had every weekday night for the last six months.

The next day, up, clothed and apparently untroubled, Joe announced that he wanted to visit his parents to tell them his news. Once more, he preferred to be without her company. Christy phoned him three times to assess his mental state before, judging it sound (sounder than *hers*), she applied herself to her own errand. Returning in good time to the Identico.UK office building, she was determined to stalk more effectively this time. She'd been too self-conscious yesterday; given the rush-hour multitudes, she could tail Jeremy Fraser at quite close quarters and remain undetected. She'd dressed this time in work clothes and felt herself moving differently in them, striving to belong once more as she attached herself to her mark, matching her pace to his and keeping him always within touching distance. In the confines of the Northern Line train, the two of them stood in the same aisle, not quite close enough for her to read the emails he thumbed through on his phone. When the train was held in a tunnel, her own impatience escalating with that of the collective, he remained utterly cool, almost grave. As others turned and sighed and complained, he was fixed on his task, a man who had learned not to look up. She glimpsed the background image on his screen: a smiling redhead.

At King's Cross, he left the Northern Line and switched to an overland commuter train. It was uncomfortably crowded and, separated from him by almost the full length of the carriage, Christy feared she would miss him making his exit. But several stops up the line, the crush subsided, he was still there and when at last he stepped towards the doors, she did the same.

They were about as far away from Lime Park as you could get within the limits of the city.

He walked from the station through a succession of residential streets at a pace far faster than her natural one, clearly a man with something – someone – to hurry home to, before at last approaching one of a row of pretty workman's cottages on a road so far from the station it must have been equidistant to the next one up the line.

As he let himself into number 223, she cursed the lengthening nights, for the moment the door closed again there was nothing to see, only curtains drawn at every window.

After waiting half an hour or so, she returned to the station and made the long journey home. Joe, in front of the television with a beer, was happy to see her. He told her that his parents had reacted to his news with a compassion that had surprised him. Christy, however, would have expected no less: when your parental ambitions were exceeded to the extent that theirs had been, there was likely an element of relief in being presented with evidence of ordinary human frailty. ('It's not like I'm *really* in trouble,' Joe said. 'Not like Rob.')

In turn, she told him that her meeting with a new headhunter had gone well and that she'd met Ellen for a quick drink after work. In truth, of course, there'd been no meeting and Ellen had scarcely been in touch since the two women had ceased to occupy adjoining desks. Christy would be lying if she said she hadn't – predictably, no doubt – contrasted that indifference with the concern of Amber Fraser's former colleague Imogen, who long after the two had parted ways professionally had crossed town with a young baby in search of her missing friend.

'Perhaps today's meeting will lead to something and you'll be earning again soon?' Joe said. She could not begrudge him his air of joyful abdication; she could not protest the logical equation of one Davenport's unburdening of responsibility with the other's stepping forward to claim it.

'I hope so.' And fictitious meeting or not, she *was* hopeful about a final-round call-back, even if it did involve psychometric and aptitude tests (these, she feared).

She fetched herself a beer and joined her husband on the sofa.

'There's been more drama here,' Joe said.

'What, with Rob?'

'I haven't seen him all day. No, a huge argument in the street between Joanne and Liz, in front of the kids and everything.'

'Joanne and Liz? But they're really good friends.'

'That's what Joanne thought too, but it turns out Liz has been having an affair with her husband.'

Christy was flabbergasted. '*Kenny.*'

'You won't believe how it came out. Their dog had been hoarding some piece of underwear, a bra I think, and, here's the scandal: *it wasn't Joanne's*. She confronted Kenny and he confessed. Seriously, you couldn't make it up.'

Christy recalled her visit two days earlier: *Poppy! There's no one there!* Had Liz been in the house then? (Perhaps Christy's interruption had led to the stealing of the bra.)

'Do people really do this?' she asked Joe. 'Have affairs in their own homes, right under their partner's nose?' She remembered too the dog hairs on Liz's chaise longue; no doubt there'd been plenty of clues if she'd been following that particular whodunnit.

'Maybe they use the spare room? I don't know. But anyway, Joanne's thrown him out – or at least he left. And

Caroline knew, from what I could gather, so Joanne is upset with her as well. I watched it all from the window upstairs, like Jimmy Stewart. I was just going up for a nap after I got back from Mum's. I had a superb view. I can see now why you got so obsessed.'

'I got obsessed because there was something serious going on,' Christy reminded him, but not sharply. 'I can't take all of this in,' she said, and sighed, emptying her lungs of another day's emotions. They sat for a minute or two without speaking, faces turned to the TV screen. Then she said, 'Do you sometimes think, Joe, that if you compare the contents of your mind now with the days before we moved in, there's nothing the same? It's like everything we used to know was deleted and a whole new life's worth of stuff entered in its place.'

'I know what you mean, yeah,' Joe said.

She waited. The next suggestion could only come from him.

'We're going to have to sell this place, aren't we?' he said. 'It was lunacy to buy it. Someone must have been spiking our food.'

Christy took a mouthful of beer. 'I've been thinking about that today. I wondered about a lodger, like Dad joked about in the beginning? But then I thought that wouldn't bring in enough money. So why don't we rent out the whole house for six months, or even a year, while we decide what to do?'

Joe cocked his head, interested. 'That might work. Rent somewhere ourselves for half of what we get for here, so we're covering mortgage and rent?'

'I think we'd be lucky just to cover the mortgage – think how enormous it is. Why don't we see if we can move in with my parents for a little while? We could leave the furniture, lock up all our personal stuff in one of the rooms at the top. It wouldn't be for long. I could commute in for interviews and the rest of my St Luke's sessions. I don't want to let them down.'

What she was suggesting was humiliating, but she, for one, was becoming practised in the absorption of humiliation. In the end, the world didn't stop turning because you'd lost. Perhaps it had always been inevitable, she thought; perhaps the house was destined to be one of those cursed plots, the ones you found on every high street where businesses came and went and nothing ever seemed to stick. 'It's not like either of us is never going to work again,' she added. 'It's just short term.'

'It would buy us a few months,' Joe agreed, readily enough for her to know that if he'd take the in-laws over the law then he really wasn't going to return to corporate life. 'I'll phone some lettings agents tomorrow.'

It might be a relief to leave, she thought. If the Frasers could downsize to a small cottage in the back of beyond, then so could they. Lime Park Road was for families, stable families in which the adult roles were clearly defined and the life philosophies undivided (the occasional extramarital affair notwithstanding).

'Joe, I think having a family is more important to me than having this house,' she said, surprising herself as much as him with her directness. It was heartbreaking to think how long she'd not said it when in the end it was only a few words, just one short statement of preference. 'I know you don't agree, and that's fine, and I know there are more important things for us to worry about . . .' She paused, corrected herself: 'Maybe there *aren't* more important things to worry about, maybe that's what I'm trying to say. Anyway, it's only fair that you know how I feel.'

Joe was silent, his fingers toying with the remote control. He did not look at her. 'All of the partners at work, the married ones, they've all got the house *and* the children. I'm not sure how it hasn't worked that way for us.'

'I don't know. But I don't think it matters; we don't have to be like them and do everything in the right order. This is us. This is our order.'

He was nodding again, in the committed way of a man hoping to convince himself. 'They're all captive, Christy, every single one of them. I don't want to breed in captivity like them.'

'Breed in captivity or breed at all?' she asked, her heart quite still.

'Breed in captivity,' he said. He paused, at last looking at her. 'But in the wild, sure.'

Christy smiled. She wondered at her own lack of anxiety today in this perilous situation of theirs. Perhaps it was because of Joe's obvious equilibrium, the sense of peace that – unhelpfully – could only properly be identified as having been missing now it was restored. Or perhaps it was because of her other unresolved preoccupation, the second reason why a departure might be required. The question was, would that departure be temporary or permanent?

Well, tomorrow she would know, one way or the other. 'When did you change your hair?' he asked.

'Oh.' She touched the ends, faded now according to the Frasers' all-seeing mirror to an undesirable shade of washed-up crab. 'I did it myself to save money.'

Joe shut down the TV and flung the remote to the far corner of the sofa. 'Let's go out for dinner,' he said. 'To Canvas. We haven't been there since the first week. It's a disgrace.'

Her eyes bulged as her stomach responded with a groan. 'I'm not sure that's the most appropriate option for two unemployed debtors.'

'I don't think another hundred pounds is going to make much of a difference, do you?'

'That's exactly the sort of thing bankrupts say,' she said, but she was smiling as she went upstairs to change.

The following morning at eleven, when Joe was making his first enquiries at the rental agent on the Parade and when Jeremy Fraser would be well into his second meeting of the day, Christy retraced the route to the far-flung suburb beyond the North Circular and presented herself at the Frasers' door. Of course Amber Fraser might very well be out at work herself – who knew what had changed in their circumstances besides their address – but Christy understood by now that it didn't matter, because she would keep on coming until she had the answer to her question. She would buy herself a season ticket.

As she raised her hand to ring the bell, she felt on her

wrist the reassuring weight of the bangle, worn on this occasion to remind her to give it back to its owner; out of sight, in her bag, it would more likely be forgotten.

The door opened and Christy drew breath. Finally. The woman standing before her was incontrovertibly Amber Fraser, you could tell by the long strands of glossy red hair that had freed themselves from her ponytail and by the smooth milk-pale face that had only lucky angles to it, the bone structure of the born beautiful. She'd gained a little weight since Caroline's photograph had been taken, and was casually dressed in leggings and a ribbed grey sweater, her skin devoid of make-up. Having always pictured her as she'd looked in the photo, painted and bewitching, Christy took a moment to adjust to the more workaday version in front of her.

'Hello, can I help you?' Her voice, pitched low, was small and wintry, with no discernible accent. Her large eyes remained narrowed. There was the curious sense of her having made efforts to minimize her own impact on the senses of others.

'I'm Christy Davenport,' Christy said, too nervous to smile. 'My husband and I bought your house on Lime Park Road back in March.'

While not having expected to be welcomed with open arms, she was genuinely startled by Amber Fraser's reaction: aversion, fear, the undisguised impulse to slam the door in her caller's face. It made Christy think of Felicity's friend, the way the door had come towards her even as she continued to speak. March? It might have been the nineteenth century for how removed it felt from the here and now. She felt a tug of sorrow for the lost promise of those few short months.

Impressively quickly, Amber recovered control of her facial muscles. The door remained open. 'Can I ask how you found me?'

'Through your husband's work.' Christy was reluctant to admit that she'd tailed the man in the manner of one of those people you read about in the papers who ended up having restraining orders taken out against them, and was grateful that Amber accepted her answer in its abbreviated form. She did not, however, go so far as to invite her visitor in, apparently determined to conduct this conversation on the doorstep, which brought to mind Christy's other recent doorstep exchange with Rob.

Rob and Amber: now she was face to face with Amber she could see it, how they might be considered similar, how they might be mutually attracted; in fact, it was so *easy* to see as to have been predetermined, written in the stars.

'What can I do for you?' Amber asked. 'Is there another problem with the roof?'

'No, nothing like that. I'm really sorry to bother you, but I wanted to ask you about a situation with a neighbour.'

Amber's already defensive bearing clenched visibly. 'Which neighbour?'

'Rob Whalen.'

'I don't want to talk about him.'

'I know, I understand. But I believe you made an allegation against him?'

'I have no intention of getting into that.' Amber's

words came with a formidable firmness for someone so quietly spoken.

'Please.' Christy wrung her hands, her face, in the habit now of supplicating herself. '*Please.* I swear I'll keep coming back, you won't get rid of me.'

'Is that some sort of threat?' If Amber perceived it as such, then she made it clear with her eyes that she would meet it head-on. Christy remembered one of Caroline's confidences: *It wasn't like she'd led a charmed life*. She'd had her adversities, had seen off challengers before.

'It's a vow,' Christy said earnestly. 'Please, just talk to me now, just this once, and I promise you won't hear from me again.'

Amber frowned, closed her eyes and exhaled heavily as if to rebalance herself by some learned ritual. Only when she opened her eyes again did she part her lips to speak. 'Wait here.'

As she turned into the hallway, evidently to pluck a jacket from the hook and slip her feet into boots, she was silhouetted in profile and Christy noticed an unmistakable swelling of her abdomen. Then she was pulling the door closed and ushering Christy back down the path. 'Let's go somewhere where we can talk privately.'

'Your husband's at home?'

'No, at work.' Amber did not explain from whom then the conversation was to be concealed (or, more likely, admit that in taking her visitor into her house she feared she might never get her out again), but marched briskly ahead, her tread light, sheepskin boots silent on the pavement.

Never quite allowing Christy to draw level, she led the way to a café on the nearby main road, a colourless, down-at-heel place, and though it was barely half full she chose a booth right at the back, far from the window. 'It's too cold to sit near the door,' she said by way of explanation. It didn't seem like the sort of place Amber Fraser would choose in any weather, but that hardly mattered. To be eye to eye with the woman who had eluded her for so long and yet been impossible to get from under her skin, who had bequeathed her the keys to her house and yet never truly vacated it: she would have faced her across a nest of vipers.

They ordered tea.

'You know what happened then?' Amber said. Somehow, already, Christy had conceded the lead to her.

'Yes.'

She did not ask how and oblige Christy to mention the letter, which eliminated one of her larger fears. Seated, Amber seemed less sure of herself: jittery, blanched, under-slept . . . was this what a victim looked like? It was almost nine months since the alleged attack, and Christy wondered what that represented to her: an eternity or no time at all? When you disappeared yourself like this, did life stretch or shrink?

She realized that she wanted more than anything for them to be on the same side.

'I'm really sorry . . . about what you've been through,' she said. 'It's honestly not my intention to pry into a private incident.'

This was one of her rehearsed lines and, inevitably, it

did not wash. Amber looked unconvinced to the point of disdain. 'You do know that I retracted my statement?'

'Yes, and the police closed the inquiry.'

'Exactly. Months ago. So what is there to discuss? It's done and dusted, ancient history.' Unyielding, tight-lipped – plainly she would have ended the exchange there and then had Christy let her – she began casting frequent glances at her watch, an expensive-looking bejewelled item on her slender wrist. Already she had checked her phone once, too.

'Well, not *that* ancient,' Christy said. Not yet daring to pose the question she'd come to pose, she could only play for time. The arrival of two mugs of unappetizingly grey tea aided her cause, though she doubted Amber would touch hers, judging by the way she looked askance at it. 'Why didn't you declare it on the forms?' Christy asked, finally.

'What forms?' Amber glanced a second time at her phone.

'To do with the sale of the house. You're supposed to say if there's been a dispute with a neighbour.'

Amber's eyes flashed with heat and Christy knew she deserved the contemptuous response she got. 'You call something like that a *dispute*? As if it's some squabble over a garden fence? Are you crazy?'

Christy flushed. 'Of course not. I'm sorry.'

Amber composed herself once more, lowered her voice to a pitch that half swallowed every second word. 'As it happens, my husband handled all the paperwork, not me. We were both a little preoccupied at the time and you're just going to have to find it in your heart to forgive us.' She paused, focusing on Christy fully for the first time; her irises were the most beautiful colour, a feline golden green. 'Besides, the "dispute", as you call it, was completely resolved before we left. There was no way it could have impacted on you.'

'But –'

'Look, I really don't see how this concerns you. As you said yourself, it's a private matter, a very sensitive private matter. Why are you here? Is there anything wrong with the house itself? Are you not happy you bought it?'

There was a challenge to her manner as she discharged this round of queries, a trace of superiority that riled Christy in spite of her avowed compassion. 'But it *does* concern us, Amber.' No need to confess that she and Joe would soon be moving out, having both proved unemployable; the issue was whether they could ever return. 'It concerns the whole street. There's a culture of fear there now. There are kids not allowed to go to the park on their own or get the bus to school because their parents think there's a rapist living a few doors down. And the way you're talking makes me think they're right. *Are* they?'

Amber gasped, her eyes becoming unsettlingly wide and unblinking. 'You can't seriously be asking me that question?'

Christy held her gaze. 'I am. I'm sorry to be so frank, but I don't want to waste your time and you're the only one who knows. Are we safe living next door to him? Raising a family on that street?' With this, she gestured to the other woman's stomach. '*You* made the decision not to, after all.'

At this, tears sprang to Amber's eyes, all her previous vehemence dissolved. Her temperament was evidently changeable, even fragile. She pushed aside the tea, as if unable to contemplate it a moment longer, or perhaps to clear the decks between them. 'Fine. Let's sort this out. If I answer your question, will you give me your word that you will never contact me again? Like you said before?'

'Yes.'

'And you won't tell anyone where you found me, especially not him?'

'Yes. Does that mean he did it?'

'It means there's nothing to be gained by us seeing each other again. I'm sure you can appreciate that?' Amber gazed at her, her sudden personal appeal making Christy sting with self-consciousness, her cheeks flame deeper.

'Yes,' she repeated, contrite.

'Good. Listen to me, Christy, you must forget what you think you know and you must ignore any rumours you hear from now on. None of it is true. It was all a misunderstanding. Rob Whalen is not going to harm you or anyone else on the street – and that is my honest opinion.'

To her alarm, Christy felt a great swelling of relief, a flooding close to ecstasy. 'Thank you,' she said.

Amber was rising from her seat. 'Now, I'm sorry, but I really do have to go.'

Christy stood too, suddenly longing to express her thanks by saying something generous or gracious. 'Well, congratulations on the baby, anyway. Is it OK to tell Caroline? I hope you don't mind, but she told me you and your husband had been trying. She'll be *so* pleased.'

She regretted these remarks as soon as she'd made them – relief had made her overfamiliar. Many women loved to share their experience of pregnancy and motherhood, common gender often being the only ticket required, but Amber Fraser was plainly not one of them. She looked frankly appalled. Perhaps when it took so long to get there, casual discussion of it felt like tempting fate. It occurred to Christy also that when you were celebrated for your figure, for your flawless beauty, it was perhaps harder to come to terms with the physical changes of motherhood.

'It's OK,' she said hastily. 'Forget I asked. And I'm sorry to make you talk about the past. You have my word you won't hear from me again.' She wondered if she ought to offer a handshake to demonstrate her sincerity, and the awkward beginnings of one reminded her of the bangle on her wrist – a last shot at salvation. She unclasped it and held it out to the other woman. 'Before you go, I brought this for you. I found it in the en suite, it had fallen behind the bath.'

But again she had misjudged, because Amber only stared at the bangle with a strange, sad horror. 'Keep it,' she murmured. 'I don't want it.'

'Are you sure? That's very kind.' It meant something to Christy to have an object of Amber's not by accident (or theft), but by design. A gift. 'Oh, there's a key ring as well. The estate agent had it. It has your name engraved on it. Here . . .'

This the other woman did take, pocketing it with obvious gratitude.

After thanking her once more for agreeing to see her, Christy fumbled in her purse for the right coins to pay for their tea. When she turned around again, Amber Fraser had disappeared from sight.

Chapter 32

Amber, October 2013

I told Jeremy about Christy Davenport's visit the moment he came home from work. I'd had all day to adjust my mindset – and Lord knows I needed those hours of preparation, for I am not a mental gymnast these days, can only marvel at my previous feats of guile.

'I don't like the sound of that,' he said, taking the glass of wine I offered, and sitting opposite me at our tulip table. It was quite a squeeze in that tiny kitchen, but we were used to the shuffling and manoeuvring by now, the little collisions that invariably encouraged him to embrace me and tell me how proud of me he was. 'You told her he didn't do it, of course?'

'Of course. That's the official line. I don't want her to be too scared to set foot in her own home.'

'Let's hope she really *doesn't* have anything to fear.'

But he did not look terribly worried, not as he once would have been. Time and distance have made him less concerned about the risk Rob Whalen poses to the female population of Lime Park. These days Jeremy prefers the idea that the man *simply wouldn't dare*, not after his last brush with the law; he favours that over the possibility that such tendencies might be serial.

'What was she like?' he asked.

'Kind of neurotic. But it was hard to tell when I was in shock at finding her on my doorstep. And she was so persistent.'

'She *must* have been, to find us in the first place.'

'She got the address through your work, she said.'

He frowned. 'I don't see how when ninety per cent of the staff don't know it. Oh well, we can't stop people googling, can we? The whole world's a private detective these days. You have to change your name to really start again.'

I nodded. I had not ruled out that possibility. 'You know, I got the impression she had feelings for him.'

(And I, of all people, could identify the signs.)

'She's married, though, right?' Jeremy said. 'It was a couple who bought the house, as I remember.'

(As if a marriage certificate was any immunization against *him*.)

'Yes. I'm not saying she's acted on it – maybe she's not even aware of it yet. It's just . . . the way she reacted when I said he was innocent, it was more than just relief. It was like I was giving her permission or something.' I shuddered.

Jeremy sipped his wine, watching me. 'Are you OK, sweetheart?'

'I'm fine.'

'Try not to worry. We always knew one of them might turn up. But we should be safe so long as she doesn't go spilling our address to any of the others.'

'Thank God I didn't invite her into the house,' I said.

'She would have been impossible to get rid of, and your mother would have come back during the time we were talking, for sure.'

'Why *didn't* you invite her in?' Jeremy asked. 'You can't have known what she was going to say.'

'I don't know. It was just an instinct.'

'A good one. You're a born survivor.'

'I hope so.' At sudden sounds of activity from the monitor positioned between us, I groaned, not so much in complaint as in expression of bodily exhaustion. 'Already? It's only been forty-five minutes!'

'I'll go,' Jeremy said, happily. 'I hoped she might wake up.'

In the time it took me to stretch my arms and ease my aching spine, he was back. 'Here she is!'

'Oh Jeremy, what are you doing bringing her down? Look at her, she's wide awake!'

'Of course she is. She thinks she's missing out. Like mother like daughter, eh?'

'Come here, darling.' I smiled, reaching for the little imp. So beautiful! This is a child who will be forgiven *anything*.

Two weeks ago, on the 20th of September, Sienna Fraser was born. That's right, another redhead: to our indescribable relief, she looks just like me.

'A ginger kitten,' Jeremy said, when he first cradled her by my hospital bed. 'It's apparently a real advantage to be born at the beginning of the school year,' he added, and I knew he was going to be a splendid father. Who cared if

474

she didn't have his genes? She would have his love and that was the only thing that mattered.

(We've already talked about trying for a second with a sperm donor.)

If I sound as if I've become sentimental in my old age, I have to concede that I sort of *have*. I've learned that too much time, too much choice, was not good for me, and now I have less of both I'm twice as contented.

I've even spent time with my mother and, believe it or not, almost enjoyed it, another agreeable side effect of conception and its unique power to reboot the system – or was it some kind of post-traumatic stress syndrome at work? Either way, in the latter month of pregnancy, when I didn't want to risk running into anyone I knew, in particular anyone from Lime Park (it wasn't as if the population was legally confined to its postcode), I needed to leave town. And what more unlikely place to find me than with my own family?

I spent my days practising parenting skills on my brothers' kids, able to hand them over to their mothers or my own the moment I tired. I ate, I slept, I passed the time in easy conversation. As the days went on, I no longer despaired at my poor luck in getting the parents I did, but saw in my mother's face *her* wonder at producing a daughter like me. It's nice to feel you've made someone proud, especially after a period of – how can I put it? – *dubious* behaviour.

It was also an opportunity to hone my story about the dates. Right from the moment we left Lime Park, Jeremy and I had lied about the baby's due date, quoting a late-October one that, should Jeremy's paternity ever be challenged, would cast doubt on the possibility of a mid-January conception. (Only a court order would wring a DNA test from us now, and even then I think we'd skip the country first.) Privately, Jeremy of course anticipated *mid* October, nine months after January 15th.

I alone knew to expect an early bird. I'd had my suspicions from the moment Jeremy confessed his infertility, but these had been confirmed only when I presented myself for my first hospital appointment. Conceived in the first week of December, Sienna was in fact due in early September.

Did I say her middle name is Fern? A little nod to her woodland beginnings. Because the terrible – and, you could say, wonderful – fact is that she was conceived in love, not hate, at least on my part, for it was the night in the tree house that it must have happened. We'd been too intoxicated to take proper care, to notice a tear in a condom, to use one every time. It had been an exceptional night in all senses, my mind had tricked my body – or was it the other way around? – into thinking Rob was my partner, the one I'd selected to father my child. I had thought I loved him. As for the pregnancy test taken soon after in December, it must have been falsely negative; if I'd conceived fewer than ten days earlier, the hormone levels would not have been detectable.

(And in those concerns about the DNA test that I'd shared with Jeremy, I'd withheld one crucial anxiety, the one that drew from me the deepest shudder of all: if linked by the defence with the baby's inevitably 'early' birth, proof of Rob's paternity was going to be excellent evidence that we'd been having a sexual relationship *before* the date of the incident.)

Luck was on my side: I presented small throughout the pregnancy and Sienna was overdue by two weeks. I insisted on an NHS birth, knowing the understaffing and general institutional chaos would make it easier for me to maintain that my dates were the correct ones. Where possible, I attended appointments without Jeremy.

'It can't possibly be as far along as you think,' I would say to the midwife, always good-natured, never too forceful. 'My husband and I hardly saw each other in December. We've always thought late January was when it happened.'

'Not a chance,' would come the reply. 'But the important thing is you're progressing well. What's a few weeks between friends?'

I suppose it's possible that mine was not the most dysfunctional set of circumstances she'd been privy to in her career.

After the birth, any concerns Jeremy voiced about Sienna being premature were dismissed by harried staff who could see for themselves that she'd been born at full term; fortunately for me, the postnatal unit is a rare realm in which men's opinions do not matter.

The handful of relatives who've met Sienna have been told she was born 'a little early'. Her birth weight was light, so it hasn't been an impossible falsehood. ('Amazing how quickly they fatten up,' said my mother-in-law Katherine, when she met her. 'You must have very good milk,

Amber.') People tend not to challenge you when there's no obvious reason for dishonesty, and we're so used to being vigilant about what we say, both to family and to the few new acquaintances we've made on the street, that the lie has come to feel like the truth.

In any case, sobriety keeps me focused. I couldn't drink alcohol during the pregnancy and don't intend to start again now. It's the new Amber: temperate, discreet, self-sacrificing.

As far as she's concerned, January the 15th never happened.

Chapter 33

Amber, 15 January 2013

It couldn't go on forever: I knew that deep in my heart even as I denied the existence of those depths; it was a miracle it had lasted as long as it did. But still it smashed me sideways when Rob said he wanted to stop.

'I think we should call it a day.'

That was how he put it, and almost in a mumble, the words indistinct, careless.

'You're joking, I assume?' Having believed I'd recovered my dominion over him, reeled him back to me good and proper, I didn't move a muscle of my languorous stretch in his bed. I didn't even twitch.

'No, not at all.' He looked at me in casual surprise. 'I mean it. It's time.'

Now I moved, heaving myself upright. The sudden assault of my pulse was painful, claustrophobic. 'But why? I thought we'd got over . . .' I faltered, remembering he didn't know the full extent of my anxiety in the weeks following our house-warming party, didn't regard the period as an estrangement but rather an unremarkable interlude during which the spoiled princess had become a little irked at not having her texts answered.

'Why?' I repeated.

A part of me – a frail, feminine part – longed for him to say it was because he wanted more, he needed all of me and couldn't bear to have me on this limited basis a moment longer; everyone in Lime Park Road had fallen in love with me, that's what he'd said, and now *he* wanted to be allowed to too. But I knew that wasn't it. I knew he had been the one to end every relationship he'd ever been in; he burned for only so long before the light cut out.

I thought I'd been extraordinary, but I'd been only ordinary in a new way.

'Pippa?' I said, ice in my voice.

'Partly, yeah.' He told me that the lease on her flat would be up at the end of the month and he was going to ask her to move in with him.

'Why would you do *that*?' I said scornfully.

He by contrast just grinned, patient, affable, *supine* – as if this was no different from our standard pillow talk, wicked little fripperies to make one another gasp and giggle. It was as if the night in the tree house had meant nothing to him. 'Because I think it's crazy for her to pay extortionate rent for some pit when I've got a big place like this.'

'But it can't just be about splitting costs.' Petulance was spilling from me in spite of myself. 'You must be serious about her to ask her to move in with you?'

He shrugged. 'Maybe I *am* serious, or would like to try to be. Everyone else seems to like the arrangement, even you.'

Even you. They were the words that broke my heart in the end, the implication that I was irrefutably the least in need of traditional love of any creature of his acquaintance. And I had no one to blame but myself. I'd sold myself to him as one kind of lover and I'd done it so convincingly he would never be able to think of me as any other kind. Worse, he no longer wanted to think of me *at all*.

'You said you missed me,' I said. 'When you were in Morocco. You gave me the bangle.'

He looked at me then in an unfamiliar way: incredulous, contemptuous, *pitying*. 'The bangle is meaningless,' he said.

I fingered the clasp at my wrist. 'No it's not.'

'Come on, you don't *seriously* want to carry on, do you? We should quit while we're ahead, don't you think? It's only a matter of time before Felicity suspects. She probably already does.'

Bloody Felicity. Though the works had finished months ago, still I took her my cakes and little gifts; they were my tithe, my admission of guilt. 'What if we had somewhere else to meet?'

'Not worth it.'

Though it was true that I couldn't fund the expense of a flat or a regular hotel room without Jeremy noticing, I didn't care for the way he put it: *Not worth it*. He wasn't even dignifying us with a complete sentence.

'What?' He was growing testy, his fuse shortening. 'Look, we've had a great run, but I'm not going to be your little toy for the entire duration of your marriage.'

'Who said that's what I want?' Escaping his effrontery, his sheer arrogance, I slid from the bed and from his reach (not that he was reaching) and began gathering up my clothes, fumbling with my underwear.

'Are you sure about that? Me at your beck and call every time Jeremy's away or ill or boring you or not showering you with enough diamonds?' He wasn't even looking at me as he insulted me, but had turned to his phone, as if weary of the banality of my emotions. I imagined him tapping out a message to Pippa – 'Which day can you move in?', or, as he had once to me, so simply, so electrifyingly, '*When?*'

Now that the loose end of me was tied up, *any* day worked for him.

Sensing the heat of my glower, he glanced up, brow puckered in exasperation. 'Look, you must see that you can't keep on doing this stuff in plain sight, coming round here twice a week dressed like a whore.' He paused, his sneer making it clear it was not only how I dressed that had earned me this label. 'And the other week, when Jeremy was ill – what was that all about?'

'You tell me! You're the one who made us do it in the living room. If you ask me, you get off on the idea that he might hear us.'

He ignored my desperate use of the present tense. 'What's next? In your bedroom while he's in the shower? In the kitchen while he's mowing the lawn? On the garden swing while he's checking the oil in his car?'

'These are all fantasies of yours, clearly,' I said coldly, but my face was aflame, my temperature so feverish I was starting to shiver in the centrally heated room. Dressed now, I let my fingers fiddle helplessly with my buttons, anything to stop them from reaching to slap him, to tear his hair, to damage him physically. He had never goaded me like this before.

And nor had he finished, continuing now as if uninterrupted, the words dripping crueller and crueller: 'Hey, *I* know, check us both into your tree-house hotel and divide your time between the two rooms, see if either of us notices you're not actually there when we're not fucking you. Invite him to join us in the hot tub and watch? Ask him what the worst thing is he's ever done and –?'

'Stop!' I'd raised my voice to a yell and we stared at each other, startled. There was something sadistic in his expression and I wondered what was in mine, something that was drawing the brutality from him: pain, fear, some weakness in me he did not care to protect, only to expose and belittle.

'Calm down, Miss Amber,' he said, and the nickname, the change in tone from bullying to playful, altered something in me.

'I haven't heard you complain before,' I said, smiling. Nothing but instinct propelling me, I lowered myself onto the mattress right at his feet, blinking, pouting, appealing to him with my eyes and lips.

'I'm not complaining now.' He echoed the adjustment, the spite in his face fading. 'That's not what this is, don't get me wrong. I'm just calling time, like we said we would. No arguments. No emotions. Don't go back on that when you were the one to insist on it in the first place. You practically had me swearing on the Bible, you were such a control freak, remember?'

I remembered very clearly, just as I did the animal hunger that had obliterated all moral concerns, all common sense. It wasn't the same now, certainly, it had mutated, twisted, but it was just as powerful – on my part. It terrified me to think it might no longer be fed.

'I'm not going back on it,' I said. 'You've misunderstood. It's fine. I get it.'

With my apparent compliance, he begrudged me a half-smile. 'OK, good, so let's avoid each other for a little while, then be normal neighbours, right? We've always been completely natural with each other outside of here, we'll just continue doing that.'

I thought how utterly wrong that sounded – to me we'd been natural inside his flat, unnatural outside. 'I notice you waited till afterwards to tell me,' I said in a dreary voice, causing him to look up, puzzled more by the tone than the question. He'd assumed, of course, that I would still have slept with him even if he had told me before; he'd assumed this was pure convenience, pure pleasure, of itself and nothing besides. He was beginning to find me extremely tedious.

'What difference does it make? *Jesus*,' he muttered, turning back to his phone.

'*What* did you say?' And with a full turn of the wheel, self-pity erupted into fury; I was far more incensed than when he'd called me ugly names: to hear so plainly, so callously, that there was no difference as far as he was concerned, when for me there was all the difference in the world. Here was the final evidence that I had let myself down, betrayed myself, and somehow that meant a far worse betrayal of Jeremy than the technical one.

He tossed me a pitiless glance. 'Come on, don't go getting all bunny boiler on me. I know you've got form in that department.'

'What are you talking about?'

Now he looked at me properly, enjoying his moment of power. 'I know all about your employment tribunal. What a farce *that* was, eh?'

I glowered at him. 'I've never mentioned any tribunal to you.'

'No, but you told Felicity, didn't you? That was a mistake. "Inappropriate sexual misconduct", my arse. I can't think of a single person in the world less likely to be a victim of *that*.'

'Neither of you know anything about it,' I said. I refused to have my bluff called like this. 'There were no press there and witness statements aren't made public after the event.'

'No, but journalists have ways of getting around that. You can't expect me not to want to dig into something like that?'

'I expect you to mind your own business,' I said coldly. 'For your information, I was unfairly dismissed and that's all there is to it.'

He smirked. 'I have no doubt that's what you like to think, but that's not what the panel decided, was it? Didn't they decide that *you* had harassed him? Matt, wasn't it? The one who tried to blackmail you? Poor sucker. You wouldn't leave him alone when he'd had enough. What was the phrase the judge used about your behaviour? "Statistically uncommon", that's right, "but no less damaging for it."'

'I can't believe you're quoting this nonsense,' I sneered. 'You obviously have nothing better to do with your time.'

He continued as if I had not spoken: 'You were the woman, you were the subordinate, and you *still* managed to fuck him up so badly he had a Prozac prescription by the time you'd finished with him. And there were some pretty nasty emails to his new girlfriend, as I remember, Lesley something or other. Didn't you get some IT dope to help you send them anonymously? You were lucky they didn't go to the police.'

'*He* was lucky *I* didn't go to the police,' I snapped. 'Blackmail is a crime.'

'Yes, it's interesting you didn't tell the silver fox about that,' Rob said in mock puzzlement. 'Didn't want to risk his being tempted to look beyond the rose-tinted surface of Amber Baby, eh? Because he *doesn't* know everything, does he? He doesn't have a clue how psychotic you get if someone has the audacity to reject you.' He sniggered, waggling his phone at me. 'Well, I can tell you now that if you try any of your revenge crap on *me* I'll forward it straight to him. He'll be the judge of any tribunal *we* have.'

Under his goading eyes, my skin burned red with humiliation. I could feel my own body heat pouring from me. 'I wasn't thinking straight back then,' I said, finally. 'You know what I was like, all the drugs and everything. You met me yourself.'

He gave a malicious little chuckle. 'You didn't believe *that*, did you?'

'What do you mean?'

'I just said that for a laugh.'

I stared, astounded, disgraced. 'But why?'

He shrugged. 'I wanted to see how fucked up you really used to be. When you didn't remember but clearly accepted it as true, well, I knew the answer: *very* fucked up. I'm sorry, but the evidence just keeps on coming, Amber Baby.'

'Evidence of what?' I said, swallowing. Tears wobbled on my lower lids.

With exaggerated ennui, he peered at his phone, as if even the sight of a keypad held more interest than anything *I* had to say. 'That you're not quite right in the head,' he sighed.

'Shut up.' I lunged towards him and snatched the phone from his fingers, hurled it against the wall, not even watching as it smashed and fell to the floor, only scowling into his face, seeing his anger resurface and bloom deeper and hotter than before, challenging him to start this scene again and give me the outcome *I* wanted.

'I hate you,' I said, trembling.

I love you, a voice replied, but it was not the one I wanted to hear; only my own, inside my head, the words incarcerated there forever.

He said nothing. His mouth made vile movements, a bully's gathering saliva to spit at an object of repugnance, a victim. In his eyes there pooled pure savagery.

And then he sprang.

In a deft and practised ambush, *he* was now on top of

me, pinning me under him on the bed, I clothed, he still naked, the bedding catching and pulling between us.

'Is this how you broke up with *her*?' I snarled. It was my turn now and I was going to take every last drop of relish in my power to incense him, to contaminate his airwaves with my vitriol.

'Who?'

'The girl in college you told me about. Is this why she did what she did – to teach you a lesson for being so heartless? Did you dump her for the same reason? Because you got *bored*?'

'You don't know what you're talking about, you stupid whore.' His words were hard with anger, exciting me.

'Go on,' I taunted him, 'do it. Do it one last time. Make it hurt so I remember you properly. You have my permission – I know that's important to you.'

'You're sick, do you know that?'

But he liked it. He liked it as much as I did. Breaking one hand free, I reached between our bodies to slide off my underwear and guide him inside me. Then my hand returned to its pair, seeking his, urging him to tighten his grip, to bind his fingers tighter around my wrists.

'Come on, get on with it. I'm waiting.'

As he started to grind he had his full weight on me so I could hardly breathe, hardly move, but only whimper with the pleasure of it, the pain of it – there would be blood later, I knew – murmuring in his ear, begging him not to stop, never to stop. As he came, I hissed 'I hate you' once more, twice more, over and over until he commanded me to stop and rolled away from me in exhaustion and disgust.

488

'Jesus,' he gasped. 'I don't know what it is with you. You've got a serious problem.'

I sat up, my body sore and used but still craving contact with his. I pawed his hair, kissed his shoulders, rubbed myself against him like an animal. 'The only problem I have is to get you to come to your senses . . .' I smiled, purring now, pleased with myself, as pleased as I'd been on the day we met – and as confident of success. 'Come on, you know you'd miss me too much if I never came back, admit it.'

He spun, incredulous, freeing himself from my touch. He was breathing heavily, the skin of his chest red from the friction of me. 'Listen to me, will you: I'm not going to change my mind and we are not going to see each other again. Not like this.'

'Well, I don't accept that,' I murmured, advancing once more. 'You know you can do whatever you like with me, I don't care about Pippa or anyone else who comes along, I just want to –'

'Stop touching me!' He shook me off a second time, springing unsteadily to his feet. 'I think you should get out of here. I can't bear to look at you any more.'

Hearing him, understanding at last, I could only stare at him, emptied of my soul, utterly laid to waste. 'If that's what you want,' I said, choking.

'It is. So stop making such a song and dance of it. Put your knickers on and go. Please.'

Humiliated, degraded, I did as he said. As I left, I was already crying tears of rage. 'You will never lay a finger on me again as long as you live!' I told him, shrieking. All those months of immaculate control, not a syllable breathed to anyone, and now I had none left.

'I have no desire to,' Rob said, his voice cold and hateful, and he kicked the door shut behind me, not even sparing me a last glance.

He never looked at me again.

I blundered down the stairs sobbing, noticing Felicity at her open door but waving off her concern, dashing for the refuge of my own home, my perfectly feathered nest with all the space in the world for the chicks that refused to come.

'Amber, stop, is something wrong . . . ?'

But I ignored her. The last thing I wanted was a repeat of the time she'd found me on the doorstep, ringing his doorbell over and over, desperate and demented, an *addict*.

She'd taken me into her flat on that occasion and made me a cup of tea, brought me a little packet of tissues and watched me mop my face. Only when I'd subdued the worst of the hysteria did she say anything worth listening to.

'If you play with fire, you only end up having to cry enough tears to put it out.'

'What is that, some sort of Chinese proverb?' I'd asked. I was rallying by then, ready to excuse my distress with some fabrication or other, to give no more away than I already had.

'You could call it a Lime Park proverb,' Felicity replied.

I laughed it off. I laughed so sweetly she couldn't help but laugh along with me, coming to the conclusion, I suppose, that I could take care of myself. I was a big girl. But she made me finish my tea, look her in the eye, promise I was going to be all right.

Such a friendly street, Lime Park Road. So many doors held open in welcome, so much advice ready to be dispensed.

I prefer it here, in the forgotten little neighbourhood where our road links two suburbs, where we're never quite sure which side of the line we live on.

Where people keep themselves to themselves.

Chapter 34

Amber, October 2013

It hasn't been easy being a born survivor.

When I left Rob's flat that terrible afternoon in January, I thought I would never recover, I thought his brutality was so unendurable I might have to kill myself. On and on I wept, thrashing and convulsing, like a baby torn from her mother, and though I had stopped before Jeremy left for his business trip – it was futile and self-destructive, it upset him and debased me – I had continued to *want* to weep. I had continued to want to die.

But then I discovered I was pregnant and the miracle of life being what I now know it is – a force capable of overriding crisis, of resetting time – I was cured at a stroke. It was as if nothing bad had ever happened to me and never would.

Until Jeremy came home from the airport and dropped his bomb. The house might have been split in two with its destructive force, the whole world burned black and airless. It was deadly – almost.

I was raped: I ejected the words like vomit, the only ones that could have won me a reprieve. I think he recognized it as the solution as instinctively as I did; any other explanation and we would have been adrift, whereas this course, unedifying though it was, was charted.

But instinct is ephemeral. Obviously I hadn't thought the claim through, the risk it brought of exposure. I would have been better saying that a stranger had assaulted me. I was going to have to be ready to think on my feet if I was not to be undone – by the police, for instance.

How could Jeremy *not* have involved them? And yet in doing so he turned a convenient embellishment of the truth into a criminal offence; wasting police time or perverting the cause of justice, I was guilty of one of the two at least, perhaps both. Rob was not the one who got away with it, *I* was.

On the afternoon of the recorded interview, every false word felt ten times heavier than a true one. I think that was what made it possible to make my distress sound so real; it *was* real – only the source of it differed from the one they all accepted. It was a form of method acting, I suppose.

And my account of the attack itself was not so far removed from what had actually happened, it was simply a case of re-colouring it. When fiction tumbles out of you, you gain confidence from the interweaving with it of actual facts, just as I had during the course of the affair itself. *Rob made me a delicious coffee today, the beans were from El Salvador*, I'd say to Jeremy; or *Rob's had a great new commission from his contact at the* Guardian . . . The truthful details are what make the broader lie sound authentic, plausible.

I got into a bit of a tangle with the business of his

hands. I'd somehow accounted for both of them before he'd had a chance to unzip his trousers and have his wicked way with me. *He pressed his mouth against mine to keep me quiet*: again, the lie comes out of the truth.

Poor Felicity. She told the police she'd heard me cry 'You'll never lay a finger on me again!'; she'd even heard that yelled 'Stop!' of mine and seriously considered coming upstairs to check that nothing was amiss. She's another who's found a way to me since my disappearance; she sent a letter care of Jeremy's office telling me she has never been able to forgive herself for not intervening and will take her regret to her grave. She had an abusive husband when she was a young woman, she said, younger than me; she should have been wiser to the signs. She even admitted she'd had reservations about me during my time in Lime Park, that she'd made the mistake of sharing them with the monster himself. She deeply regretted that too. *I wish, like you, I'd had the courage of my convictions*, she wrote. Bless.

Poor Wendy, my specially trained officer, with all her exhortations to call her at any time, even when she was feeding her kids their tea or getting cosy with her husband at bedtime, to ask any question, unburden myself of any anxiety. More than once her sincerity almost felled me; all that radiant compassion, it was too much for a cheat and a liar like me.

Poor Rob. 'He's dug his own grave now,' Jeremy said, and I nodded, happy to bury him alive so long as I was not down there with him spitting earth and fighting for air. But it was a false happiness, a short-lived victory. Being asked to recount that revelation about the student rape claim was the nadir for me, for I knew as well as he did that if he hadn't disclosed it to me I would not have thought of the solution myself.

Oh Rob, betrayed by the only woman you confided in, condemned by your trust in her. It would have broken my heart if I didn't have a new claim on that organ. There are levels of duplicity and mine was the very lowest. I knew he would assume I'd done what I did for the same reason he'd been accused all those years ago: a woman scorned; in my case, a self-styled princess reacting in fury before bolting like the beggar she was. I would have liked him to know that it wasn't that. I may have been rejected but I would have accepted it in time. I had no appetite for vengeance; I was only saving my marriage and safeguarding my future.

I wonder sometimes how far it could have gone if I hadn't ended the investigation when I did, if I'd let it march onwards. Would I really have been prepared to send a man to prison to protect my own marriage, my pride? Of course I wouldn't, it would never have come to that, not least because of those incriminating texts, and the ancient testimony of that shambles of a man Matt, not to mention his lowlife squeeze Lesley. No, I knew from the moment Jeremy phoned the police that I had to bring the formalities to a halt, I just didn't know how or when I was going to be able to do it.

You know, I still think of Rob sometimes, so magnetic to the opposite sex, so natural a lover, too fearful to speak to another woman again. Except Pippa, of course. I imagine she intuited his innocence quickly enough. She's an intelligent woman and she knows what he's capable of, the brink he won't tip over, the lines he won't cross. And if not her then *someone* will help him recover his mojo. Perhaps this Davenport woman, now she knows the truth. Or at least the part of it she's interested in knowing.

No one knows the whole truth except me. Not even my husband. Especially not my husband.

Poor Jeremy. Hard though it may be to believe, given the enormous lie that separated us, I felt very close to him during those days in the hotel. Innocent casualty of men's desires, gallant protector of one woman's blamelessness: these were the roles that had bound us when we met and now they would bind us again. And I may not have been the victim of rape, but I was sufficiently damaged by the horrific mess I'd created for myself, and for him, that the symptoms must have been convincing even to the person who knew me best of all.

I didn't like to dwell on the fact that 'best of all' equated to 'not nearly as well as he thought'.

And do you know what he told me not so long ago? Just a few weeks before I was 'attacked', he'd had an anonymous tip-off that I was having an affair. He had one of his IT team trace its route and it turned out to have come from the server at my old agency. Imogen being on maternity leave, there were only two possible suspects still employed there: Helena and Gemma. No prizes for guessing which the originator must have been.

'What did it say?' I asked Jeremy.

'I don't remember the exact words. "You should keep a closer eye on your wife," something like that. Not bad advice, in retrospect.' *Still* he blamed himself for not having protected me from the wolf next door.

'Why didn't you tell me at the time?'

He was indignant. 'I had no intention of upsetting you with cowardly nonsense like that.'

My darling husband. How I wished I could reassure him that there would be no long-term psychological impairment; that he need not worry about my future sexual health or continue to book specialist counsellors to help restore my faith in man – in men. The only concern anyone needs have for me is in respect of stamina. Can I live with myself for the rest of my days if I have to perpetually play the victim? When I know I am anything but? Can I keep on spinning the lie?

Of course I can.

Yes, it was all going perfectly to plan – until *she* turned up. Christy Davenport.

By an extraordinary stroke of good fortune, Jeremy's mother was visiting that morning and had taken Sienna for a walk around the park to give me a chance to nap. Even so, I almost gave the game away. That remark of hers – *You didn't want to raise a family there* – almost had me sobbing on the spot. Bright and friendly once she knew Rob was not a violent criminal, she gestured directly to my stomach and made it explicit – 'Well, congratulations on the baby' – her mouth remaining open to ask the questions I had been dreading: Who's looking after her this morning? When was she born? *Shall I go back and foghorn the news to everyone in Lime Park?*

'Is it OK to tell Caroline?' she said, on cue. 'She'll be *so* pleased.'

It was all I could do not to sink to my knees and wail as she prattled on. This was an out-and-out disaster. Even if I said I'd given birth prematurely the day before, it was still going to create doubt among the Lime Parkers: what sort of a rape victim renewed her sex life within days of being assaulted? No one would believe that. As for Rob, he of all people would know I'd think nothing of deceiving a stranger – after all, I'd lied to senior CID officers. And she'd tell him about the baby, I knew she would; she'd go back and become his confidante, if not his latest lover. 'If it was *that* premature, why wasn't she still in the hospital with it?' he'd wonder. He'd have my address out of her in seconds.

Standing in that miserable little café, staring at her in horror, I was already rehearsing the conversation I'd have with Jeremy that evening, the one that began, *We have to move on. We have to change our name or he'll come after me. This bloody woman is going to go back there and let the cat out of the bag...*

Then she handed me the bangle and I lost my train of thought, for the sight of it produced an overwhelming sensory memory of Rob's hands on my body, his mouth seeking mine, his feverish, unstoppable desire for me.

'Keep it,' I told her, scared I might faint.

Only her producing of the key ring restored my

strength, having that dragonfly charm in my hand again, tracing the pad of my thumb over the engraving: *Amber Baby*. It had been a gift from Jeremy when he'd presented me with a set of keys to his Battersea flat, a set of keys to my new life. Now, I could attach it to the keys to *this* one, even though it was poised to change once more.

'Well, goodbye,' Christy said. 'Thank you for seeing me, I know it must have been hard. And I promise I won't tell Caroline or anyone else that you're pregnant. When is it due?'

It took me a few moments to absorb this. Stopping virtually mid-step, I stared stupidly at her, before glancing down at my stomach, comparatively svelte by recent standards but still noticeably swollen.

'Not for ages, obviously,' she added, keen to help out the gaping idiot in front of her. 'You're still tiny.' She began to look a little anxious, as if she feared she'd insulted me by mistaking greed-induced weight gain for proof of reproduction. And then I got it: she thought I was at the *beginning* of my pregnancy. I was so absorbed in my own little world that I'd expected her to understand that I was carrying post-partum weight, but having seen or heard no evidence of a baby she'd made a different assumption.

'That's right,' I said, at last. 'It's still the first trimester, we're just getting used to the idea.' And I gave her a warm smile, happy now to spare a little charm for her.

She blushed like a small child.

'Christy?' I added, just in time. My mind worked slower these days, but it was not totally atrophied.

'Yes?'

'You *can* tell Caroline – and the others. I'd like that. Tell them we're both very happy.'

'OK, I will.' I could see that she was overjoyed, so giddy she was hardly able to get her purse open to pay for the tea. She was the kind of person who liked to know other people's secrets – too dull to have her own, perhaps. 'I'm sure they'll be really pleased to know that everything's worked out well for you, Amber.'

'Yes,' I said, turning to leave. 'You can tell them it has.'

Acknowledgements

A heartfelt thank you to Sheila Crowley and Maxine Hitchcock for being such indefatigable champions of this book. Thank you also to Becky Ritchie, Katie McGowan, Sophie Harris and Alice Lutyens at Curtis Brown and to Lydia Good, Nick Lowndes and the rest of the team at Michael Joseph. Thank you to Caroline Pretty for her excellent copy-edit.

Thank you to my family and friends for moral support, sometimes the only thing that keeps a writer writing. Elissa and Karen, I truly appreciate your sympathetic ear.

And not forgetting Mats 'n' Jo!

Thank you to my sister Jane for helping me with the background on one of Amber's scenes; to Julia Harris-Voss for her suggestion about the letter; and to Richard Clifton for advice about Joe's legal career.

I am indebted to two patient and generous police officers, Nicola Hurdley and Neal McCarry, who answered my questions and read and corrected material out of the goodness of their hearts. I am really, really grateful. Any mistakes are of course mine and not theirs.

Finally, *The Art of Being A Well Dressed Wife* is a V&A publication by Anne Fogarty, passed my way during the writing of this book by Lydia Good. It is perfect 'Amberbilia'.

He just wanted a decent book to read ...

Not too much to ask, is it? It was in 1935 when Allen Lane, Managing Director of Bodley Head Publishers, stood on a platform at Exeter railway station looking for something good to read on his journey back to London. His choice was limited to popular magazines and poor-quality paperbacks – the same choice faced every day by the vast majority of readers, few of whom could afford hardbacks. Lane's disappointment and subsequent anger at the range of books generally available led him to found a company – and change the world.

'We believed in the existence in this country of a vast reading public for intelligent books at a low price, and staked everything on it'
Sir Allen Lane, 1902–1970, founder of Penguin Books

The quality paperback had arrived – and not just in bookshops. Lane was adamant that his Penguins should appear in chain stores and tobacconists, and should cost no more than a packet of cigarettes.

Reading habits (and cigarette prices) have changed since 1935, but Penguin still believes in publishing the best books for everybody to enjoy. We still believe that good design costs no more than bad design, and we still believe that quality books published passionately and responsibly make the world a better place.

So wherever you see the little bird – whether it's on a piece of prize-winning literary fiction or a celebrity autobiography, political tour de force or historical masterpiece, a serial-killer thriller, reference book, world classic or a piece of pure escapism – you can bet that it represents the very best that the genre has to offer.

Whatever you like to read – trust Penguin.

read more
www.penguin.co.uk